Also by Rob Ryan

Underdogs

nine mil

ROB RYAN

First published in 2000
by HEADLINE BOOK PUBLISHING

First published in paperback in 2000
by HEADLINE BOOK PUBLISHING

10 9 8 7 6 5 4 3 2 1

ISBN 0 7472 6120 2

Typeset by Avon Dataset Ltd, Bidford-on-Avon, Warks

Printed and bound in Great Britain by
Mackays of Chatham plc, Chatham, Kent

HEADLINE BOOK PUBLISHING
A division of Hodder Headline
338 Euston Road
London NW1 3BH

www.headline.co.uk
www.hodderheadline.com

For Deb, Bella, Gina and Gabriel

A portion of this book appeared in Fresh Blood 3, edited by Maxim Jakubowski and Mike Ripley, under the title 'Shit Happens'.

'Violence usually begins with a reason, with some principle to be defended. The real motivation, however, is a primitive thirst for blood, and as the fighting continues reasons or principles are forgotten and men fight for the sake of fighting.'

– Sam Peckinpah quoted in
'If They Move . . . Kill 'em' by David Weddle.

PROLOGUE

Neptune City, New Jersey. May 24

Special Agent Ernie Shepard was about to lose his temper when his beeper went off. He had been trying to get a straight answer out of Harold Wheeler, the proprietor of Barrels of Fun: Neptune City's Premier Gun Dealership, and Harold was squirming round the subject matter.

Shepard held up the paperwork. 'All this refers to the older guy.'

'It was the older guy who bought the piece, I'm tellin' ya. He had a purchase order from the Sheriff, filled in the form and I ran the Brady background numbers, and he came up clean, paid cash and everything. Why should I call you guys?'

'Cause he had a fifteen year old kid with him.'

'What – fifteen year olds are suddenly offensive weapons?'

Shepard looked down at Federal Form 4473. All the questions were ticked 'no' – John Wetherall had never been a drug addict, a convicted felon or an illegal alien. He filled in the form and proved he was twenty-one, showed the permit he had obtained from the Sheriff and waited while the New Brady check – a recently introduced five-day delve to see whether he had a criminal record, named for James Brady who was shot in the Hinckley/Reagan assassination attempt. This wasn't foolproof, as this case showed, but it was better than the old system when they all just assumed that any scumbag, after a lifetime of lying and cheating, would come over all honest when faced with the imposing sight of a 4473. That was all they had to do up until the mid-1990s, just tick 'no' in the box. Then they went to on-the-spot computer checks, but after the Littleton school and Fort Worth church massacres, they went back to the idea of a cooling off period.

All the Federal and state formalities taken care of, Wheeler had sold Wetherall a Glauber A-100, an automatic handgun from a Ring of Fire outfit – one of the cheapjack California companies that made Saturday Night Specials – for ninety-five dollars, and entered the make, model, calibre and serial number on the permit. At some point Wetherall had handed the gun over to his underage cousin.

'Was the Glauber his first choice?'

'Nah. He wanted a . . .' Wheeler stopped. Shepard waited. 'He wanted one of those Tec-9s.'

'Tec-9s are illegal.'

'I told him that. Ingrams, Cobrays, no deal buddy. Not legit, anyway.' He added with great emphasis. 'Not in Barrels of Fun.'

Shepard nodded. There were still a lot of fully automatic, crude machine pistols out there, but at least you couldn't walk into a gunstore and buy one any longer and pretend it was for hunting, like you wanted to pre-shred the animal you were after into elk jerky. Shepard glanced around. Barrels of Fun didn't seem to be doing too well. The many shelves that lined the wall were all were filled with ammunition boxes, which looked to be empty. A locked, glass-fronted shelf unit on one wall was filled with 'wonder rounds', the darlings of the self-defence lobby. Eliminator-X, Full-Shok, One-Stop, all expanding or multiple-headed bullets that created large, lethal – or least non-repairable – wound channels. If a dealer couldn't shift those to a discerning gun nut, he might as well pack up and go home.

A few rifles hung in cases, and beneath the glass counter in front of him most of the stock was from the cheap end of the range – a couple of the budget Davis models and others from the Ring of Fire boys, but no Glocks or Sig-Sauers. Shepard almost had to force himself to stop smiling. With the new gun control statutes on the way and litigation-weary manufacturers pulling out of the game, he knew places like this were ultimately doomed.

'So they settled on the Glauber? You didn't think – why would a guy want a Tec or a Cobray?'

'Hey, there's no accounting for taste. But when I told him a Tec was both illegal and a piece of junk, he settled on the Glauber. I mean I coulda tried to push him an AB-10, the legal Tec, but I didn't. Fuck – why you ATF guys come in here always bustin' my chops. I do not break the law—'

'Not the letter of the law.' Shepard felt a pulse start in his left eyelid. The Bureau of Alcohol, Tobacco and Firearms hit this all the time. Anyone who paid three hundred bucks could still become a Federal Firearms Licensee. There were no checks on suitability, or how they were going to run their business, and although many of them exercised due caution, there were a sizeable chunk like Wheeler who did the bare minimum and had invested in a moral responsibility bypass. Enough to mean guns were still getting into the wrong hands. As happened here.

'Listen, Wheeler, if I find that the kid had anything to do with the transaction, that the money came from him, that you saw him hand over the cash to his cousin—'

'I told you. It was the older guy. The little one was just curious. All kids are fascinated by guns. Only natural. We get them in here all the time. With the adults, I mean.'

Shepard found himself leaning over the counter.

'Hey watch the glass—'

'That kid took the Glauber to church that Sunday. He

told us he intended to kill the pastor and his parents because they had found out he was hitting on some of the little girls in the choir. That Glauber has no manual safety – you know that? Course you do. Yeah, you point and pull.'

'I didn't read nothing about—'

'Because it didn't happen. The piece of shit you sold him jammed. He nearly got the pastor anyway – the old guy, the pastor, had a heart attack.'

'Look. Agent, I sold it to the older guy and I tell you that was a good gun, he must've messed with it. One of them must've. I checked it myself.'

No concern about the boy, the parents, the pastor. No 'what happened next, Agent?' No 'Jeez, sorry Agent Shepard, I'll be more careful next time.' He wondered if the list of Fayetteville, Pomona, Jonesboro, West Paducah, Pearl, Bethal, Springfield or Paterson even meant anything to him. And most of all Littleton back in '99. Of all places, that proved kids and guns don't mix. Suddenly incensed by the thought that nearby Glendola was almost added to the tragic litany because of the jerk in front of him, Shepard was about to reach for the throat when the beeper went off.

They stood frozen for a moment, both realising what it – what he – had built up to. Shepard wasn't a big man, Wheeler thought, but he looked well muscled under the suit, and his short cropped blond hair – more FBI than the Bureau itself – gave him a mean, almost military look.

Shepard dropped his hand and consulted the beeper. It was the 'phone home' code. His cell phone was still in the car. 'Can I make a call?'

'Sure, Agent.' Wheeler passed over the handset. All was calm now, and Wheeler knew he was home free. He was glad he had had the presence of mind to wipe the security tape which showed the kid pulling a bundle of tens and

4

twenties from his jeans pocket and passing them over to
Wetherall on their final visit.

Shepard hit the Trenton ATF office number and was put
through to the duty supervisor, Dick Davis.

'Dick, it's Ernie. Shepard.'

'Ernie, yeah, we just got a call from Asbury Park. They
got a shooting, they got a gun, but they can't ID it. Don't
even seem to be able to find a serial number. And they'd like
a trace.'

'So soon?'

'Yeah, yeah, ha, ha – don't look a gift horse in the muzzle,
eh?' Both of them knew that less than ten per cent of all
guns used in a crime were given to ATF for tracing. Local
PDs were just happy to have the shooter and his weapon –
who cares where it had been? But ATF wanted to know
how these guns slipped from people like Wheeler into the
backstreets of Philly and Camden and Jersey City.

'Well, I'm about done here anyways. Where is it?'

'The Turner Terrace.'

'Wow. I mean . . . wow.'

'Yeah, I don't know too much, but take a look, eh? Nice
to get invited to the dance for a change.'

'Sure.'

The Turner Terrace wasn't so much a terrace as a giant pier
turned on its side and grafted onto the old boardwalk, its
frontage stretching for almost half a mile to the north of
Convention Hall in Asbury Park. Shepard reckoned on
twenty minutes along 66 to reach it, given that he would hit
the lunchtime traffic, so he wound up things with Wheeler
as quickly as he could, making sure the guy knew he'd be
back.

He flicked on the radio as he left the lot and punched the
seek button as soon as he heard that familiar voice wrap

itself around *The Summer Winds*. It was the anniversary of Frankie's death, and once again New Jersey was about to beat its breast about the loss of its favourite son. Been – what – five, six years now? But the citizens of Hoboken never tired of telling you what a stand-up guy he was, good to old ladies, dogs, his friends, as if this made him superhuman. Only the voice did that, but Shepard could only take so much of it in one day.

He pressed the seek each time it stopped, moving across the ads for car dealers, happy hours, hotels, fishing trips. The season was due to start, what with Memorial Day looming, and the Jersey Shore was preening itself for the annual crop of tourists, summer rentals and party kids. Oh, he was reminded, and gamblers.

'Come to the Turner Terrace' the ad began 'where we've kicked off our shoes, loosened our ties and loosened our slots. That's right, we have the loosest slots in the whole State . . .' there was the sound of coins cascading '. . . and all through May, spend fifty dollars or more and enjoy a free all-you-can-eat buffet in The Lobster Tail. And in the Turner Liner Lounge on June first and second, Celine Dion.' There followed two sentences in an Oriental language Shepard didn't know and then the announcer gravely told him it was the anniversary of Sinatra's death and to pay its respects the station would be having a ten-track back-to-back no-ad Frankathon every hour. He switched it off and popped in an old Springsteen tape, the other Jersey son.

The approach to the Asbury Park boardwalk was jammed with cars trying to get out of town. The roads of the city are oddly wide, but even so, a whole casino complex dumping its customers onto them is a sure way to get gridlock. He sat at an intersection for five minutes, listening to the chorus of hoots and obscenities, many of them in Cantonese and Tagalog – the Terrace always did draw a big Oriental crowd

– while he looked across at the big, monumental shape of the casino itself, like one of those big Miami cruise ships that had run itself aground.

The Sydney E. Turner Organisation had pulled out of Atlantic City three years previously, claiming favouritism by the gaming board towards other big time operators. Turner had then used the fact that gambling had been legalised on Atlantic City's piers to formulate the idea of the Terrace – a casino built over the water from the desolate, moribund frontage of Asbury Park. How he got it through the legislature nobody was sure – but choosing Asbury Park, long an embarrassment to the Jersey shore, was a stroke of genius. And, as Turner had promised, life had come back to the waterfront. And maybe death, too, if they needed the ATF.

Eventually Shepard snaked through a series of small gaps in the traffic, nicking the wing of his Honda in the process, and down to the twin Mermaids that framed the entrance to the Terrace. The driveway was clogged with a mixture of taxis, stretch limos and police cars. A solitary ambulance was being closed up with an air of finality, as if this was the last of any casualties.

'Do Not Cross' barriers had been hastily erected in some parts. Crowds of people swarmed around waving their valet parking tickets, but the valets were nowhere to be seen. Shepard pulled his Honda to a halt just under one of the mermaids and emerged holding his badge up so the various uniforms could see it.

'I didn't see anything. Nothing. I just ducked —' a middle-aged woman was wriggling her arm, trying to lever it from the grip of the policeman.

'Ma'am, you just have to sign something to say that, give us your details, and you can be on your way. Interviews are being processed in the Liner Lounge.'

'No, you don't understand . . .' Or maybe she was thinking it was hubbie who wouldn't understand what she was doing idling a day away at the Terrace.

That desperate I-wasn't-here conversation was repeated a dozen times as he shouldered his way through the crowd, flashing the badge continually at every curious glance from the uniforms and the detectives.

The entrance was actually a false front, a flat like you might find on a Universal or MGM picture lot. Behind it was a wide, carpeted, glassed-over gangplank, one of four, that linked the main building to the shore. The Palace wasn't actually on land, it 'floated' on huge pilings just offshore, a trick first used down in Mississippi to get over local gaming regulations. So the casino was not really on New Jersey soil at all – it belonged to the ocean.

It was hard work negotiating the eddying mass of humanity on the gangplank, but eventually Shepard reached the real reception hall, a huge space lined with fish tanks, with real fish revelling in the fact they had a depth of thirty feet or more to play with. To the left and right were the entrances to the hotel rooms and function rooms and the Liner Lounge; next to check in was the huge decorated arch – more gilded mermaids – which led to the casino floor itself. A row of the biggest police officers stood across this, like an NFL defensive line.

Again Shepard lifted his badge. 'ATF. We got a call. Who's in charge?'

The policeman peered at the badge. His expression showed he was one of those cops who considered the ATF bumptious, self-righteous and interfering. Oh, and these days especially, over-funded. 'Ask for Captain Lucas. He'll be out back, on the deck.'

Reluctantly they parted to let him through, but as he took his first step onto the gambling floor he froze. His feet crunched on broken glass. He looked up and saw a dozen fractured images of himself staring down. As he focused further back, beyond the rows and rows of machines, still flashing through the odd semi-darkness, he could see the ceiling mirrors had dropped or been forced away in dozens of places.

And then there was the smell. He had been in enough casinos to know the kind of atmosphere they generated. Industrial strength air conditioning, pumping out the most synthetic of air, still tinged with stubborn molecules of cigarette smoke and a nose-burning mix of colognes and aftershaves and perfumes and deodorant and sweat. But not here. He could feel a breeze. A real, living organic breeze. And he could smell the Atlantic.

He threaded through the aisles over a sea of debris: abandoned coin buckets, their tokens spewed across the floor, crushed plastic cocktail glasses, and food, lots of food. The Terrace had had a series of conveyor belts snaking between the machines, carrying sushi and noodles and teriyaki, all free, all designed to keep the punters at their seats feeding money into the slots. The belts were quiet now, ripped and twisted in places where people had stampeded over them or, by the looks of it, through them. Underfoot were little prawn tails, tuna, octopus and fish roe, crushed and pulped into the carpet. The rice on the floor looked like a plague of maggots. Unless they cleaned it up soon, the place was going to start smelling like a bait shop in a heat wave.

The concentration of glass shards on the floor grew denser as Shepard worked his way towards the back, until he came to a part where the ceiling had peeled down, taking with it a glass chandelier. Now there were real fish on the floor, flung from the tanks that had formed a ring around the centrepiece of the hall. They had long since given up thrashing and gasping.

Here, too, were splashes of blood and Shepard coolly visualised that glass coming down on dozens, no, probably hundreds of tightly packed people, trapped in the aisles, with nowhere to go. The blood became more frequent, the splashes bigger, some on the front of the video poker machines. It didn't touch him though. The Bureau had a way of desensitising you – the movie show of wound channels and exit holes you could lose your fist – or even your arm – in. Jesus, but the instructors at the Academy loved that one, it had the hues, the too-close rawness of the hardest pornography, the kind where you never see faces. They always handed out empty popcorn buckets just in case, because a couple of stomachs were going to be emptied, that was for sure. If you could sit through this thirty minute, R-rated show of a stream of see-through cadavers, a little blood on the walls didn't mean much anymore.

The rear of the hall was a heavily smoked glass curtain wall, darkened to keep the perma-night illusion of the casino intact, one section of which had shattered, leaving a triangular hole, through which both the daylight and the outside air were streaming in, creating that alien breeze.

Apart from the newly arrived interface with the real world, the glass curtain had three genuine exits, and at each one stood a knot of officials, police and medical people, with ashen-faced casino officials, identified by the boat-shaped badges they wore, looking like they were in the early stages of shock. Shepard guessed the grey-haired man in the tight suit was Lucas, because of the way the slow tide of people were circling round him with requests for information. Shepard strode over with his badge.

'Captain Lucas?'

The man looked up with a 'what now?' expression.

'Ernest H. Shepard, Senior Special Agent, Bureau of Alcohol, Tobacco and Firearms.' Best be formal, he figured.

'Oh, yeah, yeah. The Ness. Thanks for coming so fast.'

The Ness. Surfing the new public concern and the congressional investigation into the gun industry – the first one ever – the Bureau had lobbied hard to win more funds and prestige and responsibilities, so it had begun playing up its glorious lineage back to Eliot Ness and his treasury agents. This had been popular with a public increasingly sickened by massacre headlines. Once the gun-related death toll topped 40,000 a year, the unthinkable had happened: America fell out of love with high velocity weaponry. Especially as a hefty percentage of that total was kids. Denver, Austin, Chicago – the school massacres had just kept coming. With the gun industry reeling from negligent distribution litigation, and its defence 'Guns don't kill, people do,' sounding increasingly tired, the ATF saw the chance to restore a reputation badly dented by Waco, and had ridden the surge of pro-gun law public opinion. Not a popular move with other state and Federal agencies, so they were now taunted with names associated with the icons: 'Oh, he's a Costner,' or a 'Stack,' or a 'Ness'.

As always Shepard ignored the implied slur – it was being called a 'Kevin' he really hated – and slowly turned his head to take in the rest of the room. Casinos loved mirrors, on the gaming floor itself, in the corridors of the hotel, across whole walls of the bedrooms. And almost every surface here was at least cracked, crazed or shattered. Others had clearly atomised into dust. He looked back at Lucas who motioned him outside.

The wooden deck stretched for fifty yards, ending in elaborate railings before the slowly churning mass of the Atlantic. Next stop, Europe. A bar occupied one of the deck's flanks, a narrow stage the other. Musical instruments lay abandoned on the latter, and the microphone leant at a drunken angle.

A light movement of air played about the deck, rolling the discarded plastic cups around, fluttering the banners. It was warm and peaceful but spooky, as if an entire cocktail party had suddenly been kidnapped by aliens. But these guys hadn't been beamed up, Shepard surmised. There had been a stampede, a stampede from the rear towards the front.

'OK,' began Lucas, knowing what Shepard wanted to hear first. 'About two . . .' he looked at his watch . . . 'three hours ago, two guys walked into the casino. They had valet-parked the car, just like regular folk. Maybe a bit warmly dressed for the weather, but what the hell, all sorts of people want to throw their money away. They walked calmly to the back of the casino, produced a machine gun each and let rip.'

Shepard said. 'How many?'

'Dead? Seven.'

Seven? That seemed light, Shepard thought. Two sub-machine guns in this space, with this crowd. 'What about security?'

'Oh there was armed security all right, but all at the front end. The reception area of this baby can be sealed off in seconds. And it would have been if everyone hadn't started running for the exits. They couldn't trap them in by putting steel shutters down, could they? So anyway, the majority of casino security were at the boardwalk end.'

He beckoned Shepard once more, and they walked to the rail, both stepping as if they had lead boots on, as the sticky sheen of spilt drinks grabbed at their soles. They looked down at the eight solid pilings that supported the platform. The Atlantic was swirling lazily around them, hardly raising a foam; it was a beautiful day. 'They went down that ladder and jumped a speedboat. And I mean a *speed* boat. Man, it was gone in . . . no time. Whoosh . . .' he cut through the air with the edge of his hand. 'All agree.'

Shepard nodded. 'How much they get?'

'Nothing.'

'What went wrong?'

'Again, nothing. They didn't even try and roll the place. It was like, boom, boom, bye-bye. Gum?'

Shepard took a stick and asked: 'So why ATF?'

'OK, as they went down that ladder, there, one of them dropped his gun. Now it is pretty deep here, but see that sign? Warns that the pylons here flare out to twice their diameter a few feet down. And they don't do it gradually. There's, like, a platform. So we got lucky, well maybe lucky, one of the locals with a snorkel did a couple of dives. Came up with this.'

Shepard led him over to a table where, amid the discarded and spilt drinks, something was wrapped in a white sheet.

'None of us know what it is.'

He was on. This was where Shepard could end up looking stupid. Ten years he had been with the ATF, and seen guns of all shapes and sizes. But every now and then even he got stumped, which caused the locals a little bit of mirth. A Ness who can't tell his Astra from his Eibar. But when he unwrapped it and saw the stubby little grip at the front, and the heavily ridged synthetic receiver, he breathed a sigh of relief.

'It's a Steyr.'

'A what?'

'A Steyr. Austrian. Same nationality as that Glock you've got there.' He pointed to Shepard's belt. 'It's a TMP – Tactical Machine Pistol. You used to be able to get them as SPPs – Special Purpose Pistols which were single-shots, but it didn't take much of a machine shop to do a little tweak and turn them back to TMPs. My guess is we'll find it was imported as one of those before the ban and converted to full auto. OK to touch?'

'Well, we ain't going to get any prints off it. Seems they had flesh-coloured surgical gloves on. The car was clean, too. Stolen a month ago in Newark.'

Shepard picked up the Steyr and weighed it in his hands. Being mainly plastic it clocked the scales at a little over three pounds, and was just around eleven inches long, chambered for the 9mm Parabellum. Tough, reliable, it was a fine weapon. If you needed that kind of thing. Which, he reminded himself, no private citizen ever did. He noticed a remnant of some duct tape still on the magazine. They had jungle-rigged two magazines together, so the unit could be flipped over for easy, fast reloading. But the Siamese twin was missing.

'There is still a magazine down there.'

'I know, we saw it on the security cameras. Each weapon had two taped together. The second one must've come free in the water.' To Shepard's unasked question he said: 'We got reasonably clear images on the screen. Clear enough to know their faces were loaded with prosthetics and phoney bits and pieces. They must've looked like the Marx brothers when they came in – all funny noses and hair. But as I said, casinos are used to all sorts. Known card counters like a disguise, just in case the joint gets uppity, and half the guys at any one time probably have a rug on. The upshot is we can't do any facial mapping to match to known perps or any of that shit. Which leaves us with the car and with that.'

'It's so light you're lucky the gun stayed put on the shelf, so never mind the mag. Seven dead?'

'Yeah.'

'Seems very . . . shit, if *I* let off one of these, there would have been more than seven dead. And I ain't the best shot in the Bureau.'

'I know what you're sayin', Agent. It could have been seventy. Easy.' He sounded almost disappointed.

14

'Yeah. It don't make sense.' Shepard released the magazine, checked the breach was cleared and raised it up to firing height, his imagination filling in the noise, the smell, the constant thudding against his shoulder, the stream of people running into the crush inside. Shepard shook his head in disbelief. 'Two of these, and lots of sitting ducks and they only hit seven?'

'No, they didn't.'

Shepard put the gun down and reassembled it.

'What?'

'We got seven dead. I didn't say they shot seven. Three were killed by the chandelier coming down on them – I mean we also got close to fifty badly cut from the flying glass, too – but the others were crushed or trampled to death in the panic. They didn't hit anyone.'

Shepard let this sink in. He pulled out a pad and noted down the weapon's serial number. It was right where it should be, in the grooves of the moulding on the left side of the receiver, under 'Steyr-Mannlicher'. He would call it through to the ATF National Tracing Centre at Landover, Maryland, but he wasn't optimistic. The gun was manufactured post-1993. It was banned for private use in the US a couple of years later, so it probably came in eight, nine years ago or so. Could have gone through a lot of hands in the intervening period. But the ATF's Project Lead had been cataloguing the movements of such weapons for almost a decade now, so they might get a break.

He thought some more about the gun. Twenty or twenty five rounds in the magazine. Rate of fire somewhere around 600 a minute. Two magazines apiece. Steyr made weapons for the Austrian army and police. They were not gangster junk like the Tecs or Cobrays the kid had wanted back at Barrels of Fun. Finally he said: 'Either they were lousy shots, almost criminally bad, or . . .'

Lucas nodded. He had reached the same conclusion hours before. 'They were trying to kill the building, not the people.' And then they said, almost simultaneously, *'The Alchemist'*.

ONE

Atlantic City, NJ. Friday November 22

Ed Behr pulled his cab up well short of the Boardwalk. In front of him lay a two-inch deep lake, its surface still being ridged and troughed by what was left of the wind. The nor'easter that had hung over the coastline for days and days now had dumped so much rain the city was turning into a mini Venice. Blown out, it was down to its last few feeble gasps.

Luckily, one of the condos had put out duckwalks across the deeper sections, and he reached the ramp up to the Boardwalk with merely a dark line on the bottom of each trouser cuff. He walked up onto the walkway, puffing slightly from the exertion, and looked left and right.

Under the powder-grey sky, the Boardwalk was all but deserted. The T-shirt and salt taffy shops were shuttered, the owners having given up the thought of any business for the week, with just a few hot dog and pizza joints hanging grimly on. Clusters of the wheeled chair operators huddled outside the casinos, hoods up, shuffling to generate some heat, praying for some trade, someone who fancied a bracing push between gaming halls, perhaps, but the gamblers were experiencing their own version of lockdown. Even though the nor'easter had temporarily shut up shop, the Weather Channel promised it had a pal out over that evil-looking ocean, warming up to step into its shoes. The casinos were geared to making sure there was little incentive to leave:

Why risk getting wet, or getting that careful coiffure ruined by the wind? Here, have a free drink and a canapé.

Ed took the half a dozen steps across the still-glistening planks and leaned on the rail, looking down at the detritus-strewn beach. The storms had resculptured it as always, making a mockery of all attempts to create a stable frontage, tearing out a long section in front of Caesars, and dumping a mini sand dune around the old steel pier, the one once famous for its rides, its freakshow and its diving horses, but now just another strip of slots. Beach erosion was getting worse than ever right along the shore. He read somewhere that Long Branch was all but beachless, the boardwalk now more like a pier, with its supports dipping into the Atlantic. Even Wildwood, where most of the sand used to end up, was starting to destabilise.

He shivered. Somewhere behind the solid sheet of pewter that was the sky, the sun was going down. He could feel the last of its feeble warmth slinking away, as if embarrassed to be quitting so early in the day. He checked his watch. Time for the Friday afternoon drink at the Pole. He pulled out his little red notebook and wrote in the last fare. He flicked the pages. Today he had done two airport runs, a Margate drop-off, two lots of people over to Brigantine for lunch and a long run down to pretty Cape May. Plus a handful of inter-casino transfers. Same old, same old. He turned back, looking at the repeating patterns, his life shuffling a very limited deck of options, weeks segueing into months of fare after fare, all variations on the same theme as today.

It irritated him that he had to keep this diary. But he still occasionally had memory blanks – just an hour or two he couldn't recall, as if the access lines in his brain had gone down. Well, as the doc had said, having your head banged on a shower spigot twenty or forty or fifty times – he had forgotten to count – would do it every time.

18

He checked his pockets and found the half-eaten Snickers bar he had pocketed when he picked up the last fare, and began chomping though it. The lights grew brighter at the casinos: The Beach Club, all tropical blues and greens, its giant fake palms twinkling like Christmas trees; Bally's, as usual, spelling out its name in lights; and a new billboard outside the Taj that was flashing the total payout so far that day. Strange, they never flash up how much money has actually been played to get that total. And at the far northern end he saw the first lick of flame – the Palace's dragon was starting its hourly routine of toasting a couple of knights.

He looked at the time again, hitched up his trousers over his stomach, hoping that would prevent them dipping in the flood water this time, screwed up the candy bar wrapper and tossed it towards the sea. He had a weekly appointment to keep.

The North Pole, to give it its full name, was located on Baltic, four blocks from the Boardwalk, well away from where most of the city's customers strayed. They kept to narrow corridors – the Boardwalk and Atlantic, the well-lit strips from there to the new convention centre, and the shuttle buses and secure tunnels that fed the Marina casinos. They thought of the rest of it as the Combat Zone, all empty parking lots and dilapidated frontages and broken chain-link fences, full of dangerous shadows. Well, perhaps they were right. It was getting that way again. The nineties had been pretty good, the Y2K projects and the spending spree by the casino fund had kept the momentum going, but now? Suddenly AC had hit the buffers, it seemed to him.

The Pole didn't look too welcoming, thought Ed as he pulled up. If it had been his first time and he'd seen the spluttering Miller sign and a door with what looked like gunshots in it – which *were* gunshots, he reminded himself –

then he'd probably hightail it back to the Showboat or the Tropicana or the Plaza, no matter how much more the drinks were in the bars there.

The familiar smell hit him as soon as he walked in, the aroma of a carpet marinated in thirty years of spilt drinks, of an overworked french-frier, of stale cigarette smoke overlaid by the heavier slug of the odd cigar, of the sweat of tired, temporally disoriented workers just off shift from the halls of the casinos, their sense of time returning as they sucked back another beer before wending their way home. He stepped over Hoppitty, the three-legged retriever that was the bar's mascot. Like some kind of chameleon, the dog had gradually taken on the hue of the floor covering, so it was hard to know where sticky carpet ended and matted dog began. You just made sure your strides were big enough to clear him.

It was both offensive and comforting, thought Ed, and he started the ritual round of fast handshakes and how-ya-doings, waving to Marty, the greasy-haired guy in the corner, your easy conduit to sports betting. All in all the Pole was just your very basic drinking hole. The bar itself was an elongated oval, with a flip-up section for bartender access in the centre of one side. The circumference was padded with red vinyl, crazed and cracked and split from two generations of elbows. Unique among the bars of Atlantic City, there were no gambling machines, none of the counter-top video poker games, just a mini-bowling machine and a pinball. Even the three TV screens were considered on the spartan side. Harvey, the owner, kept one on the sports, one on the local channel and, latterly, another on the weather reports. It was enough, he said, three channels at once. Most people considered this mildly eccentric.

The other oddity was the Freedom Wall, a green felt square above the booths, perhaps eight feet each side, covered with dozens of casino ID badges or photographs, all defaced in some way and pinned on the growing pile, often with a little message: 'Taj Mahal is Indian for kiss-my-ass', 'Balls to Ballys', 'Goodnight Crapicana.' When someone left the industry, they often ended their farewell rip at Harvey's to add to the badges of dishonour.

Harvey himself wouldn't be in. This time of year he was in Florida and his son – Harvey – was nominally in charge, but he seemed to have little interest in upholding the family tradition, so Sam, a young Irishman, was tending tonight. Harvey Jr would be at the tables in the Hilton, which set him apart from most of his clientele, who saw things from the other side of the deck. Few people in here had any taste left for gambling with their own money.

Ed slapped palms with Leo, the pit boss, who as usual barely cracked a smile. It was a shame he didn't play, the man had the most perfect poker face in the city, and when he did smile you wish he hadn't. He reminded Ed of the actor Roy Thinnes, who had been in that old series The Invaders – he had the same small, hard-to-read eyes. He'd been promoted to pit boss when he caught the notorious Drop Out – a guy who manipulated slot machines using fibre-optics, teasing them into hitting jackpots then boasting about it with notes left around the casino. He'd done it in Vegas, Reno, Biloxi, Connecticut – all the places Ed had worked before these last couple of years – and twice in Atlantic City. He made the mistake of doing the third hit on Leo's shift. Leo had a rather physical version of a citizen's arrest in his repertoire. Still, the dropout claimed to have pulled in five mil over three years, not bad going.

A couple of stools along was Goodrich, his straggly blond hair pulled into a ponytail, the usual cigarette magically glued in the corner of his mouth. Goodrich was another one who proved that Atlantic City was like human fly paper –

21

once you landed, you couldn't get off. He had come down from New York City with a thousand bucks burning a hole in his pocket, and the casinos obliged by relieving him of it in three hours. Now he worked in a twenty-four-seven pawnshop, catering to players who suddenly found themselves short at two a.m., and whose line of credit had derailed. Nikon? Rolex? Tiffany? That'll do nicely, sir.

The other familiar face was Alice, of indeterminate age, who could be twenty, could be forty. She had a face that was so hard you felt you could scratch diamonds on it. Her henna'd hair was curtained across a visage devoid of make-up for once, and she had clearly thought better of trying to use the sunglasses now lying in front of her to cover up the raw blue-black streak under her left eye.

And then there was Bo. Bo was face down on the bar, his cheek and nose distorted so he looked like Charles Laughton doing Quasimodo. Saliva had dribbled out of his mouth onto the counter top, forming a small sticky pool. Bo opened one eye, saw Ed, and closed it again. There was a story to Bo, as there was to most regulars.

Bo used to be the best looking guy in the place, then he stumbled and fell, fell into the crack houses that used to line the blocks around the bar. These days you could hide a small sedan in his sunken cheeks, and his top lip had imploded where his two front teeth had come out – or been knocked out. And the dog had better hair than he had.

Bo's story was this. Two years previously his old man died and left him a three-storey building down on Brighton Avenue where, it was said, the money was hidden from some score years before. Hundred grand, claimed the rumours. Bank, armoured car, Post Office, they all said different things. However much it was and wherever it came from, it was meant to be Bo's, but his old man was so disgusted by his state he wouldn't tell him where in the house the money was stashed. 'Over my dead body,' he was supposed to have said. So that was what he did. Starting as soon as he got the ashes from the crematorium, day after day, Bo ripped another floorboard up, took down another wall, waiting to find the pot of gold. All the time the ashes sat in one corner, gloating mutely. The house was now a skeletal shell, in danger of collapse, and still no money. So now Bo was wondering whether he dreamed the deathbed scene. 'Over my dead body,' you would hear him muttering incessantly. And the frustration had turned him into the slob who was sitting on Ed's stool.

'Bo.' Ed tapped him on the shoulder. 'Bo.'

One yellowed, mad-dog eye opened again. 'Fuck you, Fat Man.'

A little ripple ran round the bar. Someone sniggered.

Ed tapped him on the shoulder, feeling the bones under the paper-thin, fat-free skin. He said, as softly as he could: 'Bo. C'mon, you know the deal.'

The eye flicked open again. 'Fat Boy? Fuck you.'

Ed felt the blood surge behind his eyes. If he sat anywhere else, if he let it lie, then he got marked down as a soft touch, a softer touch than he already was. He knew it from alley-o, he knew it from Boxgrove. There was a slot in the pecking order here, and he was about to lose it.

It happened fast, before he had time to think it through, to consider, and he used the bulk the guy was jibbing him about. He put all his weight behind the punch, driving it deep into Bo's kidneys, feeling the organs part under his first, the internal shockwave bounce off membranes and tissues. Bo tried to jump up but Ed grabbed his hair and banged down once on the bar top, sending up a spray of saliva, surfing on the wave of anger that was bursting inside him. 'You gettin' up to move, or fight?'

'MMff.' Bo even sounded like Charles Laughton now.

'What? What you say Bo?'

'Muv.'

Ed stood back and Bo got to his feet, rearranged his shirt, and limped, holding his back, over to a banquette, where he slumped in muttering dark threats. Everyone else lost interest as quickly as they had started taking it.

Ed eased his bulk onto the stool. He grabbed a Bud bar cloth and wiped up the spittle. The blood red anger was gone, diffused, as quickly as it came. A pure defensive reflex, like a puffer fish blowing up. The territoriality, the instinct of the Box, those short sharp spats you got at chow time, ten seconds of raw aggression then it's over. 'Coors. Turkey,' he said.

'There's other stools, Ed,' said Goodrich.

Ed looked across and wondered about his response. Yes, you're right? Mind your own fucking business? In the end he just flashed him the finger and Goodrich smiled and shook his head in a don't-know-why-I-bother way.

Sam nodded and put the beer and bourbon in front of him. 'So, good day?' He knew enough to put the bowl of chips in front of Ed and keep them coming. Ed liked to graze pretty much continuously.

Ed shrugged: 'Oh, couple of casino shuffles, airport run, Margate.'

'You see Lucy?'

One of the runs had been down to see her, but he hadn't bothered knocking. What was there to say? 'Yeah, Lucy was still there. Been there a hundred years now.'

'They moved her didn't they?'

Ed nodded. 'Twice. Once when they got the money together to save her, once after the arson attack a couple of years back.'

'She's great, though, isn't she? How could anyone think of trying to torch her?'

Sam was still in his late twenties, still had a twinkle in his eye, a spring in his step. Maybe he wouldn't understand that, after she got a starring role in a Bud ad, Lucy's neighbours got fed up with the constant stream of beer-swilling tourists. Word was it was one of the locals who had finally had enough, had poured gasoline over the old girl's feet and struck a match.

Ed tried to imagine the world through the young man's eyes. Well, not that much younger, he reminded himself. Ed was maybe eight years older. But Sam's were less jaded, tired eyes, that was for sure. When he saw his customers come in he must have felt like he was serving cadavers most of the time. People who had forgotten how you buttoned up shirts, how to use dry cleaners, a razor, shampoo and flat-ware, all mixed up with those guys who worked the casinos, who kept the minimum standards, but had forgotten where their soul was.

Fuck knows what he makes of me, he thought. Some lowlife who has dragged around the bars of America like this for six years now, maybe more, always finding a Goodrich and an Alice and a Sam, and a Bo. Perhaps the barkeep would look at him one day and see a terrible warning: Get out of Town.

Goodrich was watching the hockey, pleased that Joe Thornton looked like having the kind of season promised when he was picked up on the first draft of 1997 for the Bruins. 'See, I told you that kid could give the Russkie a run for his money. Samsonov fuckin' peaked too soon. Too intense if you ask me.'

Leo sniffed in disdain and said, in a voice that brooked no argument. 'And neither of them ever be as good as Andreychuk.'

'Andreychuk? Fuck – what is this? History? We going back to the last century now? Well in which case what about Bourque? Sure, he played defence, but you know he got well over a thousand assists.'

'Another.' It was Alice, ignoring what she thought of as the usual sports shit the regulars spewed like molten rock, a never-ending stream of stats, secondhand opinions and first-hand ignorance. She knew sooner or later someone would mention Wayne Gretsky and they would all start sobbing into their brews. It was worse during the ball season. Some of them were in severe danger of knowing what they were talking about. She chipped into those shit shooting sessions sometimes. Personally, she was a Mike Piazza fan, although when pushed she was more impressed by the fact the wires – the *wires*, mind – for his stereo cost ten grand than his ball play. Right now though she was too busy drinking beer and shots of something called a Neuflaymer, a kind of Goldschlager with bad attitude, to take much notice.

Sam obliged with her drinks, gave Ed a refill of chips, and then leant casually on the bar. He had yet to pick up on the nuances of any of the sports that paraded across the screens in a blur of meaningless stats, and so, unable to offer an opinion about ice hockey, he said: 'Alice, I hope you don't mind me asking, but . . . where did yous get that eye?'

If he had been a bit less relaxed – or maybe a little less stupid, perhaps – if he had even suspected there was a line to be crossed, Sam might have felt the drinkers around the bar stiffen. Ed threw back the Wild Turkey and coughed as it seared his throat. He banged the shot glass on the table, the cue to be asked for a refill. Sam didn't take the hint. 'I mean, it's quite a shiner, that one.'

Fuck, thought Ed.

Alice raised her hand and, like corn in the breeze, every figure around the bar swayed back in their stool, but she was only pushing her hair behind her ears. She leant forward. 'I will tell you Sammy, my Irish friend. I picked this guy up at Duke Mack's down on the Boardwalk. I have to work there because none of the casinos will let me in. Not by myself. You know what I'm saying? Got a client on my arm, fine, what the client wants, they want. But no cruising. Yeah? So, he didn't want to go back to his room, so we got one at the Tobago Motel, down on Pennsylvania. Now, he wants to do a lot of things – you know, a bit out of the ordinary, but he is paying top dollar, so what the fuck? Anyway, we eventually get down to the regular stuff, and I've got his dick in my mouth when he suddenly starts yelling that he has lost his fuckin' ring. He pulls me off and waves this fuckin' digit in my face and says – my ring, my ring. It must've come off. Now this guy has had his hands and fingers everywhere, but you know I had a quick feel inside me and said it must've slipped off in the bed or something. So we strip the bed. No ring. So he's convinced it is up my ass. His wedding ring is up my ass. I tell him, "There is no way we are going to organise a search party up there, baby," and he clocks me one. Biff. Decides that it's some sort of skill I have, pulling off wedding rings with my ass muscles.'

At this point Maurice, the thin, starved-looking figure who passed for a chef at North Pole, shuffled up to Ed and asked: 'A menu for you tonight, Sir?' In the years he had been coming to the Pole, Ed had never personally eaten there. Ed didn't have particularly high standards when it came to food preparation, but Maurice was still able to limbo-dance under them. During the day he fixed cars outback, and rumour was he often got the lube oil and the frying oil mixed up. Or maybe it was just the accumulated grease under his nails that lent the food that distinctive mechanical tinge. He also made cheeseburgers that looked like shrunken heads. Anyway, even if he was willing to take a risk, given the direction Alice's monologue was taking, it probably wasn't a good time for Ed to break that no-eat rule anyway. So he made his standard reply: 'Not right now, Maurice. I got some chips. Maybe later.'

Sam, feeling he had to fill the sudden silence, asked croakily: 'So what happened?'

'Well I convinced him I was no fanny-heister. If it did happen, it was an accident, and his fault for using too much damned lubricant. So he told me that if it comes out, it's worth three grand to him.' She drained her drinks and slipped off the stool. 'So I gotta watch my bowel movements – he's in town until Wednesday. Anyway, they changing the guard shift at the Palace now, and those dudes don't all know me yet, so I gotta get ready. See y'all.' She slotted on her sunglasses, flashed Sam a crooked smile and headed for the door.

'Hey Alice,' said Goodrich as she passed: 'You know down at the shop we can match any ring there is.' Then he grinned. ''Cept your own, of course.' The punch on his shoulder must have hurt, but he carried on grinning as she strode out into the dusk, slamming the door with its twenty year old bullet holes that gave Harvey his one bit of notoriety, even though it transpired they had shot up the wrong joint.

Sam looked over to Leo and Goodrich and asked: 'Do you guys believe that story?'

Leo looked at his drink. 'Put it this way – I don't not believe it.'

'Ed?'

But Ed wasn't listening.

He was watching the face on one of the TV screens, the big, bloated red face of a man he had tried hard to forget. The guy had got even fatter, fatter than Ed, bloated with excessive living and his moustache was flecked with white now. He was mouthing a speech – as usual the sound was off – to support some campaign or other, but slowly they started to lip synch with the snatches and phrases locked in Ed's brain: 'A disgrace to this community . . . running wild . . . reclaim the streets for good, honest citizens.'

The face faded, to be replaced with a shot of Cotchford, panning along the High Street, past Bailey's store, and slowly the street began to fill with Ed's memories as the people on the streets dissolved into translucent ghosts. In their place came a bunch of young kids, boys and girls, retracing those same streets as the camera. Ed imagined his own face turned to that camera, giving his side of the story.

It was a game, you see. It was the first game, you understand, the precursor of the one everyone talks about, the one that got us into all the trouble. This first one, it wasn't . . . harmful. Just an urban kid's game. I mean, a real street game, didn't really belong here at all. A kid called Grogan introduced it from Brooklyn when we was in the tenth grade. He said it was called ringolevio, but we knew it as alley-o. Whatever, the rules were simple. Each side had a base, or jail. I used to chalk ours outside Jimmy's, over on the West Side. Billy, he would do his on the East Side, right in front of Bailey's dime store, near where Woolworth's used to be. So two teams. One scattered and hid, the other went looking. You found someone, you had to get them back to jail. But they didn't go softly. Nah, it was a rough game, rough as football. Us guys who weren't jocks, but played alley-o? We got some respect, I tell you. Once in jail, they couldn't escape unless a member of their own team came running through and shouted the magic word. Alley-o. Or ringolevio. Grogan never gave up shouting his own name for it. The games lasted all day. In fact, I was talking about this once, we reckon it is extinct now. Who in America lets their kids wander the streets anymore? OK, maybe the projects, but I get the feeling the kids are too busy fucking themselves up to play games. You know what I mean? And they would be too worried about scuffin' their sneakers for alley-o. Anyways, I ain't never heard or seen it since. I reckon we were the last two sides to play it on God's earth. And you know what? The Mayor you just seen? He banned it. Not very civic minded of us to brawl and run down the street, to streak by shouting 'alley-o'. He didn't like it. So the game is banned. And guess what? We thought up a new one. A new game. And then guess what? People got killed, that's what.

Ed's internal monologue faltered when he felt a hand on his shoulder. He looked at the TV and it had moved on to floods and coastal damage. What has the mayor been doing there? Shit, the fat bastard must be running for Congress or Governor or some such. November. Mid-term elections. Shit. He shook his head to clear his mind and turned to face his visitor.

Tasker took a perch next to Ed, Ed bought the man a drink and stood him one of Maurice's hamburgers, which Tasker had an inexplicable fondness for. Maybe he liked the taste of Wynn's Superlube. Chit-chat – sports; mostly the horses and, specifically this week, The Breeder's Cup; the state of the city; the economy – was the order of the day until the burger was gone and Tasker was on to drink two. Only then he would produce the sheaf of papers from his inside pocket and lay them on the bar.

It all went according to routine this time, except Tasker hesitated before delivering the bad news. 'I checked through them. Nobody that has Cotchford, New Jersey as a birthplace.'

Ed picked up the folded sheets. These were copies of licence applications submitted to the Casino Control Commission, who must vet everyone who works in the giant gaming complexes, from cocktail waitresses to cleaners, pit bosses to camera monitors. The higher the position, the more thorough the check for a felonious background. It had been a slow time for recruitment. That business in Asbury Park, and *The Alchemist* before that, people were beginning to think there were safer ways to earn a living than the gaming industry – coal mining, perhaps, maybe stripping asbestos.

But this time Ed noticed something in Tasker's voice. It was higher than usual, there was no flatness, it had modulation. Ed had heard this before, way back. Optimism, yeah, that was it. 'But? You got something?'

'Nah.' Cagey now. 'Probably not. Just that one of the slot servers over in the Palace, she sort of fit your description, about the right age, and she was born in Long Branch. That's not too far is it?'

Ed frowned. It was maybe five miles from Cotchford. And she had been born smack on the border of the two townships, so perhaps she opted for one rather than the other.

Tasker said: 'And the name is similar. See here?' He stabbed at the details he had circled on the list. He could see something flickering in Ed's eyes, like a kind of greed. A hunger. 'Look, don't get your hopes up. I mean, it's been how long? Maybe she got a job in Reno. Las Vegas.'

Ed shrugged. He had tried all the others, worked cabs, busboy, ticket collector, anything, had talked to a dozen Taskers but he knew that, like him, she would eventually find herself back at Atlantic City. 'She'll be here. One day. She's a Jersey Girl.'

'Yeah, well this one's a Jersey Girl waitress, Ed.'

'Maybe she's going to school. Dealer school. You know? The dealer schools?' Ed didn't sound convinced himself. Tasker could feel a slight hostility, as if he had ruined the ritual by actually coming up with a candidate. He wondered why he did this, why he risked his good job at the CCC by copying each week's applications for a greasy burger and to feed the fantasies of a sad barfly. Because, he guessed, the Pole was the sort of bar where, after a few drinks, you found

31

yourself suggesting – promising – such things. This was one place you felt you were all in the same boat together, even though some of you were stokers while others got to walk the bridge. And, let's face it, Ed was down in the bilges.

When Ed had finished scanning through the list and had scribbled down the details of the circled entry, Tasker took the papers back and slipped them into his inside pocket.

'Yeah, always worth a look, Ed. Take it easy, eh?'

As he watched Tasker leave, he caught Goodrich looking at him. He raised his palm in apology and sniffed: 'No offence, Ed, just . . . curious. None of my business.' He rubbed the shoulder where Alice had punched him, more out of nervousness than pain.

Goodrich tried to light a cigarette with a damp book of matches. Ed watched the flame on each match dance and die. He pulled out a Zippo lighter that had been left in his cab and slid it over. 'Use this.' Goodrich got the light and offered the Zippo back. 'Keep it.'

'Sure. Thanks. So . . . what is this thing with Tasker? If you don't mind me askin'?'

'Just someone I've been looking for is all. I figured she'd wind up here sooner or later. You come here, you wanna job, you go to a casino – right?'

Goodrich moved to be closer. 'Atlantic City? Right now? For a job? Don't you get the feeling someone has pulled the chain, it's just that the flush hasn't hit us yet?'

Ed nodded. 'You been outside recently? Seen the amount of water on the streets? I think God pulled the chain last week.' But he knew what Goodrich meant. Since the New Downturn – or, because it all started with some currency thing in Europe that hit the US markets hard, the Dollardrums – the casino revenues had faltered, overall drops were plummeting, and all those who said AC had put all its civic eggs in one basket had been proved right. When the casinos caught a cold, Atlantic City got pleurisy with complications. Now it was coughing real hard.

Goodrich scratched his three-day growth and bought Ed another drink. 'She was like . . . special?'

Ed shrugged. Was special. Is special.

'OK, OK, I can see I am treadin' on toes here. Like I said, no offence.' As if in return for the lighter, he lowered his voice and said, 'Look, Ed, we got a shop full of gear down there, anything you want, you come by after eight, which is when I get on most nights, and I'll see you OK. The shit we got – guys come in every night. You see the looks on their faces, and they are thinking, "Well I got two, three hours to make up my losses." '

Ed had been around casinos long enough to have absorbed a few truisms. 'You never make up your losses,' he said flatly, eyes on the TV screen in case that face came back.

'You're right, you're right. Never. You're A-one fuckin' right. Dumbest way to gamble, tryin' to get back what you already threw away. But we get all kinds. I got offered a porn empire a while back. No bullshit. A whole series of internet pay-sites – guy wanted to hock them. I mean – some of the stuff. He showed me print-outs. There was this one of these women with turkey basters up their asses. Can you believe that? You can't make this stuff up.'

Ed turned to face him: 'Doesn't it make you sick?'

'Well Thanksgiving'll probably never be the same.'

'No, I mean taking these people's watches and cameras and jewellery and giving them a few bucks you know will go straight into the casino's pockets?'

Goodrich took a slug of his beer and wiped his mouth. 'Whoa, Ed. You are expecting me to make some sort of . . . some sort of moral judgement here? In Atlantic City? Are you crazy? We're all damned, my boy, even the cab drivers.

Want another? Another drink? I got time for one more before my shift.'

Ed made to get down from the stool. He had to take the cab back to the garage and then get home and change. 'Thanks. I gotta check this out.' He waved the piece of paper from Tasker.

He slid off the stool, and heard Goodrich order another beer, hesitated and heaved himself back on. His elbows stuck to the bar, sucked into the familiar dips in the crazed padding, as if held by a vacuum. His stool. Anybody else, it was just on loan. He kind of fitted in this place. 'OK, just the one. Coors. Turkey. Hey and Sam – keep those chips comin', eh?'

TWO

Binker Towers, Fifth and 51st. New York.

Billy Moon turned sideways to the mirror and pulled in his stomach. It was definitely going. He felt the little butterflies down there, the nervous energy that was – with a little help from his new gym membership – without a doubt, burning off the layer of mid-thirties fat that had started to accumulate around his middle over the last two years. Mistresses, he thought, best diet ever invented. That and an arm-and-leg personal trainer at the club. He flexed his arm and smiled at the way the bunched muscles strained at his shirt sleeve, as if it was trying to burst out. He did the other one. Not quite the Incredible Hulk. But not bad, he thought, not bad going at all.

He slipped on the jacket of a navy blue suit – a Jil Sander – he had bought from Barney's, and checked the knot of his Prada tie. Looking good, he thought. It was three o'clock now, so, if he left soon and missed the worst of the tunnel traffic, two and a half hours to drive down, an hour, maybe ninety minutes of business, and then . . .

'Don't you feel like a messenger boy?'

His wife's voice made him jump. She had come into the bedroom unheard. How much of his little preening had she seen? He turned to face her, his face, he hoped, composed: 'What?'

She sat down on the bed, kicked off her shoes, then curled her legs up under her in a way he used to find very provocative. He guessed he was suffering some sort of sexual overfamiliarity – the same way you had to buy a new stroke mag every so often because the images lost their potency after a while. Maybe that happened with people. The smell of her, lying in bed with him, the scent that used to get his dick hard in an instant, even that had the opposite effect. Nausea, that's what he got from it, a cloying sensation that made him gag. He had to fight hard not to wrinkle his nose when she was near, to keep a civil tongue in his head. However, it wasn't a good time to rock the boat, start everything unravelling. Too much going on, the last thing he needed was another distraction. Soon, maybe. 'A messenger boy? What the fuck you mean, messenger boy?'

She put a whiny sneer into her voice: 'Daddy wants something picked up from Atlantic City, so Billy Jr has to hightail it down there every week.'

'Two weeks,' he corrected.

Anne Darlington frowned. She wouldn't use his family's surname: who wanted to be Anne Moon? Sounded like a stripper.

She couldn't believe a fortnight had gone by since his last trip. '*Two* weeks, then. It's hardly high-powered work.'

Fuck. How come other guys get to do what they want, no questions asked. He knew guys who ran around like they were still single, no ties. He was out there walking the walk and talking the talk every day, and he had to come home to . . . this? He had to account for every fucking minute to this ball-breaker. 'It is none of your fuckin' business, is it? It's between me and BB.'

'What is it – blood money?'

'Yeah, Big Billy pays me to stay with you.'

She snorted at that. 'And how come you have to have dinner down there every time? That is one in two Friday nights. You know I like to go out Fridays.'

Yes, he almost said, it is one of the ways you show you are still, at heart, a Jersey girl, a b&t – addicted to the weekend, the Friday night ritual of going out and partying, even if they were at the time of their life when their party was more likely to be one of the Vong restaurants than Hooters.

'Look, I don't have to explain this shit to you again do I? Manners. Good manners is what it is. Remember those? People bein' fuckin' nice to each other. Look, Backson is waiting downstairs with the driver. I gotta go, traffic'll be murder otherwise. We'll go out tomorrow.'

Anne wasn't letting go. 'You went last week.'

'Nah, that was the construction site down in Paterson. Remember? Hospital?' In fact that had also been an excuse to see Jerry, his guy who ran the Internet network he had picked up in Atlantic City. Quite a bargain, regular income, *his* income, something BB knew nothing about. And now he had cleaned the worst bits out of it – the turkey basters, the used tampon ads – chicken blood, Jerry had assured him, but all the fucking same, sick – it was almost tasteful. And boy did it have its perks.

Anne shrugged, as if she couldn't recall the details. Billy felt a sudden anger rise in him, gush up from the pit of his stomach. He suddenly had an overwhelming urge to punch her skinny little face, to feel the bone of her nose crumple under his fist. He quickly forced the lid back on, made an effort to take the anger from his expression.

He tried to placate her, to leave on a civil note, not civil war. 'Look, I gotta run. Just do what you want. Go see Sarah, huh?' Her pain in the ass harpie friend, even more adept at chewing off balls than little Anne here. 'I'll be back twelve, one at the latest.'

'Oh, don't bother on my account.'

He spun round and grabbed her face in one hand, his

thumb and forefinger pinching her cheeks together. 'I have had enough of—'

She swung up and dashed his arm away, 'You fucking prick. Don't you touch me like that. I tell BB you knockin' me around he'll give me your scrotum for a purse and you know it. I'm not one of the pond life you spend your day impressing. Fuck off, fuck off. Go and play messenger boy.'

His presence faded, like a throbbing headache slowly softening down to a faint thrum, and then vanishing altogether.

Anne sighed, unclipped her hair and let it fall out and dropped back onto the bed, tempted to slip in between the Bennison sheets. She tried to interpret that little peacock parade she had witnessed, the pulling in of the stomach, the pumping of muscles, the sly, almost coquettish smile. Interpret, hell, she knew what it meant. Just put it together with his obvious disdain, the way he was wishing she wasn't around, and you got one answer. Which only left who, where and why.

Well, where would be pretty obvious – Atlantic City. Never before had he looked forward to being Daddy's Little Bagboy. He liked the grown-up stuff. But now he was more than happy to take his trouser bulge down there for a couple of hours.

Well maybe it was her fault, maybe she had turned from wife to an Olympic standard nagger. No, that was unfair. She'd just made sure they were going in the right direction. When he had had no idea where they should live, she had found the apartment, cajoled Big Billy to help fund it, managed to come up with a set of accounts that looked as if Billy actually earned a living, rather than suckled at the BB tit, got them through that sniffy co-op committee, had furnished it. He would have gone to Crate and Barrel or Ikea and bulk-ordered. She had scoured the Village and

SoHo for the right things, had asked Bennison to make the sheets and throws and covers to her design, and now they couldn't sell enough of them.

Who? Now that was intriguing all right. Just who could it be? Some cocktail waitress, maybe? One of the hookers that prowls the casinos looking for high rollers? Jesus, she hoped he used a rubber if it was. Or maybe it was just some twenty year old who saw the nice suits and the limo and thought she might reel him in. Oh no, honey, for better or worse, he's mine.

She hesitated for a moment. Not so long ago she had been thinking things weren't too good, had considered whether a lover might perk things up a bit. But that was different. That had been idle speculation. And anyway, that had been on her terms. She was the one who made the running, not some big-bunned waitress. He goes when she is good and ready for him to go.

Before she could change her mind, she rolled over, grabbed the telephone and punched the fast dial code. Part of her hated to do this, but the other part knew she would get some kind of straight answers, if only for old times' sake. Yeah, Big Billy, BB, he would know what to do.

Vincent Wuzel rubbed his eyes and tried to read the label on the package again. He tilted it so the light from the office's dim bulb hit the glossy address sticker, to see if he could check the handwriting, but to no avail. With a sigh he reached over and plucked his reading glasses off the desk. Getting old. Fifty and turning into a bat. Great.

He got up and slammed the window down to cut down the noise of irritated horn-honking. Outside, most of New York was either preparing to go home or filling up the bars like the one underneath his feet, the one full of young jerks. He could hear the noise coming up, the hum of voices with the occasional braying laugh of someone who was just thrilled to be part of the self-satisfied crowd. Narcotics and narcissism, that's what they dealt with down there, and neither was in short supply.

Up here on the second floor of the building, though, where he had the office and storeroom of the Paladin Agency, Wuzel knew he still had a lot of orders to fill before he could call it a day. Anyway, he didn't quite fit in down there, even though the owner, that tall blonde, had said he could jump the weekend lines anytime.

Next door he could hear the odd expletive as Edgar wrapped up a consignment of books. Edgar thought wrapping books was beneath him, that he was made for finer things. Edgar was, in fact, designed only for cracking skulls. Wrapping books was actually above him. He must remember to employ someone else for the task.

Wuzel put his glasses on and slit the parcel open, and slowly unfolded the thick cardboard. He let the book fall into his hands and gasped, even though he had known all along what was within. It was Henri Cartier Bresson's *The Decisive Moment*, the 1952 edition with a Matisse cover. Six hundred dollars he had paid for it, and it was so close to a steal as to be criminal. Once in a lifetime it happened, someone selling off a valued collection, not realising just how much photographic books had exploded in the last few years.

He could move this on tomorrow for four, five times that, but for the moment he delayed the moment of opening and he slipped it onto the shelf behind him, next to Avedon's Observations, with the introduction by Truman Capote. The next envelope was thin and flexible. A catalogue. He opened it up. Christie's annual sale of 20th century photographs. Late this year.

He flicked through on a preliminary glance, to see what

would catch his eye. Almost subliminally the names clicked over: Margaret Bourke-White; Russell Lee, a print of Lumberjacks, *Saturday Night, Minnesota, 1917*; Gjon Mili; Eliot Porter; Gordon Parks, one of the Harlem pictures from the late Forties. Robert Frank, a marching band from 1952. Ah, an Irving Penn, *Bathing Nude Soaping Rear* from 1978. A sort of arty Tennis-Player-Scratching-Her-Ass image. He looked at the estimate. Ten thousand dollars. Ten fucking thousand dollars? Jesus, hadn't anyone told these guys there was a recession on? Art market plummeting, shares wobbling, the dollar worth about as much as the rouble – how come of all the investment possibilities only his chosen field stayed buoyant? Well he shouldn't complain.

And even if there wasn't a downturn, ten big ones was far too much for a Penn of that vintage. He preferred his own Penn, the one of Regine. What would that be worth now? He thought of it in the vault. What a waste. One day he would build the extension, the little gallery out back of his house, and do these men and women justice. But the cost . . .

Then he found it. Towards the back, no fanfare, a cropped image only, eighth of a page, if that. It was a New York longshoreman, sometime in the early fifties, a genuine piece of *On The Waterfront*. The guy was maybe twenty-five and he had a big, hard body. Not the kind you see now, where people have worked out in some fancy gym just to get that *Men's Health* ripple effect on the stomach. No, this guy ate red meat and drank cheap whiskey and smoked and fucked and kept his body like that because he humped dry goods eight, ten hours a day five times a week, not because he paid 3,000 dollars a year to belong to a health club. He was looking at the camera, smiling and leaning over a big crate of something as if he was about to haul it onto his shoulder. The light was perfect on his skin in the real picture, Wuzel knew, because he had seen it reproduced much larger, but at this size he had to imagine the even, glossy sheen of sweat, and the way the photographer had captured the tensioning of tendons and sinew just prior to the lift. It was called *Necessary Dorsal Muscles*, by Bob Christopher. Christopher had made his name shooting scenes-of-crime pics, switched to reportage, joined Magnum, done a series of Americans at Work – of which this was one – and had completed twelve of a projected fifty, fifty that would have had him up there with Frank, when he was caught trying to capture the excitement of fighting a forest fire. Rumour was that the film that was in the camera when they found his body was still developable. That maybe twenty or thirty prints of the blaze that killed him existed. Now that would be a thing to own. That would complete the Core.

It was hard to explain, this centre of his collection. Sure, the Avedons were nice, but they were just pictures. The ones he really wanted captured something else, something genuinely fleeting, the interface between life and death. His favourite was those shots that captured the instant when life deserted the body, when what was a living, sentient entity became a collection of dying cells.

Capa's Spanish soldier, his arms flung in the air – assuming it wasn't faked like they said – almost did it, or the second picture of Nguyen Ngoc Loan executing a Viet Cong with a bullet through the head – not the one everyone knew, but the moment after he squeezed the trigger and the blood and brains go ker-bang – or Cedric Galbe's portraits from Sudan, those proud villagers torn down by Chinese AKs. Even frozen images from the Zapruder footage of J.F.K., they had it. It was a transition, the most important, mysterious transition of all, from this world to ... well, nothing was what he really believed, but sometimes he did wonder.

He had seen the real thing often enough, been the one to pull the trigger, had stood with a gun pressed to a man's temple and then squeezed, watched the head jerk like a turkey's, and then, nothing. But it was always over too fast, he could never stop himself blinking at the moment of the detonation. He couldn't help feeling that somewhere out there was a picture which caught what he was missing. You're alive, bang, now you are dead.

In a strange way he was sure Christopher's footage of his own demise would fall into this category, in the meantime he was fascinated by his other work. It might not all be life and death, but the guy had been seriously underrated. Up until now, it seemed. Christopher was Wuzel's own boy, he felt, his own discovery, and he groaned when he saw the price tag. 'You can't charge that,' he felt like yelling. 'He's mine – I discovered him, I sponsored the show, the catalogue, schmoozed the widow.' (Who denied the fire story, but not very convincingly.) Wuzel had five of the series, and he wanted this one so bad. Eighty thousand dollars. Eighty! He could have a fistful of Curtis's Native American studies for that. He sniffed. Eighty thousand dollars. But he couldn't close the catalogue. He wanted that image for his future gallery. But that needed big funds. What he needed, he knew, was another Alchemist.

He opened his final book. *A Year On The Streets, 92-93*, a chronicle of twelve months in New York, and it was an account of a city going down the tube. This was from before Guiliani, before they cleaned up the place and even managed to squeeze the Mob a little. He flicked through. Laurie Evans the kid was called. He was using lith printing to give a WeeGee type feel, but with the graininess softened. The effect was to make the homeless, the crackheads and hookers look like art, or at least high quality lifestyle advertising. One plate suddenly caught his eye. He recognised that sidewalk.

Then he laughed. The twisted body, the blood on the

flagstones, the neat hole between the eyes. Yeah, Jimmy Two Nostrils, that's who it was – named because his nose looked like the twin bores of the Lincoln Tunnel. When he sniffed, men held onto their rugs in case they got sucked up into the vortex. They said he had been skimming, but he hadn't – this was a don't-fuck-my-wife calling card from a client. It was one of Wuzel's last personal pops before he started farming them out – he'd given Jimmy a third nostril as a little joke. And this guy had come along and taken a picture. And a good one too. Work of art all round, he thought. Nice to be appreciated.

THREE

Ed had a familiar buzz on by the time he left the Pole. He had slopped a beer down his front when Sam had told a joke and he finally got it – skeleton walks into a bar, asks for a beer and a mop – and Ed decided to change clothes before his trip to the Palace. If it was her, he didn't want to be smelling like the Pole's carpet. And rather than risk driving his own Accord, long overdue for burial at sea or some such fate, he could hang onto the cab for a few hours. There was no shortage of vehicles for other drivers to take: the owner had overstocked two years previously, before the finances went belly up, and now you couldn't shift Caprices or Super Crowns for love nor money. Realising he hadn't eaten anything but six bowls of chips, Ed deposited his fares at the night safe on Pacific and stopped off for a box of doughnuts at the mart on Arctic.

Home was the bottom floor of a Duplex up on Oriental, the last one on the block still occupied. The wire fencing that ringed most of the site was sagging now, through neglect and the storms of the last few weeks. A couple of the 'Keep Out, No Trespassing' signs had been torn off, blown to God knows where.

Eminent domain: the phrase stuck in his head more than most things of late. He remembered old Mr Saunders, who lived above him and owned the building, explaining why they weren't going to move to make way for another casino. Eminent domain meant the city could buy you out or rehouse you and give your land to a casino, arguing that that would benefit the city more than your shitty little house. Many a night he could hear Saunders yelling into his phone: 'It is my *home*. You can threaten me all you like, I'm staying. You don't need another friggin' casino.'

He'd been right. Once the Palace was built, and things turned a little wobbly, it was clear the city couldn't support another casino while the New Downturn was running its course. So here they stayed, in splendid isolation. And, thought Ed as he kicked the bottom of the damp-swollen door to gain access to his apartment, perfect squalor.

He'd been thinking on the way over, thinking as he hadn't for a long time. There'd been false hope before, but now he had to face up to it. One day, it might just be her. And seeing the mayor on television, what were the odds of that? And the shots of Cotchford. Was that coincidence? Or some sort of pointer . . . an omen.

So you always posted a guard. We had the best. Don. Big son of a bitch, hard to get by. Weren't that many sprinters could get past him. And we had two of the best runners – Tony and Ruby. And me. I wasn't carrying the weight then of course. Even had those ripples on the stomach. Yeah, I could do a turn of speed. Then we had the ones who just hid. Honey and little Lester. Not much good for anything else, really. That was about it. We nearly always played Billy's team. Billy had Lappin, a good runner, and Small, who was definitely misnamed, he was their brick wall, the one you had to get by to release your pals. Alley-o.

He shivered and he came out of the reverie as he closed the door behind him and heard the sounds of tires squealing on asphalt, then gunshots. He looked at his watch. He had been playing when he had left, ten hours previously, he was still playing now. The room was in darkness, lit only by the greens and reds flashing off the screen. Lester was sitting at the TV dinner table, onto which he had duct-taped a steering wheel, and stamping at the pedal assembly on the floor, wrestling with the set-up as if it were a real car.

Ten hours. Only the three empty cups, which had once held coffee, showed he had moved. Ed hit the small table lamp, and watched Lester look up and blink. He didn't say hello.

'Hey.' Nothing. 'Howyadoin'?'

A grunt. Eyes still fixed on the screen. 'Paris.'

'Yeah. Those fuckin' gendarmes, eh? What you driving?'

'Renault Alpine.'

'No shit?' Ed didn't know what a Renault Alpine was. 'Guess who I saw on the TV today, down at the Pole? Fucking Mayor McKenneth, that's who. He must be standing for Congress or something. You know I started thinking about alley-o. Remember alley-o? Before the Bridge game? We played alley-o. Lester? You remember that?'

The small head swivelled towards him, quickly, nodded and whipped back to the screen. He cursed as the Renault clipped a sidewalk and he lost the back end. He corrected and hunkered down. They were bound to have blocked the roads ahead.

'You were good. Remember? Nobody could ever find you? That Billy, he always used to say you were small enough to hide in the crack of his ass and he wouldn't notice. Remember?'

Another nod. As usual the smallest exchange – well, 'exchange' was exaggerating the flow of information here – with someone glued to a screen exhausted him, and he simply said. 'Coffee?'

Everyone knew a kid like Lester. The one who hung around wherever some sort of action was, wanting to be part of the gang, always willing to go a bit further to fit in. Drink more booze, smoke more dope, play chicken harder and faster with cars and trains, rile the teachers, pull the stupidest stunts, steal the most sweets or cigarettes, probably be the first to hotwire a car, all in the mistaken belief that he would be more liked, not more despised for it. Lester had always tried too hard to go one step too far. It got him where he was today.

Ed gathered the cups and went to the kitchen, carefully rinsing them, occasionally looking in at the small, shrunken figure sitting in his chair, the face impassive even as he stared at the action in front of him, the Box Face as it used to be known. He did turn off the machine now and then, did take part in a conversation. Never said anything actually worth shit, though.

The Getaway was his life – at least, it was *The Getaway* this month, another game would replace it next month. The premise of this one was simple – you pulled a robbery in any of two dozen cities in the world, got to choose an appropriate set of wheels (a Jaguar in London, maybe, a Stingray in LA) and the local heat tried to stop you. Lester had now outrun the cops in New York, Chicago, Mexico City, Sydney, San Francisco and Paris. Well, he thought as he heard the rattle of police sub-machine guns, the latter remained to be seen.

As Ed set up the coffee filter he looked around his place with new eyes; at the stack of old foil take-out containers in the kitchen, well at least he had washed them; at the shabby furniture; the cheap hi-fi; at the big, wooden cabinet containing the TV set; at the walls decorated with a thousand splashes from ring-pulls, mouldering globules of food flicked from TV dinners, and grubby handprints; and at a bathroom that was in danger of silting up with dirt and hair. Could he imagine bringing *her* here? Explaining he'd been living this life for a while now, doing . . . doing nothing except passing the time with Lester. Well, sitting in the same room with Lester, while he explored strange cities, other galaxies or archaeological ruins, depending on which game he was obsessing on.

He handed little Lester his coffee and he reached up and grabbed it without taking his eyes off the screen. 'Hey Lester, when did you last go out? Lester? When did you last go out? Lester fucking listen to me will you? When did you last go out?'

A shrug. 'Week or two. Dunno.'

He gave up and finished his own coffee, then dumped the crumpled bills that were his tips into the trunk he kept for them under his bed, then took a shower, making sure, for once, to clean the bath afterwards and the bottom of the shower curtain, which was growing a thin film of black mould. It was as he was pulling hairs out of the sink that he caught sight of himself in the full-length mirror outside in the bedroom, saw himself framed in the open bathroom doorway, leaning over the sink, a big bag of fat, looking as big as a full garbage sack, slung around his front, hair unkempt, the rest of him wobbling, like someone had injected Jell-o under his skin. He wondered if the body retained the memory of that six-pack under there, before it was swamped by . . . well, too many six-packs for one.

He stood up and walked outside, squinting at himself. He'd split that shirt last week while lifting someone's luggage from the trunk, and most of his trousers had to have the top button moved to stop them continually pinging off. He looked at the chipped and rusted scales in the corner, and gingerly stepped on them, holding his stomach, willing his body to float. The needle stayed put. The mechanism was seized solid.

Shit, he didn't need any scales to tell him that, as with the apartment, he'd let himself go. Still well shy of forty, and he looked like the kind of warning magazines printed about what happened if you didn't put some effort into your appearance. He stood and tried to suck in his gut. Yup, Before and Before.

He shaved with a blade about as sharp as a chair leg, and made a mental note to get some more. That'd be the same mental note he made last week and the week before. He'd get it this time, for sure. Ed pulled on his best black trousers, a grey jacket – Armani, the only designer he owned, left in the back of the cab one night – and his old Bass Weejuns. He looked again. Better when he was dressed, that was for sure. But still rough. He sat on the edge of the bed and put his head in his hands. He still felt bad about hitting Bo, but there you go. The Box had left Lester a moron, it left Ed with a tendency to fight fights that weren't necessary.

He fetched Lester a Diet Coke for later – another brown ejaculation up the wall no doubt – and a packet of chips, and explained he'd be back soon. Lester looked up with a big empty grin on his face, and a synthesised voice congratulated him on having outrun the best Paris could throw at him. He pulled down the on-screen menu and selected Madrid. Jesus, thought Ed, Europe on three robberies a day.

Ed pocketed a packet of pretzels to keep him going and left without wasting his breath on goodbye.

The Palace was only about three quarters of a mile away, and he had intended to walk, but the moment he heard the freshly sprung wind rattling through the links of the fencing, he knew he would have to drive. He hadn't reached the cab before large drops of rain started to splat around him, like the droppings from a million incontinent seagulls.

He slid in quickly and through the blurred windshield saw a convoy of buses cough into life in the vacant lot over to his left. They had been on slumbering stand-by while their elderly cargo kindly deposited their money in the casino vaults. It was time to go get them now, and Ed could picture them trudging wearily onboard, maybe one or two of them harbouring a small, almost secret grin, not wanting to celebrate their good fortune and depress the fellow passengers even more. He let the buses splash by before he put the key in the ignition.

He turned on the engine and the wipers at double speed, hit demist and hesitated for a minute to catch his breath. A thirty yard run and he was wheezing, his breath burning in his throat. Not good. Not a formula for a long life. He engaged drive and slowly negotiated the storm-swept streets.

The Enchanted Palace – to use its full name – was built at the far north of Absecon Island, where the city's Boardwalk did a sharp left and headed for the marina district. It was the third in a great trilogy of casinos with which Atlantic City had ended the twentieth century, following on from the MGM and Steve Wynn's Le Jardin. Designed to out-Vegas Vegas, they were meant to be attractions before you even stepped onto the gaming floor. Hence Ed could see the dragon flames lighting up the sky well before he reached the building, as the hourly eruption signalled the start of the animatronic dragon-v-villagers scenario that formed the Boardwalk tableau, a snatch of an old Chinese (or was it Japanese? The whole thing was a chop suey of Pan-Asian themes) legend where the lone, disinherited warrior finds happiness and love by killing a rogue lizard.

This action took place adjacent to the Boardwalk, so Ed could only glimpse the light show, sparkling off the sheets of rain, as he pulled into the lot opposite the rear of the fairy-tale building. The entrance on Atlantic, landside, was guarded by a couple of giant stylised lions, their great eyes glowing red. One lion was slightly offset, as demanded by the feng-shui expert who had been consulted since the first day of construction, one reason why, alone among the casinos, dark, lustrous heads of hair outnumbered the grey, the blue and the bald. Only the new Turner place up the coast had been anywhere near as successful at tapping the lucrative Oriental market, and it had had troubles of its own. All in all, the Palace was riding the New Downturn pretty well.

Ed pulled an umbrella from the trunk, then put it back when the wind eviscerated it with a casual brutality. He hitched the collar of his jacket up and sprinted to the shelter of the great steel and glass roof that covered the driveway. He ducked down to see who the cabbies waiting in line were, waving to Harry and Mike from the garage.

The entrance was enormous, a marble cave, glistening with gilt, with enough sunken lights in the ceiling to mimic the Milky Way. Giant banners with Oriental script hung down, no doubt bestowing best wishes, long life and good luck. Ed had seen this all before, so rather than being distracted he simply scoured the faces in the hall until he had one he recognised – although he couldn't recall the name, but they had badges for that – and after a quick flick of the eyes to the guy's lapel he asked Tom if he had seen 'Rick Bevis'.

'Don't you mean Dick Bevis? Never heard anyone call him Rick.'

'Yeah, sorry, Dick . . .'

'He'll be at the slot bench, near the Casino Control Commission booth.'

He threaded through the crowd, noting the number of big men in tight suits, with earpieces in place, and uniformed guards. Since the hit on the Terrace, and *The Alchemist*, security was way up. He was even stopped on the threshold of the floor, and patted down, before being waved through. Guess he didn't fit the normal profile.

He didn't get inside too often, but Ed was ready for the noise, he remembered that much. The Palace had the loudest machines, the most flashing lights, the biggest jackpot Claxons in town. The tokens were designed to ring sonorously as they hit the collecting tray at the bottom of each game, magnifying the sound of winning ten-fold, jump-starting the adrenaline levels of the players. And it was Friday night, the weekenders had arrived, and before anything else, prior to dinner, shower, even unpacking, most were down here getting a taste for the direction of the cash flow. Inwards, thought Ed, always inwards.

He took a loop past some of the card tables, pausing to watch, but trying not to show too much interest in any one player. He knew from experience that these guys believed that every aspect of the environment influenced their luck – how often they smoked a cigarette, which side the drinks were delivered on, whether there were odd or even numbers of ice cubes in that drink. He watched them stack up the 'quarters' on the blackjack table – did they call them that so the marks didn't feel like they were actually losing twenty-five bucks a pop, just nickels and dimes, he won-dered – and he saw the stacks grow and shrink with alarming speed, like a time-lapse movie, as the action ebbed and flowed. A player got up from first base at a blackjack table, sighed and toked the dealer a chip from his meagre pile. Ed recognised him from the Pole, but he didn't see Ed, he only had eyes for the ATM machine at the far end of the section, which would obligingly tap into his cash motherlode and allow him to continue playing. There was a slight air of desperation about his stride, a let's-get-this-over-with as he went by. Ed shook his head. Like a man late for his own execution, thought Ed. He just didn't get it – maybe there was a gene for it, for gambling, or gaming as the casinos preferred to call it. If so, he thought as he made the edge of the main hall, there were a lot of people carrying it.

The slot supervisor's bench was actually a boxed-off area with a raised platform inside so whoever was on duty could survey his shiny, crashing, blinking, winking domain from an elevated perspective. Dick Bevis was sorting out an argument over comps.

'She's played fifteen dollars in three hours, and now she is saying she deserves a dinner,' said an exasperated slot supervisor, his neck craned to look up at his boss.

Dick looked down from his lofty perch and eyed the woman sitting at machine six down the aisle. She waved, a sort of grandmotherly wave.

Bevis picked up a card, signed it and handed it to the supervisor. 'Throw her a bone. Good for the $7.99 Buffet Bonanza, but not the all-you-can-eat.'

The supervisor huffed, as if this was the equivalent of pardoning major war criminals, and stomped off. Dick looked down. 'Ed. Howyadoin'? Didn't think you hung round places like these.'

Ed smiled. 'Nah, I can't remember the last time I actually came in. Hang around outside a lot though.'

'Well, no favours for customers of the Pole here. Odds are the same for you as everyone – absolutely fuckin' awful.'

'I wasn't going to play, Ri . . . Dick. I just wanted a favour. Maybe you can help. No, I don't want the all-you-can-eat. You know this girl?' He unfolded his scribbled bit of paper and handed it up.

'Girl? Well, I suppose. You want my professional judgement, I'd say that one's a girl,' he waved at a passing waitress. 'This you got here is a woman, Ed.' He nodded. She'd be mid-thirties now, so technically he was right. Not a little girl any longer. 'But she's nice. Is this a hot tip? Cause they ain't allowed to see customers—'

He shook his head vigorously. 'It might be be an old friend. Might be. I just wanna check. That's all. And I ain't a customer.'

'I suppose.' He tapped into the computer. 'She's on site.' Another tap. 'And she is working station one-niner, that's Pai Gow Poker, over yonder.'

'Thanks.'

Before he could leave Bevis said: 'Hey, Ed.'

'Yeah?'

The man was colouring up. 'I heard around you were one of the Cotchford Seven.'

'Six. We were seven. Then we were six.' No good denying it.

'Which means you were in The Box.'

'Uh-huh.'

'It's just . . .' he stopped to issue an instruction to a supervisor, 'Tell them to look at that Top Hat 2000 machine. It's been paying out for an hour now.' He lowered his voice, 'My brother was in there. In Boxgrove.'

Ed could see why he lowered his voice. The CCC background investigation probably wouldn't have thrown up a bent brother, but it didn't pay to advertise.

'Maybe you knew him. Danny.'

'Danny Bevis?'

'No, no, Danny Stowe he would have been called.'

Ed felt his stomach flip, the once-familiar fear that only a hated name can invoke. He swallowed to try and get some saliva around his mouth so he could say, 'Must've been after my time.'

'Yeah? They closed it down soon after you guys got out didn't they? He was there 'til the end. Half-brother he was, that's why we got different names.'

Ed shook his head. 'It was a big place. Divided into different units. Houses they were called. Named after famous people to do with New Jersey. We didn't mix much between.'

'You sure? He looks a little like that guy you drink with.'

'Yeah?'

'The pawn guy . . . what's his name? Goodyear?'

'Goodrich.'

'Yup, Goodrich. Bit beefier than your pal, but same kinda build and shit.'

Ed shook his head, trying to stop the face forming in his brain, attempting to throw the neural blanket over the features as they solidified. 'I was in Hollingshead House. Don't remember your brother.'

'Hollingshead? Who was he?'

'Invented the drive-in movie.'

'Oh. So you sure? Danny Stowe? He was in Edison I think.'

Not all the time, he wasn't. 'Like I said, it was a big place.'

'Just that . . . he died.'

Ed had to stop himself punching the air with joy, but he just said, 'Too bad,' before turning away.

The waitress's uniform was a modified cheong-sam, a bright, pearlescent blue with a dragon motif, but with the skirt drastically shortened. And the slit went all the way to the armpit, with a belt round the middle to stop it flapping open. It was almost impossible to wear an ordinary bra underneath, and very easy to expose flesh as you leant forward, so most of them, like his girl – woman – wore body stockings. Unless, as a few did, you realised that leaving the underwear off raised the tips by a considerable margin.

He stood behind the players for a minute, appearing to follow the action but watching her scoop up drinks, dollars, chips, and dole out Cokes, bourbons, beers, whatever they ordered. You keep playing, you can keep going. Ed tried to follow the run of the game, but it seemed like some bastard mutant offspring of poker, involving dice, a movable bank and a hand split into two cards and five cards, which had to try and beat the dealer's similar two-five set-up.

But mostly he just watched her, surreptitiously feasting upon the movement of her body, the way her breasts moved under the shiny fabric, the tight little lines around her mouth when she smiled that polite smile, the fine web at the corners of her eyes. It wasn't her after all, but it was close. She had the same sensuality, must have done the same things to the guys at school as Honey did, just the odd tease, the odd provocation, watched them getting hard in a flash before sending them that killer 'sucker' smile.

And she must look like this by now, he realised, not with the tight, smooth skin, all shiny and peachy, that he remembered. As Bevis said, a woman, not a girl. But none the worse for that, really. He wasn't a boy anymore either. She caught his eye and asked: 'Drink sur?' Even in the one word he could hear the accent.

'I'm not playing.'

She looked around: 'I can comp you if you are waiting for a seat.' Yes, somewhere South, maybe the Carolinas. A Raleigh girl. Must've moved from Jersey as a kid. He shook his head. He pointed at the olives on the tray. 'I'll settle for a couple of those, thanks.' He stuffed his mouth full and managed to say, 'Rachel is it?'

She looked down at the tag over her left breast. 'That's what it says.'

'Can I ask you, what?'

'Ask me what, what?'

'Rachel what?'

She hesitated, as if this was some kind of intricate way of hitting on her. 'Ben,' she finally uttered slowly.

'B-e-n?'

She nodded. 'Why?'

He swallowed the last of the olives and took a couple more to pop later. 'You just had a name similar to someone. I . . .' He stumbled as he thought of her, of their last time together. 'I gotta go. Thanks.' He turned and left, his cheeks burning red, as if he was a fourteen year old asking for a pack of Trojans.

FOUR

Big Billy Moon put down the pack of playing cards he had been shuffling and picked up the phone in his office with irritation. It was almost time to head off for the weekend, and his gut instinct told him this was trouble. He relaxed a little when he heard it was Anne. He had time for Anne. She had pulled the boy round a lot. 'No, no, Anne, always good to hear from you. How are you? Good. And Billy? Fine. Yeah, I got a minute.'

While she talked he looked around the office, wondering why he had never bothered to upgrade to something swankier. With an elevator for instance. Superstition, he decided. This was where he started, before the Tribeca area became all snooty and trendy and arty and 'Bobby' this and 'Bobby' that. And this was where he would stay. The last thing he needed was a big personal office that drew attention. He realised she had finished her pitch and he said slowly; 'You sure? I mean, what are you telling me here? He's lost a little weight, and he is doing a job for me down in Atlantic City. Doesn't add up to much.'

Idly he spread out twelve cards face down and hovered his left hand over them. He picked out a King of Hearts and an Ace of Spades. Blackjack. 'Anne, I'd put a hundred bucks that this is nothing. Billy has a lot on his plate. He hasn't told you? About the island? Well ask him. Listen, you wanna come over to the house for dinner tonight? OK, but if you change your mind . . . OK. Yeah. And maybe make it for Thanksgiving? No, no, I understand, wouldn't want to come

59

between you and your mom. And don't worry – eh? Promise? Sure. OK, 'bye now.'

Big Billy Moon held his fingers together in a pyramid shape, bouncing them off pursed lips, mulling over what he had just heard. He looked at his watch, wondering if he could make the next Jitney out to Sag Harbor, the one that would take him to the American Hotel and his weekend cigar.

Little Billy Moon. Couldn't even fuck a piece on the side without his wife knowing about it. He wondered why Billy hadn't mentioned the island to his wife. Should he worry about this? No, the boy was probably waiting to spring the surprise on her. Look at me. Big boy now. Uh-ooh.

God, it would have been so much easier if Billy had just got her banged up early on and left her with half a dozen kids to look after. If Anne was tied up with a bunch of rugrats, she wouldn't be analysing every pound he shed then. He thought of Anne pregnant, naked, and shifted quickly to banish the image of taut skin and engorged nipples. Behave yourself, he thought, that's your daughter in law. But he allowed himself a smirk.

He dealt out another row of cards and flipped over two, a queen and a jack. Twenty. Not bad.

He had to get Billy back on the straight and narrow, remind him what they did for a living, that it wasn't all cocktail waitresses or croupiers or whatever the girl he stopped off to see every once in a while did. There was that business at Paterson, perhaps he could sort that out, stand in for him. That would put his feet back on the ground. In the meantime, he'd better ask Backson about exactly what the boy got up to in Cotchford.

Vincent Wuzel waited until Edgar had finished frisking the figure in front of him and left, before he invited the kid to sit down. Edgar could be an intimidating presence in interviews, he knew. He never said anything, but his body language, his little huffs and tuts, always let the interviewee know that Edgar thought he was a piece of no-good shit, no matter what Mr Wuzel might think. Mind you, he might be right about this kid.

Well, he was a bit more than a kid, maybe thirty, thirty two, but still skinny, and dressed in sneakers and jeans and a Stüssy top like a kid. It made Wuzel feel old. He had twenty years on the boy and he envied him that slouch, that air of fuck-you insouciance.

It'll pass, he thought. Something'll grind the fuck out of him.

Wuzel picked up the thin file on his desk and flipped it open. There were some bare essentials, a kind of skeletal autobiography. He needed more.

'I could do with you filling me in,' he said, looking at the scrawl. 'About yourself I mean.'

'Yeah. I . . . let's see. I guess I . . . where shall I start?'

'Done time?'

'Juvenile. Two years.'

'For?'

'Arson. I didn't actually—'

'Spare me. You didn't actually strike the match. Or empty the gas tank. Or whatever. I don't give a flying fuck. No adult stuff?'

He shrugged.

Wuzel felt a sudden flash of temper, like a fast fuse ripping up his spine. He banged the table. 'What does that mean, exactly?'

'A couple nights in jail here and there. Drunk and disorderly. Suspicion of this and that. Nothing real serious.'

'Fingerprinted?'

'Huh?'

'Where you ever fingerprinted?'

'Juvenile—'

'That file will have been destroyed. Any other time?'

He shook his head. 'No. Never.'

Lucky, though, and lucky was always worth having. Chances of getting four or five busts without someone thinking of cross-checking prints were slim. 'Absolutely certain? Good.' Wuzel wrote something down. 'Alias?'

'Nah.'

'Nickname?'

The kid laughed through his nose, an unattractive snort.

'Do you have a street name?'

He picked up the tone in the voice. 'Yeah, I used to have. It used to be Pretty Boy.'

Wuzel examined the face, with its odd assortment of lumps, the misshapen brow and nose. He could see it now. Just. 'So what happened, Pretty Boy?'

'Ah, some guys thought that I needed a new monicker. So they got rid of the old one with a ten inch piece of pipe.'

'And you were recommended to me by...?' he shuffled the papers, although he knew who he was doing this particular favour for.

'Brownie. Mr Brown, I mean.'

'Mr Brown. And you had been working for him as?'

'Kind of organiser, consiglieri, counsellor.'

Consiglieri? Here was a kid who had seen the *Godfather* a few too many times for his own good. Wuzel put down the folder and stood up, wondering if his height might make an impression if his demeanour wasn't going to. He leaned his six one frame on the desk. 'Consiglieri? I would guess you can't even spell it. Now try me again.'

'OK.' The boy sniffed loudly. 'My main job was to roll winners. Not the big casinos, but, well, the gash ones, you know, private games. Sometimes for a sponsor who put a package together in the poker room of one of the Boardwalk ones, and lost a packet. Never there and then, of course. Later. Maybe hours, maybe days. At the bar. A hotel. Maybe get a woman to do it. But it was always to get back winnings. And we got to keep a percentage of what we recovered.' He smirked a lopsided grin. 'Just like insurance work I guess.'

'And?'

He shuffled in his chair, his leather jacket creaking. 'Well, work is kinda drying up down there. There aren't so many games. No more poker rooms, just the ones in the apartments and shit. Big players moved on. Big losers, too. And Brownie is . . . well, he's retired, you know.'

Wuzel was silent for a minute. 'OK, Mr Penn, I will make a few more inquiries and let you know.'

'Is that it?'

'Yeah.'

'I mean – don't I get to know how it works?'

Wuzel sighed and explained it to him, the rates, the likelihood of employment, the code of conduct. Then he hustled him out. The truth was he knew all about not-so Pretty Boy from Brown, and what he left out was just as interesting as what he had told him. Like the time the recovery of the gambling money – always a high-risk business – went horribly wrong, leaving the mark both poor and stiff. Well, he could worry about whether he owed Brown enough favours to throw the kid some work on Monday. Brown had been at his side from the beginning, had helped him get over his first-hit nerves, shown him the ropes. He was perhaps five years older than Wuzel, and already out of the game. Someone who had lived long enough to get the good life. Well, that was a role model to aspire to. He touched his left ear, notched with a V where a stray round had gone through it on one of the jobs he did for BB. He'd been lucky, too. Somehow he got the impression that

Penn wouldn't be around long enough to start worrying about his investments maturing.

Wuzel put the once-Pretty Boy out of his mind, poured himself a Scotch and, with his feet on the desk, pulled out a photo reportage book on Kosovo. Plenty of material in here, he thought, as he settled down.

FIVE

The Enchanted Palace

Ed had always thought it a design fault, had seen too many near-misses and mini-gridlocks. True, space was tight on the frontage the Palace had given themselves up here at the top of the Boardwalk, but the architect must have been able to come up with a better solution than discharging traffic from the car parks onto the same driveway where the cabs and valet drivers worked.

Even so, he never thought he would be there when it happened, but it felt like one of those dreams, the ones where you watch helplessly as a plane full of people goes down right behind your house. (What, he sometimes wondered, did people dream about before planes? Rail wrecks? Wagon train disasters?) The black limo came out of the parking shute like it had been fired, or, given the amount of water it was throwing up, like it had just come down one of those wild rapids rides they have over at Six Flags.

Harry was just doing his job, he'd dropped off a fare and was circling to take his place at the back of the line-up, sure that, with the rain and all, he would get another customer within five, ten minutes. The loop took him from under the big glass cover, out into the curtains of rain. Maybe he hesitated too long before hitting the wipers, maybe he should've gone round a bit faster, but the next thing he knew he was blinded by the lights of the limo as it all but aquaplaned from the exit ramp and swiped the front of the

Caprice, buckling the front wheel and tearing into the fender.

There was a screech of mating metal as the two cars, interlocked like tired boxers who can't or won't break, careered as one towards the centre island of the driveway and smacked into a dragon-topped lamp-post, which swayed uncertainly as if it were trying to make its mind up where to fall. It settled for a dangerous-looking lean instead.

Ed waited a second, listening to the hissing and clicking and squealing as hoses split and engines stalled. He ran over, wondering which he should go to first. But Harry was out from behind the wheel already, gesticulating at the limo driver without being able to find the words to express his full anger.

'Harry, Harry, you OK?'

Ed went to touch him, but he shrugged him off. 'Jezuz fuckin' Christ. Did ya see that? The guy was practically surfin' back there? Hey you, what was that – Hawaii Five-O?'

Ed couldn't see if there were passengers in the back because of the smoked windows, but the driver seemed to say something over his shoulder before getting out. 'You OK?' he said, echoing Ed.

'Yeah, don't worry about me, worry about next year's insurance premium. I got a witness here . . .' Harry pointed a thumb at Ed. 'That's right, isn't it Ed, you'll tell the garage?'

Ed nodded. It was a matter of loyalty, and he was fairly sure it was the limo driver's fault. The window in the rear inched down a fraction. 'Can we get going here? We got some appointments, ya know.' It was a deep, chocolatey voice – almost a late night jazz radio voice – but not a sweet chocolate; sort of sharper, menacing, with a hint of impatience.

The driver looked at his wheel and the rim. 'Thing is, Mr Backson, I only got one of those compact spares, you know, the doughnuts. I don't want to be driving on that in this weather.'

'And we have to wait for the cops,' added Harry.

Ah yes, thought Ed, every traffic accident had to be reported these days. That'd take an hour or two.

Mr Backson spoke to someone in a low voice, just the bass notes registering through the window. He turned back and asked, 'Can you get us another cab?'

Harry looked at Ed. 'Where to?'

'New York.'

'Via—' began the driver.

'No, Manhattan,' interrupted Backson. 'Straight to Manhattan.'

'How much?' asked Harry, as if he was in the market and his Caprice wasn't half crushed.

'Two hundred cover it?'

Harry turned to Ed and made a sly wink. 'Three?'

'Two fifty,' said Backson flatly.

'Plus tolls?'

'Yes, yes, plus tolls.' Irritated now.

'You got yourself a deal. Ed, you got your cab with you?'

Ed didn't want to drive to New York, not in this storm, but he could feel Harry's eyes pushing, imploring him. He knew Harry didn't want to risk giving this to some Joe Schmoe who might not play ball – ie. cut him in – if he just called it in to the garage. Ed found himself saying, 'Sure, it's in the lot across the road. I'll bring it over.' As he left to splash across the road he saw casino staff hurrying over with umbrellas. Not, he suspected, for Harry and him.

When Ed was lined up alongside, Mr Backson stepped out, and, as Ed had envisaged, he was big barrel-chested man, built in the James Earl Jones mode. The man buttoned up his overcoat against the rain, ducked under the umbrella the casino flunky was holding and opened the trunk of the limo. He lifted out a large, square case, the sort you carry files in, and transferred it to Ed's cab.

Backson tapped the side window, and only then did the other passenger emerge. He, too, checked the buttons of his overcoat and accepted the offer of the umbrella. As he moved towards the back of Ed's cab, their eyes locked. Ed realised he was standing slack-jawed, suddenly oblivious of the rivulets of rain streaming down his face. It was the eyes he recognised. Small, close set, with eyebrows that almost ran into each other, forming a monobrow. He rewound the images he had projected onto his TV screen back at the North Pole of the street game, the kids running along the sidewalk with their heads back. He focused in on the third one, panned the camera, looked at him straight on, then superimposed the visage with the man opposite him. Unmistakable. Alley-fucking-o. Billy Moon, was all he could think. After all this time. Billy Moon.

SIX

'Hello. Hello. Honey? That you? Yeah, it's bad. Bad line. Must be the weather. The weather, the rain, the storm, you know? Screwing up the signal. OK, listen, Hon, you ain't going to believe this, but we just had an accident. No, a traffic accident. Bang. We hit a cab outside the casino. It's going to take a while to sort out. No, the limo's fucked I think. So we'll get a cab. Thing is, I'd better nix tonight. I know, I know. I'm real sorry. I know it's been two weeks. What do you want me to say? I'm sorry. OK, Honey. Honey, don't . . . stop, just stop. You knew what the deal was. I never said it'd be easy. Yes, you're right I never promised you a rose garden or whatever that shitty song is. Look, hold on, hold on . . .

'Backson, Backson . . . just pay the man, eh? Pay him. Whatever it takes. I don't want to have to fill in any fuckin' police accident forms. Get a cab and we'll go straight back. All right? Great. And fuckin' hurry it up, eh?

'Hi, Honey, yeah. OK, now listen, I was thinking I can get down Tuesday, during the day. No, just the day. No, I can't stop over, you know that. Or maybe you come up to town. No, that'd be great, but . . . well, maybe I will soon. Just be patient, eh? Look, I gotta go, we got a cab to catch. And I'm sorry, eh? I'll make it up to you. Yeah, go and buy dinner on me, somewhere nice. Great. And I'll log on later, see what's what, eh? Yeah. See ya, Hon.'

Billy clicked off the cellphone and stepped out of the cab into the rain, quickly taking shelter under the umbrella the bell hop was holding. He could feel the animosity oozing out of Backson. He didn't like changes of plan. Well, he was paid not to like change, but he was also paid to make the best of it.

Billy looked at the cab driver, some half-wit dribbling in the rain, hair plastered over his face, his jacket and shirt compressed by the rain so that his beer belly was protruding over his pants. Was he going to trust his life to an imbecile like that? Shit, no time to start arranging anything else. He should have gone back and got one of the Palace's cars. Oh, what the hell. 'Hey, buddy – we going to New York or are we going to see what gets us first – pneumonia or drowning? Let's get outta here.'

SEVEN

Selin Court Condos, Cotchford, New Jersey.

She put the phone down and bit her lip. Bastard. It wasn't much to ask, was it? Seeing him once a week, instead of once a fortnight. It's not like she was on the other side of the country. Fifty minutes by car, perhaps an hour by train from Manhattan, and here she was left out on the Shore like he was some goddamn fur trapper who had to go off for weeks on end.

Still, there was a good side, she wouldn't have to listen to him reminisce about the good old days in Cotchford, wouldn't have to join in the Golden Memory Parade he liked to indulge in before he got down to the business. She lit a cigarette and considered who she could call. There weren't that many here in town, and with the weather she didn't really care for the idea of a long drive to Trenton or Philly or Paterson. She moved to the window, and watched the raindrops hurl themselves at the glass, like a swarm of insects hitting a windshield. She could just about make out the shape of the shoreline, and the lonely finger of the long-defunct lighthouse, with the boats of the marina clustered at its base, the few lights on board bobbing wildly up and down. She was glad she wasn't at sea.

Remembering what she had been doing before the call, she killed the cigarette, quickly returned to the bed, and pulled up the silk shirt which was the only item of clothing she had on. Carefully she positioned herself so she was fully

71

in the frame of the camera on top of the closet, and opened her legs. Just for a second. Just a quick flash of snatch. She hadn't even checked if anyone was logged on, but it was Friday night, and the number of hits on her page normally went up over the weekend. Again, legs open, a quick stroke this time, a big smile and a wink, and she rolled off onto the floor and walked to the bathroom. She could just imagine the surfers going shit, shit, shit, waiting for her to reappear. Let them wait.

She took a long leisurely shower, trying not to think about the disappointment with Billy. This was better than what she had just a year before, down to being a chop-out girl for some dealer in Camden, hustling a few bucks by letting the kids down the hall take Polaroids of her, and being one of the live-link girls for a web-porn broker. Although she shouldn't knock Cyberslutz; that was how Billy had found her.

And his suggestion of setting up her own web page, of changing from live strip streams to one of the home girls, had been the best move ever. Sure it was crude right now, and she wasn't as famous on the Net as the legendary Jennicam or Amy's Place or Renee, and she was older than most of the cam-girls, but she knew from her e-mail that plenty of people out there preferred their women not to look like it was all one step away from paedophilia: www. honicam.com – what a gas.

Billy, though, he was a strange one. He was somewhere between a pimp and a lover. What did that make her? Half-way between a whore and a mistress? Probably. Fuck it, he paid the bills, she got to do what she liked. And right now that was pretty much of nothing. Shop in town, buy from the art gallery. Flirt with the kids in the comic store. Regular middle-class motherfucking straight arrow. Come back, do the stuff. OK, in some ways it was a dulling, monotonous routine, but think about the money. A year of flashing the pink and she'd have enough cash to move on.

She dried herself and went back to the bedroom, making sure that she dropped the towel and bent low to the bottom drawer of the bureau next to her bed. Jerry, the guy who had created the web site and webcam, had tutored her in all the moves, the ones that got the nerds at the other end of the line hot and bothered. For a moment the image flashed of some sixteen year old frantically masturbating in front of a glowing computer screen, but she suppressed it.

OK, let's rock, she thought. She threw the case on the bed and opened it. The lid and the base were lined with loops through which were fitted a wide variety of vibrators and butt-plugs. She smiled at the camera and ran her hand over them, as if unsure which one to choose. The pink or the blue? The Love Leviathan or the Double Trouble? In fact, she only had one or two regulars within – some of the dildos she wouldn't even try and insert without anesthetic, but her viewers didn't know that, they would just think: 'Damn, she's gone for the little one again. Maybe next time.'

This bit hadn't been Billy's idea, though he knew all about it. What Billy didn't want to do was star in the show himself – they always ran a tape of previous highlights over the Net whenever he was around. The e-mail showed that, although a small number would like to see the girl at the Honey Trap page get humped, for most who logged on and paid their $19.99 a month to watch her eat, sleep, drink and masturbate – especially the latter – they wanted Honey to be *their* lover, not some stranger's.

The mail also showed what her next step would be. They wanted AVIs and MPEGs, vivos with full sounds, maybe even a mail order CD-ROM or DVDs – moving images that they could access whenever they logged on and the Honey Trap was in darkness and there was nothing to jack off to.

She could just imagine her fans out there, the thoughts running though their heads as she touched each item in the case, not knowing this was like Mission Impossible – the old guy at the beginning always had a big stack of photos, but every week he chose the same faces from the pile. No, the guys will be thinking: 'Oh, Honey's gone for that blue one. Must be her favourite because she used it last time. Maybe she'll stick it up her ass, that would be cool. Ooh, great, she's lying back now. Oh well, not her ass. I don't think. I must get a higher res screen, pictures just not clear enough. Oh . . . oh . . .'

And Honey laughed to herself as the little blue helper slid home.

EIGHT

Saturday November 23

The Atlantic City Boardwalk is four and half miles long. The first version was built in 1870, after a proposal by the appropriately named Alexander Boardman, that a proper surfaced walkway would stop sand tracking into local hotels and ruining the carpets. The first version ran just one and a half feet above the beach, and was dismantled every summer. No buildings were allowed within thirty feet of it.

Ed Behr started his thinking walk at the Absecon Inlet end of the modern Boardwalk, the bleak section where no businesses fronted onto the planks, and the wind was free to blast in off the Atlantic unblocked. The rain had stopped, and in the yellow pools of the beachfront lights the surface of the wood looked newly varnished. Four and a half miles. Ed knew that by the time he reached the other end he would have made a decision, right or wrong. It is what he normally did when he faced a crisis he considered too big for what passed for a brain these days.

It was going on three in the morning by the time he parked his car by Captain Starn's pier. He had finally made it to the garage, where he confirmed Harry's story about the accident, before going home to put the money into his stash box under the bed. For the first time in a long time he pulled the trunk all the way out and looked inside. It was full of screwed up knots of money, and not all singles at that. There were fives, tens, twenties, even a couple of fifties. He started to smooth them out and count, under the quizzical eye of Lester, who had come in to see what all the noise was. He stopped when he reached three thousand dollars. There was at least that left in there. How had it got to be so much?

Ed paused by the rail to catch his breath after a couple of hundred yards. The sea was foaming, layers of froth whipped up by the wind, gnawing hungrily at the sand, sucking it away into the dark night to deposit it god knows where. He could feel himself wheezing, his underused lungs burning. It was a long time since he had done this walk, a long time since he had had anything quite as important to think about.

It was the twenty that had done it. As he dropped them off, Billy had unpeeled the tip from his billfold and thrown it through Ed's window. Ed had watched it hang there in the air, as if some mild thermal had been set up in the cab. It fluttered a little, before slowly swinging down into his lap, sitting on his crotch. There was no thank you, just this token, the twenty thrown so disparagingly to another little, anonymous man.

He watched warily as another figure approached, head down against the gusts, hooded top up and tightly drawn, so just the eyes showed, with something in a brown bag under his arm. Ed stiffened into a defensive posture, but the man clearly felt the same and moved to landward to give Ed as clear a berth as possible, probably thinking anyone out here on a night – a morning – like this was clearly fucking crazy.

Beyond the man Ed could see the new stretch of houses built with casino money, waiting to be occupied. Next to them was a cluster of old-style rows, windows boarded, all except for one that was heavily barred. Lights shone in that one, and a few cars had pulled up. The door opened to reveal some kind of fortified lobby area, and a customer slipped in. Ed didn't know what they were selling – he thought most of the crack houses had been cleared – but it certainly wasn't legal.

He remembered when he and Lester first pulled into town, he had spent some time fronting a house pumping out some heavy duty West Coast shit. Oh, things had got physical – he had had guns, knives and bottles waved at him. But that happened every day in Boxgrove, or if it didn't the threat was always implicit. After some of the shit that happened in the Box, you think that was going to throw him? He knew from the start, though, it was a job like World War One fighter pilots – a limited lifespan. Sooner or later someone pulls a Kel Tec or some other little pocket rocket pistol and vents his anger, his poverty, his habit and his whole fucking life on the face in the doorway. Luckily the cab company came through with a position just in time for him to legally keep Lester in Coke and games.

He started walking again, breathing deeply this time. Why should he feel so demeaned by that gesture, the throw-away note? After all, Billy hadn't recognised him. Why? He understood why he might have not ID-ed him at first, what with the rain and all, but later, when he had dried out, how come he didn't notice, or even clock the voice? Even if he had put on a few pounds, changed shape, the voice was the same voice, the movements the same movements as when they ran together. He looked down at his gut. *Ran*, there was a joke.

Billy, he looked much the same. Filled out, sure, but at least some of that was muscle and he was still good looking, still with great teeth, still with that East Side glow, the sort money gives you, the sort he and Lester and Tony and Ruby and Don never had. And the clothes looked good. Billy was the first boy he had known with hundred dollar sneakers. Well, the first one who had *bought* them, anyway.

Ed hadn't said much the whole trip, just asked them

ROB RYAN

where they wanted to be dropped in the city, so maybe Billy
didn't get to hear the voice much at that. And maybe he
didn't see much more than the back of his head.

So why hadn't Ed said: 'Hey, Billy, it's me, your old pal
Ed,' when the bill came floating his way? Cause Ed wasn't
his old pal, he was his old fall guy, that's why. He felt the
familiar anger hit him, and realised he was panting from
more than the effort of walking in the wind. Because we
should have all stuck together, and you left us, Billy, you left
us. Me and Lester and Tony and Don, and let's not forget
Honey and Ruby. They got the fallout too. But me and
Lester and Tony and Don and Bird, we got Boxgrove. Billy,
you got Gibbs. A day at the fuckin' beach, man, day at the
beach. OK, so Bird got the Bell House, the soft option. But
look at Lester – dead meat now, a pixel pixie, barely able to
function away from the TV screen. And it was partly his
fault, he had to admit, he always knew he could make Lester
do stupid things. But that one photograph, that was one
dare too fucking far.

But we could have told, he thought. Billy told on us, and
we could have told him. Tony wanted to, Tony thought fuck
him. But they didn't in the end. They kept quiet. Even when
someone has ratted on you, doesn't make doing it to them
any better.

He reached the Palace, where the animatronic dragon
had temporarily crept back into its cave, and the slayer was
off sharpening his sword somewhere, leaving the rows of
Chinese lanterns swinging wildly as if they were going to be
torn off any minute. It was – what? – seven, eight hours
earlier that he had been on the other side and seen the
accident, had seen Billy. Why not just forget it? He'd never
had much trouble forgetting anything else. Forget Billy.

But he couldn't. His brain was filled with snapshots of
the old Billy, each one lit up for a few seconds as if this were

some strange arcade game, like he was caught under a strobe, briefly illuminated and then in total darkness. He could see his face laughing, carrying Lester under one arm, hauled out from his hiding place, the grim anger as Tony came out of nowhere to release his friends, sidestepping and feinting all Billy's best; alley-o. And Billy's grin when he reached into the freezer, and they told Lester what they were going to do.

All because of a game. Of sorts. After alley-o, the Bridge Game, the one that caused that look of bewilderment on his face when they heard the crashing, smashing, churning of vehicles off in the darkness below the bridge, listening to the tortured tearing of metal as vehicles mangled together, Billy with his mouth open, horror in his eyes, wondering what he had done. Then the last image flicked off, leaving just a dying red glow and the smell of burnt plastics in Ed's nostrils. He walked over the rail and threw up, splattering a mix of donuts and pizzas and Hershey bars onto the sand. That smell, it did it every time.

Ed spat his mouth clean, picked some pieces from his teeth, and knew he had to fill up again. At least life had come to this part of the Boardwalk with the opening of the MGM and the Palace and for him the best part of that life was a franchise of Max's Hot Dogs out of Long Branch on the North Jersey Shore. And open twenty-four hours. Forget Billy, get some food.

Ed pulled the door open against the force of the storm and stepped inside, the sudden quiet making his ears hum. He took a seat at the U-shaped counter and rubbed his hands. The hard core of Atlantic City's twenty-four hour workers were scattered around either side of him, mainly casino workers getting a breakfast before or after their shift. He nodded at one he recognised, a young black guy with bright eyes who got him tickets for shows now and then. What was his name? Keith. It came to him. Just like that.

'Hey, Keith,' he found himself saying.

Keith was just finishing up, he wiped his mouth with a napkin and came over. 'Ed. What's happening? You workin' nights now?'

'Insomnia. I just fancied a dog.'

'Yeah, they do some bad shit in here. I'm from Long Branch, y'know, we used to hang out with Celia at Max's all the time.' He lowered his voice, 'They better up there though.'

'Everything is better up there.'

'Damned right. Listen, I'm happier than a two-dicked dog here, cause I got ten tickets for the fight. Next Saturday? You wanna pair?'

Ed shook his head. 'It's not my game.'

'One-fifty the pair.'

'Thanks.'

'Mercury Rev?'

'Who?'

'Some band playing at the Taj next week. Hot ticket apparently.'

'Maybe. You still at the Showboat?'

'Nah, the Palace, man, got to get done up like Charlie Chan. I tell you, have those guys got their racial stereotypes confused or what?' He wiped the corner of his mouth with a napkin and slid off his stool. 'See ya, Ed.' He paused for a moment. 'Get some sleep, OK? You look beat.'

The waitress had been hovering for a minute or more now and she sighed when he finally turned. 'A dog—' he began.

'One up!' she yelled.

'No, I'll have a couple—'

'Two up, guy can't count!'

'And a Miller.' He thought about his weight. 'Make that a Lite.'

Within seconds the long toasted tubes of meat were in front of him and a frothy glass of beer. He swilled the beer around his teeth like mouthwash, then ordered a burger and fries, too, and another beer. It was closing on four when he resumed the walk.

When they had gotten out of Boxgrove, Cotchford, the old running ground, wasn't the same. Downtown was deserted, almost all shut up. The marina project had failed. Schools going to shit. Jimmy Jazz just about got by over on the West, but other than that it was a wasteland. It was becoming a welfare town. Everyone who could go had gone. Changed again, now, of course. Bankers, stockbrokers, all kinds of corporate HQs had moved in, drawn by the easy commute to Manhattan and bargain prices, putting life back into Downtown, upping the snooty quotient by a factor of five or ten. Even the West Side had been spruced up, although it was still the poor relation, didn't have the antique shops and the restaurants – it still majored on graffitti'd walls and had cornered the market in old wire trolleys.

But too late, his old crew was gone. Billy for one. And Bird had only done eight months in Boxgrove, then he had gone out to California. And Honey. Honey had split, too. She had left him with a memory of one night, one single fucking night on the beach at Bay Head, and a promise of more to come. But she stopped writing, the line went dead. And when he got out the trail was cold. All he had was that ambition of hers, in the last letter, the grimy, worn letter he still read now and then, and an even more creased photo of a shiny, smiling blonde, looking like Candy Clark, the image slowly fading with the years.

The letter told him she was going to make it as a dealer or a croupier, earn herself some real money, and she'd settle in Atlantic City. He stopped himself reaching for his wallet. Every time he pulled out the picture it lost a little bit of its life, another fold, another crease added to its network. He could conjure up the image, the head and shoulders shot, the blue sweater matching the blue eyes, the bobbed blonde hair, the slightly lazy, crooked smile, innocence slowly sliding into sensuality. Or so he liked to think. But she went.

So Ed moved on, too, because Cotchford didn't forget the boys who had put it in the newspapers, didn't forget just how sick they were. Killed an innocent family, and then . . . For those who stayed, it was still a talking point. And they treated Lester like he was some dangerous retard. Even Lester's parents shunned him, embarrassed that their little kid had turned into . . . that. So he took him with him, rather than let them dump him in the institution down at Tom's River. They started to move to wherever gambling was legal, wherever Honey might be training, looking for the girl that had boldly unzipped him and put her hand in his pants all those years ago. Until the cold, cold trail brought him here, because this was the end point she had talked about.

'What do you want to do here, Ed?' he asked himself. 'Stop listening to that churning in your stomach, the conflicting voices, the whirl of images. What do you want to do? What can you do to someone who just tosses you a bill without even recognising you, pays you off like that? What can you do? Kill him? Maim him? Kick him in the shin? What? Say it. You're a man now, you may not feel it, but you aren't that fifteen year old kid that Billy screwed.' But he *was*. He was the same person, burning with the same shames and desires. Arrested development, he thought, that must be the diagnosis. Twenty fuckin' dollars. A dollar a year for the time since it happened.

The sea along the main stretch of the Boardwalk was booming through the piles of the garden pier, now an extension of the MGM. He didn't like the sound. It reminded him of another hollow boom, the sound of that cement block hitting metal and glass, the sound they all thought was so funny. Light a joint, take a couple of tokes, and let's go and play on the Bridge. It had been their replacement for alley-o once the Mayor had banned that game.

Just past the Taj was the twenty-four hour Pawn, across the road from the Dublin House. The frontage was shabby grey, with the usual promises of best cash offers posted in the window, and the detritus of people's lives washed up there. Ed walked down and peered through the glass. Goodrich was inside, arguing with a couple of sixteen, seventeen year old kids who bolted past him as soon as he stepped in.

Goodrich smiled. 'Ed. How are ya? Late for you isn't it? Or is it early? Beer?'

Ed nodded and Goodrich pulled one off the six-pack he fetched from the ice box under the counter, then one for himself. Ed looked around at the display cases and cupboards stuffed with the desperation of the vacationing gambler and the down-on-their-luck city residents. Stereos, BB guns, gold chains, personal hi-fis, watches, rings, clocks, artificial limbs, CDs, tapes. And musical instruments. Ed pulled his eyes away from a Fender Jazz bass, but Goodrich had seen him.

'Yeah, sometimes even the bands down here, the little ones that play like the lounges and the bars in the casinos? They get sucked in. Lose the lot.' He took a slug of beer. 'Nice guy owned that bass. I tried to talk him out of it. Said, pal, you can make money with that. You ain't gonna make shit at the crap table. You play? Music, I mean, not craps.'

Ed shook his head. There was a time, long ago, when he had fantasised about it. But there was never the time, and then never the will, and now he never would. He asked, 'What the kids doing?' and pointed at the door.

'Car stereo with no bill of sale and no proof of ID they

could show me. At gone four in the morning. I'd get shut down within the hour, man, I touch that. Within the hour. You need something?' He waved the can of drink around to indicate the display cases.

He shook his head. 'Just saying hi.'

'Hey, howdya get on with that girl? You know, the one you told me to mind my own business about?'

'Wasn't her.'

'No? Too bad. Look, you want me to keep my ears open? We hear everything in here.'

'No. I mean, yeah, I guess so. Can't do no harm.'

'Abso-fuckin'-lutely. Y'see we get all sorts, the public and the cops, always looking for hot gear they say, but usually they come in for a present for the wife or girlfriend or both. We give 'em a good discount. Goodwill – you know what I'm sayin'? Tell me who you looking for. On the QT of course, I'll keep an ear to the ground.'

'She's called Honey.'

'Honey?'

'Honey Bea.'

Goodrich laughed and scratched his scrubby beard. 'Well, that isn't a name I'll forget in a hurry. Honey Bee.'

'Rachel.'

'What?'

'Her real name is Rachel Bea. B-E-A. Honey was like—'

'A joke. Right.'

'When did you last see her?'

He hesitated and counted, shocked as the years racked up. 'Must be . . .' He hesitated. Two decades sounded like too long, too embarrassing. Best cut it down. 'Fifteen, sixteen years ago, I think.'

'Fuck, man. Sixteen years? Jesus Christ. And you think she is going to end up here?'

'We did.'

'Yeah, but Ed, we're fuckin' stupid. You know what I mean? Fluff for brains. Otherwise we'd be somewhere else.'

Ed shrugged. 'She always said she wanted to be a dealer. Had an aunt who did blackjack. Worshipped her.' As he said this he could feel the hollowness of the words, see the look of disbelief on Goodrich's face.

'Ed. Fuck, ten, twelve years ago I wanted to be a rock'n'roll star. I wanted to be Bono and Bon Jovi rolled into one. Look at me now. Jesus, give that one up, why doncha?'

'I just . . .' He let it tail off. He just what? Had lived with a gut instinct for a decade that she would show eventually, whichever town he was in, like the second coming. It was an act of pure faith.

'Why here?'

'The gambling, like I said.'

'This isn't the only gaming town.'

'I know. I been to them all. Vegas, Reno, she ain't there.'

'Well, you know, gambling ain't what it was. Look at Asbury. Nobody goes there now. And *The Alchemist* ruined the offshore trade.' *The Alchemist* had been one of those ships that pulled the cloth off the gaming tables the moment it got out of NYC jurisdiction. Unfortunately somebody had figured a floating casino was also a floating bank, and hit it. 'Maybe she took up another career.'

Ed doubted it. 'Thanks for the beer.'

'Hey, look, Ed, don't get huffy man. I'm . . . I mean, look at yourself. Don't take this the wrong way, but you look fuckin' awful.'

'So there is a right way to take that?'

'I mean I am just trying to be a friend, is all. You look like you been attacked by wolves or somethin'. Go home, get cleaned up, and get some sleep.'

'Yeah, thanks. See you.'

'Yeah. Hey – just take it easy. And Ed – I will ask around, see what's what.'

Goodrich watched the door close behind him and realised he was getting soft. The guy was a fat mental defective going nowhere fast, and it wasn't his place to act as a social worker. But he had a soft spot for the great lunk. So Rachel Bea, Honey Bea. It was worth putting the word out on.

It was around about the Tropicana, towards the southern end of the Boardwalk, daylight reluctantly softening the sky, when Ed realised what he had to do. It had been there all the time, fluttering around in what Goodrich would doubtless call his fluff-for-brains head. He needed a centre of gravity. His world was spinning out of control, and he needed someone to pull him back down, give him direction, listen to his heart and tell him whether it was false. Bird. He had to see Bird.

Bird had done time. Even though he wasn't there when the block hit, he had been stupid enough to get caught up in the aftermath, but when he got out he had gone to California, and come back flush. He had managed to sell some computer system to Microsoft or one of those guys for a big wad. Bird had always been the clever one, the one from the wrong side of the tracks who would make it. He'd been tested at Boxgrove, an aptitude test, and he got, like, A-1 scores and was put into Bell House, which was just like a fucking school really. No kids to bang your heads on spigots there. More likely to bore you to death with math. So he did all right. All that money, though, he could have done anything he wanted, lived anywhere. So why did he have to go and buy himself an elephant?

NINE

the e-mailSender: davidm@mailzip.com
Received: from zap.zap.net (post-10..babel.net[194.217.
123.39])
by dub-img-5.zip.com (8.8.6/8.9.7/2.10) with SMTP id
EAA27865
for honicam.adult.net.com>; Sat 2 Nov.001From:
davidm@zapzap.com
Received: from babell.com ([158.152.210.188])
   by goodtime.adult.net.net id aa1006532; 2 Nov 8:55 EST
Message-Id: <zzp.1120@fastmail.com
Content-Type: text/plain; charset=ISO-8859-1
Content-transfer-encoding: quoted-printable
X-Mailer: TFS Gateway
/300222222/311001002811/3000120141/300202356/

Message:
I saw what you were doing tonight, you fucking whore. You
are all over the Internet, sluts showing themselves off where
innocents and children can find them. You should be
ashamed of yourself. Three hours I sat and watched you
play with yourself, put things up yourself, laugh and smile at
the cameras as if you were enjoying it. Don't you know you
are a sex slave? A slave to all the men out there who ogle
your body, who want to own you? It's sick. Also, why don't
you have MPEGs on your site?

the e-mailSender: jfutters@MailServe.com.

Received: from mailserve. net (post10.mail.CompuServe
.com
[194.712.242.39])
by dub-img-5.zip.com (8.8.6/2.6.8./2.10) with SMTP id
EAA24765
for honicam.adult.net.com>; 2 Nov From:jfutters@Compu
Serve.com
Received: from CompuServe.com
by zip.mail.adult.net.net id aa1009592; 2 Nov 9.05 EST
Message-Id: <zzp.6654@zipmail.com
Content-Type: text/plain; charset=ISO-8859-1
Content-transfer-encoding: quoted-printable
X-Mailer: TFS AccessOne
/31111111111/300102811/98716374648/300202356/

Message:
I loved the show tonight, I really did. Best yet. I just wonder
why you feel you have to do this. I mean, you are a good
looking woman, clearly, and could get all kinds of employment. I know the labor market is bad and all that, but there
must be lots of work out there. If you were my girlfriend you
wouldn't have to do that sort of thing. Only for me, I mean.
Why don't you ping me back? Maybe we could get together.
I'm in Borderline, New Mexico. Where are you, Honey?

the e-mailSender:f.alump@demon.co.uk
Received: from qik.mail.qikmail.net
by dub-img-5.zip.com (8.8.6/8.8.6/2.10) with SMTP id
EAA24765
for honicam.adult.net.com>; Friday.001From: f.alump@
demon.co.uk
Received: from qikmail.com ([158.234.66.777.888])
   by post.mail.adult.net.net id aa1009592; 2 Nov. 9.05EST
Message-Id: <zzp.1120

Content-Type: text/plain; charset=ISO-8859-1
Content-transfer-encoding: quoted-printable
X-Mailer: FFF THRUPASS
/5000100001/500102811/500102841/500202356/

Message:
Look – I have spent close to a hundred bucks on your site,
and not once have I seen you use that big mother on yourself.
And touch your ass, will you? Either that or I'm going back
to Amy's Place.

the e-mailSender:bmoon@aol.com
Received: from sidesaddle.net (post-10.mail.aol.com
[194.217.242.39])
by dub-img-5.zip.com (8.8.6/8.8.6/2.10) with SMTP id
EAA24765
for honicam.adult.net.com>; Sat 3 Nov. 1.00am1.001From:
b.moon@aol.com
Received: from aol.com ([158.154.333.666.888])
by sidesaddle.adult.net.net id aa1009592; Sat Nov 3,
Message-Id: <zzp.1120@fastmail.com
Content-Type: text/plain; charset=ISO-8859-1
Content-transfer-encoding: quoted-printable
X-Mailer: TRANSAMERICA
/7111100011101/700102811/700102841/700202356/

Message:
Hi, Honey. I logged onto the camera as soon as I got back,
but it was all darkness. Decided against using it tonight? I
am sorry I screwed up meeting you, but I just took it as a
sign that tonight was not a good idea. So near, yet so far as
someone once said. Miss you. I'll call Monday. Billy M.

TEN

Absecon Island, New Jersey.
Saturday November 23

Driving south from Atlantic city on Absecon Island, you come to the well-to-do enclaves of Ventnor and Margate, both named for English seaside towns. In contrast to Atlantic City, the homes are neat, expensive, with manicured lawns, painted fences, hefty security systems.

Ed had done this run dozens of times. Both had a smattering of good restaurants the fare might want to be driven out to, or some of the Margate residents liked to gamble, have a drink in AC and get a cab home rather than drive. And there was Lucy the elephant, which people still asked to go and see, even more so since that ad for Budweiser had made her a national celebrity.

She had been built as a stunt to generate home sales in the area in 1881. Three storeys high, covered in grey tin, the beast had been variously a summer home, a tavern and a museum, until she fell into disrepair and, when threatened with demolition, was saved by the people of Margate who stumped up for her restoration and moved her to a safer place.

Bird had always been obsessed with her, had wanted to buy her, but the Save Lucy committee was worried about the bizarre-looking pachyderm falling into the wrong hands again, and said no. Then there was the arson attack, and Billy offered to move her and secure her on Longport at the south of Margate, bordering the One Hundred Acre National Reserve, an area of salt flats and sand dunes. That way the tourists who came to see her and have their photo taken would disturb nobody. The clever bit was getting Anheuser-Busch to stump up the moving costs.

You could see Lucy as the houses thinned, sitting amid a smattering of pine trees on her stone plinth, her crazy eyes staring out to sea, a startled expression on her pachyderm features, as if wondering how an elephant got to be on this side of the Atlantic.

Bird had opened a café-bar on the howdah which he ran March to October when you got a great view along the shore, and birdwatchers would often sit up there nursing a cold one, while scanning the flats for plovers and snow geese and peregrines and the hundreds of other migrants that used Absecon as a watering hole.

The sun was up by the time he saw her, although the sky was as grey as her skin, and she looked a trifle lonely and forlorn. He turned his car onto the gravelled driveway and bumped up the road to the plinth, listening to the laughing gulls giving their raucous comments on his mission. Fuck them, he thought. This wasn't funny.

The door was in the left front leg and he rang the bell, hoping Bird hadn't joined some of his feathered namesakes and flown the coop for the winter. Five minutes later the door was opened by a tall, tousled, yawning figure with a gown pulled around him. The skin had stretched on Bird a little, accentuating the hook of his nose, the tight lips around his mouth – in fact he didn't have a top lip at all, giving him a slightly mean look, one he didn't deserve. As usual, Bird hardly batted an eyelid at this early intrusion. It took a lot to faze him. Always had.

'Ed. You look awful.'

'So I've been told.'

'Come in, then.'

They climbed up the leg to the living room in Lucy's

belly, and Bird raised the blinds. Ed had been here once or twice before, and he liked it, it was full of heavy Indian-style furniture, carved tables, an expensive hi-fi, Bird's huge record collection and a baby grand piano. The piano had been put in before repair of the fire damage was completed. It wasn't ever going to come out.

'Coffee?'

Ed, still wheezing from the climb, nodded and Bird went up to the next floor where the kitchen was located. He heard the hissing of the machine.

'Put some music on if you want,' Bird shouted down.

Ed hit the play button on the CD when he eventually found it and grinned as he heard the once-familiar sound of Kenny Burrell and his guitar. Strange, most of them had merely tolerated this kind of music back when they were kids – you want a toke of dope, or a glance at some of the mags Jimmy kept under the counter, you have to listen to Blue Note and Prestige and Atlantic and all that shit – but Bird, Bird he got to like it.

Bird returned with two cups and sat on what looked like a round leather footstool, while Ed took one of the sofas. He looked around, at the paintings, the wall hangings, the carpets, all rich colours and intricate patterns. A lot of them featured moustachioed Indian warlords riding into battles on Lucy's ancestors. Bird had been spending his money. He looked well, too. Still had those thick-framed round glasses that had gone through several stages of fashionability and were currently back again. Bird had a quizzical expression playing permanently around his eyes, mainly because one eyebrow seemed to have been positioned higher than the other. He couldn't help this 'Oh yeah?' expression, but it could be unsettling.

Also disquieting was Bird's habit of not saying anything. He would wait for you to gush and stutter and make small talk, while he just kept that eyebrow up there, until he felt you had dug your grave deep enough and then spoke just enough words to push you in.

Well not this time, thought Ed.

So they both sat there, sipping hot coffee and smiling frozen smiles.

He won. Ed couldn't believe it. He won. 'Well, Ed, what brings you here at the crack of dawn? Not my fine coffee, I fear.' Jesus, he always did speak like that, as if auditioning for some 1940s film. Basil Rathbone, maybe. Leslie Howard. All he needed was a fucking cravat.

And then Ed let it all out in a long stream: the accident, the ride to New York, the eavesdropping, them mentioning a cancelled stop-off in Cotchford, right down to his bone-numbing traversing of the Boardwalk. Even the unreasonable rage he had felt at the twenty dollar bill. Everything. Well, almost everything.

When he had finished after fifteen minutes of non-stop talking, he felt his throat constrict with the effort. He gulped back the rest of the by now lukewarm coffee.

Bird got up and began fussing, straightening straight pictures, wiping already dust-free surfaces. Over his shoulder he said: 'And you are sure he didn't recognise you?'

'Would you? I took a good look at myself in the mirror for the first time in a long time.'

Bird shrugged. 'We've all changed.'

'You haven't. He hasn't, not much. Me? Forgetaboutit.'

Bird rubbed his forehead and squeezed his eyes shut, as if trying to wake up. Ed was a mess, it was true. But surely... 'You know he probably didn't even notice you. Billy is rich ... or his old man is. You're just staff. What is it that riled you so much? The fact that he tipped you, or that it was only twenty dollars?'

Ed shrugged. 'I dunno. I've been wondering that. I just

see the note hanging there, mocking me, that look of pity on Washington's face —'

'Jackson. It's Jackson on the twenty I think you'll find.'

'Whoever. But, look, don't you think it's all so fucking weird?'

'What?'

'OK, start with Harvey's, the North Pole. I go in there, and there is that cocksucker mayor on the television. On the TV in the Pole. I been going in there maybe three years now, more or less. What are the odds of that happening?'

'Better than you'd get in any casino. He's tipped as the next governor. You won't be able to move for his face over the next year. Can I just plump that cushion? Thanks.'

'OK. Then there is a waitress with the name Rachel Ben. Almost Bea. Born at Long Branch.'

'Almost. Almost her. But it wasn't her.' Bird was impatient with Ed's fascination with his old flame. Why, she didn't even qualify as that, not really. 'Was it?'

'No,' he conceded, 'Obviously brought up in the South somewhere. Then there is the shift supervisor Dick Bevis. His brother. Danny Stowe. Danny fuckin' Stowe.'

Bird remained silent. He'd had it easy. But little Lester, and Ed, they'd got the short straw.

'Stowe was the one who banged your head in the shower, wasn't he?'

'You know he was.'

Bird shook his head. 'What about him?'

'Dead. Dunno how. Dead is good enough for me. Anyways, I come face to face with Stowe's half-brother and bing-bam, there's Billy Moon.'

'Well . . . what can I say? Synchronicity?'

'Oh, screw you, Bird. You keep missing the point.'

'Which is?'

'That . . . that this thing has come to, like, taunt me. Look what you did with your life. Zip. Oh, here's Billy, look what he did with his. It isn't *fair*.' Spittle licked his lips and he ran his tongue over them to clear it up. The sudden outburst hung in the air between them, the unnecessary force of it giving it an odd after-echo.

'Ed, Ed, OK. Calm yourself. Another coffee? You've gone quite red in the face.'

'You got anything to eat?'

'What?'

'Eat. I'm kinda hungry.'

Bird glanced at the clock. 'Well. Breakfast?'

'Waffles?'

'Yes, waffles. Anything on them?'

'Honey?'

'Yes. I think so.' Bird made fresh cups and toasted some waffles, arranged them perfectly on a gold-rimmed plate, and brought them down. He was dressed now, in one of those well cut English style tweedy suits he affected, with a shirt and tie, formally dressed even in his own home. There was another silence, more comfortable this time, as Bird mulled it over and Ed munched away. Bird eventually said, 'Fair is a hard one. I don't think you should be looking for fair. What have you done so far?'

'Nothing.'

'Often best to do nothing.'

A favourite Bird saying. 'Bullshit. You think I am going to walk away from this?'

'Walk away from what exactly?'

'Billy Moon, right under my nose. Our nose.'

He tapped the end of his impressive proboscis. 'My nose is fine, Ed. Just fine. Well, nothing a little rhinoplasty wouldn't fix.'

Ed swirled the coffee, watching the surface spin, climbing the sides, like he felt he was climbing out of a deep pit.

'There was something I didn't tell you.'

'Oh?'

So Ed told him about the case, and what he thought was in it.

Bird scratched his head. 'And this will be . . .'

'What?'

'Revenge?'

'Restitution.' The smell came for him again and he took a hit of coffee, holding it in his mouth, letting it fill his nasal cavities until the threat receded. 'We covered up for him.'

'It was the right thing to do.'

'Maybe.'

'So what next?'

'I tell the others.'

'Others?'

'Tony, Ruby, Don. I told Lester already of course. Didn't register too much. You have to preface most things by telling him you are going to be talking about the letter Z and the number four, or writing it across the computer screen.'

Bird suddenly changed the direction of his pacing and darted over to the hi-fi, turned off the Burrell and put on some trumpet. 'Dave Douglas,' he said, by way of explanation, but Ed's knowledge of jazz ended with his association with Jimmy, so it meant nothing. Sounded like Freddie Hubbard with electronics to him. Bird said: 'You don't think you should get some professional help for Lester? I mean, I know it is expensive, but I could contribute—'

'Don't change the subject. Look, maybe all it is, is, I want to remind Billy Moon that he left some dog shit on his shoes when he stepped up a couple rungs, and that dog shit was me and Lester and the others. Maybe not you – you did OK.'

Bird shrugged: 'And me? What do you want me to do?'

Ed remembered how Bird would watch the alley-o games and never joined in, devised the Bridge game that caused all this, but would never do it himself. He was one of life's bystanders. 'Tell me, where can I find Don?'

Bird hesitated. 'Why?'

'I'd like a second opinion, Doctor.' And someone to keep guard for him again, maybe: with the bulk of Don around you always felt a tad safer, he remembered.

Bird scribbled down a couple of addresses on a pad and tore the sheet off. 'These may be out of date.'

'Thanks.'

'Ed, don't do anything rash.'

'If I do, you'll be the first to know about it.'

'Now, you promise?' Like a fucking School Principal, thought Ed.

'Yeah yeah, promise.'

'Ed, I have something for you. Came months ago, but I knew I'd see you sooner or later, and the ringolevio thing, it reminded me.'

From behind the hi-fi cabinet he brought out a brown paper parcel, tightly wrapped in string, about six inches deep and twelve square. He solemnly handed it over. 'I got one too.'

Ed weighed the package. 'Jimmy?'

'Yes.'

'Shit.'

'He isn't dead, Ed. Shut the store, moved in with his sister. Got all his stuff on tape, and they need the room.'

Ed smiled: 'I thought—'

'He's probably only sixty, sixty five, and he isn't ready to go yet. Just got tired of fighting to make ends meet. He owned the building, and got a fair price for it, so he's going to take it easy, maybe move down south.'

Ed nodded. He put the parcel down and they hugged, in

a way they hadn't done for many years, with Ed just at the taller, thinner man's chest level. Without saying any more he descended Lucy's left leg, clutching his bequest from Jimmy Jazz. He didn't look back to see Bird quickly go to work, fluffing out where Ed had been sitting, straightening his clothes, erasing all evidence that his domain had been entered.

ELEVEN

Binker Towers, Fifth and 51st, New York.
Saturday November 23

Billy Moon snapped his eyes open dead on seven a.m. as usual. And, also as usual, he cursed his father. This was the watershed when he was a kid – seven was a lie-in, half the morning gone, a real luxury, and his father would shake him awake, ruin the day, before he disappeared. As often as not, though, it was six-thirty, six forty-five. He wouldn't have minded if his old man had hung around and played ball, coached little league, helped with model kits or taken him swimming like most other kids' dads. But no, it was 'get up, and get busy, I have work to do'. No wonder he ended up hanging around Jimmy's so much.

Still, it came in handy when he was in Gibbs. They had a six-thirty start for cold showers. It slammed a lot of the kids' heads, made them disoriented, more pliable, but Billy, Billy knew all about early starts, he was one step ahead of that little ploy.

There had also been that one time, however, when his dad didn't wake him. Just once, when the old man hadn't appeared. Billy recalled sliding out of bed, hearing the noise in the basement, going down to see his father with a stack of clothes in front of him, feeding them into the furnace. There were little bits of white glinting on the clothes, stuck on with some kind of paste. Bone, he knew at once, and the paste was a mixture of blood and brains.

Big Billy had looked at him and carried on stoking. 'Always get rid of the evidence, son.' he said sombrely, as if advising on how not to get a girl into trouble, 'They can't touch you then.'

He felt Anne stirring next to him, yawning, her eyes puffy and ill-focused. 'What time did you get in?'

'Early. Ten-thirty. Eleven, maybe. You were good as dead.'

'I took a pill.'

'I was ready to go out.'

'Yeah well, you told me you wouldn't be back until twelve, which usually . . .' she yawned, trying to clear the mists swirling around her brain '. . . means two or three, and I didn't want to be woken up. How was I to know you'd change your mind?' She sat up and reached for the water. The tablets always left her with a parched throat.

She watched Billy pad across the carpet to the bathroom and close the door. She bit her lip and vowed not to fight with him. Wouldn't get her anywhere. She had been thinking a lot, and maybe she had driven him away a bit, perhaps she did come down on him too much, and maybe her mind had wandered from the game a little. Can't be easy being Big Billy's son.

She wondered when it would be a good idea to broach the idea of a move. She knew he would feel they had only just got to grips with this one, but Sarah had come up with a real steal. It was a few blocks uptown, on 57th, eleven rooms, sixty thousand square feet or more, triple-height ceilings, black walnut flooring, a sunken marble bath in the bedroom, and a Sub-Zero fitted kitchen. And a view from the terrace of Carnegie Hall. And all for just a king's ransom.

'It won't go soon,' Sarah had said, 'you've got a couple of months, and it's my exclusive. Pick your time. Just make sure you got it before the shit hits the fan with hubby.'

Anne slid out of bed, robed up and went to fix breakfast.

Blueberry muffins, pancakes, scrambled eggs, granola – the lot. By the time he emerged from the bathroom, freshly shaved, she had it all laid out.

'I'll just have some toast and coffee.'

She almost swallowed her tongue, but managed to coolly spoon some syrup on the pancakes.

'Hey, watch that stuff. The pancakes got syrup in, the syrup got calories, we gotta watch what we eat at our age. We got any wheat bread? Oh, right, got it.'

She felt the food turn to cardboard in her mouth but carried on chewing as bravely as she could, washing the lumps down with coffee. He wasn't going to get the satisfaction of her choking on it. When the last boulder-sized crumb had forced its way out of her mouth she said: 'I spoke to Big Billy last night.' Just in case BB mentioned it, she had better get in first, she figured.

'Yeah? How'd he sound?'

'Good. He mentioned some project he thought you might have told me about.'

Billy turned from the toaster, thinking hard. 'Did he?' For his father that amounted to blabbing.

'Yeah, he was kinda surprised you hadn't said anything.'

He put a thin film of low-cal spread on the toast, and a similarly meagre amount of strawberry jelly. Now why *hadn't* he mentioned it to his wife? 'Well, you know. We ain't be so much talkin' as fightin' lately. You and me, I mean.'

'I know. I'm sorry. Tell me now. No fighting.'

He sighed and sat down. Well why not? She'd find out sooner or later, whether she was part of it or not. 'You know that they threw out the casino plan for Governor's Island?'

She frowned as she tried to remember. Yeah, the old military and coastguard base, they had tried to put legal gambling on it to compete with Atlantic City, but there was such an uproar from city and state – not to mention Trump

101

and Wynn – that they had had to shelve the plan. 'Yeah. That was a while ago.'

'Yeah, when it was Guliani's plan. You know, they threw it out because it was Rudy's. By the time of his second term, if he'd have said the sky was blue nobody would've believed him. Or they'd've voted to have it repainted, after the Diallo shit. So they tried again with the casino, but too soon. The thing is, while the lawyers were looking at leases and such, they found a very interesting thing. You know it doesn't belong to the city? The state thought it actually had possession? Then they reckoned it was Federal and they offered to sell it back to the city for a dollar? Remember that? Yeah, well that's a crock. Because it was Coastguard, they made it in international waters, so they could bring seized ships in and hold them legally. So it's basically like the UN – you know, a little bit of international, neutral territory in Manhattan. Or in this case, off Manhattan. Basically the island can act as a freeport.'

'A what?'

'Freeport. No taxes. No New York City sales taxes. So what is the big growth area at the moment?'

She shrugged.

'Getting the most for your buck. Times are hard, people go out to New Jersey or even down to Delaware to shop. And they have to spend to make up for the tank of gas they use, so they go to one of these outlet places.'

'So you want to open an outlet store in New York?'

'Right. Only offshore. Whole day out – shops, restaurants, multiplexes, theme park, ferry ride. It'll be like a daytrip but, you know, eight minutes from downtown.'

'That's brilliant, Billy.'

He grinned foolishly. But she was right.

Then a thought hit her: 'But will the City let all those tax dollars go easily?'

'Well they go to Jersey or Connecticut right now.'

'Yeah, even so,' she helped herself to another pancake, but held off on the syrup. 'Right under their noses?'

He rubbed his hands together. 'These Friday night trips? Like last night? That is what all this is about. There are people to be taken care of, paths to be smoothed. You know what I mean? Both the city and the state need to kept sweet. Expensive, but cheaper than going to court, what with lawyers' fees and the time and all.' Billy smiled, 'So if all this comes together, well, it'll be my own little bit of the empire. I mean BB and his pals are bankrolling it, but once we're up and running he'll hand it over to me.'

'You?'

'Yes me. Me. What's so funny?'

'Nothing. It's . . .' It was just that she couldn't see him as having the patience to be a glorified storekeeper.

The phone rang and spared her any more stumbles. Billy picked it up off the wall. Talk of the devil, BB. 'Yeah, fine, no problems,' he answered to the enquiry as to how the previous night had gone. 'Same old, same old. Well, a bit of a fender bender in the limo. No big deal. 'Bout eleven. Paterson? No shit. Three of them? Where are they? The Depot? Newark? How long they been in?' He looked at his watch. 'So I get down there about five? That OK? No, no I understand you are busy, not a problem. Yeah, I'll let you know.'

He hung up. 'Billy.'

'What does he want you to do?'

'Oh, just some more of his dirty work,' he said sarcastically. Very dirty, he thought to himself. Very dirty indeed.

TWELVE

Ed slumped down in the chair as soon as he got home, taking time to phone in sick to the garage before he closed his eyes and started to drift into a troubled sleep. A montage of images came to haunt him, fading in and out, sometimes merging, so Bird got Jimmy's voice, Don looked like Billy but acted like Tony, and Ruby, Ruby was tall, so tall, stretched like she was elastic. These strange chimera were playing alley-o again, running through the streets. He, Ed, had burst from his hiding place and was sprinting towards Bailey's Store ('We Sell Everything') where Billy's team always had their den. Tony was inside, he had been collared at the beginning, took three of them to hold him down and drag him inside the chalk line. Once you were in there the rule was you couldn't struggle no more, had to wait until your saviours came through. Alley-o. Bird saw him first, bobbing and weaving towards the guards. Strange. He was no player. How did he get in this dream, Ed asked himself.

You had to keep going. Even if you dragged one of the defence across the line with you, the shirt being torn off your back, hair wrenched out in handfuls, as long as you could cross the line and yell, your guys were out and home free, free to start the whole cycle of evasion and capture again. But he was slowing. The air was grown thick, his movements sluggish. He looked down and saw he had the legs and feet of an elephant, great gnarled shanks, thudding into the sidewalk. He could feel hands grabbing him, pulling

104

him down, he stumbled and the asphalt came up to met his face —

He jerked awake. He wiped the sweat from his face, thinking about the elephant. Bird's elephant. He remembered the package he had brought home from there. He looked over at Lester, who was still at the screen, piloting a Ferrari through the streets of Milan, looking for Wild Card. This was one of the many pedestrians who was, in fact, an armed undercover agent. It was someone different in each city – you never knew whether the little old lady was going to slough off her disguise and emerge as the big, unshaven mean-eyed cop who whips out the latest hardware and blasts through your windshield.

Lester had on a misbuttoned check shirt and some Gap jeans that were too short in the leg. Ed realised he must do something about that. Just because he was half crazy, didn't mean he had to dress like a loon.

He reached down and pulled up the parcel and felt it. He knew what was inside. Records. Old vinyl from the fifties and sixties. Maybe a Lou Donaldson, possibly a Sonny Rollins, certainly a Miles, pre-electric Miles, Miles Ahead maybe, or Sorcerer. John Coltrane on Prestige. They wouldn't be in good condition – scratched, or stained, the covers dog-eared and peeling, the odd yellowed cigarette burn. But they had been much loved.

He put his head back again and tried to cut out the sound of the squealing rubber from the TV. As sleep came again he heard Jimmy Jazz's voice:

'I was bad in those days. Had me some bad shit, I can tell you. I was so hip, so young. Like in the fifties – whoa. Forgetaboutit. Like a broke-dicked dog, as Miles used to say. I went all over, all over the village. Used to catch me a train from here, from Cotchford, and I would go to the Vanguard, the Village Vanguard – you kids heard of that?

But Birdland was the place. You never knew who would come in. I mean the Queen came in one night when I was there. The Queen – y'know, Sarah Vaughan, she'd come right in and, if there was nowhere else, she'd sit down right next to you. Just to listen to what was happening. I met Sonny Rollins, Kenny Dorham – what a trumpet player man. I mean, get outta here. And Clifford, Clifford Brown. You know, he would never say this, but he used to make Miles sweat. But the turnpike kilt him. Skidded off the road and kilt him. And Lou Donaldson – that's him up there. Always used to stop by and say hi, buy a few groceries. Real nice guy – and what a player. Whoo. Forgetaboutit. I was so cool back then. Zoot suits, peg pants and a '55 Chevy. Oooh-weee. And that man up there, see him. That's Prez. The President. Lester Young. It was Billy Holiday named him that. She said, 'Man, you're the *real* President of the United States.' Interesting sound. Listen, I got a tape. Hold on, here we go. Hear that tone? Gorgeous. He got it from a mixture of Bix Beiderbecke – I guess you guys never heard of him? He was a trumpet player, and Prez loved his changes, what he could do with a tune, but the sound, he liked this other cat who played sax in C, which you don't hear much these days. So Prez gets his sound, his own sound, by combining the two. Now what you boys listenin' to at the moment? Who are these guys? English? Look, you should listen to jazz, it's the only music there is. And it's American, not some phoney faggot rock music like that band you got there. Now move along there kids, I gotta serve the lady. *'Buenos días, señora. Cinco lonchas de jamón? Sí, sí.'*

Ed stirred back into real, grubby life again, with the sound of Jimmy's rasping Spanish still ringing in his ears. Jimmy was the focal point for them, all of them. He ran a little food store on Fremont, on the West Side, the other side of the tracks. The walls were painted lime green, and on them, like a folk-art version of a war memorial, was a litany of the great names in jazz that Jimmy had seen or met, interspersed with album covers and creased photographs, many of them signed. Jimmy could spend an hour telling the customers about the night Charlie Parker played with a plastic saxophone at Carnegie Hall. Strange to think of the shop gone, the hole on Fremont it would leave. Jimmy had learnt Spanish as soon as the first Hispanics appeared. That was one reason why he survived when the sprawling K-Marts and Safeways started opening up all around.

Why they gravitated there and not a soda shop or the mall or the record store in town, Ed couldn't remember, except Jimmy's was always where they chalked their alley-o den, the one Don would guard so zealously, and Jimmy himself was always free with the candies and drinks. If Don was out there alone, hot and gasping in the sun, a cold Coke would come out every half hour or so. Jimmy would even take over the spot while the Don took a leak.

And over the course of a year or so, Jimmy gave Lester his name. And Bird. Lester, because he liked *Goodbye Pork Pie Hat*, which was playing in the store most days. Lester's real name was Mike Sugarman, but when he came up with this theory that *Goodbye Pork Pie Hat* was homage to an item of headgear going out of fashion, well, Old Jimmy just cracked up. Called him Prez or Lester after that. Lester stuck. 'Could've been worse,' he used to say, 'I could be called Pork Pie. Me, a good Jewish boy.'

Bird, because he was podgy at that time, like Charlie Parker, but taller, and because he played saxophone for a while in the marching band. Tony the Tiger, that was from Jimmy Jazz too, because Tony Zed fought like a tiger during the games. Tony was one of those Star Wars freaks that collected all the little figures, whose main aim in life was to own the Princess Leia that Carrie Fisher had objected to and had been withdrawn after only a few shipments got out. Worth over a thousand dollars. Tony the Tiger would comb yard sales, waiting for his Princess to come to him.

Ed didn't need a nickname. Jimmy just called him The Behr. Made him laugh for some reason. Billy never got a name either, but that might have been because, although he hung around the store, he was an Eastsider really. Jimmy always suspected him of slumming it, but there wasn't any great chasm between Billy and them, not like with some of the kids. And anyway, if you weren't a jock or a jock groupie, nor a dweeb nor one of the bookies, you tended to end up with the little crowd that hung around Jimmy's after school, listening to him talking about people and places that were as mysterious as the dark side of the moon. You just nodded a lot and took the candy bars and the sodas. And after you moved on from candies to serious shit, to booze and acid, Jimmy had rules. You couldn't come around drunk. You couldn't come around wired or tripping. But now and then he'd sell you a ready-rolled reefer. He believed it was the lesser of all the evils. Especially crack – this was the time of the Chambers brothers in Detroit and the Morrises in Camden. He hated crack. And smack, too. Turned into a regular Jimmy Swaggart on the subject.

'Drugs ruined too many jazzmen. Took them too young or just sucked their talent out. A little bit of Mary Jane never harmed anyone. But coke? Crack? Smack? Dust? I catch any of you kids doin' that shit, you don't come round here no more.'

Ed opened the parcel and skipped through the records. A few surprises. Dave Brubeck. He thought Jimmy always hated that white college-boy shit, almost as much as he hated The Clash and the Beastie Boys. An electric Eddie Harris record. Some European avant-garde stuff. And at the bottom, the album *Mingus, Mingus, Mingus, Mingus, Mingus*.

Ed shuffled over to the old Japanese hi-fi, ten, twelve years old, scuffed, battered and with various knobs and dials missing. So different from that aristocratic number Bird used. This was the aural equivalent of white trash. Maybe Goodrich down at the pawnshop could fix him up with something better. He put the album on the turntable and dropped the stylus into the groove – *Theme for Lester Young (Goodbye Pork Pie Hat)*. Ed remembered Jimmy telling them it wasn't the original, but he thought it was the best cut of the tune by the bass player. It was hard to hear the horns above the spits and crackles and the cacophony from *The Getaway*, but eventually they managed to rise above the sea of static, to state the theme majestically, poignantly, like a requiem not only for an old jazzer but a bunch of kids who used to play a game outside a store way back when.

Honey looked at the time and at the camera. Yeah, almost there. Five more minutes. She fetched the trash bin from the living room, and quickly cut up the print-out of request e-mails, screwed them up into balls and dropped them in. Just like the lotto draw. Honey's Request Time was on every Saturday at ten a.m. Eastern Standard Time. Send an e-mail, and pledge an extra five bucks, and your request will be put in the metal bucket and, who knows, Honey might just act out your proposal live on air.

Yeah, 'might' being the operative word. The guy who wanted her to play with a speculum, his bells weren't going to ring this morning. No way was he going into the draw. Nor the man who had the thing about animals – she didn't care if his favourite site was www.horsecum.com. Gross, that's what that was.

It was getting tougher, because she swore her threshold levels were going up. Only last week she had put a request for her to pee into the trash bucket in there. Then worried whether she would be able to go if it was chosen. So she had drunk four cans of Coke, which meant she had to squeeze hard to stop herself going anyway when it was a straight-forward call for her to shave herself on screen-that won.

She settled down on the bed in a loose, cross-legged position, adjusted her dressing gown high up her thighs, smiled at the camera and made a great show of plucking out a slip, unfurling it, and turning her mouth into a big round 'O' when she read the request.

She went to the bathroom, fetched her manicure set, picked up a buff envelope from the desk, shed her gown and settled onto the bed. Slowly she took the clippers and eased off the first of her toenails into a perfect neat little crescent, then placed it in the envelope. She carried on until all ten slivers were inside, sealed the envelope and wrote the address on it. Howard from Pensacola, this really was your lucky day.

THIRTEEN

Atlantic City, New Jersey. Monday November 25

When Ed walked in the Pole the first thing he saw was Bo hurtling towards him like he had been catapulted. Payback for that sucker punch. Trapped in the doorway, unable to move, all Ed could do was raise his fists, but it was too late, Bo was on him, arms round his neck, his mouth reaching for the side of his face, ready to rip his ear off, like Tyson did to Holyfield. Ed started to thrash in anticipation of the pain.

'Ed, I love you, man. Love you.'

It froze him. Ed stopped moving and peeled Bo from his neck and held him at arm's length. He looked him up and down. Fresh shirt. Nice trousers. Rockports.

'What?' asked Ed.

'I fuckin' love you, man.'

Brain damage. Trauma to kidneys. Blood clot. 'Yeah, Bo.'

'I do, man. I found the money.'

'What?'

'Hunnert and fifty grand. Drinks on me. I found it – thanks to you. What'll y'have? Anything you want.'

Ed looked at him again. The madness in his eyes had certainly been turned down a notch. He'd shaved. Combed the wild thatch of hair. 'You found your old man's stash?'

'Yeah. Yeah, that's what I'm sayin'. And it's thanks to you.'

'Yeah?' Cautious now. This didn't smell right.

'After you hit me the other night. I wanted to kill you.

Fuckin' kill you. I wanted a gun, and Goodrich said he'd get me one . . .'

Ed looked over Bo's shoulder to where Goodrich was sitting. He gave an apologetic, a-sale-is-a-sale shrug.

'But I didn't have no dough. So I went home and raged at my old man's ashes, at this little urn he made them put his ashes in. I swore and I cussed and I remembered what he said to me. 'You'll get that money over my dead body.' Over his dead body. *Click* – it came to me. So I took the lid of the urn and I smashed it. And there was a safe deposit box key and instructions inside the lid. Over his dead body, see?'

'That's great, Bo. Can I get a beer?'

'Hell, have two, man. Hunnert and fifty grand. And I tell you, Ed. Money does make you better.'

'I hope so, Bo. I hope so.'

He managed to squeeze his way by to where Harry the cabbie was at the bar, having a one-sided argument with Sam about the previous day's football game. Goodrich was talking earnestly to Alice, and some kind of trading was going on, probably to do with the missing ring. There were even some tourists, a couple who had decided to be brave and leave the Boardwalk and were rewarding themselves with beer. Maurice was circling like a vulture. Another round and they would be hungry.

Goodrich broke off and said to Ed, 'That's what you call a lucky punch, eh?'

'Yup. Wanna try if it works on you?'

Goodrich furrowed his brow. Then he got it. 'The gun thing?'

'Well, you know, why didn't you just shoot me for him?'

'Old Bo – the old Bo – would never have got past question one on the form. I was trying to, you know, pacify him.'

Ed nodded as if this made sense and Goodrich turned his attention back to Alice. 'Harry.'

'Ed.'

'The cab damage – how much?'

'The shop reckoned about eight hundred bucks all in. I gotta do the paperwork and send it to this guy.'

Ed pulled out his wallet and counted out a thousand and slid it over to Harry, whose jaw was dangling in his drink. Ed's beer and bourbon arrived and he slammed back the shot.

'Fuck, Ed, whatcha doing? You win the Megabucks or what?'

'Ain't mine. The Palace said they'd pay for the damage. All I gotta do is get a receipt and send it to your man – the driver of the limo. I figured adding two hundred on for time and trouble is on the level.'

'Yeah. A receipt?'

Ed took out a piece of Enchanted Palace hotel stationery and passed it over with a pen. 'All you got to do is say: 'Received one thousand dollars in full and complete settlement of any claim.' Then give me the guy's address and number and I'll run it up to the Palace. They're just taking care of the guest, you know, the guy in the back. He's a high roller, plays premium slots.'

'Great. I mean, fuckin' A, what with the fare and all that was quite a nice little bing with the car. I might hang around that parking garage exit more often.'

'I think this is a one-off deal, Harry. And not to be spread around. They was real clear on that – or next time it's by the book.'

'I guess. Listen, I hope you don't mind me askin' but . . . you looked a little, well, a little shaken, a little *shaky* after New York, when you dropped my cut off. You know what I mean? I was worried about you.'

'And how do I seem now?'

Harry passed over the receipt and the contact numbers

and address of the limo driver. 'Well, you seem good, Ed. Real good.'

Wuzel put the phone down and swore. Well, he had done it now. Lodged the bid with Christie's for the photograph of the docker by Bob Christopher. Ninety big ones. Outrageous. He might not even get it at that, of course, and then he would be kicking himself he didn't go all the way.

He opened the desk drawer and pulled out his small accounts book, the one that gave him the broad brush strokes. The photo business was OK, better than he expected given the economy, and the other stuff was ticking over nicely, pulling in five, ten at a time. So he had just spent nine jobs' worth of money. And what if he lost it at ninety-two, ninety-three, how gutted would he be? Plenty. He was about to call up and increase the bid when the phone rang under his hand. 'Billy, good to hear from you. How are you? Well, if it's a problem I can help with, then I'm your man. Always glad of the work, you know that. Sure, sure. Look, there is a gallery near your place, the Pines. You know it? Good. I could meet you there tomorrow. say, eleven-thirty, before the lunchtime crowd? No, I wanted to see the show anyway. Catch you then.'

Wuzel put the phone down and thought for a minute. This meant more work. A bit more cash. Not exactly another *Alchemist*, but Billy paid well enough. He picked up the handset and dialled Christie's. He could risk going one-ten, just in case.

FOURTEEN

NYC. Tuesday November 26

Billy stood on the pavement with his overcoat pulled up around his neck. The light was going fast, and there was frost in the air. He thought of the three guys, and shivered from deep inside. Not from sympathy, just his body imagining what they must be feeling. Pricks, they should know better than try and stiff BB.

The car pulled in front of him and he waited for Backson to lower the window and show himself. You don't get into any car, his old man always said. Billy climbed in the back. 'Mr Moon,' Backson said, 'This is Andy, standing in for Shawn.'

'Good afternoon, Mr Moon.'

'Yeah,' Billy said curtly. Then, to Backson: 'You got the stuff I asked for?'

Backson said: 'Take the East Side Highway and the Holland, Andy. Some shit at the Lincoln.'

Andy nodded.

'Yeah, I got it.'

'Plates on the car?'

'Garbage like you asked. Who's at the Depot?'

'Omah and Spike been doing the minding.'

Backson nodded.

'How's your wife?'

'Yeah, fine, thanks for asking. Showing now, a lot.'

'Must be weird, huh? Having something growing like that inside you? You know, it's a bit like that movie. Alien.'

'Yeah, well she's kinda hoping it comes out the more

conventional route.' He knew Billy wanted to relax right now, to ease into things. The Big Calm they called it. Kind of Zen and the Art of Mutilation. So Backson said: 'Hey, this guy dies and goes to Hell, right? And the Devil welcomes him and says, "The first punishments last for a thousand years apiece. I will show you, you got three to choose from. Room One . . ." And he takes him in and there is this guy being whipped by this big mean ugly-looking bitch. "OK," says the guy, "so what's number two?" So he goes in and this guy has these nipple clamps, and body piercing shit all over him and he says, "OK, last one . . ." And they go in and there is this beautiful blonde giving this dude a blow job, really going at it. And the guy says, "hey I'll take room three." And the devil goes over and taps the blonde on the shoulder and says, "OK, you can stop now, this guy is takin' your place." '

The Town Car filled with their combined laughter. Billy wiped his eyes. 'Where you get this shit?'

'Joke of the day on laugh-dot-com. Log on every morning before work. Start the day with a smile, know what I mean?'

Andy said: 'So there is this old guy in the Jewish old folk's home, and they give everyone a dose of this new wonder-drug, meant to give you your sex drive back. Like Viagra with a rocket. And it gets them hot. So Benny he says to Ellie, 'Fancy coming back to my room, for you-know-what?' And Ellie says 'sure', and they waddle off down the corridor. And when they reach the room, she gets all embarrassed and says, 'Look Benny, I gotta warn you I've got acute angina.' And Benny says, 'That's just as well, cause tits you ain't got.'

They made the Holland Tunnel with a second round of laughs. Billy said: 'Can you go to 4th, near the bridge, Andy?'

Backson raised an eyebrow. 'Depot is other side of the river, ain't it?' he asked tactfully.

'Just wanna pick me up a couple of body warmers, you know what I mean?'

'Mean?' said Backson with a smile. 'That is downright wicked.'

The elevated section of the railway cast a black slash of deep shadow across the street. The trains flashing overhead created a strobe effect within it, flickering on the faces of the women who prowled the dank space underneath, their bare arms goosebumped, their breath coming in clouds like racehorses. Like sick racehorses.

This was the current hangout for the girls, and it would last another week or two before the cops moved them on. Newark was cleaning itself up, the girls were being pushed to the fringes, just like Manhattan in the late 1990s.

Billy told Andy to slow up as they approached, and wound the window down a fraction. A ripple went through the bodies, a pheremonal signal that there was custom, and out of the little pits of blackness, from alleys and doorways, from behind girders and boxes, from under the bridge itself, the parade stepped forward to be inspected.

Billy knew what he wanted. Or rather he knew what he didn't want. He looked at the skeletal limbs, the red-rimmed eyes, the uncontrollable streams of snot coming from noses, the breasts collapsed and imploded, the needle-scarred legs and arms and necks. They looked like they had been punctured with screwdrivers, some of them, sure sign that the one-shot syringes had been used over and over again until they were bent and blunt and it was a miracle if they could penetrate butter, let alone scarred and abused skin.

Black, white, Hispanic, they were all there, all sharing the same desperate need. Along the street he could see a couple of vans. Maybe cops. More likely the scavenging dealers, ready to dish out the shit and take the money as soon as these girls got their twenty bucks for a blow job with a condom, fifty if they fancied entering the lethal lottery of skipping the rubber. Or maybe the vans contained the pimps, keeping warm, listening to K-SILK, your smooth soul station.

A few weak lights flashed off and on in doorways on the far side of the bridge, and Billy could just make out faces hunched over a cigarette or a pipe. No, they were the pimps he guessed, a little nearer to the action, able to check who is getting what, keeping a tally.

Billy pointed to one of the more warmly dressed ones, although that didn't mean much more than a Gap hooded jacket over a blouse and short black skirt, and she leant forward. 'An hour,' he said, 'How much?'

'An hour? What, all of you want to do me?'

'Just an hour of your time. No nothing. How much?'

'Hundred and fifty?'

He looked at her face. How old? Twenty-something, hard to tell. Very light-skinned, probably one parent white, cheeks still intact, no major scars, an unbroken nose, all her teeth, but heavy, tired, flat eyes, the eyes of an old woman.

'Hundred. Get in if you want it. In the front.'

She whooped, ran round and climbed in.

'Don't touch nothing,' said Andy tersely. He didn't like low-rent on his leather seats.

'You got a friend?' asked Billy.

'I thought you said—' she began, a tiny touch of panic flashing in her eyes when she realised she was in a big fancy car with three big guys.

'Someone like you who doesn't look too fucked up?'

'Why, thank you,' she said sarcastically.

'Yet.'

'Maureen under the bridge. She's pretty new. Only started doing stuff when they killed her mom—'

'Go get her, same deal.'

Maureen was white, a little older, and despite what her friend Lisa had said, she had been out on the streets for some time. Her dyed blonde hair looked like old electrical wire, and her pallid skin was yellowy. But they'd do. He made Maureen climb in the front and perch on Lisa's knee. Andy shuffled far away from the pair, he was almost driving from the outside when they pulled away.

Backson told his devil joke and passed them the vodka bottle and hundred each and they giggled. One to tell the other girls.

The Depot used to be an old bus garage, but like its neighbouring buildings had fallen into jagged disrepair. There were no lights shining anywhere on the block, apart from the faint glow of a small fire lit by some bum on one of the upper floors of a warehouse. The sidewalk was strewn with the dumped detritus of the surrounding neighbour-hoods, bits of old cars, wire trolleys, stained and torn mattresses, all sprinkled with a dusting of glass shards from a thousand broken bottles.

Andy pulled up and turned off the engine, Backson retrieved the near-empty vodka bottle, and they stepped out into the threatening silence. Billy opened the trunk and handed Backson a large knee-length puffa jacket and put one on himself. He then passed across one of the two big holdalls, took the other, slammed the lid, and motioned for the girls to follow. He headed down what had once been the forecourt of the bus garage, stepped through a small access door in the big steel shutter that shielded the inside from the street, then walked down the ramp onto the maintenance floor, footsteps ringing on the concrete.

There was light here in this windowless semi-basement, coming from a string of low-wattage bulbs looped over the steel pillars that ran floor to ceiling. Apart from four of these clustered near the centre, the space was undivided, big enough to turn a bus round in. It was meat-locker cold, an atmosphere with no sunlight and no wind to disturb it, so chill as to be almost vicious. The two girls, one in a short skirt, the other tight jeans, both with thin tops under zip-up jackets, began to shiver.

At the centre was a table piled high with the vestiges of fast food meals and beer cans. Omar and Spike were smoking, leaning against one of the central pillars talking in low voices, but they stood up when they realised they had company, and who it was. Backson snapped round and clamped a hand over Lisa's mouth when she started to scream. She had looked down at floor level and seen what were at Omar and Spike's feet, barely visible in the shadowy gloom. Three human heads.

For the first time in nearly ten hours, Honey switched over the camera to running previous highlights and slumped back on a bed now covered in the paraphernalia of her job, and wondered what Billy was up to. Probably planning a cosy dinner with wifey. Jesus, but it wasn't fair. She was beginning to feel just a little like a prisoner of the device across the room. She needed a smoke.

She gathered up the piles of creams, lubricants, and various implements, took them to the kitchen and washed and dried them, before doing the same to herself, then sitting down on the sofa and rolling herself the slimmest of joints.

She was trying to cut down, but it was another way of purging the performance from her brain, by wrapping it in a soft haze of cotton wool and rocking it to sleep. Sometimes she wondered how she had managed not to turn into a complete fuck-up. She thought about her friends over in Philly. Melissa, the one with the tattooed breasts, who ended up injecting in her nipples, and who had either jumped or been thrown out of the window of Duke's place where they all went to score. She remembered her listing her daily requirements just before that happened: Methadone; one hundred milligrams, Xanax pills; twenty a day, washed down with booze, crack; one to two hits a day, shooting cocaine five to seven times a day. Where was her little daughter now? Jade, that was it. Where was Jade? Going down the same road? More than likely.

She took another drag. And that Lisa. Didn't believe that one-hit-and-you-are-hooked shit. Thought she could be a huffer like her mom – just going for the odd quick breathy high. Within a week she was collecting broken-off car antennas to use as a stem. It was the despair in her eyes that made Honey get out. Whenever she thought she had gone wrong, had made a mistake by going with Billy, she thought of the weight of Lisa's eyelids, and that mouth, and the ache in her bones, and the flies crawling on her skin when there was nothing to stick in the antenna.

Nope, she was lucky. Near miss. Whenever she thought of it she thanked Billy. This existence might be a narcotic, but it wasn't too bad at all. She took another pull on the joint. Not at all.

Backson said 'Whoa, whoa, girls, it ain't what it seems. Look.' He took his hand from her mouth and the two edged forward. Billy was already at the side of the heads, putting down his bag, zipping up his jacket. Backson had seen this, or variations on this before, and it was fascinating. When Billy had to stand in for his old man, he became Big Billy, same walk, same cool mannerisms. Backson pushed the girls further forward and they instinctively reached out and held hands. Both realised they had undersold themselves for a hundred bucks. This was weirder shit than they had ever seen.

The heads were, they realised, attached to bodies. One of the old bus inspection pits had been flooded with a thick black liquid, a mixture of water and sump oil and axle grease and detergents, its surface a swirl of dull bluish and purplish hues. The three men, two white and one black, were up to their chins. Backson knew their hands were behind their backs, tied, and their feet attached to hollow cinder blocks. The buoyancy of the gritty, viscous liquid was such that, with a little effort, they could just keep their chins above its surface.

But the vile brew they were suspended in was also cold – cold enough to seep through their naked skin and chill their very core, for the muscles to shiver for an hour or two and then give up, shut down, while the blood was shunted away from the surface, causing the lips to turn blue. By now the core temperature would be dropping, and hypothermia would come calling.

Billy knelt down. 'Well, guys,' he said. 'How long you been in now?'

They stared at him, but either didn't or couldn't speak. There was little light in their eyes, just torpor. Billy looked at Omar, the man who would have trussed them up and sunk them.

'Four hours.'

'Four hours. What is the record, Omar? What is the longest anyone has lived?'

'Five hours, Mr Moon. Five hours ten minutes.'

'So, guys, you have, at most, one hour ten minutes left. Now, I suppose Spike here explained why, exactly, you find yourselves . . . well, in the shit? Yeah? If I mention the names . . . Spike?'

Spike pulled out a list and started reading off names, ordinary-sounding names, Italian, Irish, Russian, Poles. Billy put up his hand to stop him. 'Just regular working Joes.

Yeah? Well, working for me on the hospital anyway. Good money, too. And *overtime*. Guys, you got greedy. OK . . . making up one or two non-existent workers, pulling down wages for them, it's kind of accepted practice, know what I am saying? Bit of padding. But fifty?' For the first time his voice rose, bouncing off the walls. *'Fifty extra fuckin' guys?* . . . And overtime. Tut, tut.'

He stood up and looked at the girls, beckoned them over, made sure all three men could see them clearly. For the first time something stirred in their eyes. Curiosity.

'The thing is, guys, that a handwriting expert costs two hundred bucks an hour. That's the very best, the Joe di Maggio of handwriting experts. A fuckin' bargain you ask me, when you trying to find out who's stiffin you for fifty or more Gs a week. Didn't take him long to come up with you three bozos as the forgers. I mean – I heard of multiple personalities, but this is ridiculous.'

He paused and hunkered back down. He had their attention now. Only the nearest white guy was tuning in and out, thin black trickles coming from the corner of his mouth where his head had dropped and some of the fluid had got in, burning the soft membranes of his oral cavity. 'You know, guys, I can't take any credit for this set-up. My father used to use it back in the days when things were really tough. Not here, of course. North Philly, mainly, and it was all kinds of pits and pools, but this is perfect, don'tcha think? You know, the Germans used to do something like this with Russian prisoners. They would put them in barrels of iced water and time it. See how long it would take for them to die. Because they wanted to know how long a Luftwaffe pilot in the sea would survive. Then they would see how best to bring them back from the brink. Hot baths, blankets, you know all kindsa shit. But the shock of the hot water often killed the fuckers, and the blankets weren't enough to save them. You know what they found worked best? Nah, you'll never guess. Lemme tell ya. You couldn't make this stuff up, guys. Women. They used to get women, two women, to wrap themselves around the frozen Joe, and bingo, back to life. So . . .' He stood up and walked towards the girls, and said in a low voice. 'Show 'em. Give them a little taster. Just to your underwear.'

Lisa said: 'You promised there was nothing. It's fuckin' freezin', mister.'

'Another hundred. And there is some fine rum in the car. Warm you up a treat.'

He stepped back, and Maureen wriggled out of her jeans, while Lisa pulled the side zip and stepped out of her black skirt. There was no underwear in either case, to make business quicker. They started on their tops but Billy held up his hand. Judging by the goosebumped flesh down below, their tits might have the opposite effect to what he intended.

'OK, now one of you gets to be the meat in this very nice sandwich. One wheat, one pumpernickel, right? Think of all that nice warm flesh rubbing up against you. What do you think, guys?'

The nearest head mouthed something, and Billy leant down. The cold jaw muscles were slow, sluggish, and the swollen tongue made the words come out thick and ill-formed. 'Nah, didn't catch it. Wanna try again?'

'It was Willoughby,' the mouth finally spat, the teeth chattering like castanets. 'He made us do it.'

The other two heads risked nods, the black oil splashing over their chins.

Willoughby had been a shift foreman. 'Yeah, Willoughby. Tricky one that, because Willoughby has gone. Disappeared. Smart guy, you see. But where does that leave us?' He thought for minute. 'You know I hate to mention my old man again, but he had a motto. Well, he had two, but only

one is appropriate just now. *Neca eos omnes. Deus suos agnoscet.*'
Yeah, sorry about the accent. It's Latin.'

Billy walked over to the first holdall and took out a red
plastic container and took his place at the edge of the pit
again, towering over the three heads. 'It comes from a
Crusader siege at a place called Beziers. Thirteen hundred
and summin'. You know, they figured this town had a fair
number of heretics inside it, but once they got in, well, they
was fucked if they could tell the good guys from the bad.
What do we do, they asked this guy Amal Ulric, their leader.
What the fuck we gonna do. It was like that movie Spartacus.
Who is Spartacus? I am. Who's a Christian here? We all
are.' He unscrewed the cap on the container and the smell of
gasoline hit him immediately. He splashed it on the first
head, and watched the guy's eyes screw up in pain, and the
oily surface ripple as the man struggled and thrashed. He
tried to dip under to wash it off, but the pool was having
none of it. It forced him to the surface and like a cork he
popped back up. The waves his struggle set up started
plopping into the faces of the other victims, causing them to
spit and splutter.

Billy doused the other two, making sure that a trail of the
light gasoline on the top of the pool linked the trio. They
were shouting now, a torrent of names and abuse, pleas and
promises, but he had filtered them out. Too late. He was
aware of the girls backing away, trying surreptitiously to get
back into their clothes.

'So, he said,' continued Billy, fetching the box of matches
from his pocket. From The Mark. Hey, maybe a good place
for dinner tonight, he thought. 'This guy Amal Ulric, he
says: *neca eos omnes*. Kill them all.' He struck the match and
stepped back as the fumes ignited, a huge whoosh spreading
over the surface of the pool, illuminating the corners of the
vast room, the crackling heat almost scorching his face. '*Deus*

suos agnoscet.' He watched as the hair and eyebrows and eyelashes sizzled and caught, the heads engulfed in flame like baked alaskas, the skin blackening and blistering, the screams masked by the greedy roar of the flame. 'God will know his own,' he finished.

He reached down into the hold-all again and took out a set of ear plugs which he squeezed home and then hoisted out the Benelli Nova, a polymer pump shotgun, less than eight pounds, but loaded with three-and-a-half-inch rounds. Billy shouldered the weapon. The faces were almost unrecognisable now, and the room was filling with flecks of charred hair and flakes of skin. The screams were still building, though, reaching a pitch that could shatter glass.

Omar, Spike and Backson moved back as Billy primed the gun and fired, watching the pool erupt like a depth charge had gone off, splattering his puffa jacket with multicoloured specks. The sound was hard and steely, thudding from concrete surface to concrete surface.

As the last of the droplets rained around him, he fired again, creating another mushroom of fluids and flesh, and then a third time, till the room was roaring from the blasts. As the sound died away, the low tones of the weapon's report were replaced by a squeal. The two hookers, arms wrapped around one another, were screaming their lungs out.

Backson stepped forward, raised the NAA.32 and shot them both quickly in the head, one tap each, and, like a single body, they slumped to the floor. He looked at them, could see the needle marks in the last dying flickers from the pockets of gasoline still spluttering on the pool. A release for them, he felt.

The cold and the quiet and the dimness slowly returned, only broken by the heavy breathing of the men as they sucked air in through their teeth, trying to keep the oily, repulsive odour from their nostrils. The air was still filled with delicate showers of singed keratin, gently wafting to settle onto the concrete, like black dandruff. Billy was positively warm now, and he shucked off the splattered jacket and brushed at the stains on his trousers. Have to burn those. He didn't look at the pool again, but Backson couldn't help himself. 'Son of a bitch,' he said quietly.

Billy unzipped the second hold-all and threw coveralls to Omar and Spike and lifted out the small chainsaw and slid it across to them. 'Get rid of the evidence,' he said, using his father's second motto. Then to Backson: 'Remember to make sure this guy Andy changes the plates back in case any of the pimps made a note.'

He looked at his watch. Still plenty of time to make that dinner.

FIFTEEN

The Blue Balloon, New York City.
Tuesday November 26, pm

Ed sat in the booth playing with his napkin, sipping the beer slowly, trying to eke it out. He didn't want to get ripped. He had to stay clear-headed. So no shooters, no shots, just snacks. He had been here ten minutes and the waitress had already replaced the little bowl of nuts three times. It wasn't big enough. Two decent handfuls was all. When he got nuts he liked a pile of them, like at the Pole.

This bar had been the driver's choice, his after-work place. Ed had been to it before, here on 8th, but it hadn't been the Blue Balloon, it had been a hardcore C&W bar, Lady Kitty's. There not being many hardcore cowboys in this part of Eighth Avenue, it attracted the usual assortment of pimps, hookers, their johns and people who looked as if their rig had been stolen, and they'd stumbled in to make a call and become mesmerised by how awful Lady Kitty's Swing Sisters really were. Now it was very, very slick, not a word you could have used about Lady Kitty's. Sticky, that was the appropriate term back then.

The Blue Balloon had antiqued walls, well padded booths with the stuffing actually on the inside of the seats, a cigar room at the back, the sort of waiting staff who looked as if they had had all-over liposuction, and drinks twice the price they should be. And no band, either. He wondered what had happened to Lady Kitty. Busted most likely – Guiliani's nightlife crackdown had probably included running bum transvestite singers out of town.

But now it was a real nice place. Not the kind of place he belonged. Maybe the driver – Shawn, his name was – was out to impress him.

He was nervous because the ruse seemed so flimsy. He called the number Harry had given him and pushed out the story. The cab garage didn't want any more trouble with its insurance company, would prefer to do this off the books, would they take a cash settlement? Sure. How much, Ed had asked. Fifteen hundred bucks, the driver had said. Ed wasn't sure that was the real price or whether Shawn had chivied it up. If he had loaded the bill it'd only be by a couple of hundred – limo tires and rims don't come cheap.

So, fine. Well, said Ed, I got to bring the cash and you got to sign for it, and I am up in New York anyway – can we have a drink? Sure. Well, maybe the guy thought people wouldn't make a story up like that, not unless they had a trunk with six or seven grand under their bed and an ulterior motive. But I'll be down again Friday week. Can we do it then? Nah, I'd rather get it settled, and, you know, off the record, when you ain't working. OK? Yeah, that was OK, Whatever.

Ed saw him come in, recognised his shape rather than his face. He had the classic broad shoulders, arms-held-out pose of someone who works out, and his off-the-peg suit looked tight under the armpits and around the waist. Ed raised a hand and he slid in opposite. They shook.

'Howyadoin'? Appreciate you coming.'

'It's OK. No paperwork? Cash payment? Cool with me.'

'Drink?' Shawn hesitated, and Ed had a terrible thought. 'You working tonight? Driving I mean?'

'Nah. Chivas, rocks.'

Relieved, Ed placed the order and got himself a second beer and some more nuts. If there was to be any hope at all, the man had to have a drink to loosen him up. While they were waiting Ed talked about driving in the city, the state of New York roads, the Lincoln Tunnel, and – no offence meant, he stressed – the cabbies, all the bugbears of any professional wheel man. Shawn asked Ed how he came to be in AC.

'Just lucky I guess.'

Shawn grimaced and took his first sip of the drink. 'I don't much like it myself.'

'You gamble?'

'Dollar here, dollar there, while I am waiting. I'm a born again Christian. I mean not, like, obsessive, but I believe in moderation.'

Ed felt the ground slip from under his feet for a second. He never did know how to deal with Christians, regular or born-again size. Does this mean he was the non-violent type? 'Oh, right,' was all he could manage.

'Can't drink, cause I'm drivin', and what else is there to do in that place? You drink, and you give your money away. End of story.'

'How often you get down?'

'Like I said, the Friday run, once every two weeks, and then maybe one other time. Still too much.'

Ed handed the brown envelope of cash over, and asked Shawn to count it. 'No, I'm sure it's all there. Anyway, I know where you are if we're short here, don't I?'

Ed laughed as good naturedly as he could manage and ordered another round. 'Yeah, I guess. Anyway I did all right out of that night. I mean – it was a good fare. And your man, Big Billy is it?'

'Billy Moon.'

'He seemed a bit pissed we didn't stop at . . . Cotchford? Is that the place?'

'Yeah.' Ed watched his lips seal like a ziplock bag. He'd come in with that one too soon. Much too soon. Change the subject. Fast. 'Look, thanks for the money and the drinks, but I gotta get going—'

'Sure. I only ask because I was born there.'

'Cotchford?'

'Yeah. Changed, though.'

'I dunno. All we see of it is the car. Call in at a place called Starboards. You know it?'

Ed laughed. 'They still serve you with the trays clipped to the car doors?'

'That's the place.'

'Used to be good burgers.' He had to stop himself licking his lips at the thought of one of those juicy mothers.

'Still are. Still are. Look . . .' He was almost gone, almost out of reach. Ed wanted to grab him, pull him back. He felt that Box anger rise, and capped it. No time to blow a fuse.

'You gotta sign this. Just to say you received it.'

'Right.' Shawn sat down again and scribbled his name.

Ed had to push it now. 'Not that good, though.'

'What?'

'The burgers aren't worth breaking the trip for. From AC.'

Shawn laughed suddenly, and his shoulders shook. 'No, no they're not. *We're* there for the burgers. The boss?' And then he changed his mind. An off-guard remark was almost out, and he had stifled it. 'Like I said, I gotta go.'

And with that, Shawn loped out. Twenty-five minutes the man had stayed. And Ed knew precious little more than before he arrived. No, that wasn't entirely true. He knew the man thought he believed in God. And he knew what he had to do next.

SIXTEEN

Newark, New Jersey. Wednesday November 27

Down Walnut, cut through to Olive, then back on Chestnut, Kennedy, Garden, New York and back on Walnut. Still there.

Try Ferry, Prospect, Congress.

Still there.

Don looked in the mirror of the BMW, and watched the Cutlass turn the corner with him. They wanted him to know they were there, that was for sure. Shit, he knew the suits had been a mistake. Twelve hundred lousy bucks.

After ten more minutes he was getting dizzy, watching the street signs blur as he circumnavigated the cluster of blocks to the west of the rail terminal. Eventually he pulled onto Ferry and parked up, scraping the tires as he did so, and watched the Cutlass glide past, the two occupants – white, mid-thirties, sunglasses even though it was getting dark, straight from central casting, he thought – turn to stare at him as they cruised by and pulled up ten car lengths down. They executed a lazy U-turn and positioned themselves opposite him, but by then he had stepped into Bolo.

Bolo was one of the oldest of the Portuguese/Spanish restaurants in the Ironbound District, and still had lighting from the days when anything more than a five-watt bulb would overload the system. Don peered into the gloom, waiting for his eyes to adjust. He could swear this was taking longer – he had to go and get them checked. Or maybe they just turned the lights down some more – it was probably the only place in town where the waiters needed seeing-eye dogs to get around.

'Mr Keah,' said Gilberto, the maître d', looking up at the bulk of his most regular solo customer, 'your usual table?'

Don nodded. The usual table was at the side of the bar, on the far wall from the door, close to the kitchen and the rest rooms. In many ways it was the worst spot in the house, because of the amount of jostling, but it was certainly the finest if you wanted to make a quick exit. Don didn't think he'd be making fast exits. They'd be in soon. They'd have a quiet word, and then they would take him outside. Maybe they would do it there and then, maybe they would take him in the car out to one of the old railway sidings. Either way, this was probably his last *riodizio de churrasco*.

He squeezed between the tables, taking a cloth with him as he went, scattering glasses and flatware on the floor in his wake. Tables too close together, he had always thought that. Gilberto got him seated where he could do no more damage. Don asked for a bottle of Dao to go with the *riodizio*. Still, he mused, it had been quite a month.

Every eight to ten weeks the Newark police sell off various vehicles – either stolen/recovereds that have not been claimed, or those used in pursuance of a crime, or tow-aways that are not worth the two hundred and fifty dollar reclaim fee, plus a few unmarked, high mileage cop cars.

It was how Don made his money these days. You could pick up a car for a few hundred bucks, run it through a shop, and front it for fifteen, maybe even two grand. Especially if, as sometimes happens, you got the old muscle cars which were collectable, or fancy foreign marques. Like the Beemer. The one that was going to cost him his life.

It came though the line as a white 5-series with high mileage, but it hadn't been a cop car, it had been a tow-away. It had sat in the pound for months, and a fine film of cement dust from nearby factories had settled on it. It looked like shit, but Don gave it a quick going over. The leather was unmarked, and the engine didn't rattle when started, so the ends hadn't been run. A slight blow on the muffler, but that could be fixed easily.

It was a slow night, just six or seven dealers and a couple of ordinary Joes who had read the books on how to pick up cars cheap. They were the ones to watch – they always pushed the bidding up too high. But they couldn't see under the dust, so Don had got it for eight hundred dollars, cash sale. He put it through the car wash, took it out on I-78, and decided it was a steal. OK, the white was yellowing here and there, but a quick blast-over would soon fix that. Wind the mileage and he reckoned two, two and a half. But it drove real nice, so maybe he would keep it for himself for a while.

Two days later he noticed two things. Firstly, the air freshener wasn't working too well against the smell of mould. He had found this in lots of cars over the years – damp in the carpets sets up all sorts of growths. And also the front right tire was illegal. And he hadn't checked the spare. If that was fugazi, then he'd be out of pocket straight away.

It was as soon as he cracked the trunk and the rancid odour hit him that he knew there was nothing wrong with the carpets. He could almost see it creeping out in waves. Gingerly he raised the lid and slammed it again.

Whoever was in there had been dead a long time.

He parked the car round the side of his house and tried to figure out what to do. Would the cops actually believe they had had a vehicle in their possession for months without checking the trunk? And in that trunk was a stiff. Who clearly didn't climb in himself and pull the lid down.

It took three paint-spraying masks and a couple of garbage liners to equip himself for his version of a post mortem. Head turned away, he reached in and found the inside pocket of the jacket, only too aware of how the flesh was yielding and parting wherever he touched it.

He pulled the wallet free, slammed the trunk – his nail was still black from where he had caught it – went inside and wiped the surfaces of it with a wet cloth, trying not to gag. He thought carefully about what he could have picked up from the body. Hadn't he read something in Monozine about those flesh-eating bacteria? He went and took a long, hot shower, scrubbed himself all over and dumped his clothes in the machine on an extra hot setting. Only then did he go down into the kitchen, make himself a coffee, and sit down to see what he had.

American Express. Mastercard. Chemical Bank ATM, NYC Library card. Visa. Driver's licence. Dry Cleaning receipt. Bits of paper with phone numbers and shit on them. Thirteen hundred dollars – well that would get him a new tire.

Lawrence Kenneth Milne, what had you done? No clue here. Nothing that said drug dealer, loan shark, gambler, pimp. No clue as to why someone should put a bullet in his brain or a knife in his ribs and bundle him into his car and leave him to be found by the police. Who seem to have missed this one, the guys responsible were doubtless thinking. Been scanning the small stories in the papers looking for it, have they? Bottom of page six, seven, eight. Nothing.

And what about his family? When the cops wrote and said, we got your car, why hadn't a wife or daughter or son or mother said – hey, have you got my Lawrence as well? I don't know, ma'am, we'll just pop the trunk and look.

Because nobody cared. Nobody missed poor Mr Milne.

And Don owning up wasn't going to change that, was it? In the meantime he had two credit cards, an ATM card and a whole bunch of signatures to copy, plus cash.

All he had to do was lose the body.

OK, this was not going to be easy. He knew from just one exploration it was about as solid as a cream puff. But if he did it, well, the police ought to thank him. Imagine the embarrassment otherwise.

So he made the call. To the Engineer. He fixed things. For a fee. Usually losing cars for insurance scams, that kind of thing. This was just the same idea. Only fleshier. It was the worst forty minutes of his life. No contest. Worse than the very worst moments of Boxgrove, that was for sure. But where they left the poor stiff, nobody was ever going to find him.

OK, so the rule was this – small purchases, no need to phone anything through. The first ones would be the worst, because the credit and charge companies pick up any unusual pattern of activity on an account, and this one clearly hadn't been around for a while. But a few CDs, a couple of cinema tickets, some dental work, two new tires for the car, his prostate check – he was still five years outside the danger zone, but fuck, it paid to be cautious – and routine blood checks, three or four meals, all went through fine. So someone must have been paying the bills, too, while he had been out of circulation, otherwise they would've been cancelled by now. Maybe they went out of the guy's checking account automatically.

It was only after he bought the suits that he realised there was a downside to this.

What if whoever had popped him suddenly realised that Mr Milne seemed to have come back on line? That would be awkward for the guys who hit Mr Milne.

'I tell you, we did it and put him in the trunk. He was chilling nicely.'

'Well he ain't there now, and he seems to have warmed up, guys. He seems to be eating at Bolo a lot and is walking round in a couple of expensive Barney's suits.'

The suits were the biggest purchase. Maybe they rang bells somewhere. Maybe someone called at his home and found the bill with all these purchases on it, dated after Mr Milne went trunk-side.

His food arrived and he asked Gilberto to go and see if the Cutlass was still there. Gilberto came over and nodded gravely.

Maybe he could reason with them. Sorry I made you look like jackasses, boys. Can we work this out? Blam, blam. It seems to be all worked out now, Pal.

'Hello, Don.'

He looked up from his food and quickly wiped his mouth. The light from the wall fixing behind him barely penetrated to the edge of the table, and the face was mostly in shadow. He squinted, trying to put a name . . .

'It's Ed. Ed Behr.'

'Fuck, Ed. Ed – you . . . you pick your moments, you know that?' Don struggled to his feet, just catching the wine as it started to wobble. 'Sit down, sit down. Great. Great to see you. You look . . .'

'Big.'

'Well you put some weight on. Shit, when did we last . . .? It must've . . . How did you find me?'

'Bird.'

'Bird?'

'Yeah.'

'I haven't spoken to him in . . . I dunno.'

'Bird knows everything. He said try here or the Rusty Nail down on River Street.'

Don nodded. That about described his life these days. 'Ed, it's great to see you an' all. But . . . I'm in a bit of . . . it would be better if you weren't here. I think something bad is going to happen, and I don't want . . .'

He was used to this. Something bad was always going to

happen with Don. His heart stopping, lungs collapsing, meteor hitting the earth, that kind of thing. 'Tell me.'

'Ed, are you all right? I heard . . . heard you had a few problems. You know, you and Lester . . .'

Ed leant forward so the bulb illuminated his face, staring hard at Don, concentrating on looking tight, together. 'And how do I seem now?'

'Good, Ed. You seem good.'

'So tell me.'

When he had finished Ed asked for an extra glass so he could have some Dao and a beer on the side. He swilled the wine around his mouth, swallowed and said: 'And these guys are outside? The ones who are tailing you?'

Don nodded: 'It's no good trying to reason with them—'

'OK, OK. Just be quiet for a while.' Ed thought for a minute. 'How are you, Don? Otherwise?'

'OK, I guess. I had these headaches . . .'

'Yeah? You see the doc?'

'Sure. You know what he told me – that brain tumours very rarely start as headaches.'

'No shit.'

'No, it's true. Memory loss, numbness, tingling, disorientation, that kind of thing, that's the big clue.'

'You got any of those?'

'Nah.' he laughed. 'Not this month, anyways.'

'You ever had one of those tubes down your throat?'

'Throat? No. Up my ass, yes, when I had a cancer scare.'

'God, I hope they clean 'em between ends. You had cancer?'

Don looked shifty and said quietly. 'Not exactly. I had haemorrhoids. But the symptoms are—'

'Yeah, spare me that one.' Ed had heard enough. Same old Don Keah. Built like a brick outhouse, with the constitution of an ox, and the sunny world view of a turkey at Thanksgiving. He recalled Goodrich's baster. 'Can I get some bread here? And some olives?'

Don ordered some over and Ed quickly stuffed his cheeks so he looked like a chipmunk, and managed to say, 'Give me the credit cards. Come on, hand them over. I'll get dinner if you ain't got enough cash. Now order me a chicken piri-piri. I'll be back.'

'Yeah – with or without holes in you?'

Ed tried to look strong and purposeful as he left, but he could feel the comical wobble of flesh round his middle, the soft ballast that made his gait roll like one of those self-righting toys. He thought back to the days when he used to run those games through Cotchford, when he was fit and thin, and he pulled himself up, felt the gut tighten a little. He could still cut it, he was sure. He used to keep door at a dope house, for fuck's sake, he knew what was what.

After the gloom of the restaurant even the remnants of sunlight leaking through the slashes in the clouds hurt him. His eyes streamed, and it took him a while to locate the Cutlass. This was a hunch, based on the behavior of a kid he knew a long time ago. Maybe Don had changed. Maybe he was right. Ed went over to the car, his heart pounding, frantically trying to swallow the last of the bread so he didn't spit over them.

The driver lowered the window as Ed crouched down.

'Hi,' said Ed.

No reply, the man carried on eating a packet of peanuts.

'My friend who drives that BMW, well he has this crazy idea that you guys are tailing him.'

They looked at each other. 'Yeah. So?'

'So, he'd like you to stop.'

'We will.'

Ed might be new to this game, but he was fairly sure that was a little too easy.

He waited until the kicker came: 'Just as soon as we have finished with him.'

'Now look, he knows he may have been a little dumb—'

'That really isn't our business. You know? Dumb or not, it's all the same to us. We just carry out the instructions.'

Ed looked at them. Something was wrong here. A false note. A cracked bell. Sure they looked like hard men, but hard in an oddly weary way. And the clothes were not exactly cheap, but not what he would have expected if . . . he was tempted to smile. Good old Don. Hey, here's a stick – now can you grab the wrong end for me?

'Can I have a peanut?'

'What?'

'A peanut. Can I have one?'

The guy poured a small heap into Ed's open hand and he threw them to the back of his throat.

'And what instructions would those be?'

'Look, we are being reasonable here, letting him finish his meal. When he comes out, we'll hit him and be on our way.'

'Just like that?'

'Yeah.'

'In broad daylight.' He looked up at the darkening dusk sky. A street light spluttered on near them, glowing a deep red as the gases started to heat up. 'Well, in the street.'

'Wherever – at home, here, we give him the papers and the rest is up to him.'

'Papers?'

'Papers.'

'What kind of papers?'

'For alimony arrears. Court papers.'

Ed laughed. 'Court papers?'

'Yeah. So we deliver, ruin his day and leave.'

'Process Servers. Great. You ruined his day already. How much we talking about?'

The driver looked in the envelope. 'Twenty-six hundred dollars.'

Ed counted out three thousand and handed it over. 'I'll need a receipt.'

'We aren't authorised to—'

'Course you are. Deposit it with the court as a sign of good will. He will be leaving town for a few days, so this is just to keep you off his back. The receipt only needs to be for the two-six by the way.'

They looked at each other, wondering whether this was a sting. One of them looked up and down the street and at Ed. 'Give us a minute, willya?'

Ed walked away from the car and became very interested in a piece of grating in the road. He knew what they were arguing. Was this a set up? Was Ed a plant, they were asking, a bit of authorised temptation, a sting? But they might just take a chance.

After a couple of minutes the Servers signalled him back and, anxious to be on their way all of sudden, Ed had his receipt in twenty seconds. He hardly had a chance to step back before the car pulled away, leaving him standing in a settling cloud of exhaust.

Ed turned to go back in and as he reached the sidewalk outside the restaurant he snapped the credit cards in half and dumped them in the garbage bin. If there was one thing he remembered about his old pal, it was that, in any given set of circumstances, he could always be relied upon to come up with the darkest, most desperate interpretation.

Ed sat down back at the table once he had groped his way across the room, and took a mouthful of his chicken. Don waited a heartbeat before saying: 'Well?'

'They took the cards. They want you to sell the car. You are to leave town for a few weeks, while they convince their employer that the problem is solved. If they even suspect you mention this to anyone else, you can expect to join Mr Milne. That's the gist of it anyway. But for the time being, you lost your tail.'

'Fuck, Ed. That's ... that's great. Jeez, man.' He was so happy he almost managed a smile, but waved his arms and finally knocked the wine bottle over, which dumped its contents on his trousers. He stood up and a lugubrious waiter strolled over to wipe him down. When the worst was mopped up and new seat brought, he sat down with a thump, let out a long sigh of relief and said, 'Ed, old pal, I owe you one, you know.'

Through a mouthful of rice Ed said, 'Funny you should say that.'

SEVENTEEN

The Galleons Hotel, New York City.
Thursday November 28

Galleons was the most discreet hotel Billy could think of in
New York. Sixty listed rooms, with another four on the top
floor that were never acknowledged, where calls were never
put through, where enquiries about who had the penthouse
drew blank looks from the staff. Which penthouse would
that be? Even the way in and out was tucked away round
the back of the hotel, where only one car at a time was
allowed through, since the occasion when two limos had
simultaneously discharged a husband and wife, unfortunately
from different cars and with different partners.

Now just a single vehicle at a time was allowed to glide
around the back and pull up close to the bank of four express
elevators, which delivered the clients straight into their
suites. Room service could be provided by a butler, or
through a hatchway, if real anonymity was desired. There
were the usual refinements in the rooms, but nothing –
nothing at all from handcuffs to extra bodies – was too much
trouble for the staff.

All this for five big ones a night. Bargain, thought Billy.

Honey was dozing, sprawled across the bed, legs slightly
open, a favourite pose for Honicam clients. He wondered
again why he wasn't jealous about that, because he could
do a good line in green-eyed envy when he wished. Maybe
it was because all those sad fucks just got to look and jerk
off, whereas he got the almost legendary web wonder to
himself. And anyway, it was kind of his creation. She was

his creation. So instead of jealousy he felt proudly proprietorial. When he had found her, looking for rival
operations to his own newly acquired empire, she had been
one of the Cyberslutz live video feed circuit, one up from
the nickel encounter booths you got on Pacific. He had
bought out her contract, put her on his roster, thought that
Honicam could become one of the cults. Hadn't the
Mandicam girl made the Sports Illustrated Swimwear
issue? Honey wasn't going to do that – Mandy was barely
eighteen – but it was a sign of the power of the voycam
market. Between them, him and Jerry, his webmaster, were
doing pretty good, steady business.

He sniffed and caught the smell of the Depot. Some stray
molecules must be clinging to his nasal hair, just giving him
an olfactory reminder. It didn't worry him. That side of him
was there, the person lying on the bed now, that was here.
Two halves of the same coin but separate – never see them at
the same time. His father had taught him that, too. The first
time they'd had to do someone was down in the lower levels
of Grand Central. Twenty-three he must have been. Wuzel
was there. It was Wuzel who arranged it all, found out from
his guys on engineering which lines were live and which off.
They took the guy down where only the tiny maintenance
lights illuminated the tunnels, where the air tasted of steel
and asbestos. They tied the guy to a live rail they knew was
switched off, and doused him in water. He had to talk before
the current came back on and griddled him. He didn't, and
it didn't, so Wuzel had pulled out a Para-Ord, one of those
Canadian .45s, and handed it to Billy. Big Billy had nodded
in a first-time-for-everything kind of way. He remembered
what his father had said – you drain yourself of emotion,
deflate, look for the Big Calm.

He looked at the guy who had sneered at him as if to say,
'this is man's work,' like he couldn't do it, and that was the

signal. He stepped forward and raised the gun, squeezed the trigger.

'Safety,' advised Wuzel when nothing happened.

But now the guy was scared, because he knew the boy could do it, so he took his time finding the safety, flicking it off. It was a lesson. Let them know what you are capable of. The next thing he knew the tunnels were booming with gunshots. And then the body started to jerk and fizz and smoke and glow as the power came back on anyway.

'Fuck,' said Wuzel. 'Wasted a couple of rounds there, kid,' and laughed that scary laugh.

Billy padded across the suite, took a beer from the minibar and swilled it around his mouth, before going to the window. Galleons was down near the south-eastern corner of Manhattan, just a block from the riverfront, and theoretically he should have been able to see Governor's Island clear as a bell, but a low mist was obscuring almost everything, including the whole of Brooklyn. Every so often the shrouds would lighten, and he would see a hint of its shape, but for the most part the only evidence of life beyond the grey curtains were the Staten Island ferries shuttling to and from the South Ferry.

'Billy?' She was sleepy, happy, he could tell by the tone.

'Yeah?'

'Whatcha doin'?'

'Looking for my island.'

'Your island?'

'By next year. It'll be mine. Look.' He walked around behind her on the bed, pulled her up under the armpits and pointed into the murky distance. 'There.'

'Can you get to it?'

'Sure, by boat. It's beautiful. Part of it is like a historic site, with a fort and stuff, but really, you know ... it's an oasis, that's what it is – wonderful lawns and houses, fantastic mansions – one of them will be the premium fine dining experience.'

'When is this?'

'Oh, once we get permission for the mall.'

She wriggled free and spun to look at him. 'You want to put a *mall* on it?'

He looked at her. Someone who makes her living chewing dildos in public suddenly gets an attack of aesthetics? 'A very tasteful mall.'

Very low rise, very early colonial. No cars, just golf carts to ferry those who couldn't – or didn't want to – walk around. It was going to be a goldmine. Once they got the planning and zoning approved. That would be the end of the Atlantic City runs, of course. And of Honey? Well she could operate from anywhere, even Manhattan – one of his other girls, Jerry told him, did her show'n'tell from a swanky Upper East Side apartment. Millicam, that was her.

He checked himself. He wondered whether the whole thing wasn't beginning to drive him now, rather than vice-versa. Did he really want this liaison? Before sex, the answer was always yes, yes, yes. Afterwards, his enthusiasm shrivelled with his dick. Sometimes he wished his two halves were the same, that he could deal with the women in his life the way he dealt with those three suckers in the pool – calm and detached. But you had to open yourself up to women, and that's when they got in.

'Wow. Like Madison?'

'Without Madison prices. And great food. Very upscale.' Even now he knew Big Billy was talking to some interesting names – the McNallys of course, JGV, Nieporent, Peyton – to help launch the food and beverage operation.

She yawned and stretched like a cat and rolled onto the corner of the bed. He began to realise she acted like there was a camera on her even when there wasn't. Holding a pose for a second longer than necessary, turning this way and that to get the best angle, the most coquettish look. Her life was a show, like she was something from a SoHo gallery, a walking exhibit. 'I have a hankering for something upscale.'

'Name it, Hon.'

'JG 2? I heard you talk about it enough.'

'I'll call down, they'll send the menu up and we can—'

'I don't want take-out. Not even fancy take-out. I want to go to Jean-Georges' place. Go-to-the-place.' She spelled it out like semaphore, in case he missed the point.

He frowned, feeling his forehead furrow, pulling little patches of tension across his temples. He knew he didn't look at his best like that. His two eyebrows became one, his features began to take on a simian aspect. 'I can't . . .'

'Look, Billy, I feel like I am in the Federal Witness Protection Program. Either stuck in an apartment in Cotchford or holed up in a hotel in New York. Nobody is going to whack me out there, are they?'

He thought of all the familiar faces lining the banquettes at JG 2, the smiles, the slight hesitations, the way the maitre d' and the waiters would be the soul of discretion, not so much as a puzzled look, but how the information would be filed away in their heads for a later gossip. 'And did you see the blonde that Billy Moon had with him? Not quite the finesse of Mrs Moon . . . but, well quite a looker in her own way . . .' And there was always the possibility that when she got to hear about it – as she inevitably would – Anne might just whack *him*. Or get BB to do it. Never marry a woman your father likes. Best keep some tension there, he had decided.

He watched her push her bottom lip out as if she was fourteen, fifteen again. Not attractive either, she was too old for that ploy to work. He felt irritated. She was cracking the edifice, not playing the game the way she should.

Billy felt a wash of cold come over him, grip his heart, the shutters come down, sectioning his brain. She had crossed the line. He could do violence to her now, he knew, if she didn't do it his way. The same compulsion to smack Anne he had the other day, that rose up in him. Calmly he put it away, pushed the shutters up, softened his feelings. He couldn't let his love life get on that level. All the same, he knew at that moment that moving her to New York would be a terrible mistake. Honey really only existed for him out in Cotchford at arm's length, close to the old streets and stores. Away from there she was just another ... responsibility. And, from her behaviour, liability. Sometime in the next few months – maybe once that pre-sex eagerness had become blunted – she would have to revert to being just another name on the Home Girlz menu.

Ed examined his new haircut, wondering if it didn't make him look like Forrest Gump after a six-month eating binge. Like everyone else in the world who ever submits themselves to a clipper-happy barber he chanted the mantra of the freshly shorn: It'll Grow. It'll Grow.

He finished off the four-dollar special he had picked up at the Subway franchise and then ripped open the packages and stood between Lester and the TV, the only failsafe way to get his attention. He held up the Dockers and the Calvin Klein underwear and the Tommy Hilfiger top and the Brooks Brothers shirts and Nike trainers that he had bought in New York.

Lester nodded benignly. Ed could be showing him prize-winning vegetables from Idaho and it would get the same response.

He reached over and flicked off the TV, and, ignoring the whining protests, pulled Lester to his feet. Ed propelled him towards the bathroom, unbuttoning his shirt as he shuffled across the carpet.

'A few days late with this, Lester. Sorry, man, I had a few things on my mind. OK here we go. Arms up. No, up. Right. OK, let's get the water.'

He reached in and turned on the shower, adjusting it until it was the temperature that he knew Lester liked. Tepid. Any hotter and he shouted and screamed, as if the water was scalding his skin. Just a memory of scalding, that was all. Lester did what he always did when confronted with running water, he went limp, as if all the life had drained out of him, or he had temporarily shut down all functions for the duration.

Ed helped him into the bath and ducked his head under the stream of water, rotating his scalp until all the hair was wet. 'Best get you a haircut here as well, boy. OK, close your eyes.'

Ed lathered it up, and before rinsing, he began sponging the body. It no longer hurt, Lester told him, but Ed couldn't bring himself to rub or scrub. He used a dobbing motion, as if he were applying splodges of paint. You could no longer read the individual words. The first few obscenities and insults that were carved on his body had once been legible enough, but they eventually began to run into each other, the letters forming strange runic patterns rather than words. Frustrated, Stowe and the others had created homemade dyes in the kitchen to tattoo the later profanities, to make them stand out, but they were only partially successful. Now Lester's torso was a mass of scar tissue that looked like the map of a subway system for a giant metropolis, with odd bursts of faded colour. It had originally reminded Ed of a living Pollock drip-painting, but now it was bleaching out, the colours losing a minuscule amount of brightness with each shower.

When Lester had complained to the authorities at The Box about the first one, the simple, stark four letters scratched into his chest, he had lost privileges for self-mutilation. Stowe and co. only did the torso, arms and legs. His face was always intact, never anything to arouse the guards, nothing unless they came into the showers. Which they rarely did.

Ed finished the sponge-down, rinsed the shampoo off, led Lester out and wrapped him in a towel, threadbare and scratchy. Must get some more, he thought. Something big and white and fluffy.

He roughly towelled the hair, liberally sprayed some deodorant over his body and under the arms, then helped him into the CK T-shirt to cover the worst of the scars. Ed didn't speak as he dressed him, just in case Lester realised he was crying again.

EIGHTEEN

Lucy, New Jersey. Thursday November 28

Bird looked at the two of them sitting on the the sofa. Don had always been a big boy, now he had simply coarsened a little, thickened around the edges, as if life had been buffeting him all these years, and his epidermis had swollen to compensate. He had a stoop, too, as if the weight of of his head was too much for his neck to bear. Whether life had been good or bad would be almost impossible to ascertain. Donald Keah would say it had been grim, unfair, capricious in the extreme. He always had and he always would.

Bird had once when they were – fourteen was it? – tried to explain the concept of a self-fulfilling prophecy. By assuming things would always work out badly, Don had a way of making sure they did. Of all of them, only Don had been pleasantly surprised at the trial by the length of the sentences. He'd been expecting the chair. Even though you couldn't be executed under eighteen, Don assumed they'd find a way, a loophole. They did for everything else.

And Ed. He'd been thinking about Ed a lot. He had seen him around, sitting in this cab and that, hanging on the Boardwalk, practising his own version of the thousand-yard stare. Bird was amazed the whole thing had hit him so hard. He was sure there had been little physical damage to him from his time in The Box. Yet he had grown flabby, despondent. However, now it was like the old Ed was wriggling within, trying to reach the surface through the blubber. There were flashes of his former self – he had a direction. Shame it was such a stupid one.

Don cleared his throat. 'Nice elephant,' he said, in a way which suggested Bird needed help real quick.

'Thanks.'

'Hard to heat?'

What is this, thought Bird, *Home Improvement*? 'Well it isn't exactly economical, because we have to feed in hot air from an outside unit. Fire risk, you know.'

Don nodded sagely. 'All this wood.' He swivelled his head as if looking for the nearest fire exit.

'You OK, Don?'

'Yeah, can't complain. Well, I mean —'

'Right.' Bird stood up suddenly, knowing that a complaint was coming. 'Coffee?'

Don looked at his watch. Maybe a proper drink could wait. He nodded.

'You got anything to eat?' asked Ed.

'Such as?'

'Cookies?'

'I'll see what I can do.'

'You sure you OK with this?' asked Ed when Bird climbed the stairs.

Don shrugged. 'Like I says, I owe you one. I figure I am one step ahead of the game now, so why not? Tell me again – when did this all happen – the accident?'

' 'Long time back. At least it seems that way. Last Friday.' He went through the abbreviated version, just so it was fresh in both their minds.

Bird returned with the coffee and a measly two cookies for Ed, which he didn't even give time to get comfortable on the plate. They settled back in their respective chairs. Bird suddenly leapt to his feet again and came back with a little vacuum gadget and sucked up the few crumbs that had escaped from the cookies onto the floor. 'So, just like old times. What do you think, Don? About Ed bumping into Billy – or was it vice versa?'

'You know, I have tried not to think about Billy too much these past years. Is that Cotchford?'

Bird swivelled to look at a view of mainstreet at dusk, one of the few non-Indian pictures on the wall. 'Yes. Old.'

'Still do the photography?' asked Don.

Bird shook his head. 'So Ed told you what he wants to do?'

Don nodded. Then he thought and shook his head.

'What's that – a yes and a no?'

Ed: 'I told him what we going to do. I haven't told him how.'

'Oh.'

Don: 'Or when.'

'I know when. In around three weeks.'

Bird thought for a minute. 'Ed, I'm not really—'

'No. It's me and Don and maybe someone else. My call, Bird.'

'You don't think this is all water...' Bird stumbled, realising how inappropriate his metaphor was.

'... under the Bridge?' finished Don.

Ed stood up, slopping coffee on his pants. 'We gotta go.'

'No, hold on.'

'Bird, if you ain't with us—'

'Ed, I am not against you. It was an option I wanted you to consider. Now tell me what you know. Sit down, sit down.'

Ed told him what he gleaned from Shawn.

'That's it?' asked Bird when he had finished. 'That's all you have? It isn't much. Let me think about it. Meantime . . . Ed, one other thing. You gonna do this thing, you've got to get in shape. The kid who did the alley-o jail runs? He's buried deep.'

Ed almost quoted Bo: money makes you better. But he just nodded. 'I'll call you,' he said.

'And Ed, don't think this will be like alley-o. A re-run of old times. This is serious.'

Don stood up and buttoned his jacket, and thought for a minute. In his slow, lugubrious voice he said. 'I know, Bird. It won't be like the old times. But it'll do.'

Back at Ed's they took slugs from a can of beer and watched Lester try and get somewhere through the Bangkok traffic. Ahead, to the left, the noodle-stall guy suddenly ducked down and came up as . . . Wild Card. Lester squealed as the guy raised the shotgun and the windshield of his Honda NSX exploded into virtual shards. Ed had brought him a pizza, and it lay on his lap, broken and chewed, but hardly eaten. He had drunk three Diet Cokes, though. 'Shit.' was all he said, and he re-booted the game.

'So is Bird right?' asked Ed.

'Fuck knows.' he paused for a minute. 'Right about what?'

'We should leave it alone. Let it lie,' he mimicked Bird's precise tones: '"Best do nothing."'

'Oh, that.' He thought for a minute. 'Fuck knows.'

Ed nodded and scratched his stomach. He was hungry again. The pizza hadn't really hit the spot. There was a donut delivery service on Atlantic. Maybe he'd give them a call. 'I tell you something.'

'What?'

'I'm gonna do it. If only for him.' Ed pointed at Lester who turned his head to look at them, aware at last that he was being talked about. He pushed himself to his feet to go and make a sandwich. Maybe donuts later. 'Just like there was this guy sittin' in my stool the other day. Wouldn't move. Remember in the canteen at The Box? They'd sit in your seat deliberately. Had to fuckin' move them. It was an affr-

affron-affrontery. I had to get the guy off. Seeing Billy, same thing. Gotta do it.'

Don said quietly. 'You know, Bird was right about one thing.'

'Oh yeah?'

'You ain't skinny no more . . .'

Ed slapped his gut and listened to the hollow sound. 'Kinda late to do anything isn't it?'

'Nah. What you need is some M&Ms.'

'Hey,' said Ed. 'Now that sounds like my kind of diet.'

NINETEEN

The Rotunda Café, The Pierre Hotel, E 59st, New York City. Friday November 29

Anne and Sarah waited for the server to pour the first cup of tea each and deliver the tray of sandwiches and pastries, before they resumed the conversation. Around them was the accumulated fallout from an intense, giddy shopping hit, mainly at the Asiatica collection at The Mark. Sarah had spent over her self-imposed limit on a black evening dress that looked like a block of ebony until the light caught it just right, and you could see the intricate patterning, the whirls and circles dancing over the surface. Anne had gone for a Mihon blouse, a kind of patchwork of traditional kimono patterns, at half the original retail price. Add some Arai pants for her, a Shibori jacket for Sarah and they were several thousand dollars down each. Both were thrilled.

The Rotunda was quiet, the tables under the trompe l'oeil walls uncharacteristically deserted. The regular clientele had temporarily decamped to Conran's new place on Madison, the Salon, but they would be back. For the last fifty years this had been the site for exchanging moneyed gossip – years of lethally polite conversation and intrigue and skilfully oblique insults were ingrained in the plaster. If these walls could speak, they would be pretty foul-mouthed. Yet somehow the contrived air of European grace lent gravitas, dignity, to the most tawdry of confessions.

Sarah resumed her story. 'So I was showing this guy an apartment, a pre-war brownstone, three hundred and twenty K. Nice. Marble, maple, you name it. So I said to him, "Ben Affleck is interested." Yeah? he says. "You told me Ben Affleck was looking at the last one you showed me." Well, I said, "It just goes to show what great taste you have – because Ben has a fantastic eye for a bargain.'"

'And he went for that?'

'Went for it? He bought the goddamn place.' As a realtor, Sarah was very good on the minutiae of the city. She really did know where Sean Penn or Matt Damon or Ben Affleck was looking to buy. She could point at an anonymous building anywhere from Wall Street to 125th and tell you what kind of action it has seen in the last five years, since she got her licence. She had found Anne her place, and the professional relationship had turned into friendship, mainly because Sarah fitted nobody's idea of how a realtor should behave.

Anne cleared her throat. 'You know I said . . . you know I suspected something was wrong with Billy? Little Billy?'

Sensing something fairly momentous was about to be revealed, Sarah leaned forward and put a lightly curled fist under her chin in her best you-can-trust-me pose.

'I think . . . I think he is definitely having an affair.'

Sarah leant back calmly and took a sip of her tea. Last time Anne voiced a suspicion it had been 'maybe,' and 'possibly,' followed by 'surely not'. Now the state of readiness had moved up a level. Code Red. 'Are you sure?'

Anne shrugged. She had tussled with that one for hours on end, wondering if it was paranoia. She had decided that all she could do was trust her instincts. 'How can I be sure?'

'You can catch him with his dick in her mouth. That's usually a big clue.'

Anne managed a smile. She knew that was how Sarah had discovered her first husband's infidelity with the interior designer she had hired to make over the apartment. 'Yech

. . . maybe it's nothing. Maybe we just aren't getting along. Big Billy said—'

'Hold on, hold on. Big Billy? You told Big Billy?' Sarah looked genuinely shocked.

'Well . . . yes, I told Big Billy.'

There was a silence while they both sipped and Anne added. 'Kinda dumb, huh?'

Sarah shrugged. 'He's his *father*. He may treat him like dog shit on his shoe, but then he's his old man. You're just the wife, maybe just the first wife, who knows?'

'Thanks.'

'You know what I mean. Big Billy *likes* you, huh?'

'I reckon.' She felt herself colouring. Sarah used the word 'like' as if it were a blade, but maybe she was just fishing. It was only two or three times, before she had married Billy. The father may be old, but he still had that magnetic pull. They never referred to it now, even when they were alone. It was as if once she had married Billy, she was off the menu and out of the memory banks. It had also occurred to her that maybe BB saw it as simply breaking her in for his son, checking he approved, something close to his patrician duty. She reddened some more. She imagined Billy saying: 'It's OK, son, she can suck cock with the best of them.' Except she was one hundred per cent sure Billy Jr didn't know.

'So keep it like that,' continued Sarah. 'Don't moan and whine to dad, "I think my husband is playing hide the salami in Atlantic City." He's as likely to say, "That's ma boy." Isn't he?'

Anne sighed. Sarah was two years and two marriages older than her, and she knew strategy. She expected the first marriage to be a trial run, it was the second where you pinned them down hard. Well, Anne didn't want to move on just yet. Because for the moment everything was Big Billy's. The son hadn't yet made his mark. Or his own mortgage payments. And, as Sarah would doubtless remind her, there was that new place on 57th to secure first. That was where she wanted to make her stand.

'So I should forget it?'

'Are you kidding? No, all you got to do is put the pieces together, and let him know you know. That will usually make their minds up.'

'How come?'

'Well once you know all the ins and outs, if you'll pardon the expression, where is the fun for them?'

'So I should hire a private eye?'

'What, and throw good money after a bad man? Bad men I should say – private dicks and husbands. Just remember this: when you do find out, you have a powerful weapon. Use it carefully and he will do anything, anything to make you forget it. Even buy you an apartment opposite Carnegie Hall.' She giggled. 'Course if the slut he is fucking needs a place, point her in my direction—'

'Sarah, for chrissake, this is my marriage we are talking about, not the chance of a two-for-one commission.'

'Hey, business is business. If it wasn't for the kept women and their little bolt-holes I wouldn't be selling zip at the moment. The mistresses are keeping the Manhattan housing market afloat. That and the sickos. I got an exclusive on a two-bed on West 11th. This guy goes around looking at the ceilings. I mean, there are these great floors, and he's walking round like he's on the lookout for low flying pigeons. Starts asking me about joists and soundproofing. Wanted it for a dungeon to strap his women to hooks or something. I told him, I would not do it. I would not sell it to him even if he could make the price. Which I doubted.'

'Since when did you get so picky?'

'Look, this was one of the, like, lightest apartments in the whole of Manhattan. I told him I didn't care if he liked sex with alligators, just that it would be a crime to paint the walls black and shutter up the windows. Hey, he wants dark, we got no shortage of dark in this city. So he's looking at a basement on Charles tomorrow. Thirty thousand less, too, so we should both be happy. Where were we?'

'Confirmation.'

'Confirmation, yes, that your husband really is playing touch football somewhere else.'

Anne shook her head. You had to realise that it was no good expecting your feelings to be spared with Sarah. She told you what she thought, she expected you do the same to her. This was not a woman to go out with when you were trying to hide a spot – 'hey, bad zit there,' would be her opening line.

'What about mail, you checked that?'

'Nothing out of the ordinary.'

'Wallet? Movie stubs? Credit card bills – you know, florists, that sort of thing?'

'They all go through Big Billy's office. Corporate cards. I never get to see them. I could ask—'

'No, No. Don't go asking Big Billy if you can see your husband's Amex transactions. Please.' She took one of the fancy rectangles of bread that passed for a sandwich at the Pierre and took a dainty, unsatisfying nibble. 'What does he do at home? Does he have a computer?'

'Uh-huh.'

'Well, this is probably a long shot because everyone deletes their stuff these days. Everyone whose got any sense.'

'Well that might rule Billy in.'

They laughed. 'OK, next time you have a few hours, go for a little stroll round it. This is the modern world, Anne. Chances are he is sending lurve e-mail to his squeeze. I found out all sorts of things about Marty – he was another one too dumb to delete. Turned out he was having a virtual affair – or maybe that should be virtual whoring – with some women in chat rooms. I sent a couple of messages on his behalf. Never told him and he never asked, but I reckon he guessed from the horrified replies. I bet he had to look up coprophagia in the dictionary. And he still probably thought snowballs were a drink.'

Anne waited a beat before she admitted her ignorance. 'What are they?'

'You don't want to know, darlin' – just one of those male fantasies involving two naked women and their dick. Anyway, he sold the computer and got a Palm Pilot personal organiser instead. But go in, have a look.'

'Won't there be passwords and stuff?'

'Maybe. But they're always easy. Birthdays, your name, his name.'

Anne felt her stomach contract, and she put down the smoked salmon sandwich she had been about to eat. She suddenly realised this was serious. 'And what if I find something?'

Sarah leant forward and her mouth split in a wide predatory grin, 'Call me, honey, and I'll be right over. More tea?'

The Pines gallery was a huge, clean, pristine space. High ceiled, plenty of downlight, and a beech floor with a South Pacific good luck charm inserted as a piece of parquetry. There were fifteen photographs hanging on the walls, two stone benches in the centre, one bored assistant near the door and just two customers, at the far end, conversing in low voices.

Big Billy asked: 'What do you make of it?'

Wuzel grunted. He was disappointed. This exhibition was called Infamous Alleys – the corners of cities where horrible, underbelly activities take place. There was one of a mafia hit, another of the (empty) side street where a rape had taken place, other assorted garbage-strewn and dangerous thoroughfares. The one in front of them was in Seattle, where a little girl had been taken hostage the previous year. But the colours were too vivid, the brickwork too sharp, the man had been playing with the computer and hadn't known when to stop. The kid's abandoned doll in the foreground was clearly a dropped-in prop, and robbed the scene of any poignancy. Photoshop, it was killing the art form. Which is why he specialised in things from the pre-Mac age. Like the Christophers. And that guy who took the one of his hit, Evans.

'Overworked,' he finally said.

BB laughed. 'Yeah, me too. They want fifteen hundred for that?'

Wuzel nodded.

'Looks like a goddamn Polaroid.'

Wuzel nodded again. He had been hoping for a new Eugene Richards or something like Joel Sternfield's wonderful On This Site: Landscape in Memoriam, which chronicled parts of the USA where terrible, gruesome things had happened. Even the sense of menace Ray K Metzer brought to Chicago and Philadelphia would have been a bonus – anything but this this unreal, garish approach. Ah well, what did he know? In two years these would probably be up there with his beloved Christophers in price.

BB said; 'You collect this stuff?'

'Not this stuff. Some.' He indicated the stone bench and they went and sat down opposite two solarised views of the same alley in Pittsburgh. *Cop Killer 1* and *2*, as if the place had killed the officer in question not, as the caption explained, some spaced-out psycho released onto day care. 'I just got a few people I like. And, you know, I like to have everything they do. This guy won't be one of them.'

BB shook his head. 'Me, I never got the collecting thing. You know, having all the programmes for the Yankees or the complete works of Sinatra or dozens of cars. I'm a one of everything kind of guy.'

Wuzel nodded. They had had this conversation before, and he couldn't explain the compulsion to BB or anyone else. It was a sense of emptiness that forced him to try and fill it. He was sure a shrink could wrap it up for him real neat, but he preferred not to know. Some people collect, some don't.

'Now Billy, he used to do it. Bubble gum cards. Baseball players, movie stars, that kind of thing. Then model kits, tanks and shit, then pennants . . . something different every year. Used to drive me crazy. Cause I could never keep up. I'd buy him this great Sherman tank for Christmas and he'd look at it like it was a pile of vomit, because he'd moved on to Indy 500 cars, shit like that.'

'How is he? Billy?'

BB rubbed his chin. 'So-so. Doesn't collect any more. Lost interest when he was in Gibbs. When we had that . . . trouble. But he's fine. I keep waiting for him to spread his wings, set up his own little piece of the action. Did a thing for me the other day, and done good I heard, so shouldn't complain. There's just a little . . . entrepreneurial spark missing, you ask me. I have to admit, he's got this Internet shit going now, thinks I don't know about it, and that might be a good sign. But then he's got that broad in Cotchford.'

Wuzel had tailed Billy junior on the first two of the Atlantic City runs and had reported the Cotchford stop-over, and advised against it on security grounds, but BB reckoned Backson was enough of a pro to be able to handle anything serious. 'Between you and me? That girl in Cotchford, one step up from a whore. Or should that be down?'

'But you got something planned for him. Right?'

BB nodded. It was true, he had this one thing where his son might just really earn his salary. Only he wasn't sure little Billy would see it that way.

'That's what I want to talk to you about. I may need you to perform a task for me.'

Wuzel nodded. A task. He always used that word. Ever since the first one, all those years back, when he asked Wuzel if he felt up to taking care of a problem, a little task. He was doing it for a friend of a friend. It was like laying off bets, they asked him, he asked Wuzel. Wuzel had been a rank amateur. He had needed help. That's when he went to see Brownie, who was legendary in Atlantic City in the problem-solving department. Brownie had told him how it would change him forever, he would cross a threshold, a line where different rules applied. Once you killed a man, then everything shifted. You not only knew how transient the flesh was, you also knew that you yourself were damned.

Wuzel had laughed at him. It was the right response. Brownie said he would help.

He still remembered the place, down in Chinatown. It was called The Bar B, but the walls were bare brick, the lighting was a collection of uncovered bulbs, and instead of a hint of fine cigar smoke and seared steaks the name suggested, the aroma was Mekong whisky, cigarettes and soured armpits.

It had been easy. Brownie got them through the door with some bullshit – they weren't the first gweilos to think they could get the hang of pai gow – and out came the weapons. Back then they had started out with shotguns, before they got a taste for real hardware. Just a motley pair of pumps, the sort that went with duck calls. But it didn't matter. Out of the end still came a spray of lethal ballbearings.

There were ten or twelve people around the table – on the rare occasion he did talk about it to Brownie neither of them was entirely sure of the number, the scene in all their minds a grainy, flickering image, like some badly restored silent movie reel or a cheap porno flick from the fifties – and maybe three around the outside. They had known the trio were the ones to worry about and had hit them without warning.

Once Brownie started, it all seemed so painless. At least for the shooters. The people, the victims, just blew apart. One minute, living, breathing, screaming, swearing, going for their guns, the next picked up and flung against the wall, splattering blood as if they were made of porcelain and shattered on impact. The noise was awesome, like a jumbo jet starting up in the room next door. The real surprise was the smell. Blood and bone and – especially – the contents of guts and stomachs ripped apart, coupled with the shit of those who realised what was going on as the pumps worked and the spent shells threw out and the barrels swung to face them and there was no time to get up from the table before something tore into their chest. He just stood there staring at the aftermath, wondering where all those animated people had gone, wondering what had left these lumps of meat in the process of killing. Brownie had taken him by the arm, steering him up the stairs, thinking he was in shock. But he wasn't, he was in gruesome fascination mode.

'Vince?'

Wuzel looked at him and smiled. 'I was just thinking of the first task.'

BB nodded. By doing the favour he had got his first haulage contract. The next one got him a public building job. Wuzel had done it himself for a few years – with, as often as not, Brownie – before he realised that the real money lay in being the middleman. So if you wanted any kind of talent – safebreaking, cat burgling, industrial espionage, a hit, a heist – you went to Paladin, Wuzel's company, and they put the team together. Flew in people from the West Coast or Chicago or Miami. Or did the same in reverse. For a cut, of course. Just like a legit job agency.

'If Billy did OK recently . . .'

'Different. Simpler. I want to keep Billy away from this one. Too involved. I would rather it was through you. It has to be done right.'

Wuzel put his arms out in a big-hearted gesture. 'All the same to me.'

Big Billy nodded. It was true. He took out his pack of cards and on the bench space between them dealt two face down to Wuzel, who picked them up and looked at them. Billy put one of his own face down, and another showing. A jack. Wuzel motioned for a card. He bust. BB turned his down card over. Ace. 'Blackjack,' he said. 'I meant to ask you this once. You ever turn anything down?' He repeated the deal.

Wuzel thought. 'Yeah. A guy wanted a couple of containers torched.'

'Blackjack. Arson? Don't tell me you don't keep arsonists?'

'Oh, we got explosives experts and pyromaniacs coming out of our ears. Problem was what was in them. See, it was the Victor Vasarely exhibition at the Museum of Modern Art. Remember that? A few years back? Well, it was going overseas. England I think. And this guy wanted it . . . destroyed.'

BB thought it was an extreme reaction to art, but there were times he could sympathise with it. 'Why?'

'Nineteen. Mine. He had some Vasarelys, bought very early on. He couldn't afford the rest, but he figured if he got them taken out of the marketplace, the value of his own would rise.'

'Twenty. Sounds like a plan.'

'Yeah, well I ain't in the market for destroying art either. I told him he'd have to look elsewhere.'

BB dealt again, trying to remember if he had heard of a Vasarely shortage. Then he tried to recall if he had heard of Vasarely.

'Bust. Shit. But he didn't?'

'No, he did, and was going to go ahead. So I decided to have him – the arsonist – removed from the marketplace instead. As a public service. Kinda charity.' Wuzel cracked a smile and let out his trademark laugh, the one that made the hairs on the back of your neck stand up. 'But I don't like to talk about it . . . Now, wanna tell me why we playin' cards?'

'Oh, just keeping my hand in,' said Billy.

'OK, wanna tell me what this task is?'

'Blackjack. Of course.'

Barnegat Peninsula, New Jersey.
Friday November 29

It was one of those days you couldn't believe the ocean could do anything so cruel as pound this shoreline. A cool, wintry sun glinted off a richly textured surface dotted with resting seabirds. Tiny waves fell on the sand, exhausted, as if all their energy was spent, content to dribble away the last few yards, dissipating in a froth of tiny bubbles. There was no wind, and only the triangular drifts of sand obscuring the tarmac testified that weather had been lashing the thin twenty-two-mile strip of the peninsula for the best part of two weeks.

They were in Don's new car – he had swapped the Beemer for a Neon – but with Ed driving. He took them up to Tom's River and over the bridge to the barrier island to Seaside Heights and turned north. The strip had that hibernating feel that all beach communities suffer in winter. Boats were under tarps, windows boarded, motels and diners closed, waiting for the injection of life that spring would bring.

The houses between the resorts were modest, well-kept, many home to year-round residents who were used to road wash-outs and fallen power or telephone lines. Some were out on their stoops, enjoying the feeble heat of the sun after a month of grey days.

Ed was about to speak when there was a low rumble from the seat next to him, and a pungent smell pervaded the interior. He hit the window button. 'Jesus, Don.'

'Sorry. I got Irritable Bowel Syndrome.'

'Yeah? Do that again and I'll get Irritable Ed Syndrome and you can fuckin' walk back to town.'

'Sorry.'

'Irritable Bowel Syndrome?'

'Yeah.'

'Nothing to do with the two bowls of chili and the tacos you had last night?'

'No. it's a medical condition. I followed the checklist in *Monozine*, and I definitely have it.'

'Yeah, so does most of Mexico I hear.'

'Really?'

'Don, you're going to live to be a fuckin' hundred. Stop worrying. How are the headaches?'

'Oh, fine. But I got this stiff neck. You know when you get to our age, the joints go. "Ankylosing spondylitis," it's called.'

'Our age? You ain't forty yet. And you slept on the couch. Isn't that a known medical condition?'

'Oh yeah – it could be that I guess.'

Ed turned on the radio, hoping there would be no emergency medical bulletins and settled on a country station as miserable enough to keep Don happy.

'Hey, I gotta get something. Burger King OK?'

'You go ahead. I best give these guts a rest. This'll be the new slimline Ed will it?'

'Don't worry, I'll have half the usual.' Ed pulled in to the drive-through and ordered a Whopper and fries with a Whopper on the side, picked up the order and ate as they continued. Through a mouthful of bun he broke a ten minute silence: 'So you got married?'

'Yeah. How'd you know?'

Ed shrugged, remembering there was only one way he could have known – the court order the guys were serving. He tried to gloss over it. 'You hear things.'

'Yeah? I don't remember posting it in newspapers.'

'I guess Bird must've told me. Didn't work out though?'

'Worked out just fine. Worked out it would be better if we never saw each other again. She used to drive me crazy, is the truth. Always look on the bright side of life, that was her motto. Gets you down, you know what I mean? Now she is chasing me for maintenance. Of what I don't know. Her fuckin' sunny disposition maybe. Stop light ahead.'

Ed slowed down, but it changed before he came to a standstill and he pressed the throttle again. They were approaching Normandy Beach. He pulled a piece of paper from behind the sun visor and looked at the scribbled address. 'Must be just up here.'

'What about you?'

'What?'

'Married?'

'Married? Fuck, I hardly get laid.'

'Bird?'

'Got some thing going with one of his summer waitresses – I mean, he lives up to his name, even his sex is seasonal.'

'We didn't exactly turn out to be Wilt Chamberlains did we?' said Don.

'Who?'

'Ball player. Reckoned he'd poked twenty thousand women.'

'Twenty?'

'Yeah, some smartass reckoned it meant doing one-point-five a day, every day, including Sundays.'

'What's point-five of sex?'

'Frustrating I would guess.'

'This must be it,' said Ed.

'Hey Ed. Mind if I don't come in? Me and Ruby, we never . . . you know.'

'Never what?'

'Hit it off. I always felt she didn't like me that much. You know, just kind of . . . tolerated me. I always thought she preferred Tony there.'

Ed sighed. It wasn't true, but if that was what he thought, he could play it any way he pleased. 'Sure, it's my show, Donald.'

The house was on the bay side, a single storey clapboard number, with a dinghy and a beat-up Blazer in the driveway. Ed pulled up but left the engine running. 'Give me thirty minutes and come back, hit the horn. There's a good coffee shop about a mile on your right.'

She answered on the first ring. She had on a pair of too-big Levis and an Atlanta Braves sweatshirt cut off at her waist. Only when she moved aside to let him in did he see the curve of her belly.

She didn't speak until he was inside. 'I was kinda surprised to get the call.'

He shrugged and followed her into the living room, admiring the view across the bay to the mainland. There was the faint sound of music seeping through the place. He sat down in a big rust-coloured sofa, felt it envelop him.

There was an awkward silence. She offered coffee and he refused. He felt stupid now, wondering why he had come, what he was going to say. Don was different, Tony would be different again. But Ruby? Ruby was straight-talking, straight-shooting, no nonsense. At least she used to be. Mother had been a Qantas stewardess, her father flew those planes that trawled messages along the beach in summer, but the mother had long gone by the time he met her, and the father had fallen from the sky and into a bottle.

'You got fat.'

No, she hadn't changed.

'You'll be there soon.'

She patted her stomach. 'Yeah, I'll be thin again in six months. You'll probably just explode.'

'Thanks.'

'Don't mention it. Really, Ed, whatcha been doing with yourself? Apart from spilling ketchup on your shirt.'

'Shit. Got a tissue?' She handed one over and he spread the two big blobs into a pair of much bigger, paler ones.

'So? What has Ed Behr been doing?'

'Nothing much.'

'Nothing much?'

'Absolutely nothing. Living.'

'Look, I'm going to have a coffee – you sure you won't?'

'If you can add a sandwich or something. I only got half my usual lunch.'

'Yeah, the rest went down your shirt.'

While she was out of the room he scanned the picture above the fire. He could see a man and a child repeated in the frames.

She came back with an old *South Park* mug: 'Kenny Lives,' and salami in a roll, which he demolished greedily.

'So what you up to now? This isn't doing nothing. Coming visitin' I mean. And we don't do Weight Watchers round here.'

'I . . . I thought I'd look up some of the old Cotchford people.'

'What, and exchange prison gang rape stories?'

'That never happened. You've been watching too many B-movies.'

'You talk to Lester?'

Yeah, he almost said, *most days. It's getting the reply that's the problem.* 'It never happened.'

'That's not what I heard.'

'Who told you?'

'Don.'

'Don?'

'When he got out. He said Lester had a rough time.'

'Well that's true. But there are other ways of having a rough time than being fucked up the ass.'

'Wanna tell me some?'

Ed sighed. He thought about Lester's mutilated body. The tales from Boxgrove were lurid in the extreme, and some – like Lester's – were even true, which is why they shut it down.

'Listen, Don decided that he was going to get fucked and all his teeth knocked out so he could suck cocks easier on day one. But you seen the size of him. They left him alone. Lester . . . he just got picked on and picked on and picked on. You know what he was like – hanging around, wanted to join in. They just . . . went for him.'

Ed hesitated. Should he explain everything about Boxgrove? In the regime of the Houses they were in – not in Bell of course – there were six levels, and you had to earn your way up. Level one meant rough clothes, almost sacking, and backless shoes, shuffling around like some kind of mental patient. Level six was full privileges, close to normal. Blue jeans came in at two, shoes at three, proper exercise at four, decent work at five, and TV at six. But then there was minus one, where you lost everything, even a knife and fork to eat with. And that's when the CWs hit in. And Lester, he kept slipping down the ladder, like it was some crazy, rigged board game, time and time again. Sometimes he slipped, sometimes he was pushed. It became the game. Let's see if we can get Lester down to minus one again.

They never called it punishment. It was always a 'Consequence.' As in, 'the Consequence of your action is, down to level two – turn in your shoes'. And when, early on, Ed had tried to intervene with those who had been carving their initials on Lester, they had taken him to shower and played bounce-the-cranium. And he, too, had gone down for a few weeks, for causing a disturbance. It wasn't something he wanted to repeat. After that, he didn't try so hard to protect the kid. His stomach burned at the shame, the cowardice. It was why he hated himself every time he saw that torso. Like his name was spelled out on the desecrated skin.

'Ed,' Ruby finally said, 'I don't think this is a good idea. I mean, I don't know about the others, but I've changed, I . . . I can barely remember that place. Cotchford. I can't say they were the best years of my life. I don't want any kind of . . . reunion, if that's what this is about. Class of fuckin' whatever.'

Ruby had been a good track athlete, he recalled that. And female jocks were not well liked. Dykes. Pussy-lovers. The cheerleaders feted every boy who ever held a bat or a ball, but turned all their hatred on any woman who sought to emulate the boys in athletic prowess. And Ruby's high jump was legendary. And so was her alley-o sprint. Almost as good as Tony's. Better, when Tony had been on the grass for a night or two.

'No, no you're right.'

'You said on the phone you wanted to ask me something.'

'Did I?'

'You know you did.'

Yes, he thought, I wanted to know if you would risk the life of your unborn child by joining us in some crazy scheme. 'I wondered . . . if you had ever heard from Honey,' he found himself blurting. 'Rachel, I mean.' He doubted she still used Jimmy's name for her. Honey Bea.

'Rachel? Is that what this is? Unrequited love?'

'I . . .' Since he bet Billy, since he thought about the money, the urge to find her, see her, talk to her was building. 'No, I just want to touch base.'

'I ain't seen her in a long time, Ed. You know about her and Billy?'

His throat went dry. He managed to shake his head.

'Oh.'

'What?' he asked.

'I think Don knew. After he got out they . . . they ran around for a while. Honey and Billy I mean.'

'Lovers?'

She laughed at the coyness. 'Lovers? What sort of phrase is that? Did they do the nasty? Yes. But I think lovers is putting it on a somewhat grand level.'

'And?'

'She left Cotchford soon after Billy did. Billy was gutted. Fell for her in a big way – fuck, every guy with a functioning dick did. She ended up somewhere in the Midwest I heard. Did you ever see her again? After you went in?'

'No. She wrote. For a while. Stopped . . .' Stopped when Billy got out, he realised.

'Well, I wouldn't carry a torch for her, Ed. Not worth it. I mean, she was my friend and all, but when it came to little things like morals and loyalty—'

'Ruby,' he said quietly as the words stung him.

'Yeah. Well, it's the truth. You all followed that girl around with your tongues hanging out and she played you all like an orchestra. Every one of youse would roll over and fetch and stand on your hind legs whenever she wanted. I mean, we all use sex as a weapon, but that girl – she had a thermonuclear arsenal down her sweater.'

'Ruby.'

'Yeah, yeah, you too, I know, you was sweet on her. We girls just would have liked the attention spread around a little more evenly, know what I'm sayin'?'

Ed got up and looked at the pictures. In each one was a tall, handsome man, with a close blond crop. 'Who's this?'

'Jim. My husband.'

The music came louder as a door opened and there was the sound of feet. A little face appeared at the door, a perfectly miniaturised version of her mother's, although there was something about the eyes that made Ed's neck hair bristle. Ten or eleven, Ed guessed, but he was not good at kids' ages.

'Mom?'

'Ru, you are meant to be ill. Get back in your room.'

'I'm thirsty.' There was a slight wheedling whine to the voice.

'I'll bring you some milk in a minute. Now scat.'

'Ru?' Ed asked.

'Yeah, little Ruby. Ruby-Jane is the full name. To avoid confusion.'

'What does . . . Jim. What does Jim do?'

She pointed to a picture he had missed on the wall, of a man in a pressed and polished uniform. 'State Trooper.'

That explained the haircut. 'Does that mean he carries a gun?'

'Means he has to be armed twenty four hours a day.'

Ed decided it was time he was going. He was suddenly sorry he had told Don to drive off. He should have made him wait outside.

'You never had kids?' she asked.

He shook his head. 'What's it like?'

'Well it ain't an original thought, but it's both heaven and hell.'

'What's the heaven bit?'

'*Mom*' came the urgent reminder.

'Heaven is when they are asleep. No, I mean it. When they fall asleep in your arms after a hard day, and you feel your own arms or legs going to sleep, know its going to hurt like hell with pins and needles, but you don't want to move, don't want to risk waking them up, you just sit there, stroking them, and just . . . loving them.' Suddenly embarrassed, she added, 'Then you put them down and spend half an hour trying to get life back into your arm.'

'So they're great as long as they are asleep? That ain't going to win you a slot advertising the National Mother's Association.'

'No, well, I didn't tell it right.'

'She's cute. Little Ru. Jim must be proud.'

'Oh, she's not Jim's. This one is.' She poked her stomach. 'Little Ru came as part of the package. With me, I mean. He's been good to us. And he's looking forward to this one.' She shifted in her seat, suddenly uncomfortable, 'So who else you going to look up. Bird? Or that miserable son of a bitch Don?'

'Bird isn't hard to find. Don, too. I thought of Tony.'

'Tony?' She let out a roar.

'What?'

'You didn't hear? Tony got into some beef with some drug dealer. Fucked him up real bad. And the guy came lookin' for him with a few pals and a meat cleaver. So Tony – I heard this but I ain't sure I believe it – went where they would never find him. Where nobody would want to find him. Tony? If you believe the rumour, Tony's a Piney now.'

'Brownie? Hi, it's Vince. How's it going down there? No, I don't want to know what the fuckin' weather is like. I can guess. Every time I call up one of you lucky SOBs down there all you wanna talk about is either the weather or the number of tits out at the beach. Course I'm jealous. Yeah, I know, I know. It's a weakness. If I sold them all tomorrow I could move down, yeah. But then I wouldn't have them, would I? No, it's not the same. You gotta *own* them, Brownie. Like your place down there. Actually I always hankered after Baja myself. But I ain't going to, so I am up here getting soggy nuts while you probably got someone suckin' on yours. Look, the reason I am calling is not to see how an old snowbird is adjusting to life in the slow lane. No, it's your boy Penn. Pretty Boy. Yeah, well I got a situation come up, and you know I wondered if you thought he would be OK. No, thing is he'd be number two. What do you think I am up here, senile? You think old Wuzel gone soft in the head? You taught me better than that, Brownie. No, strictly number two, he'll be back-up. Edgar has the helm, as they say on Star Trek. I was wondering, do you think he got the moxie for that? Good. No, I think he's worth taking a chance on, and he's your boy, so I am sure he is A1. No shit? Your nephew. Never mentioned it. No, well, it's good he didn't want to pull no favours, I guess. No, well I don't know if it's definite, but when I get confirmation, he's on the plate. Great. No, I'll get down there sometime. You just keep putting the sunblock on – that sun, it'll fuckin' kill ya.'

TWENTY-ONE

M&Ms, Fairmont Avenue, Atlantic City.
Saturday November 30

'I ain't going in there,' said Don.

Ed didn't say anything, mainly because Ed couldn't say anything. He was on a stair machine, desperately pumping his legs, watching the little red light telling him this was very moderate exercise indeed, feeling his heart telling him this was very severe exercise indeed and stand by for something to burst.

M&Ms, which was above a row of shops on Fairmont, just down from Angelo's restaurant, was a strange hybrid. Once an old-fashioned boxing gym, it was still used by some of the lesser boxers on the ticket at the Taj or Convention Hall, but for the most part sparring, skipping and punchbags had given way to treadmills and lat pull-downs, and it survived as a low-cost club for locals who couldn't afford the casino health club prices. But it still had the smell, as if it had long ago been flooded with sweat, until the odour seeped into every wall, floor and ceiling, to leak out in pungent little parcels. And the bits that didn't smell of sweat, they reeked of medicinal oils and balms.

M&M were Munroe and MacPherson, two elderly trainers who had skin like medicine balls, noses like misshapen vegetables, and who prowled the floor offering encouragement and advice. Munroe was hovering around Ed, a slight sneer of distaste on his lips, as if nothing so gross had crossed into his domain in a long time. A year, he had said to Don, to get this one in shape. You've got four, maybe five weeks, Don replied. OK, Munroe shot back, and next time you come in bring me five loaves and fishes, I might try feeding the neighbourhood.

The machine beeped to let Ed know his time was up and the stairs lowered him to the floor. He stood there, red faced and wheezing, unable to step off.

One of the regulars, with a physique like a bag of walnuts, said to Munroe, 'Hey Sol – we doin' sumo now?'

Don turned to look at him but Munroe put his arm up and spun Don back round to face Ed. 'Ignore him. Steroids fried his brain.'

If Mr Walnuts heard he didn't say anything.

Munroe held up some papers. 'I got it all here Ed. All your VS O2 readings, flexibility, lung capacity, heart rate maximum.' He took the sheets and tore them in half. 'You know what they tell me? They tell me what I can see just by looking at you. That you are a fuckin' sixty-five Ford with a shot transmission and a run crank and totally fucked power steering. We can probably make you into a seventy-eight Lincoln with some good chrome work, but needing a new set of rings. Maybe. Maybe we can get you there.'

Ed just nodded, frightened of how his voice would come out, and wiped the sweat from his eyes.

'It means in here three, four times a week. It means no more doughnuts, cut out the beer, the shots, the French fries. Strict routine. Fresh fruit three times a day. Three pints of water every day. Vitamins, minerals, get everything including your pecker working. Follow?'

Ed nodded again, gave him the circled finger and thumb sign.

'OK, take a breather, we'll start really working in five.' He prodded him in the stomach. 'On that.'

Ed sucked hard. 'Won't go where?' he managed at last to Don.

'What?'

'You . . . you said you wouldn't go somewhere.'

'Oh, yeah. Out to the Pine Barrens. Uh-uh. I hate that place. Gives me the heeby-jeebies every time.'

Ed nodded. Boxgrove had been on the edge of the Pine Barrens, the wilderness at the heart of New Jersey State. Sometimes on work days they had had to go into the forest to clear new diversionary strips, the corridors of soybeans intended to keep the deer away from the blueberry fields and cranberry bogs which dot the Barrens. Miles from anywhere, clearing a path through the undergrowth, with strange noises around, you could well believe in the legends of the Jersey Devil out there.

'If he's in there, we got to go and get him.'

'You seen Deliverance – "squeal little piggy"? That's what that place reminds me of. You know they all descended from one man.'

'According to the Bible we're all descended from one man.'

'Yeah, not from the last century.'

'Don, that's pure horseshit. That was just the Box bullshit machine.'

'Don't make me go in. I got a bad feeling.'

Ed shook his head, felt his neck click. Body telling him not to bother, he guessed. 'You always gotta bad feeling. You were born with bad feelings. We need the numbers, Don. Who else do you suggest? Ruby? I couldn't ask her – she was pregnant.'

'Lappin?' suggested Don.

'Dead. In Miami about three years ago.'

'Shit.'

'I want Tony in on this. It feels better if we . . . keep it in the family.'

Don shook his head sadly. 'Trouble. You'll see.'

The image flashed of Tony running that great elegant, loping sprint of his down the streets of Cotchford, whooping at the top of his voice, not caring who he knocked over or shouldered aside, barrelling down the sidewalk. 'Yeah, yeah.'

'Look, Ed, I got, like, like a ... foreboding? I feel something here.' He punched his stomach. 'Just a flutter in here.'

Ed nodded. 'Don, you know what would really worry me. I mean really fuckin' *worry* me?'

'What?'

'If you ever told me everything is going to turn out just fine. That would scare me shitless.'

'You know, I'm beginning to think I should've taken my chances with those two guys outside the restaurant. At least I was sure of the ground rules there.'

Before he could answer he was summoned. 'OK, Ed,' shouted Munroe, 'Let's go. Sit-ups. Fifty.'

Ed groaned and shuffled over to the mat where Munroe waited.

'Don, hustle us up a four wheel drive can you? And a line on where he might be? Please?'

Don sighed and gripped his temples. He could feel a migraine coming on. Maybe he should go and lie down. 'OK, Ed. Whatever you say.'

An hour later Ed sat half-way down the stairs that led to street level, fighting off the waves of nausea and fatigue that took turns washing over him. His hands were shaking so bad he could hardly hold the bag his training clothes were in. He had to get down the stairs. Had to stand up and do it. Couldn't give up now. Someone opened the door at the bottom, looked in, and went away, probably figuring the way was blocked, thought Ed.

Shit, maybe Bird was right. Maybe doing nothing was

sometimes the best way. Maybe he should just go and sink a few beers and tell Don to forget it. Bygones and all that shit. He thought of Billy and that night in the rain. Billy, dapper and sophisticated, barely noticing the bedraggled cabbie he was paying well over the odds to take him home to his swanky apartment. That final gesture of the thrown note. And then the look of Lester's face in the shower, the water running over his face, the eyes dull and inward-looking, shut down until the ordeal was over and he could get back to his screen and his beloved *The Getaway*.

Then another image came into his head. Of a little ten, eleven year old girl he had thought the spit of her mom. But she hadn't been. She'd had those close-together eyes and the eyebrows that almost met. She was Billy's. Little Ru was Billy's. He got out of Gibbs and went with Honey, and then Ruby. So one way or another he had fucked them all over.

Honey: OK, maybe Ruby was right she was a bit . . . casual in the way she moved around, and yeah she could be a prick teaser. But they were all young, they did stupid things. The frustration of her being out there somewhere welled up inside him. He wanted to see her real bad, ask her what he should do. One day, for sure. And maybe, if all went according to plan, he would have the money to make it all come true.

Ed struggled to his feet and started down the stairs, one careful tread at a time, like he was stepping on eggshells. Yeah, it reminded him, did they sell Egg McMuffins this time of night?

TWENTY-TWO

21 Club, W. 52nd St. New York City.
Saturday November 30

It was, Billy Moon reckoned, the best twenty thousand dollars he had ever spent. True he had balked at the cost – this was like, what, twenty grand for an overgrown Tamiya kit? But when he saw it he had to admit it was a thing of beauty.

The model was ten feet square, with the irregular shape of the island filling most of the space, with only a small peripheral blue/green suggesting the confluence of the East and Hudson rivers (he had realised the true timbre of the water might be a little offputting, and insisted on a little colour correction).

He had a few precious minutes to himself with it while his father entertained the other interested parties in the private dining room below. He could hear the muted sounds of a slap-up 21 dinner, knew that by now the walk-in humidor was being raided for some of the rare Havanas that Big Billy kept there. Getting him to give up one of those was like pulling teeth, and it was a sure sign of his determination to see this to fruition that he would allow some of the men seated around the table to suck on his precious Punch Punches.

He crouched down to eye level and imagined himself coming in down the eastern side of the city from the heliport, skimming over the Manhattan and Brooklyn bridges and suddenly seeing the island, with its startling modernist centrepiece, a great silver sliver of a pylon, beautifully curved like a blade, rising up from the centre of the retail area.

The old houses were still there, allowed space to breathe – places such as the Governor's Mansion would be attractions in themselves – and not all of the island was built up – the nine-hole golf course, the jogging track, the baseball diamond, all illustrated this wasn't just about shifting units.

The landing jetty had been made with astonishing detail, the catamaran shuttles looked as if they might start engines at any minute. The roads were populated with the souped-up electric golf-carts that would be the only transport allowed. He picked out the buildings he would be expected to name in a few moments – the multiplex, the bowling alley, the kids' play area, and the speculative use of the big names they had indulged in – the Disney Centre, the MGM Complex, the Virgin Multimedia Experience, including the great hump of the concert hall, seating twelve thousand – the Springsteen Stadium he had wanted to call it, but Big Billy wasn't so sure, he reckoned in NYC you went Bernstein or Giuliani – and, at the heart of it, the five-storey mall – no, not mall, what had the designer called it? The Browsing Halls. That was right, as if there was no hard sell here at all, just hundreds and hundreds of window-shopping opportunities. All part of the entertainment, folks.

And rising at one end of it, in circular steel and glass, was the heart of the operation, the futuristic equivalent of an old-fashioned control tower from an airfield, so that the administrative staff could peer loftily down on their empire. Pride of place would be his suite, plugged in to every aspect of the island, with a wall of multiple screens showing running totals from all the businesses, number of people in the complex, and where they were at any one time. Everything anyone could need, all on one island. All on *his* island, he reminded himself.

There was a knock at the door and the electrician entered and gave him the thumbs up. Billy signalled for him to go. Soon, now. He ran through his notes, making sure he knew the spiel about the demographics off pat. Just getting these bullshit figures had cost a fortune – how many of the Fifth Avenue crowd are likely to go shopping for bargains, the annual per capita expenditure on fine dining, blah, blah, blah. He checked his hair in one of the gilt-framed mirrors of the function room, and then re-arranged a few of the chairs. He took out the handset that would lower the lights and start the fanfare as he began his presentation to the small crowd of investors and, more importantly, city officials, those members of the various steering committees that could strangle this baby with the stroke of a pen. Zoning, sanitation, Port Authority, Mayor's Office, New York Development Board, the Manhattan Association, and also those folks whose names didn't appear on any board list but ended in 'o' or 'i', that would have to be cut in at some stage.

So many people to keep sweet, so little time. A little voice in his head told him that give him a decent handgun and he could solve the problems in five minutes. Maybe take a couple of them down the Depot for a little dip. He cut it off. By the book his old man had said. Do this one by the book. Supposed to be moving beyond that.

He wondered if his old man could ever truly let it go, ever switch to discussion, consensus, diplomacy, negotiation. And defeat. Once you got used to getting your own way by dropping people into icy water to make them pay attention, the other methods seemed a little . . . laborious. The winking red light in the corner reminded him he had to try and ignore that all this was being taped for inclusion in the ten minute promotional video they were to commission, charting the progress from scale model to reality.

And it would become reality. He realised for the first time in a long time that he was happy. Even Anne had shown an interest in this, sitting with him while he went through the images of the model stored on a CD-ROM, a copy of which would be given to every delegate here tonight. It was the first time she had sat down at the computer, and she seemed genuinely interested in how they could pull up images, zoom, rotate and modify.

He thought guiltily of Honey for a second, realising that she really would have no part in his life once this got the green light. There was no room in his life for two mistresses. The whole thing had been some sort of aberration, he knew that now, some sort of bizarre role-playing, as strange as Honicam was sick. But he still had time to dismantle it, to let her down gently. A few more weeks of dragging down to AC, before he could put all his energies into this.

This was important to him because it would finally make him his own man. It was clear that when he did things like the Depot, he was just an extension of his father. It was how he got respect. Do exactly what the old man would do, no surprises. This time he would be free to improvise and innovate. Yeah, and maybe he ought to come up with a variation on the Depot, just to stamp his own mark on that side of things.

The noise from below grew, and he heard a deep, basso-profundo laugh. That deep rumble belonged to Thomas Tom, he knew, the man they had to convince first and foremost. Of all the zoning and planning people, he had the squeakiest clean reputation. Was it good for the city? Was it good for the people? were the two questions he wanted answered, not how much money would it make for the people around the table.

The small group were outside the door now. He took a quick sip of water, fixed a grin on his face, and headed for the door. Time to shit or get off the pot, as BB liked to say.

TWENTY-THREE

Route 206, New Jersey. Sunday December 1

Ed and Don pulled into the lot of The Grand just as the last of the daylight was extinguished. Something that looked like snow was falling fitfully – small, ill-formed blobs, merely fetal flakes, hitting the windshield with an almost audible plop. Ahead of them Ed looked at the forest, dark as always, just the odd naked bulb showing between the trees. This was the very fringe of the Pine Barrens, the interface between the outsiders and those who called themselves Pineys – but hated anyone else calling them it. These were the people who worked, or didn't work, the forest as it pleased them, whose needs seemed different from the great bulk of the population, which is why they were always treated with suspicion. These people, on the whole, weren't concerned about having this year's car, refrigerator or jacket. Weren't too bothered, in many cases, about such things as electricity and telephones. There were times when such an attitude sounded tempting, thought Ed.

He looked at the big metal windowless box and thought how misnamed The Grand was. Maybe the interior was better, but from the outside it looked like some kind of agricultural shed. The kind of place broiler chickens are crammed into, where short lives are spent in unspeakable misery. In fact, perhaps not a bad description of some of the drinking joints that lined the highway.

He reached for the door handle, but Don made no attempt to move, apparently content to listen to the Ford Explorer he had borrowed from one of his shadier dealer contacts clicking as it cooled down.

'Don?'

Don nodded and turned to look at Ed. 'This guy . . .'

'Yes?'

'He don't do anything for free.'

He'd already made that point, but Ed just said: 'Who does?'

Don moved his head from side to side, as if considering the philosophical arguments for and against the statement. 'He's called The Engineer.'

'Yeah?'

Don took out a match and started worrying the end of it with his teeth, spitting tiny splinters out with his tongue. The car shook as a big rig passed by, bouncing its way over to the far end of the lot. The guys who got out were truckers – big, booted and beer-bellied with enough facial hair to stuff mattresses. The Grand was one of the places that pulled in a mixed crowd – travellers who had turned off the Turnpike looking for drink, truckers who preferred the backroads, wildlife management people, some military straying from Fort Dix, officers from Garden State Youth Correctional Facility and some women looking to service all of the above. At one time warders from Boxgrove may well have drunk in there. It didn't bother Ed none any more. He could only assume that was what was getting to his friend.

'Wannna tell me about him? The Engineer?'

'Well his real name is Dupree. First or last or both I don't know. He ain't a Piney, but he's lived around here for twenty years or more. Mostly he deals in poached deer and so on. He'll meet you here, agree on a price, twenty, thirty, forty dollars, for your kill and then he'll sell it on to a diner or a burger bar. You get great burgers around the

Barrens, you know that? As long as you watch out for the buckshot.'

Ed waited. Don wasn't really worried about a man who minced the wildlife for a living. There had to be more.

'I met him because his sideline is fixing ... situations. You want to lose a car? The Engineer will get rid of it. It might turn up in a swamp twenty years later, more likely he'll torch it and the cops'll blame kids. Thing is, it was him who helped me bury the guy. From the trunk.'

'You didn't . . .?'

'What, hamburger him? Shit, no. Don't worry – it's safe to eat in here.'

'I'm supposed to be off the burgers anyway.'

'Yeah. Mr Slim. How's it going?'

Ed smiled. 'You ever tasted that low alcohol beer? It's like drinking sweat.'

'So this guy—'

'What?' asked Ed irritably. 'What about him?'

'His face. It's kinda weird.'

'How kinda weird? Has he got one?'

'Oh, yeah, yeah. Just that it don't work too good. Told me he once borrowed his dad's hunting rifle without asking him, went out to shoot raccoons or something. He came back, his old man was so pissed with him he opened up the side of his face with a combat knife. Severed all the nerves. So when he smiles ... well, he can only do half a face.'

'Yeah, well I'll keep off the jokes.'

'I thought you ought to know.'

Ed sensed that he was really stalling. 'Don, is this a problem?'

'No. Really. I just thought you ought to know. It's not something I'm proud of—'

Ed interrupted. He really didn't care about all that, he

realised. Selfishness was to the fore these days. 'And this guy will know where Tony is?'

'Yeah. Well, if anyone can find him out here, you know what I mean.'

'So?'

'Ed, it was . . . every time I think of the body—'

'Don, it's over, eh? You're straight with the mob or whoever, you said they'll never find him—'

'Out in The Barrens? No way.'

'Is it Boxgrove?'

'It's all of it Ed, all of it. I've been having these dreams—'

'Don. You want to back out? You want some of this fuckin' money, the money Billy *owes* us, or not?'

'I guess.'

'Let me tell you again. It's a *lot* of money,' he reassured him.

Don fell silent for a second. 'You sure?'

'No. I can't say that. Look, as far as I know, nobody offers a Heist 101, so I am guessing a lot of this. Y'know? But a guy turns up once a fortnight at a casino for something. He leaves with what looks like a heavy bag, with a heavy dude to carry it. I can tell it weighs a lot from the cab shocks – you know, when they put it in, when they take it out. I know from humping luggage. And I've been doing some checking. A million bucks in hundred dollar bills weighs twenty and a half pounds. A million in twenties weighs one hundred and two pounds. Now, the bag, I would guess, came in somewhere in between. Maybe it's a fuck of a lot of money. Maybe it's mixed bills.'

'Hey, good it's not in quarters.'

'Twenty-one tons,' said Ed.

He could see the concentration on Don's brow. 'And you think they move this every time?'

'Hey – how the fuck can I be sure? I would put money on

it, if I was a gambling man. But as we used to say in the wood shop at The Box: measure twice, cut once, not the other way round.'

'Meaning?'

'Meaning from the talk in the cab that night I got the impression we got three, maybe four runs left. We stake them out twice until we have the rhythm, and then lift whatever is in the bag.' Although part of him – a small part it had to be said – didn't care what exactly was in the bag. As long as it was something Big that Little Billy would miss real bad. But money would be a nice bonus. He had to switch the Honey image off quickly before his dick gave an encore.

Don nodded, running it through his mind. 'What if you are wrong? And the next time or the time after there is no money?'

'OK, Don, look on the bright side, eh? There will be. But if there isn't . . . well, we don't want to do this half-assed. I think we have to assume there is, and they won't want us to have it. I doubt Mr Backson is any kind of walkover.'

Don was silent thinking about the big guy in the limo that Ed had described. A pro. Bound to be armed. Had Ed considered that, he wondered? Probably not the best time to bring it up. 'So if you are right, you guess, what?'

'I would stay at a million. But it might be more.'

'Split . . .?'

'Let's see how many we got first. Which is why we are here, remember?'

Don nodded. 'A million bucks? You know, it's going to make someone . . . well, Billy at least, I mean someone is going to be real pissed. You know? Real pissed.'

He knew what Don was getting at. He thought about the vein-popping rage, the fury, that would engulf Billy, his father, the casino guys. 'Yeah. Isn't that part of the attraction?' Without waiting for a reply he got out of the car into the cold embrace of the evening.

✿ ✿ ✿

Inside The Grand, the decor did not improve. It was functional in the extreme: scrubbed wooden bar, stage, table area, big dance floor. The place was about a third full, the customers almost exclusively male. The jukebox was cranking out music in a certain style; George Thorogood, early Springsteen, the Bosstones, Tom Petty, Guns 'n' Roses. Meatloaf and pot pies were coming out of the kitchen. Ed thought it made the Pole look like the Rainbow Room.

They took a table near the door, and the waitress brought them a beer and a soda. Nobody paid them much attention. Don scanned the clientele, and keeping his voice down, said: 'FUDs and TUDs.'

'What?'

'Fat, Ugly and Dumb, and Thin, Ugly and Dumb. TUDs tend to be locals – you don't get fat living on squirrel and cranberries.'

'Don, shut the fuck up, eh? Anyone hears you, we got zip chance of finding Tony, and a good one of getting our heads pounded.'

Don shifted uneasily and lowered his head, the way he did whenever he was about to admit defeat. 'Yeah. Sure.'

Ed had heard all the stories too. This was, after all, where the Jersey Devil was meant to have been born, a mutated spawn of the Devil, the local equivalent of the Blair Witch. It was where incest and poverty were, until recently, supposedly the main pastimes of the locals, where squalor and stupidity were the bedrock of the community. It was hardly surprising that the place fostered such lurid tales – there was something spooky about having a wilderness dropped in the middle of the most populous state, and one full of ghosts and ghost towns at that – but, as always, it was ignorance at work on the part of the outsiders, not the Pineys.

Don took a slug on the bottle. Ed passed him the glass,

but he shook his head. 'Tests by the CDC show that twenty per cent of all glasses in bars are contaminated with human urine.'

Ed shook his head; 'Well, they ain't the only thing full of piss—'

Don suddenly stiffened and Ed knew their man had come in. He walked straight over and sat down. Ed almost smiled. He had been expecting someone big and bulky, a reassuringly Casey Jones figure, but this Engineer was all skin and bone, with greasy black hair swept hard back on his head and a pocked face. He wore a T-shirt and stained chinos, with a Lee check-lined jacket thrown over his shoulders. He nodded and lit a cigarette.

'Don.'

'Dupree, this is Ed.'

Ed wondered a second about the etiquette here. He had been serious when he had said about Heist 101. There was no Mingling-With-Scum 101 either. So did he play it cool or . . .? The Engineer helped him out by offering his hand, and they shook. Ed ordered him a beer. He couldn't help looking at the face, and sure enough there it was – a silvery scar running from under his eye, meandering like a river down his cheek and disappearing off his jawline. Looked pretty normal to Ed, though.

'So. Hunting season,' said Don by way of clumsy introduction.

'I hate it. They can all go out and shoot 'em up legal, and take them direct to the diners and things. Cut out the middle man. Me. You a hunting man?'

Don shook his head.

'Good.'

'Dupree, I never did thank you—'

The Engineer shot him a look that silenced him. 'For what?'

'For, you know . . .'

'I don't know what the fuck you are talking about. We did some auto deals a way back I remember. Nothing recently. Don, do me a favour willya?'

'Sure.'

'Stand up.'

'Stand up?'

'Yeah, stand up.'

Don got to his feet slowly. The Engineer just kept looking. Then he said: 'Raise your hands over your head. Right up. Don't worry about the bozos in here. Go on. Yeah, now turn around.'

'What is this—?'

'Just fuckin' turn around.'

It didn't brook much argument, so Don did as he was told.

'OK. Now your friend here.'

Ed did as he was told.

'OK. Excuse me.' He reached over and ran his fingers through the lapels, pockets and zips of their clothes. Satisfied he leaned back. 'Always tell by how a man moves if they taped a wire to him.'

'Dupree—' Don started.

'Shut the fuck up. You show up with Fat Boy here and launch into some shit I know nothing about. Makes me edgy.'

Fat Boy? Ed wanted to protest but kept his mouth shut.

'What you saying?' asked Don.

'I'm saying if you mention that business again, you'll be joining the guy. OK?'

Don nodded.

'OK, then. Shall we take it from the top?'

'Information,' said Don. 'We need information. Local stuff.'

'Information. OK, nice clean work, I like that. What kind exactly?'

'A friend of ours out in the Pines somewhere.'

The Engineer took a slug of beer. 'They all say that.'

'What?' asked Ed.

' "A friend of ours," ' he sneered. 'They're always a friend. Never some guy who owes me money or poked my wife or shot my dog. Always a friend of ours who has lost his way, and we are here to help. But it's no business of mine. But finding "friends" isn't that cheap. Even here.'

'What if we said he's a scumbag who fucked both our wives and we wanted to hog-tie him between two cars and drive in opposite directions?' asked Ed quietly.

Don raised his eyebrows.

'Well, maybe a small discount for honesty,' conceded The Engineer.

Ed said, 'Well we don't, I was just curious. Thing is, he's South Asian, kind of. Dark skinned. Could pass for a Latino, too, at a push. We haven't seen him in . . . a while. He got into some trouble, came to hide out about three, four years ago.'

The Engineer nodded. *Changes*, the Tupac version of Bruce Hornsby came on the jukebox and Don and Ed exchanged glances. The original, way back when, was their fatalistic anthem, the refrain that was everywhere when they were put away: 'That's just the way it is.'

The Engineer pulled out a pad and scribbled some things on it. He asked a few more questions about Tony's real name, his age and description. 'Latin, you say?'

'Indian. The other kind, y'know. Father was a cab driver.'

'What, like the ones you can't understand?'

'Not this one.' Ed remembered Tony's father, a proud man who spoke perfect, albeit archaic, English.

'Tony the Tiger.'

'Tiger? Like the big cat?'

'Yup. Got his name from Jimmy . . . from some guy we knew,' said Ed.

Don said: 'His real last name is Rajadhyaksha.'

The Engineer shook his head. 'That's easy for you to say. Raja-what?'

'He'll answer to Tony. Or Tig.'

'Ah well, I suppose it could be worse. I could be looking for Simba.' He tore out a sheet, wrote on it and pushed it across to Don.

'OK, I'll see what I can do. This is the price and the number to ring in three days. If you don't agree with the price, don't ring.'

Don looked at it and frowned. It was a different number from the one he used before. Well, he guessed changing phone lines was all part of the craft in the man's line of work.

Without knowing the charge, Ed said confidently: 'We'll ring.'

'What if we don't?' asked Don, with a predictable spin on things. 'I mean, you'll have done the work for nothing.'

The Tupac was followed by the Run DMC's *It's Like That*. Ed wondered if some dude up there was practising creative programming and knew the 'that's just the way it is' refrain linked it to the previous track, or if it was the jukebox equivalent of throwing two sixes, a random pairing.

The Engineer finished his beer and stood up, and for the first time Ed noticed how weighed down on one side Dupree's jacket was, as if something heavy was in one of the inside pockets. He leant forward and Ed could see the knurled handle of a pistol. As he leant he smiled, and Ed watched horrified as just the right side of his face lifted into the appropriate expression, leaving the other smooth and unlined. It was a deranged spectacle, especially as it altered his speech pattern, and he now spoke out of the corner of his mouth in a low, threatening whisper. 'No. You said he was hiding out. Well, if you don't want the information, it sounds like there is someone out there who does.'

Don grabbed his temples almost in a reflex, and for the first time Ed found himself afraid of what he had started. His stomach flipped, maybe with fear, maybe not. As he watched Dupree walk away he looked at his partner and said quickly: 'What you reckon the food's like in here?'

That night Ed woke up at three in the morning with the fear in his heart, the hopelessness. It was a moment of sudden clarity of the kind that strikes in the darkness, that illuminates the world the way no sun ever can, the moment when you face the fact that you are completely alone. He felt the weight on his chest, crushing the breath out of him. No God, no Jesus, no afterlife, no retribution, no reckoning. Just a great big impersonal universe that doesn't care if you are Adolf Hitler or Ed Behr. Or Billy Moon. Just a brief spark of light and life and then back into the cold, back into the molecular pool.

In which case, what did it matter? What did it matter either way? He either got the million, or died in the attempt. All the same in the end. He thought of Honey again, what she would think of a guy with a million, or at least a share of a million, in his pocket. Get the money, he could pay properly, maybe even Pinkerton's, to find her. Top class detectives. Now that was worth going through anything for. He felt a hard-on stirring against his leg at the thought of her fingers wrapping around him again. Yeah, she'd be older and wiser, but it'd be all the same to the Old Man down there. Million or bust. Maybe he *was* a gambling man after all.

TWENTY-FOUR

Monday December 2

Thomas Tom liked to drive into the city. He knew it was madness, knew it meant leaving home an hour before he would if he got the train like every other commuter in his town, knew that the Lincoln Tunnel was bad for his blood pressure, knew that the parking charges he faced were tantamount to extortion. But it was the only place he could think, could order his thoughts for the day. So he had to swallow the downside.

It was barely light when he walked down to the garage and opened the door, shivering against the sudden thwack of cold which hit him. Sleet had fallen during the night, but had faded away to leave a thin, icy sheen on the roads. He backed the Chevrolet out and looked up at the window of his house, worrying he would see one of the kids staring out of the window, woken by his nocturnal prowlings, and at the same time half-hoping for a last glimpse of their faces before another day of papers and meetings and arguments.

He turned up the heat, switched on the car lights – he reckoned he would need them for another fifteen, twenty minutes – pulled out onto the street and headed for the highway. He decided that this morning he would take the George Washington Bridge, just in case the construction that had clogged the Tunnel on Friday was still in place. He had checked at the office, knew it was meant to have finished over the weekend, but it had looked way behind schedule to him. He glanced at the clock on the dash. Nobody would be in the engineers' department yet to confirm or deny.

As he made a left out of his street, he checked his mirror and saw the white panel van pull out behind him. It registered, but barely. Mainly he thought that all kinds of folk seem to be starting work earlier and earlier these days.

Aware that the roads were treacherous, he gingerly made the right and left that got him onto the highway, and slid into his lane. Once he was settled down to a safe cruising speed he hit his voicemail on the car cell phone. A dozen calls had come in overnight, mostly petty complaints about projects he had slowed or stopped altogether, plus one from Billy Moon, assuring him there were no hard feelings over the Governor's Island approval. Or lack of it. Thomas Tom didn't want anything built out there, he wanted a recreation park with maybe a few rides, not a floating mall. Of course, it wasn't his decision alone, but he had made it clear when he saw that bloated model at the 21 Club that he would fight them until it was a tenth, a twentieth of the size.

The others had stayed on to help try and make a larger dent in the club's walk-in humidor, but he had come home. As usual, there was too much money sloshing around this scheme, money that was there for the spending, but not upon anything concrete, on things such as familiarisation tours – let's go and see how Nassau does it, or the Cayman Islands, or St Martin, or Hong Kong. No, thanks, guys, it's a brilliant idea, and it'd work, but an offshore retail outlet that big is bad for the city. And therefore bad for me. But Moon's voice on the machine was all reasonableness – let's meet and discuss what would please you, and maybe we could take that to the Mayor.

The fuel warning light flashed at him. Damn, just when he had got the temperature up inside and his breath had stopped coming in clouds. He signalled, changed lanes, and swung into the gas station.

❖   ❖   ❖

Inside the white van Pretty Boy Penn tried hard to fight the seething mass of dull, ill-focused pain behind his eyes. As usual his self-control had let him down the night before. He had known he had to be clear-headed this morning. But one beer led to another which led to brandy and then that guy had offered him a line and in the john he had pulled out too much in the semi-darkness, and spent a couple of minutes trying to scrape it back into the wrap, but all that did was flick more out. In the end he had shovelled it all into one big mass and done the lot. It had kept him talking one-hundred-proof crap until two in the morning. A few hours ago, really. And now the toxins from that and the brandy were busy trying to find a way out of his brain via his eyeballs.

To cap it all the guy in the passenger seat was being a real asshole. Maybe he knew Penn was feeling fragile, but he had been on him ever since they met at the rail station, after the guy had caught the milk train out here. Had he done this kind of thing before, he asked. Was he clear that they were meant to make this an accident? That it might take two, three, even four of these runs in different vehicles before they were actually sure how to pull this one off? Maybe even a home or office visit? You're too close. You're too far behind. Move up. Move back. Pull over on the left. Slow up, there is ice. You got a piece? Well, keep it hidden. It got history? Better hadn't have. Where did you get the van? Is it clear you follow my lead? Yak Yak Yak.

Edgar. He remembered now. It was the guy who frisked him back at the Paladin office. Skinny, weasely looking guy, but kind of hard with it. Well, Penn had rolled more people than Edgar, he would bet – he was doing it once, twice a week up until earlier this year, when Brownie got tired and pulled the plug to go and spend some of his stash down south. OK, so a hit was different, but only marginally.

He shivered and reached to turn up the heat, but it was already on full. Ahead he saw the mark indicate towards the gas station. He looked at Edgar who shrugged. Maybe he was thinking the same thing – this could be an opportunity, a chance to cut all the cat-and-mouse shit down to just one day. Penn shook his head as if it would fling off the headache. He had to stay sharp.

Tom groaned when he realised there was no full service isle. It meant he had to get cold again. He popped the gas flap and stepped out of the car, rubbing his hands together to try and generate some warmth. Just as he was about to close the door and walk around to the pump, he heard the sound of an engine over-revving, the valves bouncing as the driver floored the accelerator until the kick-down came in, and the tires finally gripped on the ice-slicked asphalt, hurtling it forward. It was a moment, a fatal moment, before he realised all that noise, the screeching, the smoke, it was all coming right at him. His brain refused to move his limbs. All it took in was a freeze-framed image, like a movie still, imprinting into his visual cortex, the last neural composite it would ever form: the contorted face of the driver, partly hidden behind sunglasses, and a passenger yelling and spitting wildly at him.

This was not going to be State Trooper John Mitchell's morning, he knew it. It was bad enough having to go into the city, but finding out that Ruby had all but drained the gas tank was the final straw. There couldn't be more than a teaspoon left in it, he realised, tapping the gauge. Ah well, they say pregnant women get forgetful. She had forgotten he had an interview with the Department of Transportation over at Federal Plaza. He only had a couple of miles to go before he could park up and catch a train, but he daren't risk it. He decided to pull in and fill up. He swore he felt the first hiccup as the carb – probably fuel injectors, he corrected himself – sucked air and he eased off the gas to let it roll into place. He had just switched off the engine when he heard the painful screech of an accelerator being floored.

The fender smashed into Tom's solar plexus, pushing his bent back through the glass of his door seconds before it tore off its hinges and spun away. The door was thrown clear, spinning in a crazy, unbalanced arc, sparking on the floor as it bounced, but Tom wasn't so lucky. Caught by the front tire, he was pulled under as if on a conveyor belt, and the weight of the truck burst his abdomen like an overstuffed sausage and crushed his chest, his ribs spearing his heart and lungs in a dozen places. The double rear wheels that clumped over his inert form just made sure the job was done.

Inside the van Edgar smacked the driver on the side of his head, and Penn angrily yanked the wheel as he felt it thump over the body. The front tire lost grip and slid towards the gas pump island, just catching the rim hard enough to peel it back and break the tire seal. They both heard the loud pop as the air fled through the new opening. The front of the vehicle dropped and started to vibrate wildly.

Pretty Boy looked at Edgar in horror, his throat tightening with the realisation of what he had done.

'Stop, we'll get another car,' Edgar said coolly.

As soon as the van slithered to a halt, Edgar put the gun to Pretty Boy's head and pulled the trigger. The driver's side door window shattered and turned red at the same instant and the blast threw Pretty Boy's head out into the cold morning. A crimson mist seem to hang in the chill air, like a dying breath.

Edgar stepped out of the van and quickly surveyed the scene. There was nobody in the gas station office that he could see – probably lying down. There was a guy over at another pump, car keys in hand, getting ready to fill up. He hoped the guy was the cautious type who topped up whenever the needle went to half. He had to get going. He needed that car. As he strode across the forecourt he raised the gun and aimed it at his head to let the guy know his intentions were strictly dishonourable.

Edgar couldn't believe it when the man raised his own heavy duty weapon and let off two rounds, with the kind of grouping in the torso that the State Trooper excelled at on the range. Edgar felt the two big punches in his chest, but didn't even have time to register the pain of the bullets tearing his insides to mush. He felt the blackened shutters come down even as he staggered back towards the abandoned van.

Honey woke with a head full of smoke. She had had two big joints and watched some movie on HBO into the early hours, pausing only to give the obligatory hourly show. And now she felt like shit. Oh, yeah, there were a couple of beers too.

She pulled back the covers and scowled at the camera, rolled off the bed and went for another shower. It was what she did a lot of, as if trying to clean away the thoughts of all those guys out there. Jerry, of course, wanted to put a camera in the shower, because hidden cams – the ones the girls weren't supposed to know about – were the coming thing, so to speak. Not with her. She wanted a little bit, just a little bit, of privacy, and the shower was where she washed away the hours of posing, not added to them. When she said they'd be putting one down the john next he had said 'Funny you should mention that—' but she had cut him off.

One thing she had discovered about this game, you always had to up the ante. Girls had to be younger, tits bigger, twats stretched wider open, the sex acts more depraved. Whatever you desired in your darkest moments, from lactating pregnant women with dildos to asses with whole arms disappearing up them, some site somewhere was providing it.

She towelled herself dry and went over to the PC in the living area, logged on and hit her own site. She wanted to see what had been added and how many hits. She accessed the Homegirlz page and clicked her little pouty photo, the one that made her look ten years younger than she was. The garish blue backdrop came up, then the curly Honicam script, and the little blurb about what she loved to do. She smiled at how those jerk-offs out there could fall for this.

There was a small repeating image of her, flicking between three stills to give the impression of a movie. It was her sucking her fingers. Yup, sucking fingers, every woman she knew always rated that as a number one sexual activity, guaranteed to get you buzzing. Just like sticking your tongue out like that guy from Kiss and licking your lips, oh and sucking your own nipples. Yet it was what the punters wanted. Sucking her own nipples gave her a crick in the neck though – OK for some of those engineered bitches who could fling them over their shoulders if they wanted.

Then came the little 'Previously on Honicam . . .' trailers, showing her bending over, lying in bed, hoovering naked. Oh, this was new she thought. A banner for a credit card company: *'Ever been turned down by a company for bad debts, criminal record or wrong zip code? We guarantee to give you a credit card with just one phone call.'*

Yeah, at the kind of interest rates that makes the Mafia

look like a Credit Mutual no doubt. Then she saw the next little thumbnail and shouted in disbelief. Honey picked up the phone and dialled Jerry. The Webmaster answered sounding sleepier than her.

'Jerry? Yeah, it's Honey. Look what the fuck is that link doing there? Which one? The one I told you not to put on my page. The one about the horse, Jerry. The horse. It's sick. I don't care if it's fake, I get enough fuckin' weirdos as it is. You'll get the SPCA on me. Look, look, I don't give a shit if it is on every other girl's page. You ask them, they'll tell you the same. I mean, what's the guy paying – two cents on the hit or all the hay you can eat?' Her temples started to pound and she lowered her voice as Jerry told her what the deal from the sponsor was. 'That much? Shit. OK, yeah – put a disclaimer on mine saying that the girl on the end is not Honey. OK?

'Who got the most hits over the weekend? Angel? What'd I get? Third. Which one is Angel? The girl who does that stuff with the two lighted candles? Yeah, well she's earned the hundred dollars bonus s'far as I'm concerned. I suppose it's an easy way to do y'bikini line at the same time. And listen, get a dictionary. It should say "inveterate perverts", not "invertebrate". Although I guess half your customers are completely fuckin' spineless. Nothing's got into me. Oh ha, ha, yeah. No, I'm fine. Just a bit tired. Another hard day at the orifice – yeah right, Jerry, I bet you say that to all your girls. In fact, you say it to me every time. Ah, fuck off.'

She put the phone down and went in search of some Tylenol. She threw open the window and breathed some of the fresh air coming off the sea. That was what she needed – something to blow the cobwebs away. She would go out tonight, give herself a little treat.

❉   ❉   ❉

They watched him come threading through the trees on his third circuit of the grounds, his feet shattering the frosted leaves. His breath was coming hard now, they could both imagine how it was burning in his tubes, how the blood in his ears was the only sound.

From up on the Lucy's howdah they watched Ed disappear again. Bird asked, 'How is he?'

Don shrugged. 'He's lost about three pounds.'

'Very good.'

'And gained four.'

'Oh.'

'You know, I think those rolling totals on McDonald's would be a lot less if they took Ed out of the equation.'

'And is he still fucking crazy?'

The profanity took Don aback. Bird was normally more circumspect, priggish even, in his choice of language. 'So what was he before? Mr. Well-Balanced?'

Bird shook his head. 'What did happen to him? Were you there?'

'With Billy?'

'At Boxgrove.'

'In The Box? Nah. Just him and Lester. He tried to intervene when these guys were roughing up the kid, and they bumped his head a few times. Then they used the CWs . . .'

'You get any of that?'

'Nope.'

'Good.'

'You?'

Bird laughed. 'In Bell House? You got library privileges taken away. That was their version of the Spanish Inquisition.'

'Well, we had the CWs all right. You only got it if you caused trouble, and after the fight, they reckoned both Lester and Ed there needed calming. So they brought out the

Chemical Warders. Whatever was in that stuff kept them pretty fucked up for quite a while.'

'I thought there was a class action against the state about their use.'

'Yeah, and I heard it'll get through about in time for *next* millennium.'

The crunching and the gasping grew louder as Ed pushed himself around for the fourth circuit of the elephant's grounds. 'Come on Ed, you doin' good there,' Don yelled, but Ed didn't acknowledge him.

'Don, do you think this is wise?'

'Hey, am I the guy to ask about wise? I know what you all think of me.'

'That's not true.'

'What's not true?'

Bird hesitated. 'What we think about you.'

'I ain't told you yet. Must be pretty obvious, eh? Big dumb Don. Only good for standing in one spot and catching whatever shit comes by. Is that it?'

Bird stayed silent for a minute. 'You're changing the subject. You know what I mean,' he said finally.

'Yeah, "best do nothing," ' he said, mimicking Bird.

'Quite.'

'Just one question: if I say, yeah, it *is* wise. You gonna help?'

'Yes.'

Don put his hand on Bird's shoulder for extra emphasis. 'It's wise.'

A sudden crash of undergrowth broke their concentration, and they looked down to see Ed, his face scarlet, clutching on to the trunk of a tree, his chest rising wildly with each breath.

Don raised his cup and shouted: 'Breakfast of Champions, Ed. Come on up.'

There was a long pause before Ed could rasp out. 'Two bowls, do me two bowls.'

Bird sniffed in that snooty way he had. Finally he said: 'Then I'll help.'

TWENTY-FIVE

The Pine Barrens, New Jersey.
Monday December 2

Cold had settled on the woods like a chilled blanket. Even the evergreens looked sadly depleted, as if half their needles had moulted. Frost had lasted through the morning, but it had none of the sparkly charm it would have in other woods. Ed shuddered as they skirted the acres of dwarf trees – vast tracts where, for some unknown reason, no tree would reach above shoulder height. He knew what Don meant about the place. There was something oddly primeval, slightly twisted about it, as if too many spells, too many dark arts and too many black hearts dwelt within.

The entrance to the area took them past the cranberry bogs, square reservoirs where Sea Breezes started life, the sides raised up to form a grid of elevated paths for the machines to move around. The harvest was long gone, the bogs flooded now to protect the plants from the savage frosts which ravaged the Barrens in winter.

They bounced along a sand road stiffened by ice, the Explorer bucking at each pothole, Ed wrestling with the wheel, negotiating the pines and cypress swamps, some of them hung with brittle strands of moss, and the ghostly spindly undergrowth of huckleberry, sheep laurel and wintergreen. Away from their bizarrely stunted cousins, the trees here were twenty five or thirty feet tall, the long trunks blacked as if someone had taken a blowtorch to them. Pitch pines, Ed remembered, trees that thrive on fire.

Don huffed and puffed over the map, which he had

managed to fold into a giant pyramid, and prayed and cajoled and demanded signs from a higher being. Occasionally they passed a small house or shack, many of them held together by rotting sheets of oil paper, hardly any of them painted, their yards full of junked machinery. Smoke rose from a few, suggesting occupancy, but neither wanted to throw himself on the mercy of locals yet.

When they came to a crossroads Ed hit the brakes, feeling the pedal judder as the ABS kicked in to keep him on the straight and narrow. 'We been this way before, Mr Keah.' He pointed at the burnt out grove of trees ahead, the rusted frame of a car just visible at the centre. Another torch job, but one that either burnt itself out or was brought under control before it ran away with itself. Down the road to the left he could just make out the fire tower that probably raised the alarm.

'Is that fire tower marked on the map?' asked Ed.

'Probably. I just . . . no, no, maybe that's it. In which case I think we are here. . . .' he stabbed the map, '. . . and that is Jagular, which is about two miles that way.' He pointed left. 'And then it is a couple of miles south to where he said Tony was.'

The flat, thin sound of a gunshot managed to make itself heard above the engine. Hunting season. They hadn't seen much evidence of the hunters themselves, but every so often they heard the discharge of a weapon.

The call had come late the night before. The Engineer had told them where Tony was holed up, south of a small community called Jagular, too small to be on most standard maps. They had managed to get themselves something more detailed, but the forest had a way of bamboozling you. They had already wasted more than an hour circling the area.

Ed spun the wheel and took them down the track, heading west, deeper into the Barrens. There were things in here, he knew, that botanists would kill for – carnivorous plants, strange orchids, obscure, primitive mosses, but right now all he wanted to do was get to see Tony and get out. He turned up the heating once more as another shiver hit him.

The dirt road suddenly became tarmac – oiled, as they said around here – and the forest gave way to a small clearing, with a dozen houses and a store-cum-gas-station in the middle. Despite the cold, several under-dressed people were gathered around smoking – with scant regard to the gasoline – and chatting.

They stopped and looked at the big brute of a vehicle as it shouldered its way into their hamlet. Ed pulled it up alongside the pumps and hopped out. The air stung his face with cold. He rubbed his hands together as he ran round to unlock the filler cap.

It was obvious from the various levers on the ancient, chipped pumps that this was full service. He nodded to the small group of people, three men and two women, and they nodded back. After none of them made a move he stepped into the store, where two kids were sitting at a counter sipping soda, and a middle-aged woman appeared to be making sandwiches. The shelves were full of packets and tins of food, washing powders, car paint, bleach, medicines – human and animal – dyes, acids, alkalis, all mixed up in a seemingly random order. Two big old refrigerators hummed and huffed in one corner. The two kids stared at him intently. The storekeeper just said: 'Gas?'

He nodded.

'Pull the green lever up, lift the nozzle, pull the red lever down. Pay me when you finished, I got this big order to do for some folks at Hog Wallow.'

Dismissed, Ed went out, trying to remember green up, red down, and after some fumbling managed to get a flow going. The citizens had dispersed, crunching back to their respective homes. Don opened the door. 'You ask?'

'Ask what?'

'If we on the right road for . . .' He checked the name. 'This . . . Fisher's Gate.'

Ed nodded and went back in. The two youngsters were making loud noises as they hoovered up the last of their soda through the straw. The woman was frantically cutting slices of bread into inch-thick chunks. Ed put ten dollars on the table, and waved his hand when she went to reach for change.

'I'm trying to find a place called Fisher's Gate.'

'No you're not,' said the woman, going back to carving. Ed looked at her hands and realised she was older than he had thought. Her face suggested somewhere between forty and fifty; the discoloration and pattern of veins under the skin added a decade to that.

The two boys laughed, at a shared joke or at his expense he couldn't be sure.

'I'm not?'

'Fisher's Grate.'

'Great?'

'Grate, yes. G-R-A-T-E. Fisher's Grate. 'Bout three miles away from here. Named after old man Fisher. That there is one of the family.' She pointed at one of the boys, but they both turned away quickly.

'Fishers?'

'Yup. Fishers were big iron people. Made a lot of money. Servants, everything.'

He glanced over at the two figures at the bar, who had stopped slurping now. Neither of them looked to be from a prosperous family. 'Iron.'

'Yup. this place used to supply all the navy's cannonballs. Well, nearly all.'

Cannonballs? When did the navy last use cannonballs? 'When was this?'

'Just recently. Oh, the furnaces at Fisher's Grate were going right up until ... 1850 or so. Moved onto charcoal after that. Then flowers. Then turtles. Now it's all cranberries and huckleberries. You hunting?'

He shook his head. She nodded hers in approval. 'Don't much like outsiders coming in and shooting our deer myself. So you don't need any cartridges?' She pointed at a stack of darkened cardboard boxes, on which he could just make out shell sizes.

'No, we're just here looking up an old friend.'

She nodded and went back to the sandwiches, the conversation over.

'Fisher's Grate,' he gently reminded her.

'Two miles that way, by a stand of red maple and black-gum, you'll come to Cobb's Hole, which was a fine watering hole once, although once Cobb was found dead in it people kind of stopped using it—'

'How will I recognise it? I guess it'll be frozen now, I mean.'

'No, it ain't there at all. Just disappeared one year. But there is an iron pole, about yea high there. Look carefully you'll see a sand road leading off to the left. Bit overgrown, but I don't believe you will have any trouble in that ...' She gestured at the SUV whose silhouette all but filled up the store's side window. 'Mile, mile and a half at most. Not much there, though. A homestead, an old saw mill, a couple of good producing berry bogs, that's about it.'

Ed thanked her and left. The two boys laughed again, and this time he was sure it was at him.

They missed the iron pole the first time. It might have been 'yea high' but it was also shrouded in brown moss. It had faded into the forest cover, more vegetable now than mineral. When there was four miles on the trip, Ed turned the Ford round and headed back east. He almost missed it the second time, and just managed to stop level with the turning.

Don looked at the mass of brambles that had grown over the entrance, obscuring the turning. 'I guess there's another way in.'

Ed looked at him. 'Why?'

'Nothing much has been down there in a few months. And look, I can't afford to get this thing too beat up. Those branches do some serious damage, you know.' He pointed at the threadwork of shrubs that hugged the ground between the scorched trees.

'I'll stand you a paint job.'

'Yeah, out of your share? You fuckin' generous with that man's money, Ed. Especially as we ain't got it yet.'

'Well, I still got enough of my own to put some colour on this thing.' And that's about all, he thought. The money under the bed was fast dwindling. He had lost the heart for cab-driving, and those hours at the gym were costing, but working. Even he had to admit he wasn't quite the lumbering blob he had been. He could run on the treadmill for four, even five minutes now without fearing a massive internal haemorrhage. Another few months and he would be able to look Honey right in the eye again. With a full wallet, too. The old Ed. If it didn't all kill him first.

Don suddenly asked: 'Well?'

'What?' asked Ed.

'We going?'

'I guess.'

They both winced as the huckleberries speared and scraped the side of the utility vehicle, occasionally pinging up and whipping the windows. The wheels scrabbled for a hold on the soft, shifting sand, which seemed to have been protected from the worst of the frost. Ed felt the vehicle drift to the left, the back moving out, before the traction control pulled him forward and into a clearer area, where prostrate blueberry plants lay dormant to either side, and the trees thinned to every few yards.

'What do you think Tony'll be like?' asked Don.

'Like the rest of us. Older.'

'But . . . well, you know what he was like.'

'What was he like?'

'Impetuous, foolish, loud—'

'He was a fuckin' kid. Can it.'

Ed scratched his chin. If the chips were down, who would he rather have at his side? The plodding Don, always complaining, always about to come down with some obscure terminal disease – or at the very least a bad dose of haemorrhoids, always figuring they were off to hell in handcart? Or Tony, if Tony was still Tony: bouncy, twitchy, nervous but fast – and liable to do what you said without stopping to tell you why this was a bad idea like Don. Probably too close to call. What he needed was a cross between the two of them, but he reckoned he had left it a little late to figure genetic engineering into the solution.

He realised that, of course, he was thinking who he would have on his alley-o team. Not who he would have by his side on a million-dollar heist. But he was getting the same feeling. Whenever he used to wake up on a game day, there was a spark in the air, some strange flux in the atmosphere, washing back and forth over the town, summoning the players and the spectators, drawing them to the railroad tracks where the rules would be checked, the dens delineated (always the same, but you had to make sure) and the boundaries set. This would be nine, nine-thirty in the morning. It could be a long day, maybe eight hours taken up with hiding and running and fighting and clawing until one side was completely imprisoned in a jail. Shit, perhaps if they had realised they would all end up in the real thing they might not have embraced the game quite so enthusiastically.

The track suddenly started undulating wildly, the Explorer bucking and twisting, squeezing protests from both the chassis and Don. Ed urged it forward as the ground rose, the earth disappearing for a moment as the windshield filled with sky, before it slithered down the other side.

At the top of the second rise Ed stopped, panting from the exertion of fighting with the wheel. 'You think this is right?'

'I guess.'

Ed carried on until the trees thinned, and he managed to accelerate a little. The vegetation was whipped out of their way. It was just as the automatic shifted up a gear that the pale figure stepped out into their path.

Ed braked and swerved, thwacking into a stand of blueberries which clawed at the underside of the vehicle, trying to drag it to a halt. They burst through onto another uneven sand road, and Ed kept going. Don looked over his shoulder, trying to see clearly between the spindly branches. He had an impression of a young boy or girl, dressed in white, just standing there, face impassive, waiting to be run over.

'What the fuck was that?' started Don, before another apparition stepped in his path, this one a boy in blue coveralls. Ed instinctively swerved again, unable to override his instincts, taking the Ford over a sweet pepper bush. This time he heard part of the muffler tear free and the engine note switch to a thick unhealthy boom. He pulled up at the top of a small hillock.

'Who . . .? What the fuck? Were they *real*?' asked Don.

The explosion rocked the whole body of the car, throwing them both back in the seat. Ed felt the front lurch down on one side, barely had time to register the smoke of shredded rubber and steel thrown into the air when another charge slammed into them, bursting the second front wheel with a deafening, concussive thud.

They ducked as part of the windshield transformed itself into a sagging spider's web. Ed released the handbrake and powered the stricken vehicle down the hill. He felt something burn his neck, and looked in the rear mirror just in time to see the curtain of tailgate glass fall away from the vehicle.

There was no steering left and the Explorer rammed into the undergrowth like a rogue elephant, tearing its way through the brambles and berry bushes. Above the howl of the engine they could hear the scraping of body work as the vegetation slapped, grabbed and sucked hungrily at the metal. Ed hung on, trying to keep the bucking wheel straight as the Ford rolled lumpily on, before it finally lurched nose-first into a huge trough, sending up a spray of cold grey water, the engine screaming as the vehicle settled at forty-five degrees.

Ed pulled himself off the windshield and touched his ribs where the wheel had dug into him. He flicked the key to turn the motor off and they were left with the creakings and groanings of a fatally wounded beast settling into its final resting place, the mud under the water already pulling it down deeper. He looked out at the albino trunks of the white cedar rising from the greenish water that surrounded them, the trail of moss reaching down like tendrils. Swamp.

Don seemed unhurt. He unclipped his belt and steadied himself against the dash. Ed thought he was checking for damaged bones, too, when he suddenly pulled out a large automatic pistol from under his jacket. Ten minutes before Ed would have been surprised to know he was carrying. As the Ford gave a final judder, he was very, very glad.

* * *

Don tried to open the door, but the edge of it rammed into a sunken bank. He motioned to Ed, who managed to heave his side open a few inches, and heard the water gurgle in. There was no way he could get out there. Don re-belted himself in and used his feet to kick out the already shattered windshield. Not thinking about the cuts he was liable to get, Ed pulled himself through the resulting space, rolling down the buckled hood, and felt the air fly from his lungs as he hit the water.

Don came after him, sliding into the swamp up to his knees, gun held high. Together they tried to make progress as best they could towards firmer ground, sludge pulling at their shoes with each step, trying to put some space between themselves and the doomed off-roader.

A ridge took them onto solid earth, and they shook as much of the swamp water off as they could. 'Hypothermia,' warned Don cryptically, 'Always a danger. Stay as dry as you can.' But Ed was sweating, not shivering.

They pushed head-first into the thickest of the under-growth, ripping off snagged branches with their hands, or simply letting it tear the clothes as they walked, the pain and the cold temporarily forgotten in the adrenaline that was surging to keep them alive.

Ed felt as if his heart was going to come bursting through his ribcage. Any minute he expected to feel the back of his head pop like the front tires of the Ford, bits of blood and brain and skull splattered in the winter air. Don kept swivelling at the waist waving the gun in a rather sporadic arc, more just to show who was looking they weren't entirely defenceless, Ed figured.

When they were fifteen yards away another shot caught the top of the Explorer and a section of the roof carrier system tore off and spun in the air, shedding sparks as it cartwheeled, like an out-of-control Fourth of July firecracker.

Don hesitated a second, stood up and fired two shots to his left before ducking again. The twin booms hung in the air, bouncing from the trees as the reports slowly faded. Ed heard some raucous bird cries, saw their shadows flit away to the left. There was no return fire.

They pressed on to the first small clearing, and Ed took the chance to lean against a tree and pant hard. Don took a place next to him, and also leant his head back.

'You think you hit them?' Ed asked in a hoarse whisper.

Don shook his head. He thought about the broken-backed Explorer, expertly eviscerated like a great elk driven to its death. 'Nope. Made 'em think we can bite back though.'

The crossbow bolt rammed home deep into the pine trunk exactly half-way between their heads, three inches from each eye.

Ed felt his lunch taking the expressway to the surface. He leant over and was sick on his shoes, and as he stayed bent double, he was transfixed by the swirls of steam coming off the pile at his feet. He heard the voices and didn't dare look up.

Vincent Wuzel put the phone down, his ear still burning from the verbal roasting he had just received. So much for old friends. Big Billy had turned extremely nasty. Violently nasty. Against *him*. That was taking a chance. Showed just what a snit he was in.

No payment on this one, of course. And he had lost both operatives. Brownie's nephew, well, he had an idea that any fuck-up could be laid at that door. But Edgar. Edgar had been with him for years now. Edgar was a pro. Of course, he would have no ID on him, so it would be difficult to trace him back to Paladin. Difficult but not impossible. And if Billy carried out his threat of spreading the word that Paladin no longer delivered the goods . . .

Of course BB was right to be angry. Now it looked like a hit, and guards would be up, hackles raised, law enforcement agencies consulted. People would put two and two together and realise that Tom had been hit because of his opposition to the Island project. What had he been thinking of with Penn? Never do a friend a favour, that should have been his motto. Shit, he had been relying on the fee to buy the Christopher at Christie's. Well BB still owed him some of the money for the casino scare over at Asbury. He couldn't welsh on that, could he? He'd better wait for him to cool down before reminding him.

In the meantime he had better do some cleaning up, just in case the cops came round with the shocking news about how Edgar supplemented his income.

Christ Almighty, but that fuck-up Brownie owed him one for this.

TWENTY-SIX

The Pine Barrens, New Jersey.
Monday December 2

It was a big house that had seen better times. Two storeys, eight rooms, grand in its day, but it needed paint and pesticides and a new roof. It had once been in a large clearing, but the forest had slowly colonised a lot of it, so it looked threatened and hunted. A collection of buildings were sprinkled around it, all the way down to the fast-flowing stream that cut through the sandy soil on its way to the Aker River.

They pushed Don and Ed into what had once been the main living room, now filled with crude homemade furniture. Ed felt the rifle butt hit him square between the shoulders and he went down hard, puncturing his hands with splinters from the boards. They did the same to Don, and he landed heavily next to Ed, making him wonder just how strong the floor was. They pulled themselves upright and looked around.

The walls were damp, with what had once been floral wallpaper, but now was blackened by mould, peeling off the walls. The ceiling was cracked and bowing alarmingly. The only decorations were two full gun racks and a selection of hunting bows and crossbows.

The two men were both tall and weatherbeaten, somewhere in their mid-forties Ed reckoned, and both dressed in rough workwear, baseball caps (one John Deere, one Ocean Spray) and Caterpillar-style boots. There had been six or seven in the woods, but these were the two that had brought them here, Lou and Fred, but he didn't know which was which, they hadn't volunteered much information when they herded them forward with a shotgun in their back. It didn't matter anyway, they looked pretty interchangeable, with chiselled cheek bones, thin lips and blue, blue eyes under brownish hair that looked like it had been cut with a power tool.

Don examined the cuts and bruises on his arms, dabbed at the nicks on his cheeks the undergrowth had made. 'I need a tetanus jab. You got anything for these cuts?' he asked.

'ATF,' spat Lou or Fred suddenly.

'Fuckin' jackbooted Nazis,' said Fred or Lou.

'How many of ya are there?' The accent was strange, not New Jersey, somewhere further south.

'Two,' said Don.

Ed rolled over in time to see him kicked.

Ed stayed calm. One had a Marlin rifle, the other a Remington shotgun. Too easy to provoke them into killing the two of them and burying them with the Explorer. Wouldn't be found until . . . well, wouldn't be found.

'We ain't ATF—'

'Fuckin' jackbooted Nazis I said!' The Marlin barrel thwacked across his cheek and Ed spun back round, his head bouncing off the floor. He stayed there breathing hard, trying to contain himself. He could feel that anger there, telling him he was down, down in the pecking order, had to fight his way back up. Not against rifles, though.

'Look Lou—' began Don.

'Fred,' corrected the man. OK, so Fred is the one with the slight cast to his eye, the big silver American Eagle belt buckle, and the rifle. Fine, thought Ed.

'We come looking for a friend,' said Don.

'You ain't got no friends out here, Mr Government Man. No friends at all. Fuckin' jackbooted Nazis, that's what you are.'

'Listen you big streak of shit—'

Ed winced as this piece of diplomacy was cut short by the butt of the rifle thumping into Don's forehead. He grunted and slumped back down, dazed. Fred stood over him and worked the bolt on the Marlin and caught the round as it ejected.

He held up the shell between thumb and forefinger. 'Know what these are? Black Talons. By Winchester. You bastards banned them. Rarer than hen's teeth. The nose here has a bunch of crosscuts in it, which means the copper casing peels back to make these little prongs. You know what medics called them when the first wounds appeared? Flying scalpels. *Flying-fucking scalpels*.'

Fred cocked the rifle and a Black Talon entered the breech, and he shouldered the weapon, pointing at Don's head. 'Streak of shit? Streak of shit? Wanna say it again big boy? Huh?'

Ed watched the trigger finger tighten. Maybe coming for Tony hadn't been such a good plan after all. He started as the gun fired and the boom filled the room, drowning out Don's scream.

The phone rang for the first time in twenty four hours. Vincent Wuzel felt like he was being shunned. He wasn't even getting any legit customers for the books and pictures, and how the fuck would they know he was behind that gas station thing out in Jersey? He picked up the receiver cautiously.

'Vince?'

'Yeah. Who's this?'

'Max Middleton. Denver.'

'Oh, hi.' Another photo book dealer, one he saw every year at the Chicago fair.

'You OK?'

'Yeah, yeah. I think I just caught a cold, is all. You?'

'Good. Look I got something for you.'

Wuzel sniffed. Maybe he was getting a real cold, as well as a metaphorical one. 'I ain't sure now is a good time for me.'

'There'll never be another for this. Listen, Christopher's widow. She died. Cancer.'

He pulled up in the chair slightly. 'Yeah?'

'Yeah. Now, she – they – had a son, Al.'

Wuzel licked his lips. 'Go on.'

'So it turns out that film exists. The one we talked about? There are dozens of frames of it. Starts at the fire station, with the alarm and all. Ends up with the fire that killed him. I seen some photocopies. Even the copies look good, Vince.'

'Jesus.'

'Thing is, he wants them to stay together. He thought about splitting it all, but he thinks it's real – what? – poignant if they are seen as a whole. So no auction until he approaches a few dealers. Starting with me.'

Wuzel felt his stomach sink. 'You in?'

'Nah, I thought of you. Too rich for my blood.'

'How rich?'

'Well you seen that one in the new catalogue?'

'Yeah. Stupid money.'

'He wants six hundred thou for the lot. Prints, negs everything.'

Wuzel laughed.

'Hey – it ain't that bad—'

'No, Max, I know. Just . . . it's a lot of money, is all.'

'What about liquidating some of your other stuff?'

'What's our time limit here?'

'I got to get back to him in two days.'

'Six hundred?'

'Yeah.'

'Let me think about it, eh? Give me a couple minutes, I'll call you back.'

Wuzel replaced the handset and ran the figures through his mind. He had got a quarter of a million for the hit on *The Alchemist*, but much of that was gone – Richard Longs don't come cheap any more, he thought ruefully. He had earned the same amount – and was still owed half – for the Asbury Park disruption. And there was the Warren business, that earned a decent whack. There had been talk of a third hit, though, which he had planned to keep rather than spend on his collection. That would be out now, too, he guessed. Big Billy would get some other talent in.

The thought of the two tasks drew his mind to Edgar, who had been instrumental in both. Edgar had warned about Pretty Boy and he hadn't listened. Had made him go along with it against his better judgment. Sorry, pal, you was right, I was wrong.

OK, so it was unlikely he would ever get a big earner again soon. And sometime or other the cops might be calling. If he could get his stock together, ready for shipping, he could build his gallery anywhere in the country. Down in Mexico, even. Somewhere in Baja. He picked up his desk diary and flicked back to a few weeks previously then counted forward. Perfect. And Brownie, Brownie owed him now.

He picked up the phone to tell Middleton that he had a deal.

Ed had to move faster than he had for a long time, as fast as he did in the days of alley-o. Don was still screaming, because a large splinter of wood had entered his cheek, thrown up from the jagged hole made in the floorboards by the Black Talon. When Ed stood up he was so close to Fred that the guy couldn't get the rifle around to draw a bead on him. Ed did what instinct told him – he put his arms around Fred and squeezed, locking the man's arms at his sides. He could smell the tobacco on his breath, could see the puzzle in his eye and he used his full weight to clasp him tighter.

Ed spun and glared at Lou as he heard the Remington rack a shell.

'If you got buckshot in that you'll kill us both!' shouted Ed. He could see Lou's mind working. 'Don't do it Lou, don't do it. Lou we all gonna die. Lou, Lou see sense, we ain't ATF. Lou, Lou don't do anything stupid.'

Ed just hoped shouting at Lou would stop him hitting the solution to this predicament before Don moved. If Don moved. The race between the two brains was painful to watch. Also he had miscalculated about Fred. The man had whipcord-strong muscles, and he could feel his grip loosening, his fingers being forced apart. Ed stood on tip-toe, drew back his head and butted as hard as he could, felt the warm blood splatter over his face as the nose burst, and Fred went limp for a second. He saw a sudden burst of stars on a black backcloth and shook his head, trying to clear his stunned senses, trying to hold on.

If Lou realised he should kill Don with his first shot, then all was lost.

He was aware of Don wresting the Marlin away from Fred's slackening grip. From the corner of his eye he saw the big fingers trying to work the slide, jamming it half way up. Don was going to trap the shell in the breech if he wasn't careful. He spun Fred so he blocked Lou's firing line. He had ten seconds before Lou decided, he reckoned. 'Easy, Lou, we all go if you fire that thing.'

He risked a glance at Don. A thin red river was running down his face from the shard still embedded in his cheek, there were flecks of blood near his eyes from smaller splinters. Maybe he couldn't see. Then the spent Black Talon flew out and bounced at his feet and he knew Don had cleared it and they were in business. Don levelled it at Lou. 'I mean – do we look like jackbooted Nazis?'

the e-mailSender: bmassey@quickmail.com
Received: from post.mail.quickmail.net (post-10.mail.devil.net [194.217.242.39])
by dub-img-5.zip.com (8.8.6/8.8.6/2.10) with PPTTS id EAA76598
for honicam.adult.net.com>; Nov.001From: bmassey@quickmail.com
Received: from rrtquickmail.com ([158.152.210.188])
by post.mail.adult.net.net id aa 1009592; 12.55 EST
Message-Id: <zzp.5564@zappermail.com
Content-Type: text/plain; charset=ISO-8859-1
Content-transfer-encoding: quoted-printable.
X-Mailer: POD
ACCESS/311111111/309835644/300102841/300202356/

Message:
Hey, baby – the horse link. Am I glad to see that. Did you put that up for me? But look, it ain't you when you click though. It's just some skanky pussy whore. You know what I mean? You get these junkies doing this stuff and what does that do for you? Nothing. Zip. I like my women to be normal. Normal, but sucking horse's cocks. It's not too much to ask is it?

❋   ❋   ❋

the e-mailSender: jerryweb@homegirlz.com
Received: from homegirlz.net (post-10.mail.devil.net
[194.217.242.39])
by dub-img-5.zip.com (8.8.6/8.8.6/2.10) with PPTTS id
EAA76598
for honicam.adult.net.com>; Nov.001From:
jerryweb@homegirlz.com
Received: from rrthomemail.com ([158.152.210.188])
by post.mail.adult.net.net id aa1009592; 12.55 EST
Message-Id: <zzp.5564@quickmail.com
Content-Type: text/plain; charset=ISO-8859-1
Content-transfer-encoding: quoted-printable
X-Mailer: POD
ACCESS/311111111/309835644/300102841/300202356/

Message:
OK, so millicam also complained, so we have changed the
click through on the horse, so it doesn't look like something
you and Mr Ed got going in your spare time. I wonder
though – if you all so squeamish, why do you do this job?
Oh, I was forgetting. The money. Cause this is the last time
we change this stuff. Listen – you thought any more about
that camera in the shower? Make you a bundle, Honey.
Let's do a trial run. Just you and me. Huh-huh.
Later.
Jerry.

Don wanted a tetanus jab real bad. Ed wanted a beer and a
dog, but they sat there listening to Lou and Fred almost
apologise before launching into a justification for scaring the
shit out of them.

Fred still had crusted blood around his nose, but was
pretty sure it wasn't bust up. He said they had no hard
feelings if Don and Ed didn't. Don and Ed weren't so sure.

Fred suddenly said 'You know that there ain't no police out here? Oh, some State Troopers, but there's no police force here. In the Pinelands. None. Not enough people, you see. Not enough crime. We take care of it. We are the law. But you know what the government is doing out there? I don't have to tell you two boys. Confiscating all handguns is on the books. Guns are the only piece of property protected by the constitution. You know that? Notice it's the Bureau of Alcohol, Tobacco and Firearms—'

'Fuckin' Nazis,' said Lou, with as much venom as the first time.

'In that order? Well, they tried to ban booze once, and they are after our smokes. First they set up pseudo health organisations like the Center for Disease Control ...'

Don almost spoke, but Ed quickly poked him. Ed knew it was his favourite Federal organisation, the monthly bulletin his required reading. But Fred was in full, well practised flow. He wasn't quite the country hick he appeared.

'... which sponsor research designed to convince us that smokers are antisocial because they use up tax dollars with health care. What tax dollars? Listen – there is no constitutional obligation to allow or even permit any state or Federal government to treat its citizens. But no judge ever takes that into account. None. So they don't *have* to spend the money. Well CDC are now saying, hey, if cigarettes are a health risk, well, lookee here – so are guns. How do you feel about that?'

Ed opened his mouth to say that when the ATF did come, it was no good shooting at them, they have a record of shooting back, but Fred carried on.

'I know we remote here, but we got TV, we get newspapers, we know what is going on. Oh yeah, and I know the evil things that happened in our schools, but you have to understand taking our guns won't help. Armed guards might. Armed teachers would be a better idea. More gun clubs, not less. Proper training. What if students knew that teachers were actually a well-armed, well-trained militia? Do you think there would be all the trouble that there is now? No. No. But these are not popular views. Most others are against us – including the lawyers, who just see big bucks from suing the gun companies. And that weaselly NRA, and the Republicans.'

Fred stood up and motioned them to the window. They could see the kids that had appeared in the woods playing some game marked out in the hardened surface of the compound. 'That is the sawmill, still working, water powered. Over yonder are the cranberry bogs. We sell to Ocean Spray, the cooperatives. Oh, we ain't big time, not like, say, the Haines, but we get by. There are twenty-two of us Fishers left, and they want our land. Extend the bombing ranges they say. Federal officers come in here with papers, saying it is emi . . . eminent . . .'

'. . . Domain,' finished Ed. 'Eminent domain. Ain't nothing you can do.'

He looked at the grey, weatherbeaten faces of the men, could tell they knew this was all going to go eventually. Maybe they wanted the ATF to shoot back, finish them off quickly.

'Fishers came here before the Revolution,' said Lou, the first sentence he had uttered that didn't have the word Nazis in it, thought Ed. 'We made the cannons and the balls that defeated the British. Now those Nazis want to drive us out.' Spoke too soon.

Fred sighed, as if he had said too much and suddenly said: 'Best get you boys cleaned up.'

Don said: 'Is there a doctor here? I could do with a jab.'

'Time for that afterwards.'

'After what?' asked Ed.
Fred raised an eyebrow: 'After you see your friend.'

TWENTY-SEVEN

Cotchford, New Jersey.
Monday December 2, pm

She walked into the River Bistro and hovered uncertainly, waiting for one of the staff to catch her eye. It was Daniel, the co-owner, who finally did so, escorting her over to a corner table with a good view of the split-level dining area. There was no bar; like many places in town the bistro had no liquor licence. Daniel quickly took her order for a bottle of Chardonnay and sent out to Mr Chu's.

She scanned the menu and asked for some sushi while she decided if she could face anything more substantial, and sipped an Evian until the wine appeared.

She felt pretty good.

She had done a couple of hours of Honicam, been to the gym, showered, sauna-ed, steamed, gone home, changed (in front of the camera again), smoked a joint and come out to treat herself. Just herself. She would be seeing Billy this coming weekend, and she tried hard to dissect her emotions about it. She was slowly coming to terms with the little voice in her brain that was telling her to end it. End Honicam, end Billy. But not until she was ready, not until she had something else lined up. But deciding to move on, to be proactive, not the kept little out-of-town woman, that was the key. The night at the hotel had told her what she needed to know – that being seen in public with her was not on the Moon agenda. She had also begun to wonder whether there were any others among the cam girls he liked to entertain like this. Once a fortnight – he could get

234

through a whole stable of them on that basis.

OK, so look on the good side. Before Billy, she was spiralling down. Billy moved heaven, earth and the Internet to find her, to bring her home (or did he mean to Homegirlz?), as he liked to remind her from time to time. So she kind of owed him for that. It was definitely a move upward after Camden, after the sort of corridors most people thought only existed on *NYPD Blue* or *Homicide: Life on the Street*. She had lived down one of those dark, stinking, defaced hallways, where shitheads lurked on every corner, every doorway. So she owed Billy. But the debt was close to being paid in full, she figured.

She was suddenly aware of being stared at, could see the perpetrator from the corner of her eye, on the lower level of the restaurant, but did not look directly. She waited until Mr Chu arrived, and she had to reach down to her purse for the money, to take him in.

She studied the freeze-framed image in her mind while Daniel opened the bottle and poured her half an inch. As always Mr Chu hovered in the doorway waiting while she took a sip and smiled her approval. He nodded his thanks and slipped out of the door.

She let the image settle in her brain, filling in the odd detail with a half-guess. About thirty, fair-haired, cut reasonably long. Quite narrow features, and the sort of stubble that looked like it took a lot of maintenance to keep down. Dressed in a white shirt, nice cut, maybe foreign designer, and chinos. Hush Puppy loafers, a couple of seasons old, scuffed but not scruffy. Not bad, she thought. She'd do all right as a witness on one of those reconstruction crime shows.

She risked another glance and modified the picture. Hair a shade darker than she had thought – must be the lights – and the shirt was cream. She could feel an odd tingling in her stomach and realised, with some surprise, it was the beginnings of some kind of lust.

She sniffed hard, wondering if she could catch his aroma, pick up a few stray molecules that had burst free from his body. Lust. Something she hadn't really felt for a long time. Sure, she liked doing it with Billy, but she realised that was just an extension of Honicam – an extended piece of play-acting. Enjoyable, satisfying in a weird way – with the sense of a job well done – but there was none of the real, low-down hormonal howling. Killed by the daily sexual grind, and too much reliance on battery-powered pleasure. But if it wasn't a howling she was feeling, there was certainly a low growling kicking in.

She ran with it for a while, wondering what he looked like stripped, what it would be like to feel his weight on her – what, a hundred and sixty? – rolling on her, pinning her, what it would be like to lick the sweat as it formed on his brow. She squirmed, she hoped, discreetly.

The sushi arrived and she demolished it greedily. The place was filling up, mainly with couples. She wondered if he was waiting for anyone, but guessed not. He had a book and newspaper on the table, the sort of paraphernalia that signals, 'Hey, I like to dine alone. By choice. It isn't that I haven't got any friends, just that I don't have a problem with my own company. OK?'

She looked at her own paperback, some sleazy true-life Hollywood confessions, and smiled. She knew that feeling.

Daniel took the order for the main course. She decided to stay Asian, and went for the pan-fried noodles with bok choy. After he took the order Daniel hovered for a while.

She raised an eyebrow in an is-there-something-else? mode.

'I'm sorry but the gentleman over there . . .' she didn't turn to look, '. . . was wondering if a whole bottle of

Chardonnay wasn't too much for one person.'

She snorted.

Daniel smiled nervously. 'It was his line, not mine. I wouldn't normally—'

She raised a hand to stop him. 'I know, I know. Tell him I can handle one bottle of wine easily. But thank him for his concern.'

Daniel nodded, looking relieved. She hesitated and wondered about him. He only ever saw her with Billy. Billy always tipped well. Would he report anything else to Billy? But with the new mood upon her she decided to take a chance. 'But tell him, if he wants to join me for the second, he'd be welcome.'

Billy Moon sat pushing the noodles around his plate, trying to finish them. Anne had made an effort, cooking Thai. Cooking. In New York. Cooking her own food. This he did not see the point of. Well, it was kind of worthy, he guessed. She had even tried to do her own spring rolls, and even though they looked like split intestines, he had appreciated the effort in a detached, distant way. Still, telling the stupid bitch he could get better Thai for four-fifty down the street was probably not straight out of *Easy Marriages, Volume One*.

'You OK?' she asked.

He took that as absolution and wiped his mouth with the napkin. 'Yeah. Food's good. Someone died, that's all.' It wasn't the someone dying that upset him of course – he never did like the holier-than-thou prick anyway – just the timing and method was all off. He wasn't meant to die like that. BB said he'd taken care of it. How could he get it so wrong?

Anne furrowed her brow. 'Someone I know?'

'No, no, someone we did . . . we had some dealings with.'

'Was it sudden?'

He almost laughed. 'Yeah, it was real sudden.' He looked at her across the table and managed a weak smile. He had to admit she had been on top form recently. No snits, no snidey remarks. Even cooking, something she had gradually left behind as they could afford take-outs and maids and cooks and eating out. He wondered what Honey was doing, thought about logging on, felt that familiar little twitch in his trousers. He shifted in his seat.

'Want to talk about him?' she asked.

'No. He was pri—'

The rest of the word was drowned out by the telephone. Billy stood up and strode through to his small office to take it, instinctively kicking the door shut behind him.

'Yeah?'

'Billy?'

'Yeah, Dad. I meant to call.'

'I thought you were going to swing by on your way back from Paterson.'

He had gone to pick up his Homegirlz money instead. 'I . . . I know. Did you see the paper?'

'About Tom. Yes, I know. Lousy.'

Billy scanned the sentence for the usual signifiers – emotion, sadness, but it was just a bald collection of words. He knew. And the old man knew he knew. But the old man had also warned him about talking out of line on the telephone. 'Any news on how it happened?'

'The police say hit and run of some kind. Some guys in a van lost control on the ice, skidded into him, panicked and got into a firefight with State Troopers.'

Or as the headlines had put it, 'Slaughter at NJ Gas Station'.

'Billy?'

'Yeah?'

'It is unfortunate, but it doesn't really change anything.

Applications go ahead. I will meet with the Port Authority this week as planned about the ferry licence, and with the state and federal reps about the lease. Look, I'd like us to go out to dinner sometime soon. Just you and me, out of the office, we have quite a lot to . . . discuss.'

'Sounds good.' Christ, it was like a conversation between two refrigerators.

'Fine. Oh Billy?'

'Yeah?'

'Love to Anne.'

'Sure.'

He put the phone down and stood for a moment. Love to Anne. Very pointedly. Love to Anne. Why would he say that? He wondered if Backson had been shooting his mouth off, or the driver. Shawn. He'd find out if they had. He'd paid Backson a good whack for his discretion. And the punk driver . . . no, it's part of their job. Like priests or dentists or doctors. Don't spill the beans. Love to Anne. From Big Billy. Mr Emotive himself. He went out to try it on her for size, see what she had to say about it.

TWENTY-EIGHT

The Pine Barrens, New Jersey.
Monday December 2, pm

'I was strung out b-b-bad by then. Fuckin' dying. Look – I know you guys never did much of that shit in The Box, but by the time I got out, I was ... I was ... susceptible to things. You know I had w-w-w-wasted most of my teens and my early twenties, everyone I ever knew either got a job or went to college or joined the army. I ain't g-g-gonna give you a list, but let me tell ya, the thing becomes like your job. That's all there is. Occupation? F-f-full time drug user. You get up in the morning and the first thing you do is have to find like three hundred bucks' worth of dope. The first thing. Look – you sure you weren't followed? OK, three hundred, then four hundred and all it does is start you up. After that you can function. But you ain't high. N-n-not at all. By this time I couldn't get high on smack. Didn't work. So you smoke crack, cause at least it gives you a lift. I mean – I fuckin' hate cocaine, hate the hardness of it, but that and m-m-m-methadone, they were the only things that worked. So one du-du-day I find that I've knocked around my woman, stolen her last fifty bucks and I am in the car going to go out into Camden to score. And it hit me like a wave. Washed over me. "Scum," it said. "You have become scum. You have hit a woman. You have robbed. You have dealt drugs to m-m-minors. You are scum." So I decided to c-c-clean up. There and then.

'The thing is, I am still a junkie, yeah? Still think like a junkie. It's kinda hard to explain. Any of you guys ever split up with a woman? You know when she tells you she's leaving, there is one thought goes through you head. Will she give me one last fuck? One last b-b-b-blowjob. It'll help ease the p-p-p-pain. It's a g-guy thing. Well, this is a junkie thing. One last hit and I'll give up. F-f-fifty bucks buys you a decent sized rock, enough for maybe five good hits, almost a whole du-du-day's worth. So I thought I'd go out in style. So I goes in search of Warren's kids, anyway. You know W-W-Warren? Yeah, hard. B-b-basketball player. Never made it to a s-s-scholarship, though.

'So I cruise down Hammer Street, where the projects are, and spot PD, who's, like, this kid, a runner. And I pull up to P-P-P-D and place the order and he goes off and I am sitting there, talking to myself, engine running, got that little hum of anticipation of getting high one last t-t-time, when this fuckin' big gu-gu-gun comes through the window against my head. Hard, I m-m-m-mean, I thought my neck was going to snap. I'm surprised there ain't still an im-imprint in my skin. And it's Warren. Seems like I ripped Warren off for five hundred's worth of shit the week before. Now I have forgotten this. D-d-don't remember at all. You think I would've tried to score offa Warren if I'd've known? F-f-fuck no. So I hit the power window button to try and shut him out, but it traps his arm. Must've pinched a nerve or somethin', cause his hand goes all stiff. He can't squeeze the trigger. So I get the gun away and floor the car. Thinking he'll, like, p-p-pull out. But he can't. He's t-t-trapped. And I'm driving down the road with this badass n-n-n-nigger hanging off my door. So I go faster and he's screamin' and you can see the whole n-n-neighbourhhood thinks this is as funny as shit. I'm panicked, I don't know what to do, every bend I go round he's like slappin' against the window, his nose is bust, his feet d-draggin on the ground. Eventually I see how to do it, so I hang a right and just as we going round

I hit the window button and it rolls down and off he goes like he's been fired from a ca-ca-catapult, rollin' and tumblin', bump bump bump. Well, you don't mess with Warren. I know he be coming back after me. So I drove and I drove and I drove and ended up here. F-found this place and holed up. Lou and Fred, they came across me after two days. I was just a fuckin' wreck. They saved me.'

Ed nodded when Tony finished his story. They were in a small two-roomed shack, sparsely furnished apart from a modern TV. Lou and Fred had washed them up and led them down a trail, through the blackened pines to this place and their old friend. He seemed to have shrunk, probably from all the drugs. He had short, stubbly hair on his head, high cheeks, haunted eyes. And twitchy, like he still wanted some dope. Like dozens of invisible creatures were running over his skin, leaving little imprints that popped and pinged out, and occasionally bit so he had to scratch. He couldn't keep still for a second.

Outside he could hear Fred and Lou pacing around, weapons back in their hands, like they still didn't believe the story Ed had given them about some kind of reunion. The reason for all the suspicion was clear now – they might have accepted they weren't ATF, but they could always be Warren's boys. Once they had searched them, though, they let them in to see Tony.

Don was sitting on a chair clearly made in the sawmill. Ed was standing behind him, Tony was opposite on a threadbare sofa, scratching his chest through his shirt, so hard it was starting to bleed. 'Look, g-g-guys, I'm sorry you got roughed up by L-L-Lou and Fred. But they kind of feel responsible for me. They watched my back these last coupla years. We got this call sayin' the Feds are after us.'

Ed felt a surge of hatred, that Box temper. Gun or no, he'd like to punch The Engineer's lamps out right now. He had clearly thought they were wired after all. Ed looked at Don who shrugged bashfully.

Tony opened his shirt and looked at the red weals he had created, and started pulling an ear lobe instead. 'I-I-I mean, g-guys. Been a long t-time. What the f-f-fuck do you want?'

So they told him.

TWENTY-NINE

Long Island. Tuesday December 3, am

Big Billy Moon walked down the lawn towards the imposing brick wall that separated him from the beach on the other side. He could hear the waves hit the shore, could visualise the water pulling at the sand, the dune grasses waving in the stiff breeze. It was barely dawn, but he couldn't sleep and here he was risking pneumonia. He wrapped his overcoat round him tighter, for underneath were only thin pyjamas. He still had slippers on his feet, and they were busy absorbing moisture from the grass.

He wished he had put a gate in so he could step straight out onto the sand, but the security adviser said it was too risky. Sure, he could see the sea from the house, which was at the top of what had once been a sloping farmer's field, but he couldn't walk straight out onto it. So he usually ended up driving around his own property. Stupid. He would get a door put into the wall. And extra cameras.

He looked up as a flock of birds passed overhead, heading south. Little late, what with Christmas nearly here. Maybe, he thought, that is what he should do. Go down to the Carolinas for a while. Play those games of golf he promised himself. No, he couldn't do that, he remembered that he had a zoning meeting early January about the plot next door. Yet another Long Island field about to sprout a mono-crop, a single, giant Palladian-style villa. January was when any smart developer presented the plans to the various agencies, because most residents were off at their other homes in warmer climes. So objections were few and far between, until the absentees came out for the summer and found their view blocked by a house built by an architect who always thought Versailles a little on the modest side. Well not this time. He would be there to object ... forcefully.

He looked back at his own relatively modest ranch-style house, the Christmas tree still alight in the window. He saw movement in the bedroom, a shadow passing. He must have woken his wife. She would put coffee on. He should go and warm up.

He thought about Tom. He tried to think rationally, reasonably, but it was no good. How could Wuzel have screwed up so badly? *Accident* was the key word in the brief he had given him. Electrocuted by a toaster, slid off the road in ice, fell down stairs, out of window. Anything that could've been a freak accident, so it didn't look like he was being taken out for political reasons. It had cost him lots of money to put a lid on some of the stories, and to get the view promulgated that Tom was just in the wrong place at the wrong time. He had managed to get the blood samples of both bodies from the van dosed with smack at the morgue, so the prevailing theory was they were couple of wired junkies who lost control. And Tom was in the way. Well, with a bit of luck it was the last time he would need Wuzel for quite some time. And Wuzel could forget about the cash he owed him – it would just about cover his expenses on this.

He walked back up to the house, the wind at his back, feeling every tired joint and knotted muscle. He stopped and walked around the side of the house, onto the drive where his S Class stood. He stepped into the garage and hit the light switch.

The model of Governor's Island had been brought here and reassembled a few days ago. He wasn't quite as taken with it as little Billy, but he could see the care that had gone into it. He walked around smirking at the tiny vehicles, the majestic tower, the intricately rendered retail units.

He must have that talk with Billy, he reminded himself. Had had to cancel it a couple of times. Or was he just putting it off? He had finally realised what it was he wanted Billy to do. It had come to him when he found himself looking at the train sets in Schwarz's. All he wanted him to do was give him a grandson. Jesus, he'd pay him just to do that. And he wanted him to have it with Anne, not piss around jumping from slut to slut. Bang the girl up, he thought.

Best be honest with him, he decided.

He went to the workbench and scrabbled under it. It took him a few minutes to drag out the object from the boxes of wiring and tiles and old tools, but eventually he freed it. He weighed the sledge in his hands. He had to be careful not to pull anything in this cold. He stretched a little, flexed his muscles, took a few deep breaths and swung. The first blow landed right in the mall complex, imploding it like a giant earthquake had struck the model. The whole framework shuddered. He inspected the damage, smiled and swung again, watching with satisfaction as the modernist tower split in two, the miniature electric cars bounced in the air, and a huge crack appeared in the golf course. He carried on until the garage floor was a mass of shards and splinters and the smell of strong coffee was coming through the connecting door to the house. He nodded his satisfaction at the carnage strewn across the concrete floor and switched off the light as he went through for breakfast. And now he could get the S-Class back in, too.

Ed smiled as he looked at his watch, taking the corner at the Palace from his starting point in less than three minutes. It was, what? Ten days ago when it would have taken him best part of an evening to walk the Boardwalk. Now, he could do it in under an hour, and with a heart that felt like it might just stay in his body, even one that was still stiff and bruised from those dipshits in the woods. He looked at the sleeping dragon as he went by, the Christmas tinsel stirring quietly in the onshore wind.

The early morning was distinctly cool, but he was sweating under all the layers, revelling in the feeling of the hot stew caused by real exertion, not by a metabolism straining at even everyday movements. He was happy, he realised, happy and scared shitless at the same time.

It had been late by the time they got him to come out, and Tony crashed at Don's serviced apartment on Atlantic. It was just like old times. The Odd Couple. No, the Odder Couple. Don was still convinced he had caught a fever from the Pinelands and was going to stay in bed for a day or so, rising to get a course of jabs for all those diseases he picked up. Tony was spooked, it was strange for him, being away from trees. It was like doing cold turkey all over again he kept saying. If he was going to stay out, he suggested, how about bringing Lou and Fred into the plan. Yup, said Ed, they'd fit right into Atlantic City, it'd be like a re-run of the Beverly Hillbillies. Only with Black Talons.

He reached the Taj, also in a strange cross-cultural clash – decorated for Christmas. Everywhere was promising Santa specials, super-loose slots, Xmas bonus payouts, guaranteed comps. Yeah, people were saving the money for the holidays, and the casinos were trying very hard to suggest, with just a little luck, this could be your best Christmas ever. Or, Ed thought, it could be industrial turkey roll by candlelight.

Past Ripley's Believe It or Not, past the turning for the North Pole. A cyclist came by at speed, causing him to swerve, and a hand came out in apology. He upped his pace from fast walk to gentle jog. 'Don't overdo it,' the M&Ms had said, 'that vascular system has had some mighty abuse these last few years – shock might just be the end of it, and you.' He readjusted the belt around his chest under his clothes and pressed the pulse monitor on the watch. One hundred and forty. OK, he'd live. He watched it creep up, one notch at a time, until it reached one hundred and fifty-five, and then slowed again. There was one good thing about this exercise, he had discovered – you could eat twice as much at the end of it without feeling half so bad.

Ed knew he'd have to get back to the garage and drive the cab for a day or two. He was down to a couple of thousand dollars. And he had to help pay for the Explorer. That was lost forever, Fred had said. Come spring, the Barrens would just swallow it, never to be spat out again. Don said the guy he borrowed it off would like seven big ones for it sometime soon.

He thought of that old song, *The Creator has a Master Plan*, the one that Jimmy used to play a lot, the cacophony of percussion and overblown sax that resolved itself into . . . what? A Tarzan soundtrack meets Duke Ellington. Does he have a master plan for me, he wondered? He could see another jogger, a blonde, elasticated crop top, tight shorts, a good muscular stride. Honey. That was how he really wanted to find her. Walk into somewhere one day, and bing. And this one could be her, she had the same coloured hair, same athletic grace he recalled. She had looked like that actress Candy Clark, only more toned. And yes, it could be her coming right at him.

But as she got closer he had to remind himself she was too young. This girl was twenty, twenty-one, Honey would be well into her thirties. Honey would have aged. Well not in his mind. The fresh-faced girl didn't so much as glance his way as she pounded by, and he made a mental note to make sure he saw Tasker sometime for the latest CCC recruitments. He would find her, he knew he would.

She awoke blurry eyed, the wine toxins and tannins stabbing at her right temple, tapping out three-bottles-is-too-many in a repetitive tattoo, and touched his side of the bed. He was gone. She remembered he said he had to get up at six, had to be in Manhattan at seven, seven-thirty. She leant over and sniffed the pillow, catching the intertwining aromas, some kind of perfumed product, maybe hair gel or a cologne, mixed with his sweat and sleep. It was the kind of smell she had fantasised about in the restaurant, the kind of olfactory arousal that made you want to run your tongue over the body that produced it. Well she had and she would again. Like a stab of lightning through a dark sky came the riposte: Billy. She closed it down for a second. She didn't want Billy in here, not now, walking into their bed, their lovemaking, her post-coital glow.

But the spell had been broken. She looked at her watch. Nine. The *Honicam Holiday* video had been running for almost twelve hours. Too long. She pummelled the pillows back into shape, and re-set the bed to make it look like she had slept alone, went to the closet, flicked the equipment to 'live', and jumped back under the covers, hamming up a waking and stretching that made her breasts pop out of the nightie. Probably nobody out there, she thought. She threw back the covers and rolled around a little, inventing new little ways to make her outfit ride up over her ass, before she started laughing to herself at the ridiculousness of it. Matt was making her realise one thing – for the past six months she had been play-acting her whole life, every last moment of it. It was time to get real.

She lay still for a minute. When they were talking at two in the morning Matt said he had friends in Atlantic City.

Maybe he could get her a job down there. Maybe even dealers' school. Twenty, thirty, forty thousand a year. Yeah, Atlantic City might be a good option. Once she got rid of Billy.

THIRTY

Tuesday December 3, pm

Vincent Wuzel made himself a coffee and went into his living room to think this through. On the table in front of him were the albums of his own efforts of photography. He started to flick through while his mind ran over how to deal with this sudden crisis in his life. One minute, top of the world, next your old friend sounds mad enough to pop you. And if there was one thing he knew about BB, it was that the guy liked to keep a grudge simmering.

He flicked open to the most recent stuff and grimaced when he saw the image of the guy lying on the table. Not because of the picture itself, which he thought caught the utter hopelessness in the guy's eyes really well. But what happened subsequently.

They had picked him up off the street, outside a bar. Brownie had been with him, he remembered, and he had walked up behind the guy, put a piece in the small of his back, got him in the car where PD was waiting. Brownie hit him twice, short, sharp punches that made him docile while they gagged him, and they took him to the old restaurant they used. It had been closed a year, but all the kitchen was still intact and they tied him to the big stainless steel table. When he came to, he was looking at them, pleadingly. Wuzel set up the camera, a Nikon F3, on a tripod, talking as he did so, telling him what they were going to do and why, because BB didn't like being fucked over on a deal. It was then he took the picture he was looking at in the album now.

'OK,' he remembered saying, 'What we got here is an experiment. When we do this thing I want some pictures to preserve the moment. Think of it as being captured for posterity.'

The guy started to thrash, but Brownie popped him again and he dipped out. PD threw some water on him. Wuzel wanted him conscious.

Brownie took one of the big steels used for sharpening knives and a meat tenderising hammer. He was going to knock the point of steel through the left side of the chest when Wuzel said no, nearer the centre. He took some more shots of the guy's face and then inserted the cable release and switched on the motor drive. He could see PD looking queasy so he sent him away for a takeout.

Brownie started, a tentative blow that saw the body arch under the shockwave, but no penetration. You gotta hit it, Wuzel had said. The heart's protected by all kinds of gristle and bone. Hit the fucker.

Brownie raised the hammer and brought it down, just as the motor drive started to whirl. Wuzel knew he was going to get it this time, the moment of death right here, right now. There was a tearing and a gushing sound as the steel punched through the assorted tissue and bone and penetrated a heart flooded with adrenalin, pumping at triple speed, and a great fountain of crimson gushed into the air as if it had struck red oil. The guy thrashed briefly one last time, his back doing an impression of the Williamsburg Bridge. He tore the binding free on one hand in a final effort to get to Brownie, then slumped back, the handle of the sharpener protruding from his thoracic cavity.

'FUCK,' Wuzel had shouted. 'Fuck, fuck, fuck.'

Brownie, splattered with gore from head to foot, looked quizzically without saying a word.

Wuzel pointed at the camera, its lens a mass of rapidly

congealing blood. It had been splashed just at the instant he
was trying to preserve. All that trouble, and they could have
just shot the guy for all the good it did them.

He closed the book. What was the guy's name? Yeah,
Warren, that was it. His own runner PD had set him up.
Warren. Poor fuck. Nasty death, didn't even get a decent
picture. Wuzel ultimately decided to stick to buying photos
after that – the cleaning bill was savage if you tried to do it
yourself.

'By the way, Don – why didn't you tell me you had a gun?'

Ed had to balance his voice carefully. Loud enough to get
over the music playing in the restaurant, but soft enough
that such an accusation didn't reach other diners. He needn't
have worried. The four of them were in Vole's, where most
people were so glad to have a table they spent their time
hollering at the top of their over-excited voices. It was the
party season, the long, alcohol-fuelled run from Thanksgiving to Christmas. All around them small dramas which
had been previewing all year began to unfurl – flirting,
griping, small explosions of resentment quickly doused by
fellow-workers. The booze was kicking in, the volume was
rising.

Vole's was a strange place, located down the kind of street
where a car with a full set of wheels was a curiosity,
unsignposted and unlisted, it still managed to be the hottest
dining ticket in town.

Don, however, had known the family for nearly twenty
years, and had been something of a regular, dropping in
whenever the auto business brought him to town, even
staying loyal when the youngest son trained in Manhattan
and decided to expand their cooking repertoire, a move
which had caused some disaffection among long-timers.

Don, who had made a miraculous recovery from his fever

around dinner time, leaned forward and whispered over the top of the menu. 'Look, no disrespect Ed, but you told me those guys wouldn't be back, but I wasn't sure. You know – the guys in Newark the other day? They might have just said, sure we'll leave him be, 'cause you was in the way. A witness? It was when I got to realising that, that's when I got it. Well, I had it all along, it's when I started carrying. You know, it might have turned out differently.'

Tony spoke for the first time and asked 'W-what's a s-skirrion?' He seemed lost away from the forest, nervous, like a boy away from home. Wherever the Fishers were he seemed to draw some kind of strength from them. Away from them, he seemed less sure of himself, twitching more, impossible to keep still.

'It's a type of fish,' said Bird, who looked very uncomfortable in this environment.

'How was I to know his boys were going to blow my fuckin' car apart?' asked Don.

'Will I like it?'

'It's very nice,' said Bird.

'Don't do the dolphin fish, though,' said Don. 'Big cause of ciguatera in the Caribbean.'

'What?'

'Ciguatera. Makes your limbs tingle and you get real sick. Barracuda, grouper, red snapper, amberjack, kingfish. They all likely to give it to you. But dolphin, that's real bad news. I read about it in the CDC newsletter.'

Tony snorted. 'Fuckin' CDC—.'

'Jack-booted Nazis?' asked Ed.

'L-l-look,' said Tony suddenly, his face contorted into a scowl, 'Don't you knock Lou and Fred. They was good to me. G-g-good guys.'

'Hey, Don and me still got the bruises from those rifle butts. And they hurt.'

'Fuckin' A,' said Don, pointing at the yellow streak on his forehead.

Tony nodded and went back to the menu and ran his finger down the list. 'What about m-mirin?'

'Japanese rice wine,' said Bird.

Tony turned to Don. 'Will it poison me?'

'Not that I know of.'

'Is there anything here I can eat? W-w-what happened to the pasta?'

'Yeah, they changed the menu. You can get clam sauce anywhere in Atlantic City,' snapped Don. 'They have fusion food now.'

'C-c-c-confusion food, more like. OK, what's this here . . . garrotxa? Will I like that?'

'A marinade.' Bird again.

'Sounds like some sort of execution method to m-m-me. The Pines sort of don't do Asia much. I mean, the F-Fishers aren't big on stir-frys.'

'Hey, Angelo,' Don called the waiter. 'You still do a pasta and clam sauce? Yeah. He'll have that. I'll have the snapper with wasabi. Ed?'

'I thought you got this Che Guevara stuff from snapper.'

'Hey, loosen up, Ed. You gotta live dangerously sometimes.'

'Yeah, I was forgetting, Don. Tuna. Just tuna. Hold the garotting thing. Side order of fries. You still do those? Some more bread.'

Bird said: 'Grilled chicken breast. Green salad. Italian dressing.'

'Great', said Don. 'And a bottle of the Merlot.'

'C-Coke,' corrected Tony.

'Dr Pepper for me.'

'Spritzer,' said Bird.

Don huffed. 'A glass of the Merlot then, a Coke and a Dr

Pepper and a spritzer for my good time buddies.' He looked at Tony. 'How long you been out there?'

'Three years and change.'

'Long time.'

'N-n-nice people.'

Don stroked the marks on his cheek. 'Once they get to know you, eh?'

'Listen, those guys have good f-f-fuckin' reason to be worried.'

'Why?' asked Bird.

'Wuh-water. The biggest aquifer in the country is under the Pinelands. P-p-pure, fresh water, no pollutants. They tried to get it before, for Pittsburg, but managed to stop it. So now its p-p-protected by State Law. But for how long? The fuckin' Fe-Fe-Fe-Federal government is overriding the State more and more. Soon it won't be the United States. It'll just be the State of America. One law. One rule. And they'll come for that water.'

'One family?' asked Don, looking meaningfully at Ed. 'I mean, the Fishers. All one family?'

'Four su-su-su-sub-units, and there is no inter-marrying within a unit. Look, I owe them. I went through three months of h-h-hell in there cleaning up, and Lou and Fred and their wives, Ethel and Elizabeth, they got me to the other side.' He waved a knife at Don. 'So cu-cu-ut the crap, eh?'

'OK. OK. Fuck, Tony, I am not sure it was such a good idea bringing you out.'

'You didn't bu-bu-bring me out. I came out.'

Bird said quietly: 'Are we ever going to get to the point?'

'OK, Bird, you got the floor,' said Ed, relieved.

Bird cleared his throat and began in his best stentorian manner: 'I have done some digging on Billy and his father. Now, remember in the mid-nineties, all those stories about the Mob being finished? Well, that apparently was garbage.

Nobody really believed it. What they did was two things. First they de-centralised, made lots of smaller self-contained units to which they could subcontract. One of those went belly-up, the Feds never got the whole picture. Secondly they went into management consultancy. Hiring out expertise, advice, manpower.'

'So the mob is clean?' asked Ed.

Bird laughed. 'That's not the impression I am getting. Old habits, you see. They are fine and dandy until things go wrong. Everything is by the book until someone stops them doing what they want, then it's – well, let's whack him. Think about it – if someone says we could go to the Board of Appeal on this, or re-apply next year, or whatever it is. Or we could whack him. What are you going to do?'

Don said: 'Bah-boom?'

'Precisely,' said Bird.

Ed shrugged: 'I don't want a Fortune 500 company profile on the Moons. I just want to know what you think about Billy and his pick-ups.'

'I don't know what I think. All we have is third hand reports from the driver – we do this, we do that. You need to stake out the place – better still, follow him, at least once. I would say twice. Take timings, photographs, everything. You need to gather intelligence.' Bird couldn't help looking at Don as he said it.

Don scratched the side of his face thoughtfully. 'I don't know how you see this playing out, Bird, but . . . well, guns are going to be part of it. You got to face up to that.'

'That's not my department.'

Ed just said: 'We'll see.'

'What, you think you can walk up and say – hey, Billy, your shoelaces are undone, and when he bends down run off with the bag? And Billy's gonna go, darn it? How does that sound, Tony?'

'L-l-listen, if it's guns you need—'

Don interrupted: 'With just three of us, it's all down to firepower.'

Tony said; 'Four, surely. What about you, Bird?'

Bird shook his head. 'I think you are all crazy.'

'Bird's right,' said Ed.

The other three looked at him quizzically.

He didn't say anything for a moment as the food arrived. Don was also right, he hadn't really thought about guns. Well, that wasn't true, the question of them kept swimming into his mind, but he did his best to hold its head under water until it went away. He knew nothing about guns. Oh, he'd fired .22s with Jimmy Jazz at the back of the store. But big kill-'em-dead pieces? Nothing.

'I mean logically, Bird's right. Go against someone who is even a second cousin to those New York guys is probably real dumb. A million may be small change, but it's the principle. But we all got our reasons. Tony here wants to play John Grisham against the government with Lou and Fred—'

'And fuck Billy up.'

'Don . . . why do you want it, Don?'

'I was kind of figuring on spending it. If none of you do-gooders got any objections.'

'And Bird, you'll get a cut.'

Bird shook his head quickly. 'This is on the house.'

Tony said quietly, 'If you are going to r-r-rob someone, you got to use something to make them hand it over. A gu-gu-gun seems the most likely form of persuasion here.'

'That in the Second Amendment that Lou and Fred like so much?' asked Ed.

Tony half smiled, his dark skin stretched over his facial bones so thinly it looked like it might snap. 'Look, you have c-c-come this far. You came to get me. Nearly got yourself killed. You have to face it when you have passed the point where it is too late to turn back. I be-be-be-bet in the back of your minds you don't believe you will do this. Am I right? Am I right? Either of you ever see that movie *D-D-D-Day of the Jackal*?'

'Bruce Willis?' asked Don.

'No. One with some English g-g-guy. I don't know his name. It's an old movie, but when you are in a house in the woods for a couple of years, you ca-ca-catch a lot of old movies. There is this scene where he knows – the J-J-Jackal, the assassin – he knows his cover has been blown, right? So if he goes into France to kill the P-P-President—'

'Are we in the same conversation here?' asked Don.

'Listen will you, you knucklehead?' Tony suddenly snapped.

'Knucklehead?'

'Just li-li-li-listen, Don. He knows, anyway, that it is cu-cu-crazy to go on. He is there at the border looking at this big mother of a sign, France one way, and . . . Italy maybe, and he sits there and you d-d-don't know what he is going to do. The real sensible thing is to stay out of France. So what does he do? He g-g-goes ahead and drives into France. Because he wants to do it. Has to do it.'

'And what happens?' asked Ed.

'Oh, the g-g-guy gets blown away, but that isn't the point.'

Still bristling, Don snorted. 'It ain't? I suppose you are going to tell us what is?'

'The point is, D-D-D-on, he did what he felt d-d-driven to do. He got to a point where he could turn back, and he didn't. You are there now. We either sit around and talk about it until our du-du-du-dicks drop off, or we say – now, this could change our lives for the better. It is right and it is proper.'

Ed frowned. 'Right and proper?'

'We should have fucked Billy up in court, Ed. I always said that, and you guys gave me that Three M-M-Musketeers shit 'bout hangin' together. So here we are on the border, years later, and the signpost says – France or Italy. God or someone has given you the chance to stick it to him again, after he stuck it to you. What do you do?'

Don shook his head. 'Why do I know what's coming next?'

Bird smiled ruefully and spoke for the first time in several minutes. 'Because you gentleman are planning on going to France?'

The sweat was cooling on her skin, reducing to a sticky sheen, and she rolled over slightly to separate from the weight of his body. He was mumbling something, like he had read somewhere it was rude to crash straight after sex and was making a valiant effort to do the honourable thing. He was failing though, the words were fusing together, tumbling over each other, and his eyes were drooping. Within a minute the mumbling was replaced by long, slow, contented breathing.

She felt pretty content herself. In truth she had been a little disappointed with his performance the previous night when it became clear he had only plucked up enough courage to send the message over because he was well into his second bottle himself.

So was it the thought he might be there again that took her in again tonight? Damned right. And he had been. Sober. Sober enough, to work his way into her bed and get to work.

She raised herself on one elbow. The guy clearly looked after himself. His chest and upper arms were well defined, he had a jawline that looked like it had been drawn with a pencil, and, as she could testify, he had some stamina. Not bad for someone who worked for one of the big investment banks which had their off-Manhattan headquarters in Cotchford. She always thought of those guys as doughy screen-boys.

But why was a guy like this eating alone in the first place? She realised that she hardly knew anything about him. She knew he was pretty much a straight arrow. Nice family, nice college, nice job. Neat. So how come he ended up with someone who plays peek-a-pussy for a living?

She rolled off the bed to go and fetch a cigarette from her purse. She could hear the machine in the closet clicking and whirring. The 'Honey is on holiday. Here are some of Honey's highlights' tape was running. Maybe he wanted a bit of low life. Maybe he was going to get married and needed to see how the other half fucked before he took up with some socialite wife who would give him three kids but wouldn't swallow if her life depended on it.

She walked into the living room, sat down in the chair and enjoyed looking out over the sea, naked but for the Winston in her hand, watching the white tips kamikaze into the shore. There was plenty of time to find out about him. About Matt.

For the first time that night she wondered if Billy had logged on, and what he would have thought when he saw the holiday tape. Still, he was unlikely to pull the you're-contracted-to-do-the-hours schtick with her. But he was bound to be curious at why she wasn't performing at all that night.

Out at sea some lights winked irregularly. She sat trying to catch the rhythm, but there was none. Maybe some boat or buoy being tossed up in and out of sight. She heard Matt groan and wake up, maybe in the mood for more. She stubbed out her cigarette and went in to see. Fuck Billy, she thought, let him wonder.

THIRTY-ONE

Atlantic City, NJ. Wednesday December 4

When Ed walked into the North Pole these days the greetings were more effusive than ever. Word had got around about strange sightings on the Boardwalk, of a fat man pounding away night and day, and they worried. Worried that one of them was going to reach escape velocity and break out of the orbit of the bar, leaving their number depleted. But drinkers love a recidivist, and when he walked in he could have drunk for free all night.

Only Goodrich encouraged. 'Yo, Ed. How's the wagon going?'

Ed pulled himself onto the bar next to him, 'Two wheels, but still rolling along. Beer, Sam. No chaser.'

Goodrich laughed. 'Well, it's a start.'

Leo got up and threw some money on the bar. He nodded at Ed, as usual his face betraying nothing, not even the hate they all knew he felt for going on-shift again. Maurice was mopping at the carpet, and spraying around some air freshener that smelt vaguely mutagenic, trying to cover up something horrible that either the dog or a customer had done, Ed couldn't be sure. One thing was certain – best not to ask.

'So, whatcha up to, Ed?' asked Goodrich.

'I dropped by to see you. Thought you'd be at the shop.'

'Nah, night off. It was open, wasn't it?'

'Some kid—'

'The Old Man's nephew. He's OK. Waddayaneed?'

'Oh, some stuff.'

'Stuff. We got plenty of stuff. Can you be more specific?'

Ed shifted uneasily and sipped his beer. He suddenly wished he had brought Don, but he didn't want to arouse any curiosity about who his new buddy was. 'Something that can make you see in the dark.'

'What, like carrots?' Ed waited. 'Heh-heh. You mean like nightscopes, NODs, that kind of thing? Well, to be honest with you, we don't get many spook-types come in trying to trade their surveillance gear. FBI don't like their guys dumping their gear to play the slots.' Goodrich lowered his voice. 'Ed – why do you . . . or shouldn't I ask?'

Ed laughed nervously. 'There is this blonde, lives in one of those new condos by the Marina. She, you know . . . something of an exhibitionist—'

Goodrich hooted. 'Ed, you dirty dog. If I didn't know better I would say losing a bit of weight has woken the old pecker up. Is that it?'

'Please.'

'No, no, you are right. None of my goddamn business. Just a transaction. OK, I tell you what we got . . .' he thought for a minute. 'If the light is on, you won't need any kind of image intensifier.'

'There are some sort of curtains. Diffuses the light somehow.'

Goodrich blew out his cheeks in a takes-all-sorts sigh. 'Russian binoculars. Supposed to be the kind issued to their sub commanders. There is a night-time button on them for low light levels. Also, I got a camcorder with a shit-hot zoom and a low light facility. Both came from birdwatchers. You know they hold the Birdwatching World Series along this coast? Yeah, well a couple of them was clocking up their score over at the wildlife refuge across the way and saw the bright lights, big city and came over here to have a look.

Next day, I got their binoculars, camcorder, tent, raingear, the lot. Never came back for them. I can let you have both for three hundred. Or just seventy five for the binocs.'

'I'll take both.'

'My ma-an. Sam, two more beers. And . . . how many chasers?' He saw Ed's resolve waver. 'Two. So you pick them up tomorrow, yeah? I have to tell you something about those Russkie bins though. They's fuckin' heavy. I mean, if you are planning to jack off, it'll be real hard to hold them steady with one hand – know what I mean? Another ten bucks'll get you a stand for them. Yeah?'

'Yeah. And listen, you got any of those dictaphones you talk into?'

'Fuckin' hundreds, man. Every flat-broke businessman comes in, always got a fuckin' Olympus or Sony to sell. Five bucks, maybe ten we give for them. Three for fifty?'

Ed nodded.

'Nice doing business with you, Ed, you old dog.'

Ed put the binoculars to his eyes and scanned down the Boardwalk. He was standing by the Palace looking south, and the wooden thoroughfare was bright with the glow of the holiday lights, the Christmas trees, the reindeers and sleighs strung up on the lamp posts. Clear as day he could see the little pockets of rolling chair operators outside each casino, followed the progress of a party of drunks weaving, and right down the far end the police cruiser pulling onto the boards for a slow crawl.

He swung around towards the sea and a screen of darkness came down. Here and there he could see little pinpricks of light bobbing into view – just the odd boat or buoy out there. He flicked the image intensifier button and black turned to grey. Grainy grey, like an over-enlarged photograph, but he could certainly see the little boat cresting

the waves now, heading south, maybe running for the shelter
of the intracoastal waterway, because the wind was getting
up. He could see that what had been a limpid mass of water
ten minutes earlier was starting to churn, tossing the boat,
almost like the first few pushes from a bully, a warning of
what was to come if it didn't straighten itself out. He flicked
the switch again and darkness fell.

He weighed the heavy metal binoculars in his hands.
Goodrich had been right, they were no lightweights.
He looked at his watch. He had to meet Tony and Don
in two hours. Go over the surveillance one more time.
He put the binoculars in the bag that Goodrich had
thrown in, so he said, for all the gear, and hoisted it onto
his shoulder.

He looked at his watch again. So there was time for the
gym. Or there was time for a dog and beer at Max's. He
slapped his gut, hesitated and started the walk back towards
Max's. Maybe he could manage both.

the e-mailSender: davidm@fastmail.com
Received: from post.mail.fastmail.net (post-10.mail.demon
.net [194.217.242.39])
by dub-img-5.zip.com (8.8.6/8.8.6/2.10) with SMTP id
EAA24765
for honicam.adult.net.com>; Sat, 2 Nov.001From:
davidm@fastmail.com
Received: from rfastmail.com ([158.152.210.188])
by post.mail.adult.net.net id aa1009592; Dec 4 18:55 EST
Message-Id: <zzp.1120@fastmail.com
Content-Type: text/plain; charset=ISO-8859-1
Content-transfer-encoding: quoted-printable
X-Mailer: TFS Gateway
/300000000/300102811/300102841/300202356/

Message:
I would like you to know that there is an organisation
who can help sluts like yourself. It is called Save Our
Sex Workers, and it is for all those people, like you,
forced by economic circumstances to exploit their own
bodies in such a vile, repugnant way. It offers advice and
sanctuary. All you have to do is send me your name and
address, and I will put you on my mailing list. Maybe even
come round for some one-on-one-counselling. What do you
think?

the e-mailSender: jfutters@flashmail.com.
Received: from post.mail.fastmail.net (post-10.mail.Compu
Serve.com [194.217.242.39])
by dub-img-5.zip.com (8.8.6/8.8.6/2.10) with SMTP id
EAA24765
for honicam.adult.net.com>; 2 nov1From: jfutters@flashmail.
com
Received: from flashmail.com ([158.152.210.188])
by post.mail.adult.net.net id aa1009592; 2 Dec 4 20.06 EST
Message-Id: <zzp.1120@fastmail.com
Content-Type: text/plain; charset=ISO-8859-1
Content-transfer-encoding: quoted-printable
X-Mailer: TFS Gateway
/300000000/300102811/300102841/300202356/

Message:
Your my Honey
Right on the money,
Seeing you makes me all runny.
In my pants.

I'd like to hold you,
get you out of that zoo,

so you know I could be true
If you did shows for me.

Hey- I wrote that while I was watching you the other night.
What do you think? I once had a poem in Hustler. Hands
Off Monica it was called. Let me know what you think.

the e-mailSender:f.alump@demon.co.uk
Received: from post.mail.fastmail.net (post-10.mail.demon
.net [194.217.242.39])
by dub-img-5.zip.com (8.8.6/8.8.6/2.10) with SMTP id
EAA24765
for honicam.adult.net.com>; Friday.001From: f.alump@
demon.co.uk
Received: from demon.co.uk ([158.152.210.188])
by post.mail. id aa1009592; Dec 4 22.05 EST
Message-Id: <zzp.1120@fastmail.com
Content-Type: text/plain; charset=ISO-8859-1
Content-transfer-encoding: quoted-printable
X-Mailer: TFS Gateway
/300000000/300102811/300102841/300202356/

Message:
I will tell you this one more time. The show sucks. It is
about the only thing that does on your site. For real class,
you got to try the Russians. Go to www.ultranatasharaunch
– it'll give you some tips on how to behave when a man is
watching you.

the e-mailSender:bmoon@aol.com
Received: from post.mail.fastmail.net (post-10.mail.aol.com
[194.217.242.39])
by dub-img-5.zip.com (8.8.6/8.8.6/2.10) with SMTP id
EAA24765

for honicam.adult.net.com>; Sat 3 Nov. 1.00am1.001From:
b.moon@aol.com
Received: from aol.com ([158.152.210.188])
by post.mail.adult.net.net id aa1009592; Wed Dec 4 TNN,
Message-Id: <zzp.1120@fastmail.com
Content-Type: text/plain; charset=ISO-8859-1
Content-transfer-encoding: quoted-printable
X-Mailer: TFS Gateway
/300000000/300102811/300102841/300202356/

Message:
Hi, Honey. Well I know different. I know Honey isn't on
her holidays. Not unless you slipped in a quick vacation
without telling me. That's two nights now – won't your fans
start to complain? I will be down this Friday, looking forward
to it. See you then. Billy M.

'Brownie? Vince. Uh-huh. You heard then? I mean, son-of-
a-bitch. Look, Brownie I ain't going to bullshit you. It's put
me in a spot, and I could do with some help. No, from you.
Yes, I know you are out of it. Hey – you said he had the
moxie. You said it. He fucked up big time, brother. No, let
me tell you, the shit has just hit the goddam fan on this one,
it's buried it. And remember, *The Alchemist* gave you enough
so you could move down there. You ain't done that badly
out of Paladin. Yes I do think you should, you shithead.
Brownie, Brownie, you can't just fuckin' walk away. I am
fuckin' bleeding here. Don't make me mad. Good. Good.
What do I want? Easy. Can you get up for this next
weekend? Like tomorrow? The funeral? You're going to the
funeral? Well throw a handful of earth on him for me, willya.
A big one. You think I care? The sooner the worms are
eatin' the fucker the happier I'll be. No, no, it's not the only
time we can do this. Let me see. Two weeks' time? Yeah,

that'll be great. I'll explain more when I see you. Good. And Brownie? It'll pay.'

THIRTY-TWO

Thursday December 5

Not many minutes into it, Don realised he was dreaming. But by an act of will he stopped it dissolving, fading to grey. He wanted to see how this turned out. So he stood to one side, like a film director stripped of his power, able to watch the actors in the drama, but unable to move them, influence them, just watching it unfold.

It was one of those afternoons, a summer afternoon, with the sun so hot all the colour was bleached out of the town. Normally they would be at the beach on a day like this, but sometimes the games went on and on and on, especially when victory kept alternating between the opposing teams.

He could see himself, his younger self, still big for his age, solid, reliable. Some might say stupid and pig-headed. There he was outside Jimmy Jazz's. Pacing around the chalk box. Already there were two prisoners in there, two of Billy's team. Enough to make a break-out worthwhile. He kept scanning the corners, the low roofs, the little patch of bushes on the vacant lot over the street. Waiting for the charge.

Out there, he knew, Lester was hiding some. That was his job. He'd do whatever you asked him. Hey Lester, stay here for eight hours till we come and get you. Still be there at Christmas if you left him. Just too easy to be cruel to that boy. But they knew, even if they got the rest of them they couldn't claim victory with Lester out there, free,

271

tucked into God knows what crevice.

Tony meanwhile would be working his way towards the main street, towards the dime store, to see if anyone needed rescuing from Billy's jail. Because Tony had the acceleration, the devastating turn of speed, that could run rings around the guards. The baseball team, the football team, the track team, they would all kill to get a piece of Tony for just one season. Football in particular wanted a running back they felt sure could average one-ninety yards a game.

But Tony wasn't any kind of a team player really; not when guys who had made all those not-so-subtle racist slights about him and his old man, not when *they* came calling all smiling and cajoling. Join our team? Fuck you and your dog. Anyway, he just liked that feeling of powering through the chalk wall, yelling at the top of his voice, the word bouncing around Cotchford, whipping through the streets, up the stairs, boxing the mayor's ears. As good as any touchdown or home run, and without all those bullshit training sessions. Alley-o.

Then all at once it started. Don saw the movement in the bushes, another at the electrical repair shop doorway down the street. A two-pronged attack. He had to pin one down at least, maybe both. He needed help here.

Where was Ed? Ed had a turn of speed, too, when he wanted, whiplash-fast. But Ed was also a tactician back then. He sometimes held back if he suspected a mass attack. Where was he?

An unheard, unseen signal must have been given because they both broke from cover, running with that otherworldly motion, fluid and graceful, but slow, molasses slow.

Don felt himself grow, expand to block their way, a vast wall of flesh. Behind him he could hear the prisoners yelling encouragement at their would-be rescuers.

Billy was the one from the bushes. He was the one to stop and capture. The other guy might release the captives, but he would have Billy, and trading two for one for their leader, that was no bad deal.

He made his decision and turned to face Billy. He could see the look of determination on his scrawny face, the sinews ridged in his neck, the jaw clenched, revealing the lower teeth. He was tough and wiry, but Don had the strength, the bulk, the bloody-mindedness to take him down.

Out of the corner of his eye he saw a third figure. Ed. He had been behind one of the big silver dumpsters in an alley. And now he was heading to take out Billy. They didn't both need to get him. Don tried to yell that he was his, for Ed to switch to the second runner, but the words came out so low and thick as to be unintelligible.

And then they saw the black mark.

Just a little speck in the middle of the street. But on a cloudless day it shouldn't have been there. And it was growing, spreading, getting shape, a defined outline. Rectangular.

Then they heard it, a high whistling sound from above. It was a shadow.

The block was a hundred yards above them. It was clearly huge, and it was swelling to block out the blue of the sky.

All of them had stopped now. Billy, Ed, the prisoners, all staring up open-mouthed at the object. As it got closer Don could see the striations on it, the pattern of deep grooves, the jagged crystalline surface, strangely familiar. He almost knew what it was.

A chill ran over him as the shape eclipsed the sun. A few feet above them now. Closer. Closer.

As the great slab made contact with his head, pushing him down into the ground to crush him to dust, Don suddenly pulled out, straight into sweating, retching consciousness.

Only a dream, he said to himself. Only a dream.

THIRTY-THREE

Friday December 6

Billy squirmed in the back of the limo, slipping around on the leather, and tried to get comfortable. He had felt uneasy all night. All day. Nothing he could put his finger on, but a certain tenseness, a vague unease had gnawed at him from the moment he got up. He had tried to analyse what it was. His old man had blown him out for dinner the night before, but that was nothing unusual. His wife had been her usual recent pleasant, interested self – that was still a little spooky, but he was kind of getting used to it – and there were no pressing problems on the Paterson construction site. Not after the little demo at the Depot. Burn a few heads, kill them all, let God sort them out. Worked every time.

True, he worried about the island project, but only because there were so many cocksuckers who could fuck it up. The whole of the city and state bureaucracy - everyone it seemed, from the guys who empty the trash cans up to air traffic control – everybody, but *everybody* got a say. And although nobody was yet suggesting that Tom had been killed because of his opposition, every time he opened the *New York Times* he expected to see a headline implying precisely that.

But Big Billy said not to worry. He had a cover story underway. It turned out the squeaky clean Mr Tom had a few hidden vices that were slowly being leaked out. Stubs from Atlantic City, credit card bills from massage parlours, parking tickets from the wrong side of town. All false of course, but the water was being so well and truly muddied, what with the junkie connection in place with the van drivers, it would be a long, long time before it cleared enough for anyone to be able to see the island project at the bottom of the pond. So, as usual, Big Billy was probably right. So why the fuck were his guts all twisted up like this?

Billy Moon idly watched the giant billboards flick by on the causeway, promoting the usual mix of shows and singers. A Frank Sinatra review 'The Genius of Ol' Blue Eyes', 'Jersey Rocks – The Music of Bruce Springsteen, Bon Jovi and other Sons of The Garden State,' and a Motown show. And then there were the groups and singers from the last twenty or thirty years, some lured out of retirement for a few thousand dollars, others coasting on hits of ten, twenty years ago, shuttling between here and Vegas and Reno and Connecticut and the cruise ships out of Miami and the other compass points on the lounge circuit.

Backson almost read his mind when he said: 'You know, I'll be glad when this run is over. I'm getting sick of the sight of those big toothy bastards smiling out of them billboards.'

'Three more, that's it.' He reached forward and pushed the privacy button and watched the screen slide up between them and Shawn. If the driver noticed he didn't react.

'Backson – you been shooting off your big mouth about Cotchford?'

'What?' Backson tried his best to bristle.

'The stop-off.'

'Nah. Nobody.'

Billy wagged a finger. 'Well don't, OK?'

Shit, he had told BB about it. But then he was the ultimate boss. Should he mention it? He looked at the scowl on Billy's face and decided against it.

The car swung into the driveway of the Enchanted Palace and took the ramp to the parking bay. 'I mean it.'

Backson shrugged his big shoulders. He liked Billy, but he could be a pain in the ass, in that he didn't always appreciate how these things worked. Backson was thirty-two now, he had been minding people since he was thirteen, when he got real big for his age and would accompany bagmen around the Aker projects in Staten Island. Who he looked after didn't matter, whether it was some small-time contractor being leant on or the boss's son, just as long as they didn't give him a hard time. Like now. The guy who paid his wages, that was BB, not Billy, so his first loyalty was to the old man.

'OK,' he said, 'There's this old persons' home—'

'Heard it,' snapped Billy.

'Nah, this is a different one. So there is this old woman, every day she takes her wheelchair for a spin around the place. And she is just going past one guy's room and he steps out and raises his hand like the Highway Patrol. Sorry ma'am, but you're speeding, can I see your driving licence? So she looks in her pockets and finds an old cinema ticket and hands it to him and he waves her on. The next day she does the same thing and he jumps out and says, sorry ma'am you just jumped a red light, I need to see your insurance. And she looks in her pocket and finds an old pizza flyer and hands it over and he waves her on. The next day she is going along and the guy jumps out and he's buck naked and he's got this huge fuckin' hard-on and the woman says, "Oh no, not the breathalyser again."'

Billy reluctantly snorted. They were here now. Backson brought those jokes out at the damnedest times. Billy watched as they pulled into the reserved bay next to the Samurai's Club Executive Elevator, of which he was a keyholder. He let out a long sigh: 'Let's get this over with and get the fuck out of here.'

❊　❊　❊

'Four-thirty. They have parked up. Three of them. Gone inside. Nothing to do but wait.

'Six-o-five. Still nothing. What they doing in there?

'Seven twenty-two . . . no, -three. Here they come. OK, one of them has a big case. The driver is opening the trunk. He's put the case in. All three in car . . . and they are off. Seven twenty-five. Been inside close to three hours.'

The feeling hadn't gone away three hours later when they backed out of the same bay. Shawn spun the wheel and took them outside, slowing as he came out of the exit ramp in case any more kamikaze cabbies were lying in wait. As he came up to the junction with Pacific, Billy pushed the intercom button and said: 'Stop for a minute.'

Backson didn't say anything. Billy looked around trying to locate the source of this persistent nagging. 'Case is OK in the trunk?'

Backson nodded, wondering what had got into the guy this evening. It had all gone as usual: polite conversation, a couple of drinks, the pick-up and they were out in plenty of time to reach Cotchford. He was getting hungry for that burger with his name on it. Yet Billy looked as if someone had put fire ants in his pants.

'OK. Shawn – let's go.'

'Cotchford?'

He hesitated. He wasn't sure that he was in the mood, but he couldn't call and cancel again. 'Yeah, Cotchford.' Billy leant back and flicked on the stereo, selected some Luther Vandross. Maybe some smoochy soul music would lift his spirits.

'Don's tape. Testing, one, two. Seven twenty-nine. Subjects leaving the ramp of the Palace. Jesus I feel stupid doing this. OK, subject approaching Pacific. Stopped. Oh-oh. Still stopped. I can see driver

looking around. He's looking at me. Right at me. Shit. We've blown it. I knew I was parked too close. Sorry guys.

'No, no, it's OK, they've pulled away again. Seven thirty-one. I'm going after them.'

Anne poured herself a large helping of gin, went easy with the tonic and ice, and opened the door to Billy's office. It was neat, orderly, just a few scribbles on a notepad spoiling the clean lines. She looked at the doodles. Giant towers climbing out of an island. Helicopters. Speed boats. They were oddly childish, and she felt as if she had stumbled across him playing soldiers or cowboys and Indians.

She sat down and looked at the computer in front of her. She placed the drink and the cellphone down in front of her on the desk and unfolded the piece of paper in her hand. She read Sarah's looping script carefully and then stabbed at the button in the top left-hand corner. The computer made a little singing noise, followed by some very industrial-sounding grunting and groaning, as if the thing were not the product of post-millennium humanity, but something from the industrial revolution, with flywheels and pulleys within.

The screen started to fill with little symbols and a progress bar telling her it was warming up. There was a strange little tune, some dancing graphics and then it all went quiet, save for the self-satisfied hum the machine gave off.

Anne noticed her hands were shaking. Worse than reading his diary, his letters, this felt like some kind of electronic rape. She swallowed hard. If there is nothing, then no harm done. If there is something, did she want to see it?

Hell, yes.

She read the next instruction, pulled up the hard disk, clicked on the server icon, then indicated she wanted the mail centre. The modem kicked in and brought up the display. She browsed the instructions again and clicked a couple more times. Unread messages: Zero. Messages stored: Zero.

She hit the speed dial for Sarah, and, whispering even though she was alone in the apartment, told her what she had done.

'What, nothing?' asked Sarah.

'No. No stored messages.'

'Bastard. He must delete them as they come in. Hey – maybe he isn't so dumb.'

Anne suddenly felt defensive. 'He isn't so dumb. And maybe there aren't any messages. Maybe he isn't doing anything wrong.'

'Pul-eez, Anne darling, don't start giving him the benefit of the doubt now. Try outgoing messages. It'll be another little box.'

'Outgoing messages. None.'

'My, he is thorough.'

'What do I do now?'

'You shut it down, go downstairs, catch a cab and we tie one on. I've got the keys to this great place overlooking Central Park. Ice box full of champagne.'

'Nothing else I can do here?'

'Nope. Sorry – I was sure it would give you some idea of what was going on. Come on, let's party. The owners said "help yourself". I'm supposed to offer it to serious potential buyers, but hey, if you had seven million dollars to spare I am sure you would consider it real hard.'

'Well I am kind of relieved. It felt like snooping.'

'It *is* snooping, baby – that's half the fun. Now shut down and get over here.'

'How do I turn it off again?'

'Seven fifty nine. Just turning onto the Parkway and the 40

interchange. Can see Tony behind me. He is going to go ahead . . . now, and get in front, and we will change over a couple of times.

'Eight fifteen. All seems to be going OK, just going to do the changeover routine a couple of times, let's hope they turn off as expected.'

On the trip up the Parkway to Cotchford, Backson felt the mood ooze out of his boss, cross the leather between them and seep under his own skin. All in all it was pretty uneventful, only a speeding car forcing them to move over broke the monotony. He wondered what was festering inside Junior to make him like this. Usually the thought of doing the nasty with whoever he kept in the apartment up there put a smile on his face, a spring in his step and a bulge in his pants. Now he was sitting there with his eyes closed, ostensibly listening to the music, but when headlights hit his face he could see the eyeballs moving under the lids. The man was thinking hard about something.

Backson, too, was beginning to feel unsettled, but then running all that money around, same day at regular intervals, same route. It wasn't too clever, and it made him nervous. He should think about making Billy Jr change the day at least. After all, surely it didn't matter what time of the week he got to see this broad.

'Nine-o-five, Don is indicating to turn off ahead of them. Shit, the limo isn't indicating. They ain't gonna make the turn. Oh fuck. Must be goin' straight to New York. Jesus, there he goes. God, he's taken it. No indicators. That's fucking terrible driving. OK, I'm off after them. Oh, it's nine-o-eight.'

They pulled off the Parkway and headed East to the shoreline. The usual strip malls gave way to small clusters of communities, all lit up for the holidays. Backson couldn't believe how much garbage people had attached to their homes. A simple string of lights wasn't enough any more it seemed. There were waving Santas, speeding sleighs, giant Christmas trees whose lights must be sucking half the power in the entire north-east, and twinkling stars flashing at them.

Backson shifted in his seat and repositioned the gun under his left armpit. He reminded himself to stress with Big Billy that he, Backson, had never liked the Cotchford stopover. In a not very strong chain, it was the weakest link, but little Billy-boy here wouldn't let him bring any more guys out. If anyone seriously wanted to take the case, he always argued, didn't matter whether we had three, four or five guys. They'd just get more. True. The main deterrent was, of course, the old man. Nobody wanted to wake up floating in the Depot pool. He remembered the first time they used it he had taken Polaroids which were passed around like some kind of pornography. It got the message across real clear.

Word was BB was going soft now, but he knew that wasn't true. Despite his Hamptons hideaway, BB was still playing the game. *The Alchemist* was but a year past. Asbury Park a couple of months. And that guy Wuzel put the stake through – that was meant to have come direct from BB, right down to the bit where they wanted the guy alive when it went in, inch by inch. That was a bit of a message for anyone who wanted to fuck with him and his associates. He wondered if he could get some of that action rather than playing mind-the-money. Paid real well. He would have to buy a bigger apartment, now he had a kid on the way. He smiled to himself and banished the thought. Don't dwell on anything too cuddly, he reminded himself. Blunts your edge.

They passed Cotchford's only hotel, did a right at the Brew Pub and pulled into the U-shaped drive that looped around the apartment block. As usual they swung around the back of the building and stopped there. Billy didn't open his eyes, so Backson touched his arm. He started. 'We're here.'

Billy stepped out of the car, smoothed his coat down and used his key to let himself into the stairway/garage lobby. Shawn pulled away and completed the U, bringing the car around to face the Starboards diner lot directly opposite, which it shared with the rear of Cecil C's Brew Pub.

'Done my U-turn. Just driving by Starboards, coming up on left. Can see Tony coming opposite direction. They have turned into an apartment opposite Starboards. Can't really see, hold on. One guy out. Must be Billy. No case. No case. Great. Perfect. All up to you now, Ed. Shit, it's . . . fuck, my watch has stopped. Hold on, the car one says Nine twenty-three. Yeah, nine twenty-three. I'll wait and see when they leave.'

Shawn waited for a gap in the traffic and bounced straight across the road, pausing at the intercom-on-a-stick to shout their order. He positioned the limo as usual on the left of the lot, farthest away from Cecil C's, and a good distance away from the diner itself. The help would have to walk further to deliver the food, but, things were considerably quieter and they could actually see the apartment window from there, which made everyone feel better.

Backson got out and took his place in the front, where they would share the meal and listen to sports on the radio, a preview of Nebraska at Kansas State, with a profile of quarterback Michael Bishop. Backson was keen to hear how good the boy was – after all, they had the nation's top scoring defence, with a 7.8 point average per game. But Backson figured that the Wildcats had had it easy up to now, and that score reflected bullshit opposition. Which is why he had two hundred on the Huskers.

'How's the wife?' asked Shawn.

'Good.'

'Showing yet?'

'Bump city. Tell you – one strange thing. She can't get enough at the moment. Wearing me out.'

'Hormones,' said Shawn. 'I read about it in *GQ*. Pregnant women get this big surge of hormones, makes them horny as hell.'

'Tell me about it.'

'Piece also said, make the most of it, boy – you won't be chasing that tail for a looooong time once the baby comes,' Chris chuckled.

'Guess I'd better just stockpile some memories.'

'Yeah, and some Hustlers.'

Backson laughed: 'Fuck you.'

'Shit, he is out. Nine-fifty. Twenty-seven minutes. No time at all.'

The trays arrived and they clipped them to the window – despite the wind whipping through the car, they liked this now almost forgotten ritual – and devoured the food hungrily. They had barely wiped the last of the ketchup when the door opened and Billy slid back in. Backson looked at his watch. Shit – twenty minutes. They usually got a couple of hours. Backson grunted as he turned down the radio, just as the Huskers' injuries were being listed. He heard the name Mackovicka – but did that mean in or out?

He turned around and looked quizzically at Billy, who just shrugged. Backson knew better than to ask and resumed his position in the rear, looking around to check the area. Nothing out of the ordinary. Shawn dumped the two trays in the designated bin and headed off to New York. Suited him, he'd be back for a drink before eleven. He watched as

Billy slumped down in the seat, chewing his lip. Backson stayed upright, alert, trying not to think about what Shawn had said about post-baby sex.

'Nine fifty four. Looks like they are heading back to New York City. Damn.'

She sat on the bed, a little tearful. Nothing had gone according to plan. There had been a script, a long one, a slow builder, explaining gently how she had tired of the life. Of being under wraps all the time. Of exhibiting to an audience of jerk-offs nationwide. And how she was even more tired of their little rituals, which had been fun once, but now just seemed . . . tawdry. Time to wind it all down. Nicely.

Instead she felt the air crackle when he had come in. He slotted into his usual patter, but awkwardly, half-heartedly. She had responded equally badly, impatient with his talk of when they were 'just kids starting out' – what horseshit – insisting on finding out what was wrong, worried that someone had told him about Matt. Maybe Daniel. A call might have been made, to say she had been *seen*, but short of confessing, she had no way of drawing this out of him.

There was a clumsiness between them, physically and mentally. It was clear from the start that sex wouldn't be on the cards, not the way he sat there, stiff-backed and rigid, hands tightly clasped. Well, that suited her, but for old times' sake she didn't want it to end like this, not after all he had done, getting her out of the slut end of the market, giving her the apartment and all. She would have to play it better next time. Maybe she should send him a message.

She went to the bathroom and threw some cold water on her face, put on that track she always chose when she felt sorry for herself – the aptly named *Unfinished Sympathy* –

before logging on to the computer. She rolled herself a small joint as she accessed his e-mail address and started typing. Conciliatory, worried, bruised, that was the tone to take. She listened to the epic chorus 'You really hurt me, ba-by,' and sang it as she she re-read the message, nodded, took a big drag and held it before pressing 'send'.

Anne put the phone down on her friend and sighed. She looked at her watch. He would be a good few hours yet, but there was no point in going round in circles, and the drink did sound like a good idea. She was just about to leave the mail centre and log off as instructed when a small box appeared on the screen telling her that she had new incoming mail. It flickered and a progress bar appeared. Above it, a series of words informed her that a message was coming from honeybee@honicam.com. She felt her heart jolt. What did she do next? Did the other end know she was logged on? Fingers fumbling badly, Anne picked up the phone and punched the button that held Sarah's number.

THIRTY-FOUR

Atlantic City, New Jersey. Friday December 6
Saturday December 7

They finally rolled into the North Pole at around twelve, all in need of a drink, brains spinning as fast as they could. They hunkered down in a booth with a beer each. In front of them were the little tape recorders, full of timings and thoughts. They had wanted walkie-talkies or mobile phones, but Bird had required a permanent record. And he told them that you never knew who was listening.

'So?' said Ed at last.

'Well?' asked Don.

Tony, his cheek twitching more than usual, was the first to break. 'Two gg-gu-guys – just two guys, both in the car. And Billy out of the w-w-way. Gotta be easy.'

'Must be a woman in there, like the driver said,' said Don.

'Implied. Not said. Implied. Nineteen, twenty minutes he was in there,' said Ed. 'Ain't long.'

'Ain't a lot,' echoed Don glumly.

'No, no, no,' said Tony, his face twitching. 'They m-m-m-must've had some sort of s-s-nit in there. Must have. I mean, it is hardly time to bang her. And if he did, well old B-B-Billy's developed a bit of a hair trigger, you ask me. Ten minutes, we can roll the two g-g-guys in the car, and be on our way. And five'll get you ten he gives it the works next time. And I don't care how tough the ca-ca-cavalry in that limo are. Two guys? There are ways and means, believe me. Made by Sturm, Ruger and Co. And

Billy won't even know 'til he comes down.'

Ed said quietly, 'I want Billy to know.'

'What?' asked Don.

'I want Billy to know what is happening. Otherwise they'll think it was just some punks.'

Tony said, 'Then send him a postcard from C-C-Ca-Cancun.'

'No, I am going to be with Billy while it's going down.'

'With him?' Don shook his head in disbelief. '*With* him? What the fuck you talking about?'

'I'm going to be in the apartment.'

'Then we're all going to die,' said Don, then thought further. 'Well, at least *you* are. That's just dumb. Very dumb. That's like, no-brains dumb.'

'Billy went up by himself, right?'

'Right.'

'So it's just him.'

'And a girl.'

'Let me worry about that. You figure out how to do the car, Tony?'

'Well, I think we should run it by B-B-Bird. But yeah, I g-g-go-got an idea. But if you are in the apartment busy gu-gu-gu-gloating. . . .'

There was a sneer to the voice, but Ed didn't rise to it, he just nodded. 'The driver is a Born-Again Christian.'

'So?' asked Don.

'I don't think he'll be armed.'

Tony started rubbing his forehead. As usual he was a mass of tics and little repetitions. 'I dunno. Remember the fucking Cr-Cr-rusades. They were fuckin' C-C-Christians.'

'We need more people,' said Don with a depressed note in his voice. 'One minute we got three of us, now we got two. So we need one, maybe two more.'

Tony said: 'Lou and Fred?'

'*No*,' Ed and Don both said in unison.

Don pointed to his still-marked cheek and to his back, stiff and yellow with bruising.

Bird came in at that point, looking around, his nostrils twitching at the disagreeable odour. Ed suddenly realised he was hungry. Still not hungry enough for Maurice, though. Bird collected a soda from the bar, used a handkerchief to wipe the seat and slid in next to them. 'So. How was it?' he asked.

Ed talked him through it while demolishing a bowl of chips, spraying his audience whenever he got too excited.

Bird gathered up the dictaphones and pocketed them. 'I will view the videotape and pictures tomorrow. Maybe go down and take a look at Starboards again. But you need to do it again one more time, make sure it is consistent.'

'And what if next time is the last time?' asked Don, as if this were inevitably true.

'There is always Lotto,' said Bird. He reached over and straightened everybody's beer mat.

Ed was about to answer when the figure at the edge of his vision spoke. 'Hi, guys.'

It was Goodrich.

Ed did the introductions.

'How was the stuff?'

'Yeah, good. Did the trick,' said Ed.

'You must show me sometime.'

Ed sensed Bird stiffen and said quickly: 'X-rated. Not sure you could take the heat.'

'Hey – you should see some of the tapes we got in the shop . . .' He shouted over at Alice, whose eye seemed to have healed up. 'And a shot, darlin'.'

Alice took two steps over and waved a fistful of bills. 'Hey – it wasn't that good a night, Goodrich. You can pay for your own shots.'

'Just get the drinks you tight-assed bitch.' He looked at Ed. 'Well, maybe not so tight-assed, given that story the other week. Eh, Ed?'

He was saved from answering by Sam, who came over with his coat on. Ed was trying to look relaxed, but the party was growing. Alice would be over soon, at least if she ever finished arguing with the barkeep about the strength of her drink.

'Hey Goody, you drink over at the Hoop Bar sometimes, doncha?' asked Sam.

Ed looked at Goodrich. Hoop, a corner bar two blocks to the west, was not generally good news. The joke was you could buy anything in there but a drink, because the bar staff were too busy dealing out contraband this, snitched that. 'Not tonight.'

'They hit the place about two hours ago. ATF. Looking for illegal weapons.'

Ed felt the table move and looked at Tony. His jaw was clenched tight and he was breathing through his nose. 'Those . . . we gonna take that? C-c-coming into the bars now and rousting us? We should g-g-g-go there. It's our constitutional right —'

Bird reached out and pulled Tony's jacket to stop him rising in his seat. His face had gone red, and you could see the blood pressure rising, even in his dark cheeks. 'You don't understand. We've had these people sniffin' around Fishers. They are out of c-c-co-control. They're just, just —'

'Jackbooted Nazis?' suggested Don.

'Yes, yes they f-f-fuckin' are.'

Bird said as coolly as he could: 'Sit down, Tony. Just calm yourself. I am sure all the excitement is over.'

'I guess it is,' said Sam. 'I heard they took a coupla guys in and shut the place down. See ya. I'm out.'

'It's inaction like this that let Hitler in, that caused Bosnia,

Vietnam. When the ATF and their friends are running the country, when you can't fart without a F-F-Federal form, then you'll know,' said Tony, as he slid out the booth and walked out.

'He OK?' asked Goodrich.

'He's from the woods,' said Don. 'Believes in the right to keep and arm bears.'

Goodrich laughed and said: 'Yeah? Well I'm with him there.' He pulled open his jacket and they saw the dull lump of metal in there. 'Don't worry, this one's legit. Anyway, I'll leave you guys to it – I'd better go and rescue my drinks. Good to meet you,' he said to Don and Bird.

Ed was wondering about how much of a liability Tony was going to be if he went off the edge every time the ATF or other Feds came calling – what had they done to him in those woods? – when he noticed Bird looking over his shoulder at Goodrich. Bird raised an eyebrow. 'Who was that? You *will* be needing an extra body you know.'

Sarah said slowly, but forcefully, 'Log off. Get out of there.'

'Shouldn't I read it?'

'No.'

'Why not?'

'Because he might know. There might be a way of saying which messages have been read or not. You can't take the chance. Exit the server and shut down.'

When Anne was left looking at a dark screen she let her breath out. 'What now?'

'We wait. You can read it after he has. Just hope he doesn't delete it. My guess is he does them in batches, not one at a time. He'll have no way of knowing afterwards if we read it or not.'

'I don't think I can do this again.'

ROB RYAN

'Of course you can. I'll tell you what, darling – next time I'll sit in. OK?'

Anne thought about it. She knew that this was more than just an offer of friendly help, knew that Sarah would get some kind of vicarious pleasure from it. She was the kind of woman who, if there was a job opening other people's mail, reading their diaries or tapping their phones, would jump at it. Maybe she should have been a journalist. Still, she had her uses, so she said: 'Deal.'

Sarah whooped with rather too much joy. 'Now get your bony ass over here.'

When they finally got back to Ed's place, away from any more interruptions, Ed fetched a six-pack from the refrigerator. He gave a Diet Coke to Lester, who nodded and floored the throttle of a Lamborghini Countach. Ed watched as the screen went blurry to represent a juddering, wheel-spinning start.

'Isn't a Lamborghini a kinda obvious getaway car?' asked Ed.

'Fast,' said Lester.

'Which city?'

'Miami.'

Ed shrugged. Maybe not so out of place in certain circles.

They had found Tony on the Boardwalk, staring out to sea. The righteous indignation had gone, and he had returned to simple twitches, scratching his body through the combat jacket he was wearing. Bird had gone home, saying he would be in touch.

Don said to the pair of them: 'Listen, your pal. Goodyear? Goodrich. Maybe he would go for it. But I think we stick with who we know, what we know.'

Tony nodded. 'Lou and Fred, they would have—'

'*No*!'

292

Ed thought for a minute. 'Goodrich is alright. But I take your point there, Don. Though we are kinda short of options, what with Bird out of the frame. We need someone to drive the car and, or, someone to lift the case from the trunk. It isn't rocket science.'

'We could go on the open market, there's this agency that will get you any kind of talent you want. Paladin – they do a contingency scheme I hear: no take, no fee, like those lawyers,' suggested Don.

Ed shook his head. 'No, you were right, no outsiders. And especially not that sort.'

'Then who?' asked Tony.

A metallic voice boomed: 'Congratulations driver. You have just outrun the Miami Police. The getaway is complete.'

The three of them turned to look at Lester who was nodding his head wildly at the dollar sign flashing on the screen. He whooped, and then felt himself under scrutiny. He looked around at the three faces, all with strange expressions on them. 'Hey, guys. What you looking at?'

THIRTY-FIVE

Monday December 9

Brownie looked fit and tanned and he had only been out of it for, what? Two months. He looked to have dropped ten years since Wuzel last saw him, which must have been around the time of the Asbury casino raid. Wuzel shook his hand and slid into the booth beside him. Normally they would have met at Brownie's old bar, the Hoop, but the ATF raid had made that off-limits for the sort of conversation he had in mind. You never knew what those bastards left behind when they stormtroopered a place.

So they had chosen a bar in Absecon, a place near the shore, with a closed deck overlooking the water.

'You OK?,' asked Wuzel.

Brownie sniffed and wrinkled his nose. 'Yeah.' Flat, pissed off. He didn't want to be here. Didn't want to have to dig out his overcoat one more time, take one of those flights where the plane comes in jerking like it's on a string, where they have to de-ice it ten times before it takes off for the sun again. But he owed Wuzel, he knew that. Felt like he had let him down. Must be going soft – he should have told his old partner that Penn could be a fuck-up. Guess he just hoped the kid would have the sense to do this one right. 'They connect you?'

Wuzel shook his head. 'I can only guess they got Car 54 on the case, 'cause there is a fucking big dotted line leading from that gas station to Paladin.'

'But you're clean?'

Wuzel ordered two beers from the waitress. 'Yeah. But . . . well, it was a fuck-up all round, if you know what I mean. I have kind of taken it as a sign.'

'Sign of what?'

Wuzel stroked his chin. Senility? Old age? 'Time to pack up. I got some money . . .'

'Some? *Some* money? Shit, you should have got a couple of mil by now. What was your cut from *The Alchemist*?'

Brownie had used his own money wisely, he knew. *The Alchemist* – a ship named for the power to turn base metal into gold – had sailed from Highlands on a big loop heading for New York. It was a weekend thing, Friday and Saturday, gambling cruises, turning dollar bills into stacks of chips, an alchemy of sorts, and one with just the same sort of mythical status as the real thing.

Sometimes the ship – a converted car ferry – turned south, spent the whole weekend at sea, taking the punters past Atlantic City. Well, for one reason or another, the owners and operators of *The Alchemist* had upset the guys on the mainland. Wuzel had never asked. Not his business. He knew the competition for the diminishing pool of big players was fierce. Or maybe it was some old beef, something personal. Either way, on one of the weekends heading down the coast a whole fistful of the passengers suddenly drew guns. The radio was disabled, the place shot up, customers robbed. One of them had tried to resist, he was tossed overboard. A croupier and a dealer had died. Stupidly, wastefully. The ship had a hole blown in it below the waterline and was told to get to port before it sank.

The terrorists, gangsters, whatever they were then departed by waiting speedboat, leaving the ship to limp back. The Coastguard got the passengers off, and the crew. *The Alchemist* never did make it to port. Now it was an attraction for divers, who brought up *Alchemist* chips as souvenirs.

Exactly what happened to the perps wasn't clear, but Wuzel knew, because Wuzel had arranged it. They had rendezvoused with a yacht and scuttled the getaway craft. It was audacious, risky and had worked beautifully. The fee plus the takings were seriously healthy. Wuzel had organised the talent, put Brownie in charge, and gone photograph shopping in London and Paris with his commission.

They had used the same technique at The Terrace in Asbury Park – and pulled it off again. Then there was the vampire-slayer job. With two fat earners, plus a tasty enough package for the staking-out of that scumsucker Warren – Brownie had cashed his chips and left for Florida. Wuzel, though, Wuzel had spent his.

Finally Wuzel said. 'I still got the money. I just put it in photographs. Same ways you put it in bonds.'

'Then sell some. Don't fuckin' drag me back up here. Sell some.'

Wuzel just smiled. He didn't understand the compulsion, the sickness in the pit of his stomach when he had to have – *had* to have – a photograph or a set of photographs. Like the Christophers. They were his, really. He wasn't going to let anyone else have them. Now, though, he had convinced himself that with a bit of fast footwork he could have them *and* his retirement.

'It's nothing like *The Alchemist* or The Terrace.'

'No?'

'Simple.'

'Good. Cause I ain't happy—'

'One-armed man.' He saw Brownie's eyebrows rise. 'No, one man with arms. This ain't the fuckin' *Fugitive*. Maybe two. A case. Parking lot. We walk up and take the case. Might have to drop the man with the gun.' Might? No, he could ID them. No 'might' about it. Kill them all, as BB would say, let God sort them out.

'He any good? This guy with the gun?'

'Backson?'

'Backson.' He watched the thoughts flicker across his old friend's face and the pieces finally fall together. Wuzel didn't say anything while the next beers were delivered. He took a sip and said, 'Nine deliveries of one mil each, that was the arrangement. We are going to take one. Only Backson, Little Billy and a driver. One million. I need seven hundred thou of it. Leaves you three.'

Brownie finally drank some of his beer. Three wasn't much, but it just about made it worthwhile. Despite the sourness in his stomach, he felt a tiny little flutter of excitement, and it took him a while to recognise it for what it was. 'If Big Billy figures it was us—'

'Why should he? Listen, I cased that run, I told him it was wide, wide open. Stupid. But his little boy, he's poking some broad en route, and Big Billy is thinkin' "let the kid have his fun," or some such shit. Criminal, I told him.'

Brownie laughed. 'You think *that's* criminal? That's rich, Vince.'

'Yeah, well Billy said there are millions flying round AC on any given night. All the cash from the casinos being shipped off the island here there and everywhere. Who is going to risk his neck for a lousy million?'

'Got a point. A million ain't what it was. Dollar ain't what it was.'

'No, and neither is the Canadian dollar, the peso, the cruzado or the lempira. It buys a lot of those babies.'

'Lempira? What the fuck is that?'

'Honduran.'

'Shit. You thinking of going that far?'

Wuzel shrugged. 'You never know.' He slumped back. Brownie was right, a million wasn't much. But getting it was straightforward enough – all those millions he was talking about washing around AC were locked inside humongous armoured cars. This one was Security-Lite by comparison. But, of course, this caper involved an element of the personal. BB shouldn't have talked to him like that. He was lucky he wasn't taking him down for a dip in his own pool.

And with the deductions BB wanted to make from his Asbury fee, he was leaving him no choice. Shit, he should never have agreed to deferred payment. Give the casino a few months, BB had asked, time to cover their opening costs, like he was some Ezy-buy furniture store. Kill now, pay later. And now they were turning it over in one mil bites.

He looked up at Brownie, expecting to see disgust, resistance, horror. Nothing. 'No photos this time, eh?'

Wuzel shrugged, 'I wasn't planning on any. Not enough light.'

'Good. I felt like I was on QVC doing that shit.'

'It wasn't you I was fuckin' interested in.'

'Yeah, well if I ever cop it, don't go pointin' no lens in my face. OK? Now, what kind of gear we need? I'll fix it.'

It was then Wuzel caught the gleam in Brownie's eye. Despite all his talk about the sun, the women, the money, the grouching about the weather, the old bastard couldn't hide the fact that he had missed all this.

THIRTY-SIX

Tuesday December 10

It was just Ed and Bird, Bird insisted on that. Too many voices, too many opinions otherwise. Inside Lucy he laid out a plan of the Cotchford site, marking out, on one side of the road, Cecil C's Brew Pub, whose lot adjoined the Starboards diner. Across the road was the apartment block that Billy had disappeared into.

The two men sipped coffee and stared in silence for a while.

'You want to be inside?' said Bird at last.

'Yeah.'

'It's your call.'

'I know.'

'I don't recommend it.'

'I know.'

'I don't recommend any of it.'

'I know. It'd be nice if we could get Bruce Willis, but we got me and Tony and Lester.'

'Lester?'

'Yeah.'

'Lester?' What's he going to do? Serve drinks?'

'Bird. That's my problem. Now tell me what you have.'

Bird unfolded a map of New Jersey. 'First of all, think about what happens afterwards.'

'What?'

'Let's say this works, you get your million. Where do you go?'

'I . . .'

'You don't know, do you? I'll tell you. You go to where Tony was holed up.'

'With Lou and Fred?'

'Whatever they're called. From what you told me, they are totally paranoid about the law and the Feds —'

'Hey, you heard Tony. That shit's contagious.'

'They will know when anyone is coming to get you, there are thousands of acres to hide in. It's perfect.'

'I'll ask Tony —'

Bird sniffed in his superior way. 'Don't ask him. Tell him. You need a leader, Ed. It was your idea. You tell Tony what you are doing. You tell him to tell Lou and Fred you are coming in. Tell them you upset the ATF.'

'That'll do it. We'll be local heroes.'

'Fine. The rest is easy if you follow timing and procedure. Only you are the wild card. Being inside, I mean. It's risky.'

'I know what I am doing.' Bird looked at him quizzically. 'But before we start . . .'

'Yes?'

'You got anything to eat?'

The virus that infected the atmosphere throughout the city, that was pumped into air conditioning ducts, released from canisters dropped in the streets, sprayed from the banner-towing planes that flew the shoreline, finally hit Don. Why else would he suddenly want to gamble?

He explained the theory to Tony, who just shrugged and said, 'Like the end of Goldfinger? When they s-s-spray the gas around F-F-Fort Knox? You think they got a gas here? Gameathon – painless, odourless, able to open w-w-wallets and unzip purses at f-f-fifty yards? Or maybe like in The Time Machine – some siren is calling you to go where the sun don't shine?' He laughed. 'Or maybe you are just b-b-b-bored shitless waiting for the main event? Me I spent a long time where there ain't nothing to do. I'm c-c-c-cool.'

They had rented a small, scruffy apartment set back from the front, TV, DVD, CD and some sad sack pieces of furniture, but Tony was happy. He could dial out for food, he could get a six-pack on the corner, he could go and watch the girls at the titty bar at the end of the street, little things that were a real pleasure again. What they made of the stubble-headed little guy who grimaced and twitched through their performances, Don daren't think.

Don was scared of sitting still for too long, brooding and thinking about what he had got into. The dreams were getting worse now. He didn't want to follow that line of thought, he needed a distraction. And what other distractions were there in this place? Only one game in town, albeit in a multitude of disguises.

'Where you g-g-going?'

'The Palace I guess,' Don said. 'Keep it in the family, you know what I mean? Sure you won't come?'

Tony lit a cigarette. 'Nah. Be lucky.'

The words haunted him as he walked the few blocks to the Palace. Be lucky. How lucky had he been so far? He realised he was going to have to go back home soon, just to pick up the results of those blood tests he had had. The doctor had assured him he was too young for prostate problems, but he insisted. Thirty percent of people in their thirties he had read get some gyp. And he remembered standing there with his dick in his hand, waiting for the stream to come shortly after he had read the piece in *Home Diagnosis* magazine, and, well, he just knew he was one of the unlucky ones. So the doc put on the rubber glove and said it *felt* OK (he shuddered at the thought) but they would do a blood test anyway, run the PSA levels. His skin prickled when he pictured the envelope lying on the mat, with all the other mail, like a Trojan Horse. 'Dear Mr Keah . . .'

Inside the echoing entrance hall of the Palace with its trailing banners and calligraphy (like something from a K-K-K-Kurosawa movie, he heard Tony's voice say – the guy had seen a lot of movies over the last three years) he stopped at the gift shop and picked up a copy of Blackjack the Barry way. Mr Barry, the blurb informed him, was a legend at the semi-circular table, one of the few who had exploited the tiny edge that the player had over the house.

Don went to the nearest bar, ordered a beer and turned straight to the chapter on basic strategy. These were the ground rules. OK, he repeated to himself, his lips moving silently, you stand on seventeen or higher. Stand on a soft nineteen or twenty (he looked up soft in the glossary – it meant having an ace in the hand, which could count as eleven or one), stand on a pair of tens. Hit on twelve through sixteen, if the dealer is showing a seven through ace, and all totals five through eight.

He ran through it in his mind. So the dealer is showing a four on the face up card, he has, say, an eight and a six he should . . . shit, he looked at the book. Stand, he should stand.

After ten minutes he slipped the book into his pocket, drained the glass and went in search of a Blackjack table. There was nothing like on-the-job training.

The first step into the main room at any casino is always a moment of transition. Don knew this. Outside the line where the carpet changed colour, that was where money meant something. In here, it was just a unit of counting, its significance negated until you stepped back out and realised exactly what you had done. Not him. He wouldn't fall for that money-is-just-how-we-keep-score bullshit. Hundred bucks and he was gone. But he examined the odd feeling in his chest, turned it over in his mind, pulled it up where he could mentally examine it. Optimism. That's what it was. Optimism. He felt . . . well, Tony was right on the money, he felt lucky after all.

He squeezed his way through the rows of video poker games and into the Blackjack pit. It was late afternoon, most tables had just one or two players. He would prefer to make a fool of himself solo, but with no option he slid into first base on a ten dollar minimum table with a woman dealer, about thirty, with a friendly face. Eva, the badge said. He looked at the writing on the green surface: 'Black Jack pays 3 to 2.' Well, so far so good, he knew what that meant.

It also warned: 'Dealer must draw to 16 and stand on all 17s.' All seventeens. Hmm. That included a soft seventeen, he was pleased with himself to note. Don waited for his fellow player, an older Oriental woman, maybe a Filipina, to finish her hand. She didn't look up as the dealer changed his chips, shuffled the cards, loaded eight decks into the shoe, extracted the burn card, discarded it and began. He felt his heart take a hit of adrenaline and flutter with expectation.

Don glanced at the cards in front of him. Dealer had eight showing, her hole card face down. He had two eights. Two eights. He fingered the book in his pocket, but pulling it out and leafing through it was out of the question. He hit. A ten. Bust. The cards blurred away as the dealer clawed the humiliating hand back. The Oriental woman tutted, but when he looked over she was still gazing down at her hand. She got a three. Nineteen. The dealer flipped over her cards, seventeen. Dealer had to stand, it said so on the table. His tutting companion had won.

Split them. He should have split the eights. That was what the pursed lips of the lady meant. He looked at the dealer who kept the same pleasant expression throughout, no emotion either way. She might have been thinking – this guy is playing like a jerk, but none of this would get out on to her face. Then she leant over and said 'Next time, you should split the eights,' and he made a mental note to toke her.

He didn't get the chance. Forty minutes later, despite a few more nuggets of advice, his last chip went.

Don drained the last of his comp beer and nodded to the Oriental woman, who scooped up her chips and fell in beside him.

'First time, eh?'

'That obvious?'

'As a neon sign,' she said and laughed. 'Takes insurance. Doesn't split aces and eights. Hits on a soft nineteen. Read the dealer card better. You always assume the hole card – the face down card – is a ten. Always. And lean to count.'

'Count?' He looked down at her, trying to guess her age. Judging by the fine lines around her eyes, she could be forty-five, but she could easily be a decade older.

'Count cards.'

'It's illegal isn't it?'

She laughed again: 'If it is, so is thinking. The casinos want you to think it is illegal. They don't like it. It doesn't mean it's illegal. Anyway, they can't bar you for it in Atlantic City. That *is* illegal. And that book,' she patted his pocket, 'rubbish. You want Renan's book. Blackjack Supreme.'

'I'll get it.'

'Not here you won't. They only sell the books in the gift shop that sucker you. Barry's counting system is too complicated, so casinos love it. Renan uses a variation on the Red Seven. As simple as they ever get. Works for me. See you around.'

And she went off to the cage to cash up.

Don hesitated near the archway off the floor, where the colour shade of the carpet changed. You were either on the floor or off the floor. Don vacillated. Stepping over the line, he was out of the game. A hundred bucks down. He looked at his watch. Nearly six. People drifting in. OK, skip the insurance, which was the side bet you made when the dealer showed a ten face up, against he or she having Blackjack. Remember to split the pairs. Think hard and soft – that ace was the key. He would do better next time. He took out his wallet and pulled out the CB bank card. Mr Milne. He had given Ed the credit cards back in the Ironbound district, but not this. An ATM card. He fished in one of the pouches and brought out a scribble of numbers on a scrap of paper he had recovered from Mr Milne, the trunk man. Two that were obviously phones, one a cellular, but the two other four digit scribbles, they might just be the access number. What about . . .? A question began in his head. What about what? It finished. He worried too much.

He stepped up to the ATM and joined the line. There was a small notice above all the usual logos: 'five per cent transaction charge'. Great, punch in for a hundred bucks, get ninety five out. Instant tax.

Aware of the impatient bodies falling in behind him Don inserted the card, fully expecting it to be swallowed. He punched in the first number. Five, nine, zero, one. Incorrect code the screen admonished him. Try again. He punched in the second one. Incorrect code. Take your card. There was a huff from behind as he put it in the third time. His fingers hovered over the little silver buttons. Three strikes and out – if he got this wrong the machine swallowed the card. On a hunch he punched in the first two numbers of the top code, the last of the second. How much would he like? Two thousand dollars. The little screen blinked at him, asking him to wait. Hey, you're not Mr Milne, he half expected the display to say. Instead it glowed with a viridescent 'insufficient funds'. 'Try another sum?' It invited him.

'Hey, buddy, I think my dice are just going off the boil, what the fuck you doing? It's for withdrawals not deposits.' Don turned around and there was a little guy snarling at his waist, his features twisted in unnecessary hatred. Realising he had seventy, eighty pounds on him, and could swat him like a fly if he was so minded, he ignored him and tried a thousand.

The ATM clicked and whirred and out came the cash. He was in business. No insurance. Split the aces. Come on, come on.

He sat down at the same table and Eva, the dealer, gave him a wan back-already smile. The limit had gone up while he was away. Twenty-five dollars. Still, in for a dollar, in for a dime, or whatever the saying was. He hit the hostess for a bourbon, got his chips and began. It was like the tide coming in. Twenties, Blackjacks, pairs of aces, they slowly dragged more and more chips towards him. Eva pulled all the shitty numbers, fifteens and sixteens, the horse latitudes where the rules are becalmed. Then, as the pile peaked, the pull changed, first with a couple of pushes, where he and the dealer had exactly the same total, and the money stayed where it was, and then the plastic markers were plucked away again, by the dealer turning up two tens, Blackjack, soft twenties, and by him getting twenty two, twenty three, busting on what were originally ridiculously low cards, or watching a fifteen and sixteen, while Eva showed an ace. The basic strategy was letting him down, the statistics going through one of those wild, wilful phases where the cards don't know how they are meant to behave.

And as the house stole at his money – Mr Milne's money – he realised what he had done. ATM. The account active. He remembered those actions of an hour before as if it were a dream, a week-old dream. Not him, not Don, he wouldn't be so reckless. Surely the guys who tracked him down for the Barney's suits, surely they would watch the checking account. Shit, there was no way he could go back for the prostate results now. He hit on two sixes, watched a ten come out and continue the attrition. Down to a few bucks. What if alarms were ringing somewhere? Hey, this guy Milne – he just won't stay dead.

He stood, watched the dealer top his eighteen with two tens.

Stupid. There was something about this place. Something . . . where was the logic here? Pulling out that plastic card, reactivating the account, that was just dumb. And if anyone could spot dumb, it was him.

Stupid.

The dealer turned up another Blackjack.

He felt a hand on his shoulder.

Stupid.

'Hey, about the other night, coming over and . . . you know, pokin' my nose in.' Goodrich spread his arms out and hunched his shoulders. 'I went for a drink with Alice. Jeezus that woman can hold her liquor. Next day I've got this head you would not fucking believe. Now. What can I do for you?'

Ed said, 'Forget about it. Look, I need some stuff.'

'Stuff again, eh? More late night windows?'

'It's . . . a delicate matter.' Ed looked around the empty store as if their conversation could be interrupted any minute, and glanced anxiously at the TV camera slowly swivelling its black eye like some curious insect sniffing the air . . .

'Don't worry about that, there's never any tape in the fucking machine. Delicate? Delicate? You come to me with delicate? I mean, if it's delicate like, I need to sell my porno collection, then fine. If it's delicate like, I want to *star* in a porno movie – you best go see Alice or one of her sisters down there.'

'I want to buy.'

'Oh you want to *buy*? You want to buy something delicate.'

He remembered Bird's shopping list. 'A couple of shot-guns.'

The smile went from Goodrich's face. 'Shotguns? That's your idea of delicate?'

'And a pistol of some sort. A handgun.'

'Ah, a touch of finesse. We got a slight problem here. New Jersey pawnshops can't take firearms for cash. I got nothing to sell you that's been hocked. But I know a licensed gun dealer, he can get you stuff. But you got some paper-work?'

'Like what?'

'Like a Brady application. But, you know it's a formality, no problem. They ask why you want it—'

'Been some robberies in the cabs.'

'OK, DGU. Defensive Gun Use? Fine. You just gotta make it sound good, know the language. A year ago there wouldn't have been any of this bullshit. Fuckin' ATF, federal employees of the month, they make it all paperwork, paperwork. And then they run a check on you, criminal record and—'

Ed flinched. 'Wait. They check your what?'

'If you ever been inside, in trouble, you know . . . I quote, "he or she must be of good character, must not be a convicted felon, substance abuser or suffering from mental illness . . ."' Goodrich looked at him. 'What? What? That a problem, Ed?'

Ed nodded.

'You been inside? Ed Behr, master-fuckin'-criminal cabbie? What was it? Not turning on the meter? Over-charging? Throwing a lousy tip back at a customer? What?'

Ed didn't know why he said the next words. Maybe it was all those years of being the soft butt of jokes like that one. Old Ed, not capable of anything. So he said, straight out: 'I killed somebody.'

'Fuck.'

He regretted it at once, felt his feet go into reverse and the backpedal start. 'Well, kinda. But people died, so you can call it what you want.' He gave Goodrich the outline. About alley-o being banned, about bored kids hanging around on bridges. 'It began with spitting, you know like kids do. Watching it slither down, ten points for a roof, five for a trunk – that kind of thing. Then baseballs. And then . . . someone came up with the idea of pushing a cinder block over the edge.'

'Jesus,' said Goodrich.

'And one time, it . . . it hit some people. Killed them – the driver, everyone.'

'But it was like an accident, yeah? I mean – worse things than that have happened. Littleton.'

Ed shrugged. 'The courts didn't see it that way.'

Goodrich blew his cheeks out. 'Well, OK, let's worry about the legal shit in a minute. How many shotguns?'

'Two. And some double-o bucks.'

'Jeez – you planning on knocking down some walls? I know where I can get some pumps. Good shit.'

He thought about Tony's shakes. 'You got an auto?'

Goodrich shook his head. 'Nah. Not one I'd pass on to yous anyways. Just some Italian rubbish. I mean, don't get me wrong, there are good Italians, but not this stuff.'

'OK, pumps it is.' Tony would have to manage. With a bit of luck nobody was going to be firing anything much.

'Good. I gotta level with you, we gotta break the law here, technically. Seein' as you are resident in New Jersey, you need a permit for the handgun and an ID card for the shots. Now I can get hold of those. I gotta guy in Virginia, where things ain't so tight. He can get you the pistol and the documentation. For a price.'

'How much?'

'Like I say, for a price. I gotta negotiate. The problem is, the documentation will stand a casual look-over from a cop. ATF or state police run the numbers, though, shit hits the fan with a big plop. You know what I'm saying?'

'You're saying you don't want your name in the frame.'

'I'm saying my friend would not take kindly to any kind of . . . disclosure.'

'Right. I see. You can trust me.'

'I hope so, pal. This is ten years, y'know? Federal offence.'

'I know what you're saying. I appreciate what you're doin'.'

'Right. Just as long as you realise . . . this ain't like getting a parking ticket fixed. OK?'

'OK.'

'So . . . you did time you say?'

Stupid, stupid, stupid. Should have canned that urge to shock. 'I was a kid. It was manslaughter really.'

'A kid? Well they scrap juvey records after seven or eight years, don't they? I mean, there is, like, a statute of limitations on what you do as a kid.'

'I was in Boxgrove. You know? The Box? The one that went from juvee to adult. I ain't so sure the same rules applied.'

'The Box? No shit? Well like I said. I could see my man in Virginia. Pay my gas and fifty bucks on top, and you will be fully functional. Six hundred bucks tops for the pistol, coupla hundred each for the shots. Three for the documents. Maybe a little more. Two days. Maybe three.'

'Sounds good. But two days. Not three.'

'Two. OK. What do you want? What kind of hand gun?'

Ed was hardly a regular subscriber to *Guns & Ammo*, but he knew he needed something big. You got to make the other guy take notice. 'A .45. The automatic kind.'

'Nah. Colt pulled outta consumer guns back in '99, after all those lawsuits. Anyway, it was a fuckin' dinosaur. You want something light and modern, easily concealed – which, by the way, is also against the law in this fuckin' state – but capable of stopping some slimeball trying to roll you. An H&K maybe. A Sig or a Glock. Something really useful. What you need, Ed, is a nine mil.'

Up at the Silk Tiger, the high-rollers' restaurant at The Palace, Tony looked at his steak appreciatively, afraid to cut into it, as if the anticipation would evaporate, that the taste could not possibly live up to the hype his saliva was generating.

Don, eating with the heartiness of a reprieved man, sucked up some of his linguine with a loud slurp. 'You going to eat that or fuck it?'

'You know, it's a c-c-close call.' He cut a thin sliver off and savoured it. Not bad. The maître d' came over with the Oregon Pinot Tony had ordered. Tony proceeded to slice the meat into portions so he could eat with his fork in his right hand.

'You know only assholes pay in this place. The name of the game is to get comped,' said Don looking around at the tables of happy shiny people, skin and eyes flushed with a mixture of alcohol and excitement.

Tony laughed. 'Yeah, and you only get co-co-comped if you lose a lot of money. Oh, I'm forgetting – you did lose a lot of money. You didn't look much like hustling a comp when I put my hand on your shoulder. Thought you were going to swallow your t-t-t-tongue.'

Don hadn't told him where he had got the money. Or

how much was involved. He had broken up the card when they got off the floor, and dumped it and the Barry book in the trash can, feeling grateful to be alive. 'So, what are your thoughts now?' asked Don, hoping to move on from the embarrassment of his lapse.

Tony stroked his darkening beard. He was beginning to look like a swarthy pirate. It couldn't hide the little nervous ripples which were running up his cheek, though. 'About?'

'Ed and Lester.'

'Damn, this is a good piece of steer. Why?' He waved his fork and Don watched the end blur, wondering if he could hold a gun steadier.

Don reached over and stopped Tony's hand as it rose up towards his mouth, the strip of meat quivering on the end of his fork. 'You heard about that Mad Cow shit they had over in England?'

'Yeah? So what? This is T-T-T-Texan.'

'Just want you to be sure of the facts. Scary stuff. And you know why they won't take US beef in Europe?'

'Jealousy?'

'Hormones, pal, hormones. Think about what you eating. Anyway, Ed and Lester.'

Tony thought for a moment. 'No, I don't g-g-g-get it.'

'Like this is suicide. Going up against a bunch of professionals, with one fat cabbie, a tiny retard, a strung out Piney and . . .'

'And a born pessimist.'

'Fatalist.'

Tony paused before he answered, ordering his thoughts. His voice was lowered, more considered, more adult than usual. 'OK. T-t-t-tell you something else that worries me.'

'What? Billy?'

'Billy? L-Look I was the one who th-th-thought we should have thrown him to the fuckin' wolves, yeah? Hittin' Billy is long overdue, you ask me. No, it's the money. A million dollars isn't a lot of m-m-m-money any more. Something like one in five hundred people in this country are m-m-m-millionaires.'

'So?'

'So what if Ed wants to k-k-k-keep it all for himself?'

Don scratched under his chin with his free hand, looking pensive. How did he come to this one, again? He couldn't quite recall how he ended up from a restaurant in the Ironbound district to thinking about rousting an old friend for a million or so bucks. One million four ways wasn't really enough. But maybe it'd be more. Would Ed turn on them if it wasn't? He tried to imagine what an Ed double-cross would look like. Then he said: 'Nah – he wants to go into the apartment, remember? He's as fuckin' crazy as the rest of us.'

'Oh, yeah. Amen to that.' Tony glanced down at Don's hand, still clamped onto his wrist. One eyelid flickered as he looked up. 'Now can I eat this piece of steak before it grows its hoofs back and g-g-g-gallops off? Thanks.'

He started chewing and said, 'OK, one other thing. Honey.'

'Honey?'

'Yeah. Ed t-talk to you about her?'

'I know he's got this thing for her still.'

Tony nodded. 'Let me ask you something – she ever put her hand in your pants and, you know, j-j-j-jerk you off?'

Don looked a little embarrassed. 'Well—'

'Yes or n-n-no?'

'Uh. Yes and no. She did it, but I . . . I couldn't – well. It was broad daylight . . . I . . . Yeah. I guess.'

'And me. She did me. It was like her p-p-party piece.'

'You told him?' asked Don with concern in his voice.

Tony swallowed the last of the steak. 'Not me. And if *you*

do you better d-d-d-d-duck. You shouldn't mess with a man's dreams.'

THIRTY-SEVEN

Friday December 13

The phone rang and she thought it would either be Billy or Matt. No, not Billy. Wrong Friday. So Matt. Strange how life seemed brighter now he was on the scene. All she had to do was make sure that he stayed on the scene.

'Honey?'

'Yeeeaah.' Didn't recognise the voice.

'It's me.'

'Yeah?'

'The guy who e-mailed you?'

Her heart gave a thump. One of them had tracked her down. 'Wh-which one exactly?'

'Oh come on Honey, take a guess.'

He sounded normal enough. 'Hey, listen, I get a lot of e-mails. I mean, thousands.'

'I bet you do. I bet you do. Wanna clue?'

'Sure.'

He began to sing, a high, whiny voice. 'A four-legged friend, a four legged friend, he'll never let you down . . .'

She remembered the e-mails about the horse, and now the banner was on her page, this guy obviously thought it was in response to his missives.

'Oh, right, got you, er . . .'

'Call me Alan.'

'Alan. Right. Listen, Al—'

'Alan you cumsucking slut. Alan. Not Al. Alan.'

Honey began to think as fast as she could. Where would

he be calling from? Could she trace him through the phone company? She could imagine the conversation. Hello, I earn my living as an on-line tramp, and I'm getting nuisance calls. Hello? Hello?

So she said: 'Alan, how did you get my number?'

'Oh, Honey, it wasn't hard. Now area code 515 . . . that's in New Jersey isn't it.'

'Alan, I have to go.'

'So I must be real close to you. I am in Pennsylvania.'

'Alan, I have to go. Trigger is just coming up in the elevator.'

She slammed the phone down hard and then took it off the hook. OK, two things. Call Jerry and chew the nuts off him. Two, get the number changed and maybe get that call traced. Oh, and three. Buy a gun.

'It is traditional that we use fruit for this. One of those little rituals handed down over generations,' Goodrich winked to let Ed know he was kidding.

They were on the edge of the Wharton State Forest in a clearing surrounded by towering pines. The ground was brown and springy underneath their feet, dense with slow-rotting pine needles, exuding a rich smell, at once clean and oddly putrid.

The pair had walked almost a mile from the road, a distance Ed could not have managed with quite such alacrity a couple of weeks previously. The car was pulled onto the shoulder and they set off with their bags, first through waist-high brush, and then spindly, etiolated trees, before the fatter, healthier brethren appeared, bearing down on them, cocooning them, muffling all the sounds.

They had left Alice in the car, and Ed was beginning to wonder whether Goodrich was pimping her. When he walked into the store, they had been arguing, and

Goodrich had a gold ring in his hand. 'Hey, I hope you got this cleaned,' he had said, winking at Ed. 'It ain't that one,' insisted Alice. 'Guy ain't got no cash to pay me – you know, I admit, I broke the golden rule, I didn't do CBD. Cash Before Delivery. But I swear he was as surprised as I was when his wallet was empty. So I took his ring. Fuck, he's divorced anyways, only kept it out of sentiment.'

Well, maybe he was wrong. Maybe she was just trying to hock it. But there was no doubt Goodrich had a proprietorial air about him when she was around. Goodrich had given her fifty bucks – the price of turning a trick – and she had decided to come for a ride in the country, afternoons being kind of slow, she explained. Once she saw the undergrowth they were expected to walk through, and looked at the heels she had on, she decided to stay in the car and re-do her nails, which was fine with Ed. The fewer who knew what was going on the better.

Goodrich put his backpack down and took out six oranges and bounced his way across the sprung forest floor to a fallen log at the far end of the clearing. He arranged the fruit in a line.

From the pack he pulled Ed's new gun. Even in the half-light of the clearing its finish glinted coldly yet seductively. 'This is a Spitfire. Not your average piece of junk, as you will have guessed from the price. It is basically a Czech CZ75 re-cast in stainless steel. It is light, strong, with a great slide design and holds fifteen rounds. Grandfathered of course – the mag was made before the high capacity ban, so legal, y'know? Chambered for the nine millimetre Parabellum. Two safety catches, one on either side of the butt, so it can be used by either hand. What's the word? Ambidextrous. Yeah, I'd give my right arm to be ambidextrous. That's a joke, Ed. Anyway, used by some European cops, pretty

rare over here. But a beauty. Won't have any trouble selling
it on when you're done with it at damn close to what you
paid. Here.'

Ed took it in his hand and curled his fingers around the
grip, but the weapon seemed to take them and rearrange
them, placing them just right, a fraction of an inch down
here, up there, so suddenly it didn't feel awkward or alien,
but like a telephone or a handlebar, something you held
naturally. Ergonomic, that was the word he suddenly
remembered.

'How's it feel?'

'Good.'

Goodrich pointed at the fruit, which suddenly seemed
like tiny orange specks to Ed. 'OK, pull back the slide to
chamber a round. Yeah, like that. Now these babies are used
as target pistols as well as combat, so you put your arm up
and point and the bullet will pretty much go where you aim.
Hold on.' He took out two pairs of ear defenders and slipped
one set over Ed's head, then his own.

Ed swung up the gun.

'Use two hands. Hold your wrist. I know it feels kind of
jerky, like you been watching too many SWAT movies, but
it works. OK, in your own time. I ain't going to give you all
that squeeeeze shit, let's see how you do.'

The suppressed explosion came through the defenders as
Ed pulled the trigger. They watched the first orange zip
away into the undergrowth as if it had been pulled on a
cord. The second citrus fruit launched itself into the air in a
shower of wood splinters as the round thudded between its
base and the tree. The third simply exploded into a mush of
skin and pulp, leaving a fine mist settling on the tree, like a
sweet rain.

Goodrich just shook his head in disbelief. 'Fuck, who
needs a juicer? Looks like we got us a natural, Ed.'

Ed couldn't help himself. Despite his best efforts, a lopsided smile spread across his face.

In fact Jimmy Jazz had taught him to shoot, out in the yard on Sunday mornings. Jimmy kept a collection of BBs, .177s and .22s, nothing fancy, but ideal for taking pops at tins too dented for even Jimmy to sell at a discount.

'You know why I learned to shoot?' he used to explain over and over again. 'Fairgrounds. They used to hate it when you could go up to the booth and damn near clean 'em out. Ended up getting banned from some ranges – just like they ban winners from casinos in some towns. Hardly seems fair does it? Once in a while, guy comes along who can play the game and what do they say? Whoa, sorry – you're too good. You see, on those shooting galleries, you got two problems. Firstly the guns are shit, but you know, you can compensate for that – just ignore the sights for one. And two, the targets. Like if it's a duck? with a bullseye? Well you see those ducks are hinged and weighted and shit, so you can hit them one spot – bing, they go over. Anywhere else, no deal. Now you can be sure the centre of the target and this little g-spot . . . you know what a g-spot is? No, well, this little place, and the middle of the target, they ain't one an' the same. No way. But you can't help aiming for it. So you see these people thinking, goddamn I hit the bullseye that time, but it ain't gone over. Then they give up. Me, I would spend two, three dollars, just checking out the rifle or pistol, maybe changing it, and then I'd concentrate on finding the real centre, the sweet spot. Once I had them suckers pegged, then I'd clean up. I mean, often spend ten bucks for some big cuddly toy that wasn't worth two, but it was the thrill of the chase, you know what I am saying?'

Thrill of the chase, yeah. He looked at the smoke lazily curling out of the barrel of the Spitfire, and at Goodrich's admiring ear-to-ear grin. He thought of that million dollars in a trunk, and going after a blonde girl. The thrill of the chase.

THIRTY-EIGHT

Tuesday December 17

There were few things that pleased Harold Wheeler more than seeing a woman walk into his gunshop. Truth be told, Barrels of Fun wasn't always that much fun, but the little blonde looked set to brighten up his day no end. And more than that, it was a very definite potential sale. As that circular from the National Association of Federally Licensed Firearms Dealers pointed out, around twenty-nine per cent of men were interested in owning a gun, but twenty-eight percent of them already had one. With women it was nineteen percent wanted but only nine percent owned – the gap between the wants and haves had to be closed.

It was why he had that poster on the wall of the woman in the bedroom alone, and the big shadow. 'It's late. Your husband is away. The phone is dead. Who you going to call? Try your two best friends – Mr Smith and Mr Wesson.'

'Hi, honey,' Harold said to the woman.

She looked up with a start, and he wondered what had made her so jittery. Maybe a rape victim, maybe the poster was too late. Best tread carefully. 'What can I do for you, ma'am?'

'I'd like ten pounds of potatoes and a quart of milk.'

Harold looked at her quizzically. 'Ma'am this is a gunshop—'

'I know it's a fuckin' gunshop,' she snapped. 'I want a gun.'

'Oh. Yeah. OK, let's see. I take it you want a purse gun? Something a little fancy?'

'No. Not pearl handles and scrolling. I want a gun, not a powder compact that also shoots bullets.'

'OK.' Harold scratched his head. 'Can I see your hands?'

She held them out. Small, well manicured, not shaking.

He reached down under the counter to the locked trays. 'I got a Lady Derringer Mark Two—'

'No.'

'No?'

'A gun. G-U-N. Not a piece of jewellery. Imagine I am six-three with a four day growth of beard. What would you sell me then? Not a Derringer.'

'With all due respect, ma'am, it's got to be light for—'

'I'll have something in polypropylene or whatever it is.'

'OK, OK. I got something that might interest you. Expensive though.'

'Try me.'

Harold went out the back and opened the safe, taking out one of the three really top-end pistols he kept in stock. If he could sell this, he could shut up shop for the rest of the day.

He put the polished wooden box on the table, spun it so it faced her and lifted the lid, waiting to see the expression of joy as the weapon, sitting snug in its green felt, was revealed. Not a muscle moved in her face.

'Handsome devil isn't it?'

'Hmmmm. May I?'

'Go right ahead.'

She picked up the pistol, checked the safeties, and weighed it in her hands.

'Polymer frame,' said Harold breathlessly, 'Walther PP9. Three safeties, adjustable grip for different hand sizes, single or double action, cocking and loaded chamber indicator – I mean all those safety features any gun should have. German.

Gun Tests magazine said better than the Glock and H&K for workmanship. Chambered for the Smith & Wesson .40. Also comes in nine millimetre, but I'm an S&W man myself.'

'Well I'm an S&M woman now and then. How much?'

Harold wasn't sure he heard properly but said: 'Seven ninety-nine is recommended retail. I can let it go for seven plus tax. I'll throw in a box of ammo. I said it was expensive, but resale value's real high—'

'I'll take it. Put it on a Visa?'

Harold tried to keep the quiver from his voice: 'Fine. But we got some paperwork first.'

'Paperwork?' she demanded,

'Er . . . yeah. The Brady Check?' The investigation period had been reintroduced after the on-the-spot computer background check had been found to be too prone to errors. 'Five days. While they run your name through the files.'

'Files?'

'Police. Feds. See if you a convicted felon or mentally unstable. I mean, I know you're not wacko, but these fuckin' – pardon my language – these ATF guys got us by the balls.'

She tutted. Still, she had no record anywhere, so it was little more than a nuisance. 'No way round this? For cash?

Harold looked at the camera and remembered that ATF man who came last time he bent the rules. Didn't want to see him again. 'No, ma'am. You can pick it up Saturday, though.'

She threw the card down on the counter top. 'Let's hope nothing happens before Saturday, then, huh?'

Ed drove them out to the edge of the forest, away from the highway, not too far from where he had had the pistol practice. Lester was in the front seat next to him, blinking like he hadn't seen too much daylight for the last few years. Which was close to the truth. Ed was surprised he could still focus at a distance of more than two feet, the gap between him and the TV screen. Don was in the back, mumbling. He didn't like being in the back. He had decided he had motion sickness.

They pulled in at a gas station and Ed swapped with Lester, placing a cushion on the seat so he could see over the wheel. A few feeble snow flurries were whirling round the car as he sprinted round the front and jumped in the passenger side. He turned the heating up and rubbed his hands. Lester climbed in and scrunched down on his seat.

'You know this is illegal?' said Don.

'And robbing a million dollars isn't?' replied Ed.

Don said, as if Lester wasn't there, 'He never learned to drive. He's got no licence. You can hardly claim running little cars over the rooftops of Milan—'

'Turin,' said Lester.

'Where-fuckin'-ever – Christ you and Tony'll get on well. Turin, running little cars over the rooftops of Turin in a computer game doesn't exactly qualify as a driving exam in this state. Or any other as far as I know.'

Ed glared at him. 'Lester will do just fine. Won't you Les? Yeah, see? OK, so it's a computer game – but the principles are the same.'

Don hunkered down in his seat. 'Yeah, well tell that to the Highway Patrol.'

'There won't be any Highway Patrol where we are going. OK, Lester, you ready?'

Lester nodded.

'And remember, no Wild Cards here. You don't have to hit pedestrians just in case they're armed and dangerous. Shall we go?'

The squeal of tires must have been heard in Baltimore. Don felt himself submarine, slipping off the seat and onto the floor. Ed was pinned back in his seat, his face almost showing G-force marks as they left the station in an almighty plume of dust.

'Left. Left. LEFT,' shouted Ed and the car performed a four-wheel drift, threatening to enter the two-lane blacktop sideways, before righting itself. The engine skipped a beat, then caught and the car plunged on, the trees seeming inches from the windows, a blurred curtain of hard, unyielding timber on either side. They went straight over the first crossroads, causing a small truck to take off six months' worth of brake pads, and powered over the hill in front, the car leaving the ground, almost flying for a stomach-dropping moment, before it hit the ground with a jarring thud as the shocks bottomed out.

Lester overdid the brakes on the next bend, and the Chevy snaked, brushing the undergrowth, and there was a loud clang as the tail caught something, tearing out a light housing. Back on the throttle the rear was wrenched into reluctant line, the needle hitting ninety, on a road where thirty was considered reckless. Ed managed to get his feet on the dash to brace himself and looked over at Lester, who, shrunk down behind the wheel, had an expression of fierce concentration on his face, the tendons and veins in his neck etched out of the flesh. But most of all, he had a big smile across his face, which didn't deviate even as he took a corner improbably fast, losing the front end in twigs and branches until he forced it back on the road. Ten point penalty, thought Ed. He can't tell the difference between this and the screen game.

Don managed to struggle up from the back onto his seat, in time to watch Lester take a switchback in a sickening slaloming motion, slamming their heads from side to side. There was a loud Doppler effect as a pickup leant on his horn, but it was gone in a fraction of a second, receding in Lester's rearview mirror. Don managed to grasp the back of the passenger seat and lean over to Ed. 'For fuck's sake,' he yelled above the noise, 'Tell him he's got the gig.'

Anne ignored the chill air and the car fumes and leant on the rails of the terrace, six storeys above the street. She looked across at Carnegie Hall, and imagined having the view on the night of a big concert, watching the limos and the flashguns going off, staring down with a glass of champagne in her hand, imperiously perched above the seething masses. It felt good.

She was aware of Sarah behind her. 'What do you think?'

'I think,' she said slowly, 'you are a wicked temptress. You come here and lay out your goods, roll over and say, Here, take me I'm yours.'

'For a price, please – you don't get this for free.'

Anne looked back in at the living room, bare now, but she mentally populated it with furniture: an Ashdown sofa here, an Eames chair there, maybe even a Beetree coffee table, and an antique rug over the floor. 'How much is it again?'

'You *know* how much it is. Come on, Billy must have the money.'

'Not Billy,' she looked back over at the line of yellow roofs. She would put money on the fact that if she rushed down now to get one of the cabs they would all have evaporated. 'Big Billy.'

'Well, come on then. Fuck it out of him.

'*Sarah*.'

'Hey, don't tell me you never thought about it. You see it on the talk shows all the time – "I screwed my father-in-law 'cause he was more of a man than my husband."'

Anne felt herself go red. Again. 'It's a disgusting idea.'

'No it isn't. He's quite a handsome old man. In good shape. I wouldn't say no. If I weren't happily married.'

Anne raised an eyebrow.

'Well, most days I am.'

'I am not about to do that just for a fancy apartment.'

'Just for a fancy apartment? Don't blaspheme. This is my bread and butter you are talking about. And maybe yours. Look, you get this place, this is collateral. Little Billy can do what he wants, bang who he wants, get sucked dry by half the cocktail waitresses in New Jersey, but you get to hang onto the real estate. I reckon, you get to the truth, then use the leverage . . . you could have all this.'

'And if Billy is Mr Clean?'

'Oh, don't disappoint me now, Anne. I thought I had a sale.' She laughed and went back inside. Sometimes Anne wondered if there was anywhere her friend drew the line when it came to closing a deal. She watched the little figures on the sidewalk below and fought back the impulse to tip her glass over, to watch the champagne fall through the air, stretching into a fine stream, exploding in a mass of bubbles on one of the heads below. She stood up, shocked at the image, and went to rejoin Sarah, who was struggling with another bottle. It was, in truth, too good to waste on childish games.

the e-mailSender: jfutters@MailServe.com.
Received: from zap.mail.fastmail.net (post-10.mail.qik.com [194.217.242.39])
by dub-img-5.zip.com (8.8.6/8.8.6/2.10) with SMTP id EAA24765
for honicam.adult.net.com>; Dec 17 From:
jfutters@compuserve.com Received: from MailServe.com ([158.152.210.188])
by post.mail.adult.net.net id aa1009592;
Message-Id: <zzp.1120@fastmail.com
Content-Type: text/plain; charset=ISO-8859-1

Content-transfer-encoding: quoted-printable
X-Mailer: TFS Gateway
/3000000000/300102811/300102841/300202356/

Message:
I think you are a hussy
But I love your pussy
Sometimes I wear Stüssy
While I'm jacking off.
Getting better, eh?

Honey closed down the file on the last of twenty-five messages. It had been several days since she read them, and they were getting fewer. She knew she must be losing customers now, that logging on time after time and seeing a blank screen or a holding tape would drive them away. But Alan the horse freak had rather blunted her appetite. He hadn't called again, or e-mailed, so maybe she had scared him away. The number was due to change at the weekend, and her gun – her very, very expensive gun – would be legal. She must go and shoot at a range, it was a long time since she had pulled a trigger.

Billy hadn't messaged either. She knew she would see him in a few days. It was a strange feeling. Switching from one man to another. She knew she could do it with both, because they seemed to occupy different niches for her – shit, it wouldn't be the first time she'd had multiple partners – but she also knew that if she were to stand a chance with Matt for anything other than a short-term fuck, she had to put all her attention into it. Nurture it, not let it slide away.

So she had to choose. Play the whore, the kept woman, the cyberslut, or come out and play with the big boys. Risk a real relationship for once. It wasn't much of a contest, really.

* * *

None of them had noticed the route that Lester had taken, it was a succession of lefts and rights and bumps and cross-roads, with them yelling at him that it was fine, he could do it. Yes, going up on two wheels was mightily impressive, as was getting the whole car to lift clear of the road by hitting the ruts at close to eighty but could he please *stop now*.

And when he finally slewed the car to a halt and flicked off the ignition and the silence settled around them, they all looked over at the once familiar gateway with something approaching awe. Ed glanced at Lester, but he was as confused as the others. This had not been deliberate. Somewhere in the last twenty minutes of hard driving, he had traced a line, like one of those kids' mazes – doggy needs to get to the bone, can you show him the way? – he had drawn a route through the spidery roads of the Barrens and come up here.

Ed stepped out and heard someone follow him. Don. Lester didn't move, his hands were gripping the wheel, the knuckles white. The collection of buildings was slowly being reclaimed by the forest. This was once a huge clearing, with no bushes within thirty yards of what had been a very impressive fence, or rather series of fences. Most of them had gone when they had tried to find other uses for the buildings – nobody had wanted to take over something that still looked like a correctional facility.

But the truth was that nobody wanted the site no matter how much they spruced it up, put in planters and lawns. It was tainted. The agriculture people had stored vehicles for a while, but they found the cost of maintenance too high. Now the once-brutal brick arch looked terribly forlorn, with its guard tower missing, and a few strands of wire the only evidence of the high-intensity lamps that had once festooned it. Ed approached slowly, the hard crust of frozen topsoil crunching under his feet. He mentally ticked off the buildings as he recognised them – reception, the lecture hall, the gym, then the various houses that kept the inmates, and the long, low line of shower blocks. But as he got closer he began to see that the appearance of completeness was deceptive. Each unit had been systematically gutted, of glass, timber, electrics. The locals had come in and fallen on the place, like ants on a struggling cricket, tearing the heart out of it until all that was left was the shell. He had hated this place, or what it represented, for so long that he was surprised to find himself almost sorry for it, as if it had been raped. Yeah, well, it deserved nothing less.

Ed wondered if those camps you read about in Germany and Poland had this feeling, this aura. You come to them and you can feel the systematic evil; that something went on in there. Oh, not like those camps maybe, not in the same league, but still something designed to strip you of your humanity. Take you down and down until all you had was that little animal buried inside you. Except by the time the likes of Danny Stowe had finished with you, it had changed places, the animal was on the outside and who you were was buried deep, deep inside. He was aware of Don behind him, the big man breathing hard and heavy as if he had run all the way here. Actually, that might have been easier on the constitution, all things considered.

And finally his eyes were drawn to it, set way back: Hollingshead, the house named for the man who invented the drive-in. He wondered what Mr Hollingshead would think if he knew he also lent his name to the systematic degradation of Lester.

Ed remembered the dead driver of the car, Billy and how he and Lester had brought them to this place.

Don just said; 'All roads lead to Boxgrove, eh?'

Ed thought again about Billy and his cashmere coats and

platinum Amex. And then he flashed on Honey, too. Get the money, find her, in that order. Stop fuckin' daydreaming for once. Find her. 'I guess. Let's go home. We got work to do.'

THIRTY NINE

Thursday December 19

Ed woke at two in the morning, his reflexes suddenly up and running. Something had disturbed him, penetrated his brain, and the systems had fired up even before his higher centres had roused themselves. He strained his ears, but the only sound was a faint groaning of metal mesh as the fence contorted in the wind.

He pushed himself off the bed, his arms aching, rubbing his eyes, the sleep packing up and marching off. He knew it wouldn't be coming back that night. He had done an hour at the M&M gym, being cajoled and insulted, and all it had given him was sore muscles. And he thought exercise was meant to make you sleep better.

He went through to the lounge, heading for the kitchen. As usual Lester hadn't made it to his bed again. Playing the game until he had dropped, he had fallen asleep in the Laz-e-Boy, a blanket pulled over him, illuminated by the small lamp in the corner he insisted stay on. Ed stopped and looked down at the open-mouthed face, the lids twitching as the eyes underneath darted frantically from side to side, following God knew what sort of action.

Hardly sleeping beauty, Ed had to admit, but it was a giant leap forward when he had agreed to drive the car – a real car – for them, even if he had nearly killed Don and him. He hadn't even mentioned Boxgrove, just meekly moved over when Ed said he would drive them back. Ed wondered how much he was really taking in, if he understood what was going down.

And that was because of Boxgrove. It started with the best intentions and degenerated into a monstrous parody, a game of snakes and ladders where some people, like Lester, only hit snake after snake. Lester must have had an invisible – to them at least – sign saying 'victimise me' on his head, because he brought out the worst in everyone. It was as if they couldn't help themselves. Something about the eagerness to please, to be part of the gang, that exuded from him would infuriate prisoner and guard alike. And so the degrading game began, trying to make sure Lester never got the privileges, always languished at zero or minus one in the hierarchy of concessions.

Ed had found Stowe and the others one day forcing a bar of the industrial strength soap they used in the showers down Lester's throat. Two of them had grabbed him to hold him back. Someone else was painting Lester with the thick grease they lubricated machines in the machine shop with.

Ed heard one of them say something about fetching a baseball bat when he broke free and rushed over to try and do something.

Danny Stowe had grabbed him round the neck, slapped him about. Ed fought back, getting a good one in the eye. He hadn't put on so much weight then, could still bob and weave, so he broke free and smacked Stowe a few times before they grabbed him from behind again.

When Ed wouldn't stop shouting for help they had dragged him over to the wall and hammered his head against a faucet for one, two, three, four . . . the blows kept coming, and blackness finally came when his hair was soaked and matted with blood. As he went out he could hear Lester's screams, his pleas for help, hear him calling his name, but there was nothing he could do as he slid down the wall to the floor. Someone turned on the shower, and he lay there for a long time, the water swirling around him, tinged pink.

Lester had not gone then. Not that day. He had recovered well. Wouldn't even talk about it. But in retrospect it was like he had been at the top of a long ramp, and that day with the soap, and maybe the bat, Ed never found out, it had given him the push that would eventually send him sliding down into whatever little world he had been locked in ever since.

There was a look, maybe all institutions have it, thought Ed, but the Box Face was how you knew a long-term inmate. The animation leaves the face, the stare becomes cold, devoid of meaning, you betray nothing, no matter what they are doing to you. Not fear, not hatred, not pride, certainly not anything like love or friendship. Lester developed the ultimate Box Face. Still had it, really.

Ed allowed himself to play What If. What if he got four hundred thousand. They could get out of here, out of the country, somewhere warm. And get him a nurse, a helper, someone to bring himself out of his shell, maybe. If he still needed one. Because Lester agreeing to be part of this, that was a new sign. Something had penetrated the cotton wool, had flicked a neural switch, had caused synapses to spark again, chemicals to flow, emotions to register. And that was a victory, and maybe that was all he needed from this.

Ed wanted a victory right now.

He went into the kitchen and made himself a turkey and bacon sandwich with extra mayo and coffee, went back into the living room and dragged the television away from Lester and put it on with the volume down. She was there. Sitting in the bath. Honey. As gorgeous as ever, that big smile, those wonderful tits. She radiated joy. He shook his head. It was her. He must be hallucinating. He flicked channels with the remote, thinking maybe she was on every channel, such was the power of suggestion, but she wasn't there. Back again. Honey. And some guy he vaguely recognised.

Maybe she had made it as an actress after all. He rummaged around for the *TV Guide*, found it under Lester, didn't care about waking him. He looked at the clock. Two forty-five. Movie. Man Who Fell To Earth. David Bowie and Candy Clark. Her again. He remembered her from American Graffiti, he always told Honey she looked like her. Now it turned out Honey had the same morals as that character. What was her name? Debbie, Debbie he was sure. No, mustn't judge on hearsay, not on what Ruby said. Let's hear what Honey has to say.

He sat back down and he could see the differences now, the thinner mouth, eyes set closer, the different shade of blonde. Lester and Honey. Honey and Lester. What a pair of hang-ups to finish up with. He flicked channels until he found a movie less painful, an old Randolph Scott and Joel McCrea western. 'I just want to go into my house justified,' one of them said. It seemed a reasonable motto to adopt, thought Ed, as he finished the sandwich and wondered if there was enough turkey for a second.

They met at Le Cirque Sud, which was just a block away from Big Billy's office, and where, as a high spending regular, he was guaranteed attentive service. Unlike its more northerly parent, the southern offspring was not in a listed building, and the architect had gone to town, and then some, with the circus/harlequin theme. It was either repellently garish or fabulously vibrant, depending on your point of view.

They were seated on the elevated upper level, of course, the one that gave a view over a room compartmentalised by this use of folding glass screens, which gave an impression of intimacy. It was Thursday night, busy with regulars rather than the anniversary/birthday/Christmas crowd who moved in on the weekend.

Big Billy ordered them a glass of Krug each and asked for a ninety-one Corton-Charlemagne Grand Cru to be put on ice. He glanced around at the nearest tables, nodded hello to one or two faces and swung his attention back to his son.

'See the game?'

Billy Junior nodded. 'Yeah. I don't give a shit though. 'Bout who wins? I wanna see the Nets.'

Big Billy nodded in agreement. Another season in disarray because of a players' dispute – the second in five years – the NBA was starving its fans yet again. The only happy people were the ABL and the women's leagues, who were getting heavy network coverage so that there was at least some hoop action for the nation to focus upon.

BB pyramided his hands in that way so familiar to his son, the stance he took when he was about to pass judgement or impart news, some kind of defensive shield it was, to distance himself from the person in front of him. Slowly he said: 'Tell me about the girl in Cotchford.'

Billy nearly choked on his champagne and it was a few seconds before he could get a word out, during which time his skin had coloured up nicely. 'Girl?'

'Yes, Billy, girl. The one you stop off to . . . see, after the pick-up. Tell me about her. Do I know her?'

Well, kind of, he almost said, but he shook his head instead and took another mouthful of Krug. 'No.'

'How did you meet her?'

I was surfing porn on the net after I had bought the marker on Cyberslutz and I came across her – shit, it's Honey, I thought. So I tracked her down through the webmaster and set her up in the honicam game. Nooooo. That wouldn't do, either. 'Met her in a bar in Cotchford.'

'I had rather hoped we had left Cotchford behind.'

'Only physically.'

'Meaning?'

He shrugged. He wasn't sure what he meant, except he still found himself drawn back there, back to the memory of a couple of summers when he first smoked dope, drank beer, ran ringolevio and everything was a game until. . . . Boom, it was all over. He felt a sudden flash of anger. 'And who told you about her?'

Big Billy took out his reading glasses and studied the menu. The change shocked his son. The moment he put them on his stature seemed to diminish, his vulnerability rating increase. He almost wanted to hug him. How do we feel over there pop, now we are the hardman facing old age, now we are sixty, or as near as damn it.

'I'll have the grilled quail salad and . . . the striped bass. Billy? OK, two of each, fine.' The menu was removed and the fingers went back to the tent shape. 'Billy, it isn't my place, but . . . well, to answer your question I found out very early on because I did a security check on the run. Yes, had you followed. I just needed to know what the risk was. Nine runs you had to do, and that is nine chances for things to go . . . wrong. The consultant suggested we stop your little, diversion. I let it ride because Backson said he could handle it. However, I think the time has come—'

Backson? Son of a bitch. Billy blurted: 'Listen—'

'William,' he hissed, 'I give not one flying fuck about where you put your dick but I care about you doing it on my time and I care when it affects your judgement. Which I think it might. I know it has affected Anne's happiness – no, no she doesn't know, she is just aware, was aware that something had changed. I managed to calm her down, sidetrack her a little. No, it's OK, you don't have to thank me.'

Billy understood now. Hence the perfect housewife act.

He wondered if Big Billy had suggested this approach. And she'd sucked his cock more often than she ever had, excepting for the first few weeks of marriage. The way to a man's heart is certainly just below his stomach, that's for sure. Except even during that he found himself clenching his teeth. And if a guy can't relax for that . . .

He felt a hot pit of anger boil up in him, forced the lid back on. He had a lot to play for here, and he shouldn't over-react. Not when he had been thinking things had to change himself. 'Well listen, Dad, the days of that thing are numbered. You know what it's like? I mean, I don't want any details, please, but there must have been times when you wanted a break, a change from Mom? Never crossed the line to field for the other side?' Big Billy didn't acknowledge either way. 'That's all it was. Out of my system now, I am just looking for a way to break it to her gently.' Maybe to both of them, he realised. Maybe he would be better off starting fresh where women were concerned. Get one that didn't break his balls or get paid to broadcast her snatch globally.

The salads arrived, Big Billy tasted the wine and pronounced it fine, but before he put a fork into the quail he said. 'Let's play for the bill.'

This was one of his old man's favourite games. He took out a pack of cards and dealt Billy two, then put one face down in front of himself. Billy picked up. Seventeen. Son of a bitch. Stand or hit? Seventeen just wasn't good enough, but all the rules said stand. Dealers had to stand in most casinos on seventeen. Oh shit, live a little – he indicated for a hit. A king. Bust. It'd be his tab. BB turned over and showed a Queen. He dealt himself a single card. An ace. 'Blackjack. Talking of which. Breaking things gently, I mean. William . . . Billy, I have some bad news for you.'

Billy felt his heart spasm in anxiety. 'About the Island?'

Big Billy nodded gravely.

It could only be fallout from the carnage at the gas station. 'Who? Who has pulled the plug on it? The Mayor? The fucking Port Authority? Who?' There was suppressed anger in his voice as he tried not to attract attention, making it tremulous.

Big Billy had rehearsed this one a dozen times. Had considered lying, but knew the truth would out, would be glaringly obvious, so he said: 'Actually, Billy, it was me.'

Honey ran a finger down Matt's back, nervous and worried because he had gone so quiet. They were surrounded by the remains of the take-out they had ordered after sex, and two bottles of wine had gone. It was dark now, but she daren't put the lights on.

'And this guy? He's what?' She could hear the anger in Matt's voice, mixed with bewilderment. He must have felt like he'd been sucked down the drain plug into some very bizarre underworld, where his values had been completely inverted. She had been right about him – he was the guy who was good at football and ball and field and track without being star material, who studied hard, who went to NYU and got fast tracked by a Wall Street firm who moved him out to the sticks for a while to give him a taste of the quiet life, with the purpose of making him even more hungry for the world of the big players. He was the guy who had good friends he played tennis with, who went to the movies, who double-dated, who knew his wine and believed what Robert Parker said, who read consumer reports before buying a car or a refrigerator, who loved his mom and dad despite that little misunderstanding of his heavy metal years, who hadn't found the right woman yet, who had his life all mapped out. Until now. An atypical night dining alone with a few drinks brings him in touch with . . . the Dark Side. or at least a woman who could fuck his brains out, the first one he had ever met.

'He's history. Matt, that's what he is. After the next time. Promise,' she had said.

He had rolled over and faced her, run his own finger down the line of her nose. 'And all that stuff about Philly?'

'True. I was on my way down, ain't no doubt about it. Just where I was living, you know, there was crack apartments, where people could smoke if they gave a little to the tenants, there was money to be made either by cooking it up for them, or sometimes just bagging up coke. I never liked the crack side too much, I seen what it does to women, in particular. I mean, it don't do men no favours, but it seems more degrading to see what a woman will do just to get high again.'

'But coke?'

'Yeah, I was doing toot. Fuck, you mean to tell me you Wall Street types never indulged? Bullshit.'

He shrugged. 'Not on a grand scale.'

'Well, I was also making money with this camera thing. I mean, real harmless, don't get the wrong idea. Just a kind of . . . art thing. Like performance art. Living sculpture.' She had read about it being that kind of thing in a copy of *Maxim* Jerry had showed her to prove that some of the girls were becoming big-time celebs.

'What was the company called?'

'The company?'

'The one with the camera.'

'Oh.' she figured Cyberslutz wouldn't impress. 'Glam-cam. So Billy saw me, tracked me down—'

'He what?'

'He tracked me down.'

'Isn't that kind of scary? I mean any fuckin' freak could do it.'

'Only if they own one of the big cam server sites. Like he did. Still does. Some guy had traded it in as a marker in AC. Got a stable of twenty, thirty girls all doing the same thing. Anyway, the new owner, Billy, he got the details from the webmaster,' And then she knew. The tumblers clicked into place. The fucking prick. The call from Alan, it had been Jerry the Webmaster phoning up to get his own back for her telling him to fuck off. Jesus Christ, and she had just spent seven hundred bucks on a gun. Well, she was going to get it, shove it up his ass and empty a clip.

'Honey, you OK?'

'Yeah. sorry, just thinking.'

'You looked like you were thinking of killing someone.'

She had laughed as innocently as she could. 'Anyway, he sent a message he wanted to meet me. I wasn't going to go, but, shit, curiosity got the better of me.'

'And you could have been the cat.'

'Matt, I don't think you can be retro-protective, you know what I mean? What's done is done.' She couldn't help a little internal smile. She knew what was happening here, knew what was going on in his WASP brain. It was why men always fell for strippers, for whores, for lesbians, for victims. It was why women after they have been dumped are so vulnerable, so sexy to men. It was the fallen angel syndrome. Obviously she had only been sucked into this life because she hadn't had a man strong enough to help her. A man like Matt. Well, he would be telling her soon, he was here to save her, to wrap her in his big manly arms and take her away from all this. Got them every time.

'And when you met him, what?'

She had kissed him on the forehead and then run her tongue over the spot. He squirmed away, but shuddered with pleasure. You have to be a little bit dirty, but not overdo it.

'Then what happened?' he had asked.

Now he had had nearly all the truth, just like she had promised herself before he came over. Just enough. She should stop soon and get to work on those brains.

'Then, I grant you, it got fucking weird.'

'He's out with Big Billy.'

'You going to log on, see what that message was?' asked Sarah Jane.

'I . . . I don't want to.'

'You don't want to? Want doesn't come into it. You need to know. Damn it, Anne, *I* need to know.'

Her friend was shouting. Anne held the phone away. 'Sometimes, Sarah, I think you are more interested in this than I am.'

Sarah tried to keep the guilty-as-charged tone from her voice. 'Well, maybe, but this is powerful ammunition.'

'Look, Sarah, I am not even sure what I am doing. I can't even find that piece of paper you gave me.'

'Want me to talk you through it?'

'I would rather you were here.'

'Now?'

'You free?'

'Noo . . . no I can't. What about over the weekend?' Anne thought she heard a noise, maybe a cork easing out of a bottle in the background.

'Are you in that apartment again?'

Sarah giggled. 'It goes off, you know, champagne. Very short shelf life.'

'What about tomorrow? You'll probably have drunk it dry by then. And it's Atlantic City.'

'Great. I'll come over at what? Eight? Nine?'

'If you would.'

'Great, see you then. Have to go, I have some hot buns toasting.'

Anne put the phone down, fairly certain Sarah wasn't talking about English muffins.

'YOU? You did it? Why?'

Big Billy cleared his throat to keep his tone even and his voice low. 'What we are dealing with here is human nature and human hypocrisy. Hypocrisy that says there are degrees of being compromised. That if you accept a hundred dollars to kill a parking fine, then that's fine, that's almost a favour and nobody gets hurt. But if you take a thousand to falsify a birth certificate or a passport, that is a heinous crime.'

Billy could hear the words, but they were tumbling at him through a thick, thick soup, plopping into his ears, muffled, indistinct. He was breathing though his nose, and he could feel veins throbbing across his face and neck.

BB grabbed his forearm. 'Do you get my point? Now, if we go and say to these guys, we want to build a casino – casinos – here is ten thousand dollars, their liberal conscience is going to be outraged. OK, we say, how about this car, this woman, how about we get your son off dope, free of charge, and make sure anyone who ever supplies him again lives – or rather dies – to regret it. No, no, no they say. But a shopping mall? A *tasteful* shopping mall? Well, that's almost a favour. That puts money back into the city, kick starts a little section of the retail economy, provides jobs. Unfortunately it would also take twenty years to get back the investment. I don't have twenty years, Billy. Are you listening?

'Good. So you sold them, sold them brilliantly on the idea, and off they went and took their little sweeteners, those that hadn't already jumped first time, all except poor Tom, the last honest man on the block. He would have stopped you either way, you know. He just wanted a historic site left out there, unspoilt. Like Ellis Island.

'Now with him gone – not the way I would have wanted, I gotta confess, but gone all the same – we have just a couple more payments to make, and everything will fall into place. Of course when they realise it's not a mall, they will protest, but by then we'll have everything on tape or camera or video. We will have the girls, the boys, the other men's wives, the junkies, the golf club membership. In one case the yacht. Everything. No going back for them.'

'So the money from Atlantic City?'

'The nine mil? It was partly a payment for some work Wuzel and co did for the Enchanted Palace.'

'The Asbury Park hit?'

'You didn't guess? No? I thought even you would put that together, but seeing the big picture has never been your strength, William, has it? Yes, I am afraid the Palace people couldn't afford a serious rival up the shore at this stage. There is only so much Oriental business to go round these days.'

'And the rest of it . . .?'

'Has been used to go around the various authorities. Mass bribery, especially in New York City, doesn't come cheap, and since the city celebrated the millennium by putting tags on employees' bank accounts to monitor any untoward activity, well, it is back to a cash economy these days.'

'I don't understand –'

'No, there is something missing, isn't there? Why would Atlantic City invest in a rival in New York?'

'Unless . . .' Billy furrowed his brow in thought. It was almost there, he almost had it.

'Unless Atlantic City intended to move. Or at least, the people behind it. It has been twenty-five years since gaming started down there, and, to be frank, it has outlived its usefulness. They wanted Monte Carlo back then, but now everyone realises it will never even be Vegas, let alone

Monaco. The top end is going, it's all slots, slots, slots. The buses are bringing in nothing but the desperate, the welfare, the pension market. Apart from the Orientals, the type of client they are getting . . . well, it is going downhill. There isn't a poker room left in the city now. Gone. Oh, Blackjack is more robust, but even in that the gamblers prefer playing against a machine now. More slots. Roulette, craps, all down. And the big boys need the real games to keep up the mystique, the glamour. You never see James Bond walk into a casino and play the Megabucks, do you? So, some time ago, a small . . . consortium, decided that the future is an up-market resort on the tip of Manhattan. Or rather, off the tip. Very up-market – some big hotel names are interested. Not the usual suspects. So we have two very tasteful casinos. Just on part of the island, keep the rest as a historic core. Subsidise . . .' Billy tried to pull away but BB held firm and scowled. 'Listen. Hear me out. *Our* casinos will be more Monte Carlo than Vegas. Plus we will guarantee that for the first five years all the profits after costs go to the city. How can it resist? We all know that the eighties are coming again, the city might go bankrupt. Not with money from this it won't. I know – where is our angle? These.' He tapped the cards. 'It is based on a little scam in South Africa a few years back. Friends of ours own the card factory that will make the decks we use. Every pack has the tiniest, tiniest flaws on certain cards. Almost undetectable unless you are trained to spot them. However, after a few weeks of practice I can tell what is an ace and what is a ten card. That is all you need to know for Blackjack, of course. In four hours I, or someone I have instructed, can walk away from a Blackjack table a million dollars up. Maybe you. If we don't get too greedy, well, we can make a withdrawal as often as we want. I have had it all approved. Our friends are in it for the long term now. Five years to bail out the city, then a sliding reduction over the next five until the city get fifteen per cent of profits. We get the rest. Billy – you didn't want to be a shopkeeper really, did you?'

Billy Moon felt a red fog descend on him, blanking out all his peripheral vision, while his father's features appeared to distort, as if he was being viewed through a fish-eye lens. The mouth carried on working, but Billy couldn't hear the words, just see the lips twisting and writhing like slugs, spewing forth their lies and deception. And this crazy, crazy, megalomaniac scheme to all but abandon Atlantic City. Move. Just like that. No loyalty, no thanks, just fuck you – stew in your own stinking juice and plastic coin buckets. Shopkeeper? Scam their own casinos? Fuck them.

He wrenched his arm free of his father's grip and giddily he struggled to his feet, trying to keep down the champagne, and knocked over both glasses of wine. He was dimly aware of other diners looking at him, but he didn't care. He leant over and managed to spit out: 'I tell you what, Big Billy, you go and get your own filthy blood money from now on.' And he careered off through the tables towards the exit.

BB calmly refilled his glass. He had always feared he would take it badly.

FORTY

Thursday December 19

The three of them sat waiting for Ed to return. He was out there pounding the Boardwalk again, four punishing miles, brow furrowed as if he could will the fat off his frame, squinting against the squalls battering him.

Tony racked the slide of the Remington for what must have been the twentieth time and Don snapped: 'God's sake, give it a rest. If you don't know how to chamber a shell by now we might as well all go home.'

Tony threw him the shotgun, and took out a cigarette. After he lit it he kept flicking the Zippo open and closed, open and closed. Despite his complaint, Don, too, could not resist pumping an imaginary double-O into the business section. Ka-boom, it went in his mind, and his skin prickled as the memory of another boom – the one that brought them to this – came from down the years.

He looked at Lester sitting in that oversized chair, his feet not touching the ground, swinging wildly with excitement.

'Lester, you gotta realise exactly what you just did. You came out of a nice, cosy, computer-game world and decided to join in with us. The fuckin' craziest people on the Eastern seaboard right now.'

Lester just giggled. 'That's OK.' Then he furrowed his brow as if concentrating. 'Billy with us?'

Tony looked at Don, still flicking the lighter, setting Don's teeth on edge. He turned back to Lester and said: 'It's B-B-Billy we are going after. Remember?

'Bird, I meant. I meant Bird,' he said not too convincingly.
Don said: 'Bird'll be along later.'

Don got up and walked to the window, smearing clear a
swath of the condensation. He could see the rain in the
streetlights outside, twisting and looping as the wind caught
it, never allowing it to fall straight down, first driving down
at forty-five degrees and then swirling, some of it even flying
upwards, as if caught in a vortex. He had checked the
weather reports. They had the chance of a fine evening the
next night, with a second instalment of this storm coming in
around midnight. There was a high pressure system forming
in Maine, according to the Weather Channel, which trad-
itionally blocked the northerly movement of weather systems
along the Jersey shore. Which meant that if it got to build
they were in for a hell of a weekend. He hoped it was better
when they did it for real.

Lester eventually said: 'When will Ed be back?'

Don looked out of the window as the pane was rattled by
another blast and said: 'If the wind's behind him he should
be coming through that door any minute. Might even get a
chance to open it first.'

Tony was pacing again now his hands were free, trying to
burn up his nervous energy, bumping into furniture. He was
mumbling, too, going over everything in his mind. In the
end Don said: 'I got some blow if you want to calm down. In
that box. There.'

Tony hesitated, not sure whether he meant blow as in
coke or blow as in dope, but guessed it must be the latter. A
line of cocaine and he would explode, opening up all those
demons again. But a bit of Mary Jane, that might do the
trick. He opened the stash box, noticing his hands shaking,
and found a ready-rolled joint and a book of matches. He sat
down, lit up and inhaled deeply. This was something he
hadn't done in all that time out in the Barrens. There it had

348

been booze, both regular and home-made. Lou in particular knew how to run a good still.

He knew they would be OK out there lying low for a while after the job, knew how to get them in and out. The area was changing rapidly, civilisation was now within a few miles of where his home had been, but the old prejudices that still existed – the legends and stories – meant that folk still thought twice about messing with the Fishers. And Lou and Fred would help him out again. He wished they were here right now. He would feel a lot safer.

Tony sat down on the arm of the chair, passed the joint over to Don, and said, 'N-n-nice shit.'

The door opened and Ed came in, panting, his face flecked with moisture, hair blown wild. He went to the bathroom and grabbed a towel, roughly drying himself. Tony offered him the joint but he shook his head. The last thing he wanted to do was to muddy his thoughts now.

He went to the bathroom and they heard the new set of scales move.

'OK, Ed. How much?' asked Don when he returned.

'Seven pounds,' said Ed.

'Great.'

'Heavier,' added Ed sheepishly.

'Fuck.'

Tony said: 'Yeah, well, they say m-m-muscle is heavier than fat.'

'Nice try, Tony. You got the stuff Bird asked for?' He pointed at the Warner Brothers bags.

'Best I could.'

Ed tore open the packaging and started to set out the figures. Tony was giggling, which irritated him.

Don said: 'Shit, who do you want to be?'

Ed grunted after he had them all laid out. He scooped up three of the figures. 'You, me and Tony.'

'Which is which?'

He looked at Tony. 'You sure they didn't have no Gl Joes or Action Force?'

'No, it was this or characters from *Quest for Camelot*.'

Ed held up the Bugs Bunny figure – 'me'. The Road Runner went to Don and finally Daffy to Tony.

'Hey,' asked Tony in exasperation, 'Why do I have to be D-D-D-Daffy?'

'Because you bought these fucking things,' replied Ed.

'There's an Elmer F-Fudd there.'

'That's Lester.'

'I got the p-pig for Lester.'

'For cryin' . . . look I'll be Daffy, you be Bugs Bunny, OK?'

Tony nodded as if his honour had been satisfied.

'Don, you OK with Road Runner?'

'Meep-meep.'

The other two exploded with laughter and, exasperated, Ed leapt to his feet. 'OK, guys, OK.' He grabbed the last of the joint and ground it out on the table. 'No more dope until after this is over. OK? It ain't funny. A fuck-up will get us killed . . .'

The smile vanished from Tony's face and he and Don breathed deeply, trying to compose themselves. He was right.

The bell rang and Ed opened the door. The imperious figure of Bird came in, making them all feel like naughty school kids. He sniffed the air and nodded, as if he expected nothing more than the odour of sweat, and apprehension and domestic slovenliness. He had a small suitcase in his hands.

'Tony, Ed, Lester,' he said neutrally. He eyed the toys with disdain.

'B-b-best I could do,' said Tony.

From the case Ed produced the streetplan of Cotchford

and a New Jersey map. He laid both on the floor. He took out a stopwatch and put it down on the plans. 'Coffee?'

Ed obliged and Bird began to pace, hands behind his back, as if addressing his troops. Ed believed he was secretly enjoying this. 'The problem with this is that it's both very easy and very difficult. It relies on surprise and a steady nerve.' He looked at Tony who was frantically running his fingers back and forward over his short hair. He stopped and clenched his hands together. 'The Enchanted Palace is eighty-five miles from Cotchford. Eighty-five point three. Now it will take Billy between one hour fifteen and one hour twenty-five to get to the apartment. We take the moment the car stops to drop him off as Zero Hour. Clear?' He started to draw in the path of the limo and where it had parked last time on the street plan. 'Now, when you know he has left, you ring Ed on the cellphone. Two rings. Everything must be signalled like that. No talking unless you have to, unless Billy changes the route. Now, we give him ten minutes to get into the apartment, and Ed to tell him what is happening, incapacitate him. So at zero plus ten, you should be ready to roll. By that time the food should be out and clipped onto the cars.'

'What if it isn't?' asked Tony. 'I m-m-mean, what if the weather is like now? They won't have the windows open.'

From the suitcase Bird took out two small grey metal rods. 'These automatic punches will shatter any closed window. Now, Lester you are parked here.' He pointed at the cartoon characters. 'I think we will forget about using those, just in case you start thinking this is any more Looney Tunes than it is.'

'Daa-dah-dah-dah-dah-dahdahdahdah-th-tha-th-that's all f-folks.'

It was Lester.

Tony suppressed a grin then went back to wringing his

hands. He forgot for a moment that his life might depend on the little retard.

'Now,' continued Bird, irritably, marking an X on the plans. 'You are parked up here. This is the way it goes down. Zero plus eleven – Ed, you must be making your way down. Zero plus twelve – Don and Tony get out of the car. Plus thirteen, they make the edge of the parking lot – eyes on the diner as if you are going in. Don, slightly ahead of Tony. Don, you make the far side of their limo and pull the gun first, because they are more likely to be looking at the apartment.

'When they turn to look at Don, Tony, you take yours out from under your coat. Now, you put it through the window, maybe after using the punch to break the glass, depending on whether it is open or closed. They will get the message. At that moment, Zero plus fourteen say, you, Lester, will drive around and block off any chance of reversing, forming a "T" with the rear of their car. Got that? Good. Ed, Lester will pop his trunk, Don will make them do the same, or reach in and do it.'

'It's on Tony's side. We checked. Just under the wheel.'

'You OK with that?'

'Steady as a r-r-rock,' said Tony, shakily.

'Now, Ed lifts the bag from one trunk into the other, and then . . .?'

'We shoot the tires out,' said Don.

'You shoot their tires out,' agreed Bird. 'Into the car, away four blocks. Change to the pickup. Drive to Freehold. On the dirt track, right? Not the highway. Fourteen miles. Change cars again. Now, tomorrow I want all those cars in place and I want a dry run in daylight. Then I want you to do all the timings again. Then two weeks tomorrow, we go. Or, should I say, you go. Got all that?'

There was a silence while they all thought about what

could go wrong. They had never done anything like this before, waving guns. Ed looked at Don, who had a thin bead of sweat on his upper lip, at Tony, who was scratching again, worrying his wrists until they were raw, and at Lester, swinging in his chair and smiling like they had been planning a day at the ball game. These were the guys he was relying on to pull the trigger if things started to go fugazi. Just as they were relying on him.

'Got it?' asked Bird again.

Ed finally said: 'Is anyone else hungry?'

Bird had gone, refusing to countenance the thought of Chinese take-out.

The rest of them sat on the floor, the opened cartons around them, cramming food in with plastic forks, except for Lester who was honing his fast-driving skills on the Getaway game, trying to outpace the German police through Berlin.

Don asked: 'Do we have an Oh Shit Plan?'

'What's that?' Ed managed through cheeks packed full of rice.

'In case it all goes belly up. You know. "Oh Shit." '

Ed shrugged. 'Get back here as best you can, I guess.'

Tony was sniffing like he was a rabbit, twitching the end of his nose. Don wished he'd go back to the Zippo. 'Ed, the weak spot is you w-w-w-wanting to be inside. You know that?'

'Anyone else want a beer?' Ed got to his feet and fetched four from the icebox. He took a slug. Finally he said to Tony: 'I know. But you know the old saying – revenge is a dish best served hot.'

Tony scratched his head. He was sure that wasn't right.

For the third time that night he drifted off and saw the heads exploding as the gasoline ignited over them, the skin bubble, the eyes boil, the tongues shrivel even as they tried to scream. He woke up with a start. Had he done *that*? No, no, it was his old man, a voice kept telling him. He made him do it. Yeah, like anyone can make you do anything. Whatever sluice gates he had put in place to keep those images away, now they were fully open, flooding him with nausea and shame.

But it was the other shame that was burning him up. The shame of having been duped. Used. Of having to face Anne and everyone else – *everyone* else he knew – tell her the big scheme, the one that would sever him from Big Billy, it had all been just another piece of manipulative shit.

He looked out the window at the darkened harbour and the lights of Brooklyn. It had been gut instinct to run here to Galleon's, to claim one of the private suites and to think what to do next. He had ordered a bottle of bourbon on room service and was steadily climbing into it.

God, how he hated his old man for this. Of all the stunts he had pulled in his life, every little put-down and push that made sure Billy did just what he wanted, this whole charade was the top of the tree. He had known in the back of his mind that the money from the Enchanted Palace was tainted, but shit, he thought it was going to a good cause. His cause. Well that was the last of that. He was fucked if he was going to be a shitty messenger boy again. Stuff the million bucks that was in the case.

Would he ever be free of that guy? Would there come a day, maybe when the old man died, that he could at last be just Billy, without them having to explain the difference between the big version and himself? But the old man, he looked damn near immortal. Except when he wore those glasses. But he could easily live another twenty years. Billy would be old himself by then. Never be taken seriously. He would show them when he had his day, though.

Then he realised he never would get away. BB didn't trust him. Didn't trust him to deliver the goods, to know the truth. So he wouldn't trust him when he was gone, wasn't going to leave any of the businesses to him, was he? He shook his head to clear the bourbon. He went to the window one more time and looked out to where he knew, somewhere in the darkness, lay the island that should have been his. Well, he thought to himself, if I can't have it, I'll make damned sure nobody else will.

He went over to the bed and picked up the phone and dialled the front desk. 'Hi. Listen, I know it's kinda late, but can you get me a typewriter? A what? Yeah, fine, just as long as it'll type and print. And some paper. Fifteen minutes? Great.' He put the phone down and restoppered the bottle. Getting ripped could wait another hour. He had some calls to make.

It was gone eleven when the buzzer rang from below. Honey was just building up to a session with the little blue number and she cursed. Then a fear gripped her. The horseman. No, now she was sure that had been laughing boy Jerry. She would confront him with it once she had built up a head of righteous steam, enough to blow him away forever. But she wished she had the Walther right now.

She slipped on her gown and went to the intercom.

'Yeah?'

'S'me.'

'S'me?' she said teasingly.

'Matt.'

'Matt, I thought we agreed to miss tonight.'

'I know. I couldn't. I . . . I worry about you.

Yeah, where exactly did you leave your white charger and all that shining armour tonight, she thought. 'Don't. After tomorrow, I told you.'

'I want you.'

'Matt.'

'It's raining.'

'You're drunk.'

'I got flowers. They're getting wet. Need to go in some water.'

'I thought they were getting wet?'

'Wrong end.'

'Matt . . .'

'Please. I just wanna hold you. Ten minutes, then I'll go. Promise.'

Jesus Christ he was drunk. Drunk and loving and deluded. 'OK, give me a minute and I will buzz you in.' She went over to clear up the Honicam accessories from the bed and switch to pre-recorded. Leaving more dissatisfied customers, no doubt.

FORTY-ONE

'Hi, Dad? Yeah, it's me. Billy. Look, I just wanted to say . . . I know, I know. It was stupid of me. I was . . . embarrassed, annoyed, pissed off. If you'd have told me upfront . . . of course I could have been as convincing. Look, anyway, I just wanted to say my . . . my outburst. No, forget about it, I'll do it as usual. No, no, no hard feelings. Yeah, I know there will be something for me, yeah something big. No, I'm not at home, I had to come away and think. No I called Anne and explained that I would be out tonight and I would see her tomorrow. No, she's fine, she'd taken a pill so she wouldn't care whether I was there or not. Yeah, I have been drinking. Just a little. But I am OK now Pop, really. Back on target tomorrow. Promise. Yeah, goodnight.'

'Honey? It's me, Billy. Hi. Yeah, I know what time it is. Look, I made a decision. Yeah. About us. No, don't say anything, just listen. We're going to go away for a time. Me and you. No, listen. *Listen*, damn it. Yeah, I have been drinking, but it's not that. No, I am not at home. I am at Galleon's. Yes, same room. No, shit, of course I am alone. You think I'd be phoning you about this with some hooker in the bed? What's that noise? Are *you* alone? No, no, OK, OK, for Chrissake, listen. Honey, OK, the car. Your car. Well, my car. I want you to leave the keys tomorrow night on the front wheel on the driver's side. Yes, on top of the tire. Because I will need to put something in the trunk. Then I will call you from the garage phone and then you come down. No, I won't be coming up. Because we'll be in a hurry, that's why. No, I can't tell you where we are going. Somewhere nice, I promise. It's a surprise vacation. Pack a case. Swimsuits and shit. So you got all that? Sometime tomorrow evening put the keys on the tire. Front wheel, driver's side. No, we'll talk tomorrow. You OK? Good. And don't worry, everything will be just fine. Great.'

She stared at the phone in her hand for a long time, and then over at the still slumbering Matt, wondering what it all meant. Go away with Billy? He'd have to shoot her first.

Billy finished typing and pressed print. He ran them through the in-room fax to make enough copies, and then addressed the envelopes. Everything was non-hotel stationary, just to be on the safe side. Both the *Post* and the *Times* were listed in the in-room directory, but he had to get the FBI address from the concierge. They'd had stranger requests. He sealed up the three letters, stuffed with circumstantial details, but with enough for any reporter or investigator to be going on with, and arranged to have them collected and posted from a few blocks away. Then he lay back on the bed and closed his eyes. There was a long day ahead for him.

FORTY-TWO

Cotchford, New Jersey.
Friday December 20, am

They drove in three separate cars. First they dropped off the Subaru at Freehold, then headed into Cotchford in the Oldsmobile, leaving the double-cab Chevrolet pick-up a few blocks away from the apartment where they would watch and time Billy one more time.

Lester got to drive, putting in some more practice. He was good but intense, holding the wheel too hard, concentrating like he was looking at a screen. Ed suddenly said: 'Why don't we eat at Starboards.'

'What?' asked Tony.

'Just go in and eat. Then we can take our time looking at the lot instead of cruising by like fuckin' kerb crawlers. Besides, I could go for a cheeseburger.'

'When couldn't you?' asked Don. 'I don't like the sound of it.'

'OK,' said Ed, 'Don doesn't like it. It must be a good idea. Lester. Lester. *Lester*. Starboards. You remember it?' He nodded and made a right onto 35. It was as they pulled into the lot Ed saw the sign. 'Oh fuck,' he said.

'What?' asked Don. Then he saw it: 'Serving Cotchford for Forty Years. Bob and Edie say Thank You and Good Bye and Happy Holidays. Starboards' Grand Closing on Saturday 21st. Site of new Century 21 realtor.'

'J-J-esus,' said Tony, suddenly tugging at his ear. 'What we gonna do? It means it won't be here next t-time. They won't stop for burgers.'

'I knew it would all go wrong —' began Don.

'Shut up,' snapped Ed. 'Just shut the fuck up everyone.' He chewed his lip for a while, feeling the Olds bounce while Tony agitatedly changed position every ten seconds. 'The cars are in place. We got the guns. We got the timings. Tony could tell Lou and Fred we are coming, get a message to them. Bird . . . well, Bird's out of it anyway. It'll be a nice surprise for him. I guess it's our oh shit plan.'

'What is?' asked Don.

'We hit Billy tonight.'

the e-mailSender:f.alump@qikmail.com
Received: from qik.mail@qikmail.net [194.217.242.39])
by dub-img-5.zip.com (8.8.6/8.8.6/2.10) with SMTP id EAA24765
for honicam.adult.net.com>; Friday.001From: f.alump@qikmail.com
Received: from qikmail.com (158.234.66.777.888)
   by post. mail@adult.net.net id aa 1009592; 20 Dec. 11.05 EST
Message-ld: <zzp. 1120@fastmail.com
Content-Type: text/plain; charset=ISO-8859-1
Content-transfer-encoding: quoted-printable
X-Mailer: FFF THRUPASS
/5000100001/500102811/500102841/500202356/

Message:
Look – that is it, slut. Last night I sit there for ten minutes with my dick in my hand while you screw around with the dildos and you are just gonna fill your pussy and bam. Gone. Here – here's some tapes I made earlier. Not fucking good enough, you ask me. I warned you. So it's back to Amy. I asked your skanky webmaster for a full refund for the year I paid upfront. If there was a Consumer Tests section on sex

sites I'd complain. Let me tell you baby – you keep pulling stunts like that and you're finished in this business. Finished. You are what is wrong with this country – we all got standards to keep up, Bitch.

❋   ❋   ❋

They sat down in the small room, just a cheap plastic coffee table between them. He laid his tape recorder on the cup-stained surface and flicked it on. He apologised for being late, explained where he had been, how he had come to this room, this situation. The man just nodded. He was big, and still trim, mostly, except round the face, where some sagging had occurred, blurring the jawline. But he imagined someone stretching out the skin, taking up the slack, as if the collagen had never gone away, and he could see this guy had been a looker once. Without any preamble, Jimmy Jazz began.

'Heaven was all around them, you know? That's what I used to say. "Heaven is all around you boys – make the most of it." They were never bad kids. Got into some scrapes, maybe. If they'd been my age they'd have been stealing hubcaps. But they stopped putting hubcaps on cars. Maybe that was where we all went wrong – introducing alloy wheels. Meant the kids had to find something else to do.'

There was a pause while they both ruminated on this, an urban crime wave precipitated by changing auto fashions. He didn't rush him. He had looked up the court records in Trenton. Examined the clippings in the *Newark Star-Ledger*, but this old man, this crazy old man, he was going to put the flesh on the bones for him.

'I thought I was so cute as a kid. I used to hang around the Village, you know. I saw them all – Lady Day, Prez, Miles, Coltrane – whoa, that Coltrane, by the time I saw him he was burnin' up the place, all that devotional shit – it was fierce. You came out with the your head ringin', your ears bleedin', but man your heart was flyin', just flyin.' Jimmy cleared his throat. This was just a warm up, just the guy practising his scales. 'I'll tell you about the night, but you gotta go back months, maybe a year or more, before that incident.'

'They used to use my place as a jail. For alley-o. You know that game? Ringolevio they call it in Brooklyn and the Bronx. All the time they was thirteen, fourteen, some of them maybe fifteen. Sort of twixt and between. Still kids, but almost men. Almost. You remember that stage? Half of you wants to play Gl Joe, the other half wants to play with your dick. Or even better, get some woman to play with it. So they all hittin' that particular wall, and was beginning to get into other things. Still hung around my place though. Kind of social club. I tried to keep them relatively straight – you know, without being their parents and saying they couldn't do squat. You understand? So they sometimes blew a little weed, and, OK, I admit, I had some mags under the counter they would borrow. Not hardcore stuff – shit, some of it was my old collection of *Playboys*. I tell you, some of those guys got a shock when they finally realised how old Stella Stevens really was. But anyway they still played the game. Alley-o.

'Now, problem was, as they got bigger, it kind of took up more space. You know what I mean? Take that kid Don. He filled up the whole sidewalk. And Tony? He liked to – what is it when you ski? Slalom, yeah. He liked to slalom through people, cutting this way and that. But sometimes he don't make it and bam! Someone gets knocked over. An arm broken, some old lady gets her teeth knocked out. So you got complaints from the citizens and the Mayor bans it.

'So a while later the one called Bird, he invented the new game. The Bridge Game I think they called it. They used to stand on one of the overpasses over the highway and, you

know, spit, or throw baseballs over it. Mindless shit, really.
See who can hit the red car with a mouthful of saliva. Woof.
Hey, the windshield, splat, ten points, that kind of thing.
Wasn't nothing till the trucks came. You see Cotchford then,
it was a split town. Still is, really. You got this side of the
tracks here – poor, black, Hispanic, some white folk on
Wylie Avenue, where Ed was from, and down on Sixth and
Tenth with another bunch in the trailer park down on Laurel.
The other side, the East side, now, that always been where
the money, the stores, the businesses is. And the beach. You
know, at one time they tried to make it so that only Eastsiders
could go on the beach? Back in the early sixties. I tell you,
we nearly had a race riot of our own then.

'But anyway, 'bout the time we talkin' about, the
Eastsiders are doing some land reclamation, out by the
lighthouse. New marina, bring some more custom to the
town. To the East side of town, that is. The trucks used to
come with the landfill at night, rumbling though these streets,
they'd go down MLK – Martin Luther King – and then turn
left onto Highlands Drive. It meant they didn't go through
the upper town at all – past all them rich homes. Just kept *us*
awake, mostly. I was shooting my mouth off about this when
Bird came up with an idea. Scare the shit out of them.
Instead of hawking over the bridge, or dropping sticks, use
something heavier. Scare the shit out of the drivers. Piss
them off, you know? Like some kind of terrorism? Urban
guerrillas. At least that's what they said. You ask me, all kids
like tossing things off bridges, so if you got an excuse, then
great.

'So they waited until the trucks were empty coming back
from the marina, and you balanced a cement or a cinder
block on one of the bridges over the highway, just which
intersects with MLK Drive over yonder. Two, three bridges.
They changed which one they used all the time. When the

truck was below them, they would push the block off. *Boom* it would go as it hit the tip-up section on the back, and they would watch the guy slam on the brakes. First few times they screeched to a halt, wondering what the f . . . what the heck had hit them. Soon figured it out. They tried patrollin' the bridges, of course, but you know what kids is like – they always knew when someone was up there waitin' for them. Just made it more exciting for them, is all.

'So if they knew security was out, sometimes they'd do it from another bridge, sometimes lay low for a week, two. And then they did it one time too many. The kids I mean. This driver died, family, whole family. But the driver . . . shit. By the time they caught them, the Bridge Boys, they were like the town outlaws. I thought they was going to lynch them.

'Anyway the deal went like this – Billy was an Eastsider. His old man wasn't exactly rich, but you could say he was well connected, enough to get a greasy lawyer down here. Rich now I hear – did well for himself. Little Billy, too.

'Y'see what happened was this. They all got tried as adults, 'cept Billy. He got considered a juvenile. The rest of them, over fourteen in New Jersey, the judge can try them as adults, and he did. Billy went to the family court – cause he was an Eastsider, so when his hotshot lawyer stood up and explained how he had been corrupted, and when Billy stood up and said how he'd been led on by these guys, well, they threw him back and kept the other ones, thinking these were the big fishes. They even took on Bird, who wasn't there, not during the actual drop. Bird was clever, one of those kids who tran-transcends his background, you know what I mean? I called him Bird after Charlie Parker. No, not because he looked like him. But because of the way he hustled around. Bird was not really an alley-o player, he was more like, the guy who had the concessions, you know?

Like he was the guy who throws you nuts and hot dogs at the game? So he'd sell sodas for me, on commission, to the guys in jail. And later he used to buy the odd reefer offa me, and sell it on outside to the rest of them, always with a mark-up. So I knew he'd go far.

'So most of them go to this new place for kids-stroke-adults, Boxgrove – The Box – which turns out to be kinda hard. But not Billy, he goes to some soft-shoe shuffle kind of almost reform school place, buffs him up a little, he's out within a year. Gibbs, that's the place. Comes back for a while, does the usual things, and then his old man moves up in the world and he's gone. The others? Bird was OK, he was in some soft part of The Box, more like a school than a prison. Don, Tony . . . they weren't too hot, Tony got real strung out. Came round in a terrible state, arms all bleeding, track marks, I told him to leave. Lester was worse though. All Lester ever wanted to do was be liked. Goodbye Pork Pie Hat. So Long Lester, more like.

'I tried to tell the court that the kids were basically OK. But the court couldn't or wouldn't see it. I stood up as a character witness, but hell they managed to suggest I was some kind of pusher, not to be relied on, you know what I mean? So fat lot of good I did. Yeah, they tried to close me down after that. But you know what? When you tell the Mayor that his boy is your best customer, and, hell, you got it all on video camera, well suddenly they don't feel like runnin' you out of town quite so much.

'Hear this track? Clifford Brown, great trumpeter. Miles would never admit it, but old Clifford, he made the man sweat. Turnpike killed him. This one – the New Jersey Turnpike—'

His cellphone rang and he excused himself, cutting off the old man before he started his own jive-soaked version of *Jazz Greats*.

'Yeah.'

'It's me. That gun. It's moving.'

'Sure?'

'Check your unit.'

'It's in the car.'

'Well, trust me.'

'OK. Consider yourself trusted. Where's it heading?'

'It's coming your way.'

'My way?'

'Yup. North.'

'Meet me at the brew pub. You know the one? Cecil C's?'

'Yeah, I know it.'

'How long?'

'With lights going? An hour?'

'See you then.'

He started to gather up his things, telling the old man he had been a great help. It was the truth, for once. But he'd almost forgotten how to tell it.

'There is one more thing,' said the old man.

'There is?'

Jimmy shook his head. 'What they did afterwards. After the crash. *With the driver*. Wasn't in the papers. You ain't gonna believe it.'

He wanted to leave now, he had had enough of this sentimental, dewy-eyed old fool, so he said with a little too much impatience. 'Try me.'

FORTY-THREE

It was force of habit now, she realised, that she was still doing anything. That guy who e-mailed her was right – she was finished. She had already decided once and for all that Honicam would have to die. She would unplug it for the last time. Put out a message thanking all her subscribers, telling them how to get a refund, but regretting that fanny time was over for her – they would have to switch to someone else's ass. Try Renee, she seems to be doing good stuff now. And then she could tell Jerry it was his shithead stunt about the horse that made her do it. That'll give him something to chew on.

But for the moment she lay on the bed and thought about Matt and stroked herself the way she knew they loved. Crunch time for more than just Honicam. Within an hour or so she would have to tell Billy she wasn't coming with him, that she was dismantling his little fantasy castle, tearing it down. He could go where he liked with whom he liked, and so could she. And for the moment she had that big chest of Matt's to lie on, the man who was going to save the poor little bad girl. Oops, must keep stroking.

She looked at the clock. Billy would already have left Atlantic City. She felt a twinge of nerves. It was one thing having all this bravado when Matt was with her, but this was something she had to do alone. She had had to work hard to persuade Matt to leave. It was important Billy didn't suspect another body was involved. It was enough he thought the whole life had turned sour on her. She had rarely seen Billy's temper, but she knew he could do bad things to Matt if he suspected.

When the doorbell rang she groaned. She knew it was Matt, knew his male ego didn't want to skulk in a little bar around the corner, that he felt some kind of combative surge of testosterone. He wanted to lock antlers with his rival and paw the ground a bit. Well, fuck that.

She swung off the bed and went to the door, firing herself up to righteous anger. The words died in her throat when she saw the black 'O' of the silver gun barrel pointing directly at her forehead.

Goodrich sipped from a glass of Cecil C's Old Nuzzler, one of the owner's heavier brews. The pub was located on a corner near the Cotchford waterfront, a triangle of glass walls with a mediocre restaurant on one side but a good bar. He was sitting on one of the seven stools so he could swivel and take in the whole area. Ahead of him was a four-storey, low-rise apartment block. Behind him, due south was Starboards, an old fashioned diner, and to his left the long drag that led to the downtown area. He kept swivelling, feeling slightly edgy, because he had no idea what he was looking for. All he knew from the beep-beep in his car was that Ed Behr was somewhere across the road, with a nine mil and maybe two Remington pumps. He wondered if he had done this all wrong, figured Ed all wrong.

He pinched the bridge of his nose and tried to put the old man's ramblings into some kind of order. There had been a bunch of kids, and some deaths, some sick shit, and an acrimonious trial, and close to – what? – well, within spitting distance of twenty years later, it was as if the last act were being played out.

This was not what he had expected. He knew he should call for back-up, but he had no firm details to give them.

Waste another night's overtime for a Fast Response team and there would be hell to pay. It was not as if there were any in the immediate vicinity. Trenton was the nearest. Still, only 40 minutes away if things got tight. Of course 40 minutes could be very quick or an eternity, depending.

Alice came in looking as he hadn't seen her in months. The make-up was gone, the hair pulled back and clipped, the clothes plain, smart, comfortable. Even the walk was different. Gone was the ground-down slouch, the posture of a self-esteem brought so low it could squeeze through the cracks in the sidewalk. Here she was shoulders back, chest out, look-em-in-the-eye confident. ATF agent confident. She put her purse on the bar top and ordered a Coke.

She turned and smiled. 'Hello Goodrich.'

'Why hello Miss Alice,' he said, and she watched him, too, change and grow and shift and slough off his used skin.

They picked up the limo as it crossed the causeway. Perfect timing. One of Brownie's old crew had staked out the Palace, and had dialled Wuzel's cellphone immediately. Three rings and then off.

They slotted in a couple of cars behind them, Wuzel driving, nervous in the rain. Visibility wasn't so good, everyone was spraying great spumes of water which turned an opaque white in the causeway lights, cutting visibility to a few hundred yards. Plus a black limo was hardly a distinctive car to tail at the best of times, so he kept closer than he would have normally. But the weather worked both ways – the limo driver wouldn't be able to read the traffic half so well as if it were fine, wouldn't be as sharp about scoping a tail.

Brownie had wanted to stake out the stop, the one at Cotchford, but Wuzel had been clear. 'What if they had like a lovers' tiff? And it's all off? What if he got another squeeze?

Me, I reckon it is worth the trouble to pick them up in AC, and we take our chances if the system has changed.' So that was settled – if the routine didn't go as they expected, they would improvise. 'But if the odds don't look right, we do it next time. What do you say?'

Brownie wasn't saying much, just playing with the heater controls on the Chrysler. Shit, he hadn't been warm since he had come north. The cold had gnawed its way through to his bones. He would swear that his marrow was icing up.

He kicked the canvas bag on the floor, making sure for the tenth time the weapons were there. He had wanted to bring the Steyr, but caution told him it should stay where it was buried. Just in case. He was sure ballistics could match it to the casino hit. And the way Edgar dropped one that day – even if it was in the ocean – made him think maybe those machine pistols were jinxed anyway. Or was it still in the Atlantic? Perhaps ATF had recovered it and managed to trace them back to the buy in AC; maybe that was why they took such an interest in his old bar.

Still, the gear he had here was clean – two mini-SAF Chilean army numbers, basically SIGs made under licence, but a lot easier to get hold of, and a lot cheaper. Not as classy as the Steyrs, but when you are pumping out twelve hundred rounds a minute, who cares about classy? Not you, and not the poor punctured sucker on the other end.

He glanced at Wuzel every so often, but the man was concentrating too hard to notice or engage in conversation. He was an odd one alright. How could you do this – this sort of thing – to fund buying photographs? Photographs. Not art, not something one-off, not a Picasso or shit like that. But photographs.

Wuzel had spent ten years putting people in touch with other people and skimming off almost every kind of action there was on the East Coast. He must know that somewhere along the way he had helped facilitate murder, kidnapping, extortion, mutilation, robbery, prostitution, drugs and Christ knew what else. Did it make the pictures seem tainted he wondered? When he looked at some classic black and white scene of New York, did he see the red splattered over it, the blood and brains congealing in the corners, lying in the gutters?

Nah . . . did Brownie himself after all? Did he look at his house in Florida and think of the skulls and the bones and the skin that made up the foundations? He didn't even think of it all. How many had he killed? Shit, that was like adding up how many women you'd fucked – a little on the vulgar side. Too many of both. And there was only one that ever worried him, stayed with him, dared to have a walk-on part in his dreams. Not even driving a stake through a guy's heart had fazed him. In fact, he loved a challenge as much as the next man. Well, maybe not if the next man is the one having a knife-sharpening steel hammered through his sternum while another guy tries to capture it on film.

No, the only one, the absolutely only one that had worried him had been that dealer on *The Alchemist* who had screamed and screamed and yelled at people to do something. *Do something*! So he had. He had shot her. Boom. He could still see the entry hole, just beneath the badge. If he concentrated harder he could pull her face into focus, get the blonde hair piled up on top, clock the name badge . . .

'What you got us?' Wuzel suddenly asked.

'What?'

'In the bag.'

'SAFs.'

Wuzel shook his head. 'Don't know 'em. Wanna run me through it?'

Brownie reached down and unzipped the bag, pulling one of the weapons free, inhaling the familiar smell of oil and the very faint aroma of spent rounds. Fired only for testing, he had been told. Surplus stock.

'OK, it's a nine mil, mag takes thirty rounds. You got like a combined safety and fire selector on the left side here. See? Up is safe. Like now. Down is one notch for single shots, two for a three round burst. They are not fully automatic, which is good. You can control these babies. Three rounds is plenty. Magazine catch on the front of the trigger guard. We got three spare mags each. I ain't jungle-rigged them – they got these little lugs. You can clip them together. But I doubt we need to. What we got? We got one guy, maybe two. Don't need a battle tank. Got all that? Mind if I turn on the radio?'

Without waiting for an answer he flicked it on and switched channels until he found some Tony Bennett – he felt disloyal saying it, but he always rated Benedetto over Ol' Blue Eyes – then leant back in his seat to relax. What was the name on that badge?

Anne twisted the bottle and felt the cork come out in her hand with a satisfying gasp. She kept pouring and refilling, waiting each time for the bubbles to recede, until both flutes were full.

'Oh, just to the brim for me, Sugar,' said Sarah. She took a big slug of the champagne and said, 'Shall we?'

Anne had the same falling-elevator stomach as last time she entered Billy's sanctuary. But now, as they went into his office, it was tempered by something else, a little hit of adrenalin. Being with Sarah made it all feel less furtive and sordid, more like some kind of adventure, the Hardie Girls perhaps.

'So,' said Sarah, eyeing up Billy's inner sanctum. 'Kinda neat, isn't it? Tidy mind your boy has. OK, let's go. Hit on. Bing. So what's his thing? Let me guess from the books.

Cars? Nooo. Golf? No. Baseball. Noooo? Je-sus doesn't this guy have a hobby? Every man I ever met had a hobby. Come to think of it men without their little obsessions are a rare thing – maybe you should hold onto him afterall. Here we go. Right, let's go to the in box and check what that e-mail said. There you are: honey-bee at honicam dot-com, and the message is . . . a kiss. Fuck. A lousy x. It must have been a reply to something he sent. Jesus what a bummer. No wonder he didn't bother to delete. OK, we aren't beat yet, because if we come out of there . . . so, and go onto the Internet, here – can I have a top up of this? – and then wait and see what happens here. OK, yes this looks very familiar. Now see this top bar here, this is where we can see what is what, so we can either go favourites, which will be the sites he really likes, or we can go open history, which will tell us where he has been browsing. Let's hit favourites. Well, here we are. Wooo. Aimeecam, taracam, millicam, reneecam . . . now, there you go – hey, lookee here, a www-dot-honicam, and wasn't the e-mail from a honeybee at honicam-dot-com? So click on this and what do we get? Oooh-ee we get an adult content warning. I think you better sit down Sugar. Am I over eighteen? Well I guess so, and accept conditions and . . . oh, shit. Password. Password. What might work as a password? Let's try your name. No. Let's try his name. No. It's a word not a number, so can't do dates of birth. Has he got a middle name? No. Well let's just try . . . Moon. Ah-hah, accepted. I told you they were always easy. Now let's see. It's a live camera feed, I guess. Welcome to honicam, your window on the life of . . . holy shit. Lookee here. Did he ever do anything like that to you? You sure? I mean, don't be shy – after a long day at the office a little light bondage never did anyone any harm. But look, I'd say the guy . . . the guy has a gun. Anne, sugar, I have a very bad feeling about this.'

❀   ❀   ❀

Billy Moon frowned as another squall hit the car. He was going to get soaked yet again – the weather on these runs always seemed to be foul. Even the few steps from car to the rear entrance of the apartments would get him wet.

Backson could sense tension, again. Jesus, what a boss. Personally, he liked to relax, no matter what the job. 'Wanna hear today's? Chicken goes to bed with an egg. Afterwards the chicken lights a cigarette and says to the egg: "Well, I guess that settles that." '

'Heard it,' said Billy. 'Listen. We may have to go back.'

Backson shifted in the seat. 'What?'

'To Atlantic City.'

Backson shrugged. 'Why's that?'

'We were light last time.'

'Light?'

'About twenty grand off the mil.'

Backson whistled. 'That's a hell of a skim. Watcha do?'

'We mentioned it.'

'And?'

'They faxed us a count check, signed by two inspectors.'

'Like that's any kind of guarantee.'

'So this time we check it before we go back to New York.'

Backson's mind was already sorting through the various angles before he said, 'You don't think . . .?'

'It was you?'

Backson frowned at him, trying to read the eyes in the intermittent glare of passing headlights. Did he really think he was putting aside a nest egg for his kid's future? Surely he knew this would not be a smart move by anyone's standards. Not with what he knew about the depot. He didn't want the baked alaska treatment. 'Do you?'

'No,' said Billy firmly. He didn't want this situation to develop an edge.

'It was in the trunk the whole time, as always.'

'I said no,' said Billy firmly.

Backson thought about security. 'You carryin'?'

Billy shook his head. He'd considered it. Didn't think he'd need it. And guns were a problem when you got to airports.

Backson dug in his inside pocket and brought out a small pistol. 'This is an H&K chambered for a .32 ACP. Nice and light, always carry it as a spare.' He handed over a second clip and said, 'Just in case. Make me happy.'

Billy pocketed the gun and Backson just nodded, satisfied. Shit, thought Billy, maybe he should just pop him and Shawn, might be easier. Shawn was a Christian after all, so he kept saying – Kill Them All, God Knows His Own. What made him think God'd toss both of them to a guy down there without a second thought?

Nah, leave them be. In the grand scheme of things they probably deserved to die. But he shouldn't be the one to do it. He'd be long gone before they figured something was wrong. Billy felt curiously elated, high almost. He should burn his bridges more often.

FORTY-FOUR

They knew it was apartment seven. They now knew there
was a woman living there, Don had talked to the Super.
Knew she had no room mates. And Ed knew, most of all, he
did not like this.

He was dressed casually enough – big leather jacket, polo
shirt, chinos, loafers. Over his shoulder was a big square
bag, of the sort messengers use to hump bulky documents
around. It contained four rolls of heavy duty tape, a
cellphone, a large parcel and three pairs of handcuffs, the
easy-snap quick-bind kind. The Spitfire completed the set.
Unless you counted the ham and mustard sub he had picked
up at the gas station. He had to fight hard not to eat it now.
He was saving it for when all this was over.

He was in unknown territory here. It was one thing
Goodrich getting him to seriously maim fruit, Jimmy
tutoring him on how to puncture cans of beans, but pointing
the gun at a living, breathing person was different. A living,
breathing *innocent* person at that.

Well, he consoled himself, nobody around Billy could be
that innocent.

He stepped out of the elevator and scanned either side.
Getting in had been far too easy – the old trick, buzz another
door number and wait until someone hits the entry release.
Ed stood there listening to his breath, lifted the flap of the
bag and wrapped his fingers around the butt of the gun, felt
the energy leap from it into his hand. He could see why
people wanted to ban these things, they were like a drug,

pumping you full of illusory power.

He listened to the sounds of the apartment block. There was music – some violin-playing down the hall, the thump of rock music from above, and a kid shouting for his or her mother, the thrum of the heating system, and the sighing and plopping of plumbing. He felt something behind him and spun round, but there was just air. He imagined he could see a ripple in it, like a heat haze, the space where someone had been standing, but he dismissed it. Then he realised what it was – whoever had let him in was checking he wasn't an axe murderer. No, he was something worse. He felt the phone buzz in the bag. He had switched the ring off, just in case it alerted anyone. The buzzing meant Billy was nearly at the apartment block. Here goes, he thought.

It was ten paces down the hall, if you made the strides big enough. He started off, dragged along by a wildly pounding heart. He rang the bell and stepped to one side in case she looked through the peephole. If she did that he might have a problem. He had the package as back up, and the forms that had to be signed. Special delivery from Mr Billy Moon, that would get him in.

He didn't need it, the door was flung back and the face appeared, anger playing across the features. Without even looking at her he swung the gun up level with her eyes. He was about to say don't make a sound, don't say a word, but he was talking to the wrong person. It was him that gasped in shock, him that made the grunting noises. Honey. Shit, Honey. After all this time. He felt his eyes cloud with tears. She looked, looked . . . fabulous.

He had almost lowered the pistol when she said: 'Who the fuck are you?'

'Ernie?'

For a second he didn't respond, and then he realised that

Alice was talking to him. At least she got to keep her real name, which made it easier. He had spent months training himself to respond to Goodrich or Goody, and now his own name sounded awkward and clumsy, as if he was trying on the suit of a dead relative.

'Yeah?'

'Agent Shepard, you are the SAC here. Do we phone in for back-up or what?'

He thought for a moment. Being the Special Agent in Charge also meant taking the flak when – as he had done in the past – you end up with twenty men on full overtime talking about hockey for ten hours. He shook his head and took another sup of his ale. 'We know that a guy with a gun is in there. We know that guy bought the gun from Virginia. We know that because he bought it from me. And we know he is in there because there is a bug in the gun. Now we know that, since I put the bug instead of the last three slugs in the mag, and since it is still working, we know he hasn't fired it since the day I took him to the woods.'

'Something is going down. Unless you think he's taking it for a dirty weekend away.'

'Yeah, maybe he's grown attached to it. I know what you are saying, Alice. But we have to remember who we dealing with here. This isn't Frank Nitti. I mean – Ed Behr, what did you make of him?'

'Just another loser in the bar. You know, hung up on an old girlfriend, going nowhere but Fantasyville in the bottom of a bottle.'

'Precisely. I expected busts through The Hoop, through your contacts, through the store, but Ed Behr? It don't figure.'

'So what do we do?'

Shepard ran his fingers through his hair and felt a shudder of disgust. After the hit on the casino in Asbury Park the

ATF had traced the Steyr to a gun store in Atlantic City, long since closed down. But they figured the guns might have been bought local. Shepard had gone in undercover as Goodrich along with Alice, and a steady stream of small violations had kept them there. The big one had never come and he knew that by January he would be pulled out anyway. ATF needed him back as a regular operator. He was glad. And the first thing Ernie Shepard would do would be to lose Goodrich's hair.

Alice saw Shepard's eyes narrow and she turned to see what had caused the frown to appear. She watched as a long black Lincoln limo came past the Brew Pub and turned into the parking lot of the building where they knew the Spitfire – and therefore probably Ed – was. It disappeared around the rear and they could see the red of the brake lights reflected on the puddles in the asphalt surface of the parking lot where it had stopped.

Shepard put five dollars on the bar and slid off the stool. 'Alice, go get your car, bring it over here . . . there, in this place's lot, so it is opposite the apartment. Next to Starboards diner.'

'What are you doing?'

'I got some hardware in my trunk I got to get. Stay in the car. I will be right over. OK?'

As he said this the crimson reflections disappeared and the Lincoln reappeared from behind the block and bumped across the street to the side slots of the diner, only pausing for the driver to place an order into the freestanding speaker system at the entrance. The lot of Starboards was L-shaped, the longest section, with perhaps half a dozen cars, facing the diner building itself. The limo pulled into the top end of the arm, furthest away from the building. It would give a good view of the side of the apartment block.

Shepard felt a sudden jolt through his system as a cocktail

of fight-or-flight chemicals kicked in unbidden. 'Alice, hurry up, something is going down.' As he walked quickly to the door he told his body to calm down a little, to stop the twitching of muscles and sphincters, that the 'flight' option really was not on the menu tonight.

She backed in without another word, but he could hear himself making little squeaking sounds. She made it all come back to him. God she had been lovely, been perfect, much, much more beautiful than Candy Clark. And things were going so well. But he had been caught at that stage, the cusp, just leaving the childhood world, and taking those first, stupid fumbling steps into what should have been adulthood. Instead it became some kind of bizarre purgatory called Boxgrove, where women played no part, except as mythical, unknown, unknowable creatures, about as real as the Jersey Devil.

It was all down to that one night, walking the Boardwalk at . . . where? Bay Head. Fuck, it was coming and going in waves, sloshing with the blood through his brain. It had been Bay Head, by the dunes, where the Boardwalk is just what it says – a series of planks paralleling the seashore. No hotdogs or T-shirts, no carousels or casinos. He remembered putting his arm around her shoulder and pulling her to him, tentative, waiting for the arm to be swept away, or one of those little defensive moves girls seem to know instinctively.

But she didn't do those moves, didn't block and deflect, just let him in through the defensive shield. And the signs said stay off the dunes, help protect the environment, but it was getting dark and the concerned citizens that make up the community were all safely tucked away and so they left the Boardwalk . . .

'What the fuck do you want?'

The hardness in the voice shocked him out of it. She

knew enough not to scream and make him jittery, that a frightened man is more likely to do something stupid; she had also been around enough that a gun pointed at her was nothing new. When you chop and bag coke for a living such hardware is part of the furniture.

He let the Spitfire down a few inches so it was level with her throat so he could get a better view of that face, that fine-lined, cute little face. So close. So close to the real thing it was uncanny. Close enough to trigger the same flood of emotions, like seeing one of those real good Marilyn impersonators that makes you think – wish, even – maybe she didn't die after all. OK, she was maybe twenty-nine or thirty, a little younger than the genuine article, but otherwise they could be twins. It was ... bizarre. He backed her into the bedroom, walking fast towards her, forcing her to give ground until she was on the bed.

She risked a glance at the camera. The honicam was still running, and dozens, maybe hundreds of men were logging on for their Friday night special. What would they see? They would see a little play-acting, that's what they would see, something that would make them take notice. What was this, she could imagine them thinking. A rape fantasy? The first live snuff link? Five would get her more than ten that not one of them would think – woman in trouble, call 911. Nope, they'll be unzipping and flopping it out just in case it got interesting. All the same, she had the feeling that they were about to be disappointed, that he wasn't here for any of that stuff.

'Get on the bed.'

She swung her legs up and worked her way back to the bars of the bedhead. He brought out the handcuffs and clipped her on to it, leaving one hand free for the moment. He used the second set to clip the other one to the cast iron upright. Then he took the tape, bound her legs together at the ankles, then unravelled a six inch section and laid it on the bed next to her.

'I don't want to gag you. Not yet. I might have to, OK? But first I need to ask you some questions. OK? Just some questions. You won't get hurt. Did I say that? I'm meant to say that a lot earlier.'

Honey flashed him a crooked, sardonic smile, 'First time is it? What's the question?'

He hesitated and felt a thousand thoughts go through his head, freeing up neurones like a pack of escaping rats, tumbling and clawing over each other. What is the routine when Billy comes up? Are there any codes? Does he expect her to ask 'Who is it?' Does he have a key?

Instead he said in a soft voice: 'How come you look like my Honey?'

Billy wanted a cigarette, and he hadn't smoked in years. In fact, he had never really smoked at all. He had only taken it up so he could take a hit of grass at Jimmy's without all that embarrassing coughing and spluttering. But now he felt like getting something warming, comforting in his lungs. They were into Cotchford, and he ticked off the familiar landmarks. There was Bailey's, the dime store that had managed to keep afloat when everything else of its ilk – even the Woolworth's across the road – had long gone. It was where he used to chalk out the rectangle, the jail for alley-o, the very place where they would keep an eye out for Ed or, more likely, Tony the Tiger sprinting down the street, feinting and bluffing his way past the defence, almost like an ice hockey player, as if he were skating on the sidewalk. Ducking and leaping, never giving a solid target, until he burst into the chalk square and that yell of 'alley-oooooo' bounced its way down Main Street.

They banned it back then, and they certainly would never

allow it now, not decent respectable Cotchford.

They passed the Brew Pub and swung close to her apartment building. 'Here,' he said quickly, reminding them that he was getting out with the goods tonight. 'Shawn, pull the trunk.'

He stepped out, quickly rounded the back, and lifted the case. He felt a muscle protest in his arm. Christ it was heavy. No way there was less than a million in there. He scooped up the scales and shuffled his way to the door. Backson watched as he fumbled with the key, stepped into the building and pressed the elevator button. He didn't signal Shawn to go until he saw the elevator doors shut.

Billy pressed 'G' and hoped they couldn't see the floor indicators from outside. The elevator slid down and deposited him in the gloomy garage under the block. He stepped out, starting at the sound of his own echoing footsteps. He scanned the deep shadows. He wondered if anyone had ever thought of lighting a garage properly. Shit, he was sure residents would pay a few bucks extra a year not to have to walk through something that was like a set from Alien.

Relax, he thought, you're scaring yourself. He was nervous. Everybody has to go against their dad sometime. He'd just left it later than most is all. Shit, once he calmed down the old man would probably admire him for it. After all, what was one out of nine mil? Then he thought about the letters he had posted, the ones explaining about the Island, and the bribery. The ones naming names, including Wuzel and his old man. The ones that would bring the whole thing tumbling down. It had been the bourbon that did it. Too late, now. But if his old man ever found out about the letters, about who actually sent them, one thing was certain – he would kill him, son or no. So, too late to get cold feet now.

The cars all looked the same in the gloom, just deep-shadowed humps, and it took him a precious minute to locate the Toyota. He put the case down with relief when he realised it was the right vehicle, slid between the cars and stroked the front of the tire. Nothing. He went around the other side, stupid bitch must have put it on the other one. Nothing. After checking all four wheels all he had left to show was a blackened hand and shirt cuff. Fuck. He would have to go up. Stupid, stupid. He looked at the exit ramp to street level. This wasn't the plan at all. About two minutes ago he should have taken that ramp and headed off to the Scobeyville airfield, and he should have been by himself. He didn't like this development at all. Not one little bit. He ditched the scales, reluctantly grabbed the case and headed back for the elevator. Why didn't it ever work out for him? It was like his old man was there all the time, fucking him up at every step.

the e-mailSender: jfutters@MailServe.com.
Received: from MailServe.net (post-10.mail.MailServe.com [194.712.242.39])
by dub-img-5.zip.com (8.8.6/2.6.8/2.10) with SMTP id EAA24765
for honicam.adult.net.com>; DEC 20 from: jfutters@MailServe.com
Received: from MailServe.com ([158.152..111.188])
by zip.mail.adult.net.net id aa1009592; 20 Dec. 8.05
Message-Id: <zzp.6654@zipmail.com
Content-Type: text/plain; charset=ISO-8859-1
Content-transfer-encoding: quoted-printable
X-Mailer: TFS AccessOne
/31111111111/300102811/98716374648/300202356/

Message:
Hey, that's more like it. A bit of a show, some playacting.

For God's sake keep your face to the camera when he fucks you, baby. He keeps standing in the way, the jerk. You just can't get the talent.

'What in Christ's name is going on?' Sarah was watching wide-eyed as the man sat on the bed and put the gun down. He was gesticulating wildly. 'She could kick him you know. Both legs.'

'It's not real. Is it? I mean this is one of those fantasy things? God, is this what gets Billy off?'

Sarah snorted. 'This is so tame. I found some corkers on my husband's favourites list. Ever heard of beastlove-dot-com? You don't wanna, let me tell you. And there is this one with horses, Jeez. I bet you look at most men's computers you will find something on the list like that. Doesn't bear thinking about does it? All those guys whacking off in front of a screen. Think about the mess. I think you should check the front of Billy's pants now and then.'

'Don't be disgusting.'

'What, me? I'm not the one who logs onto . . . this. Any more of that champagne? Thanks. Hold on, he's gone. Look, he's taped her mouth, grabbed the gun and gone. She's staring at the camera. Shaking her head. What do you think that means? Something is happening. Look, there's another person. It's a guy. Another one, I mean. Look, next to the bed. Anne? Can you see this?'

There was a squeal and then a crash as one of the champagne flutes hit the ground. She could see all right, even in a low res image that left everyone with distortion trails bleeding out of their faces as they moved. She could see that the second man was Billy, her husband.

Tony was squirming in the seat of the car. From their position up the street they could see the lot where the limo had pulled in quite clearly, after it had driven around the side and – they could only assume – had dropped Billy off. But they couldn't see the vehicle itself, a high hedge blocked their view.

Lester was behind the wheel, looking ridiculously small. He, too, was edgy, playing with the keys, waiting to start the engine. He knew what he had to do. Roll down the street a little. Stop. Let the other two go out and approach the Lincoln, before driving forward and cutting off any attempt to reverse the limo.

Don was the only one who was calm and quiet, and that was because he was contemplating how this might turn out. Quite a hit team, he was thinking again. Hardly *The Magnificent Seven*. Not even *The Dirty Dozen*. More like the Four Stooges. Check it out, he told himself: upstairs was a sad, overweight loner with a gun holding a doubtless terrified woman hostage, waiting for one of his old pals to come in so he could tie him up and tell him exactly what he was going to do. In here . . . well, second best didn't come close. And he included himself in that. Maybe they should've got a pro involved.

He was psyching himself up. He had to remember he was once the best alley-o defence player in the whole of Jersey. You want to get to the others? You got to get past me first. That was the message he always radiated to his opponents. If only they'd stuck to that, instead of throwing cement blocks off bridges, none of this would have come to pass. Ah well. Can't change the way it's written now. He took a deep breath, felt himself grow, expand.

'N-n-now?' asked Tony. He looked at his watch. Zero plus fourteen.

Don shook his head. 'Wait until the food comes.' It had stopped raining, just a pause, and the chill air stabbing through the window still felt heavy with moisture. 'With a bit of luck they'll still do the window-tray clip number, and we can poke the shotguns through.'

'It's g-g-gone zero plus fifteen.' said Tony, rubbing a spot on his forehead.

'I always thought that was tight. For Ed. One minute'll be OK. Now don't get jittery or jumpy, eh? If anyone's going to blast them it'll be me. You take the driver. OK?'

'Y-yup.'

'I used to work there.'

It was Lester, the first time he had spoken for many minutes.

'What?' they both asked.

'Starboards. I used to work there. Bus boy. Then on to serving.'

'We know, Lester,' said Don impatiently. 'We was always hitting on you for free burgers. Remember?'

'Yeah. Wouldn't eat them myself, though.'

'Why?'

'Shit, things people'd do with them. Drop them, leave them lying around, sneeze over them. Then there was the Saturday night frisbee championship. With the burgers. Nope, wouldn't catch me eating a Starboard burger.'

There a pause before Don said, 'How come you didn't mention this hygiene crisis before? Like at the time, I mean?'

'You seemed to enjoy 'em alright, Don. Didn't wanna rain on your parade.'

Tony laughed and Don said tersely: 'You know, Lester, there are times when I preferred you in the coma.'

Tony said, 'Ch-ch-chow time.'

They watched as the main doors opened and the waitress came out with two clip-on trays. They imagined the scene as the windows were lowered, the food positioned, tips given, and sure enough within a minute she was back in view. Don adjusted his overcoat, made sure the shotgun was going to be properly concealed. His throat suddenly dry, he croaked. 'OK Lester. Let's do it before they choke to death on those burgers.'

Anne leant over Sarah's shoulder, her warm breath panting onto her earlobe. Sarah could hear the soft mewing in the throat, the disbelief at what they were watching. But this time Sarah said it first, the tone and volume rising as it came out of her mouth until it was shrill panic: 'ohmigod!' Even with the poor, fuzzy image, she could see that Billy was being forced to sit on the bed at gunpoint.

'Do something. Isn't there any way you can do something? Call the police.'

'The police? Nobody can track this shit down. It could be anywhere, any state, any country.'

'No it couldn't. It's Atlantic City.'

'You sure?'

'Well somewhere down that way – what the hell is he doing now?'

Anne grabbed the phone and punched in Big Billy's number as fast as she could. She got the answerphone. She looked up the Long Island number and tried that. He answered on the fourth ring.

'Hello?'

'Billy.'

'Who is this?'

'Billy . . . it's Anne. Listen, is . . . you've got to help. Is Billy, my Billy, doing something for you tonight?'

'Yes, but?'

'But we can see him. See him here on the computer. He is in a room, being filmed and we can see it. And someone has a gun on him. Billy? Billy? I know it sounds crazy . . .'

'OK, Anne. Leave it to me.'

Calm, so calm. The cold bastard. It was his son. In some

fucked-up situation, and it was like she had told him he would be late from school. 'Billy, I think he's being—'

'Leave it to me Anne. I have help nearby. Now switch that thing off.'

She put the phone down.

'What did he say?' asked Sarah.

'He said I should not worry and should turn it off.'

'Turn it off? Is he crazy? I wouldn't miss this for the world. And I think your Billy ain't taking it lying down. Look.'

Wuzel and Brownie stopped outside Cecil C's, the engine running. Wuzel indicated the limo, its food trays now clipped to the windows. Brownie, out of habit, checked every other vehicle he could see. From the front seat they could see the lot of Cecil's, where it fronted onto Starboards. In fact there was no real separation between them, just colour coding of the bays. He looked at each car in turn, stopping on the red Chevy with two people in, parallel with them, perhaps twenty yards away. Man and woman. Just sitting there. Just like they were. The rest of the vehicles he dismissed, a Plymouth, a battered white Isuzu pick-up, a Honda, a Cougar.

'Wuzel,' he said quietly and indicated the red Chevy. Wuzel swivelled and looked and frowned. Didn't smell right that. He looked to the front, watched the Oldsmobile up the street detach itself from the kerb and roll down the incline. Silent and, thanks to a high fence and hedge, not yet in the limo's line of sight.

Brownie was reaching down for the bag when Wuzel grabbed his arm. 'Get them ready, Brownie. But nothing yet.' The Olds began slowing, straining to stop on power-less brakes, eventually rubbing the sidewalk to come to a standstill. As it halted two of the doors opened.

The bad smell became a rancid odour in Wuzel's nostrils. But he didn't despair. Sit tight. He had seen this kind of thing before. One, two, three interested parties. Four if you counted Billy on the inside. Five with them. They had a front row seat for the show. Well, someone had to be around to pick up the pieces. Might as well be him and Brownie.

FORTY-FIVE

'Ed? Ed Behr? Is that you?'

Ed just nodded and motioned Billy in. Even in his hyped state Ed noticed how ragged Billy was looking, almost dishevelled. His composure was gone, his clothes grubby – dark patches on his knees, a dirty cuff where it protruded from his coat. He had brushed his hair back and left a greasy mark on his forehead. Ed motioned him into the bedroom, where he could keep an eye on both of them.

'This . . .' he pointed at Honey. 'Is this some kind of JOKE?' He had to keep his cool, he reminded himself. After all, this was just his old friend Ed Behr, clearly off his trolley. With his little Honey manqué. Funny. It would be funny if he didn't have that big gun in his hand. He remembered the .32 Backson had given him, could feel it weighing down his jacket. But it would take a bit of fumbling to get it out. Best choose his time carefully.

Billy had to think logically. Was the honicam on? He looked up and over at the bound form of Honey, thought he saw her nod. Fuck, the nerds were getting their sub-scription's worth. Them looking in didn't help. Nobody knew where he was. It had taken him a long time to track down this girl. Even the police would be stumped if any viewer bothered to phone them and asked what was going on. 'Hey officer, I was just logging on for my usual whacking-off session when I saw the strangest thing . . .' Best try to reason with the guy. And then kill the fucker.

'Ed, what are you doing?'

Ed smiled with a kind of twisted satisfaction. 'Right now? I'm robbing you.'

'Well that's funny, Ed, because right now, I am trying to rob myself.'

For the first time Ed noticed the case Billy had in his left hand.

Don stepped out of the Olds, the shotgun held under his raincoat. He snagged the gun on the frame, and had to try and lever it out. He staggered back as it came free, and felt his hand tighten, almost discharging it. Shit, nearly blew it at stage one. He breathed deep again to try and calm himself, and watched a shaky Tony get out, wiping his nose with his left hand over and over again. He looked at Don and nodded in what he hoped was a confident way. The wind caught Tony's coat and it blew open to reveal the gun to the whole world. He grabbed it and wrapped it back over as fast as he could.

OK – simple, thought Don. The guns go in the windows, the trunk is popped, Lester should start up and come round, blocking the exit. By then Ed would be down, having incapacitated Billy. Incapacitated Ed had kept saying. Not tie up. Not knock out. Not use the cuffs on. Incapacitate.

And for the first time Don wondered if he had been suckered. All those stories about wanting revenge, some justice, a chance to rebuild Lester's life. What if Tony's instinct was right – except Ed didn't want the money, just wanted to pop Billy, and the hell with the consequences? The hell with all of them? Go out in a blaze of Glory. He took a deep, calming breath. What the hell was all this doing to his blood pressure?

Backson was two bites into the burger and five minutes into the second quarter of the game when the cellphone rang. He looked at Shawn. Billy? He picked it up, not liking the little fluttering in his stomach.

'Yeah?'

'Something is happening in the apartment. Get up there. Now.'

Big Billy didn't have to identify himself, and he didn't have to ask twice. Backson flung open the passenger door, squeezed himself out, checked his gun was loose in the holster, and looked up at the window he knew was the girl's. He almost didn't notice the big figure turning the corner, who froze, surprised to see him out of the car. Don could see Backson was reaching for a gun, assumed it was for him. He flipped back the coat and started to raise the Remington, felt his limbs turn to lead, the gun weighing heavy in his hands, the trajectory inching up to firing level painfully slowly. Just as he had expected. All going to shit.

Ed looked at the case and at Billy. Across the street, right now, he knew, his friends were risking their lives to open an empty trunk. Waiting for him.

He pushed the gun into Billy's chest and reached for the bag.

Billy shook his head. His hand moved towards his jacket pocket. He wasn't going to let this fuck-up have his money. He'd ditched his wife, his father, his lover, everything. There was nothing to go back to. He had to have the money.

It had never occurred to Ed that Billy might be armed, and it took a fraction of a second for him to register what he was reaching for. Surely he had others to do that, to carry the weapons. But what was it he said? Robbing himself. Fuck – he was making off with the mil, for whatever reasons. Turning over his own old man. Billy squirmed away and stepped back to get a clear pull of the pistol.

It was pure, pure instinct on Ed's part. He is going to

shoot me, he thought. Kill me. I am going to die in here while my friends get slaughtered for nothing outside. The gun. The gun had control here. So, almost unbidden, Ed's finger tightened on the trigger of the Spitfire. He felt it buck in his hands, felt his ear drums spasm as the shockwave thudded around the room, watched Billy clutch his chest and go down.

Alice wanted a cigarette, but she couldn't. No lighting up in the car. Shepard was stiff as a board she noticed, wound up like a super-coiled spring, almost to snapping point. 'What you find out, by the way?'

'Where?'

'From the old guy. The guy who ran the store.'

Shepard didn't want to speak. Every so often he glanced down at the GPS system that pinpointed where the bug was in the gun. Still in the apartment. Still transmitting. 'It's . . . Behr and the others. They did time. For murder.'

'I thought he already told you that.'

'Yeah. But it should've been manslaughter. It was here. In Cotchford. They all went down except one kid. Name of Moon.'

'Moon?'

'You not heard of Billy Moon?'

Alice shook her head.

'I have, he's one of the little cellular type networks. Word is he is going fully legit. Don't they always say that? Played it smart – just expanded a little, not too greedy, consolidated what he had, kept out of all the trouble with the Russians and the Koreans. But someone, somewhere'll have his number – I'll make a call to the OC when we get finished.' Ted Vespa at the NY Organised Crime Field Office still owed him from a gun trace he had done a couple of years back that joined the dots on one of his RICO cases.

'So this guy Moon and Behr knew each other?'

'What? No, no. The Moon I'm talking about is the father. It was the son who was involved with Ed. It was the son that killed the people – he actually tossed a cinder block through the windshield of a car. Hit the driver. You know what that'd do? But Moon didn't do time. Maybe this is something to do with that.' He turned to face her. 'Who knows?'

'How come?'

'What?'

'He didn't do time?'

'Well, he did Gibbs, but you know what that is. Soft option. Basically his old man made him finger the others. You know, help the law enforcement officers by naming names – which is kind of ironic, given the kind of man the father is. But that isn't the sick part. That wasn't why they got the book thrown at them.'

'What wa—?'

The little beep from the GPS handset faltered and disappeared, causing her to stop mid-sentence. At the same time Goodrich thought – imagined, surely – he heard the distant, flattened bark of a handgun. He almost fell out of the door, shouting at Alice 'Get some back-up—'.

'About time, Shepard.'

But too late man, too late, was what she was thinking.

Shepard was up and out of the car when he saw the bulk of Don turn the corner into the lot. The guy hadn't seen him yet. At the same time someone was getting out of the limo, another hefty piece of work. Big man, moving easy. All happening too fast. Shepard watched as the coat flicked open and a shotgun appeared in the new guy's hands. The limo man was going for his piece as well.

Shepard decided to join them. He reached in and hesitated between the Neostead shotgun and the laser-sighted Colt SMG. The Neostead was a fearsome weapon, but maybe a bit of finesse was needed here. He went for the SMG, flicked it to semi-auto. At the last minute he switched again. He could finesse another time. The Neostead made people pay attention.

'Armed Federal Officers. Stay where you are!' he shouted. He didn't have to tell Alice what to do. She rolled out, using the door as a shield, and pulled out a S&W 1076 auto pistol, the big ten mil number. Always had to go one better, our Alice, he thought. Didn't like the Sig 228s because they were too small. Wanted the bad guys to know she was pointing some heavy shit at them. He must remind her that it helped in a firefight if every officer had the same weapon. Then you could swap mags and—

He heard the yell from his left. He looked over and saw something arcing through the air, a perfect parabola, spinning lazily as it went, the streetlamps catching the metal corner plates, flashing with each slow revolution.

A case. Someone had thrown a case out of an apartment window.

Brownie flicked the safety off the machine pistol and laid it across his lap. He watched the three protagonists as if it were a ballet, a choreographed performance. The guy getting out of the limo. The shotgun carrier stopping and bringing up the barrel of his weapon, clearly surprised to see this character out of the car. Then the man and woman bursting out of the Chevy to their left.

He looked at Wuzel and said: 'This idea of yours. It wasn't original, then?'

Billy felt the impact in his chest, and staggered back, losing his footing. He let go of the case. Too late to worry about that now. Such a soft impact, really. Bam. Like being hit with a BB. All the nerves must have shut down, gone into shock. The pain would come soon, he knew. His footing went as the carpet slid on the polished floor and he crashed down, the breath driven out of his body. What a fuck up, he thought, waiting for the darkness.

Ed picked up the case and ran to the window. Through the rain-streaked glass he could just make out a collection of figures. Already it seemed to have gone wrong. He could see the Olds starting to move, but clearly Lester wasn't in place yet. There was movement all around. Don had cleared the shotgun from his coat. Backson was out of the limo. Why? And what was happening around that Chevy?

They are all going to die. Over what he had in his hand. No doubt about it. Bloodbath.

Instinct took over again. It wasn't worth it. Already he had shot – no, killed – Billy. Killed a guy. He struggled with the window catch, unclipping the frame and swinging it open as wide as he could. Not much space to get a good throw in. He stepped back into the room, swung his arm with the case in it behind him, felt tendons and sinews pop and muscles pull with the weight, then, like a crazed discus thrower he pitched it forward, staggering as he went, watched it spin off into the semi-darkness of the parking lot, and fall from the sky, like pennies from heaven. A lot of pennies.

The room suddenly lit with an intense glow, and there was a deep rumble. Ed leaned out to see what was happening.

It was at that point Billy realised he wasn't dead after all, and reached for the gun Backson had given him.

Eleven pairs of eyes watched the case crash to the ground, and buckle into a twisted three dimensional trapezium. It bounced once, tumbled end over end, but it didn't split. The million stayed inside. Don turned and looked across the road to the apartment lot, where the baggage sat in a puddle, surrounded by a halo of diminishing ripples. To his right, a few yards back, he could sense Tony also looking.

The case. It could only be the case from the trunk. Billy must have taken it with him, Ed was throwing it out to warn them. What were the moves here? Think. Fast.

The Feds whoever they were, they were a problem, but maybe he could do something about them. He risked a glance over.

'Federal Officers,' the guy repeated, and racked a round into the breech of his weapon. And Don realised he knew him. Even in this yellowy light. The guy from the bar. Ed's pal. The one who sold them the guns. 'ATF. Drop your weapons.'

Federal Officers? ATF?

Who cared. Here was the big question. Had he sold them guns that worked?

Time to find out. He swivelled again, facing back towards the diner, and shouted over his shoulder. 'Tony. The case. It's yours.'

Just like old times. Don the big defender. Tony sprinting, those legs carrying him across the street, as if he were looking for a chalk circle to burst through. Only this time, no friends to liberate. Just a million bucks.

Don saw the ATF man swivel to cover the figure of Tony. He was about to put something his way when the guy from the limo did it for him. Backson had assessed the situation and decided that those with a badge had to be dealt with first. Don raised to fire.

'Fuckin' jackbooted Nazis!'

The cry stopped them all dead. The words, spat out with an involuntary venom, came from a battered white pick-up in the corner. Two men in dungarees were dismounting from the cab. Both looked to be armed. Tony slowed and looked over his shoulder. Fred and Lou. They'd come to save him, protect him after all. Fuckin' ATF – they'd been onto them all along. Still, Fred and Lou'd sort them. He'd best get the case, he thought, then thank them.

The pick-up was facing the diner, with the tailgate towards the Chevy. Fred stepped from the driver's side, raised the Marlin and loosed off a shot at the Federal Agents. Shepard felt a tug at his left arm and gasped when he looked down. A big piece of meat had gone, clawed out, as if raked by a giant beast with huge talons. He heard the second shot come by and tried to lift the Neostead. The left arm wasn't working so well, but he held it up and rested the barrel on it, ignoring the searing fire in his shoulder. Shepard heard part of the Chevy explode behind him as another round from the Marlin burst through glass and metal, showering him with debris. He finally steadied the Neostead and pulled the trigger.

Meanwhile Alice's ten mil slug hit Backson hard, sending him staggering. Five more, tightly grouped, punched into him, almost lifting his bulk into the air. He jerked for a few seconds like a crazed puppet before his strings were cut and he flopped to the ground in a shapeless heap.

The Neostead was a South African weapon designed to stop fleeing vehicles. The shell exploded on impact with something good and solid, usually just passing through flesh, leaving a big hole. It struck Fred squarely on his big silver belt buckle and detonated, severing him clean off at the waist and ejecting his flailing upper torso into the air. Lou watched, jaw agape, as the semi-human cartwheeled through the air and thudded onto the windshield of the Honda, shattering it before slithering down the hood.

'Nazis!' Lou shouted again and squeezed the trigger of his shotgun. The next round from Shepard detonated in the cab, filling Lou's eyes with needle-like shards of metal and glass. Shepard fired again, the recoil bruising his shoulder, and the third explosive ordnance hit the fuel tank, the fourth and fifth followed it close behind, and the pick-up jack-knifed into a column of flame, shattering the front of the diner, and washing the scene with a sickly orange glow as the fireball reached skywards. In the flames, Shepard could make out the twisting, waving form of a man, trapped by the splayed metal of the flatbed, incinerating in the column of fire.

Lester didn't know much, but he knew when things weren't going right. Don shouldn't have stopped like that. Shouldn't be pulling the gun out like that. He started up the car again, kept the lights off, lost sight of them all as a truck drove by. Now there seemed to be two people out of their car at the far end. As he got closer he felt a jolt of recognition.

It was the scruffy beard, the long hair. It was the undercover man from *The Getaway*. With some big fuck-off shotgun in his hand. Ed said there wouldn't be one, no plain clothes to worry about, but there he was, ready to rack up the penalty points. On the periphery of his field of vision he could see the score plummeting, the figures rolling down like the altimeter on a plane spiralling from the sky.

The huge whump of gasoline going up, incinerating the pick-up truck, buffeted him, but he kept going. They often threw distractions like that, make you lose concentration, lose points. He gripped the wheel harder.

A car swerved and he heard the horn screaming away into the night, his foot was flat to the floor, and the engine was revving into the red, filling his ears with its death rattle. He opened his mouth and joined in the chorus of stressed metal as he bumped onto the lot. A star shape appeared on the windshield in front of him. And another. Something seared the side of his head, and a clot of blood splashed onto his shoulder. His hearing had gone. No matter. Time to get that bonus. A white hot pain pierced his shoulder, wrenching his left hand from the wheel, but he kept it straight. Foot to the floor. Straight at Wild Card, the undercover Fed. He wasn't going to close this game down on him. Not now. Feet, inches away now, almost see the whites of his eyes. Game Over. Lester was smiling at the thought of the bonuses when the back of his skull lifted off and filled the rear of the car with its contents.

Above all the noise, the detonation of rounds from the Olds, the boom of a pick-up torn apart, came another sound. An engine, screeching. Don felt the door mirror of the Olds catch his back, spin him round, as it powered across the lot towards the red Chevy. Lester, full throttle.

Alice swallowed hard as the headlights bounced towards her, suppressed the urge to run, to get away, held up the S&W and as coolly and steadily as she could placed three shots right where the driver's head was. It kept coming.

Shepard couldn't reload the Neostead in time, so he grabbed the Colt SMG as best he could and began copying her grouping. He had lost his left arm, as a useful tool anyway, and his firing was erratic. The Olds fishtailed slightly and still it came. It was then that he realised they had been aiming far too high. Now he could see the driver's head and it was barely over the wheel. He put another cluster into the safety glass, lower down. Must have connected. Must have. But nothing would stop it now.

There was an anguished squeal – a monstrous sound collage of metal and human sounds – as the two cars collided. The Chevy reared and slid over the Olds' front, as if it were some terrible fatal mounting, and the intertwined bodies slewed back into Cecil's glass wall, which shuddered, cracked and exploded over the lot, like an accident in an ice factory.

* * *

Tony heard the detonations, shouts and screams behind him but kept running, kept pumping, willed those legs to shrink the distance between him and the case. He was sure Lou and Fred would do their best, would save him. Still, he had told them to meet him at the second car. A little thought came into his head. They wouldn't have come for the money themselves, would they? He felt a wave of sickly, fume-filled heat wash over him, saw the walls of the apartment block burst into light. What was going on?

Tony concentrated on running. He still had the speed, still had the stride, smooth and elegant and effortless. As he reached level with the case he almost skidded to a halt, like making a homer, a spume of water rising up as he pressed his shoes to the asphalt. In one smooth movement he bent and picked it up. Just on the exhalation of his breath he added a little soft, alley-o to himself. Victory. Not quite like old times. But it'd do.

The small smile vanished as he turned just in time to watch their getaway car destroy itself in grinding crash of steel and plastic, imploding and bursting and twisting until the two shapes had almost fused. And then he saw the immolating pick-up, though he could see a darker shape within it turning to blackened ash. No. Not Lou and Fred.

Don felt the same as he looked at the carnage, the glowing and smoking wreckage. Lester was dead, no doubt, and probably the two ATF officers were buried somewhere in there, and Lou was toast and a large chunk of Fred had slithered down the front of a Honda, leaving a red trail like a haemorrhaging snail. But they still had one car that was usable. Billy's limo. Take the limo and run. How long should they give Ed? And what had the money been doing up there anyways?

He decided such questions could wait and waved to Tony

to cross the road and he was about to spin and face their new vehicle when the bullet caught him low in the back, severing his spine, turning his legs to mush, exiting in a fist-sized hole through his stomach, bursting bits of his gut onto the wet surface in front of him with a sickening splatter. He teetered there for a minute, his large frame balancing on twin pillars of jell-o, some quirk of gravity keeping him upright. His brain sent furious messages, but there was nothing to receive them, his lower torso was cut off, silent, deserted. Slowly he pitched forward, blackness rushing to meet him as he thought, the driver. Driver had a gun, too. And him a Born Again Christian. A half smile played over his face. He had known it. Known all along it wouldn't work. Something would fuck it up. Why hadn't they list—?

It was a long way for an accurate shotgun blast, but Tony dropped the case and raised and racked the Remington anyway, his hands absolutely steady for once, and fired over the head of Don as his friend thudded to the ground, sending up a pink-tinged spray of water. The recoil knocked Tony back, and he saw one of the rear windows of the limo punch out. Fuck. Clumsily he pulled the slide for another try.

The remaining lights went out in the diner, and then in the lot itself. Someone had finally realised this was no accidental explosion that had taken out half the windows. Shots were heading their way. Tony imagined the prostrate forms glowing in the dying flames from the truck, scrabbling for cover across smashed plates, broken glass, burgers, dogs, pot pies, rivers of Coke and mush of cream pies.

The limo started up. No lights. Tony braced himself. It would come right at him, just like Lester had done to the Feds. He watched it kangaroo as it thumped over the crumbled shape of the bodyguard, then the rear wheels went into a full throttle spin, powering the vehicle across the lot, sending up chutes of water and, still reversing, bounce onto the road and carry on before executing a perfect U-turn to face the right way and roar off.

Silence was reclaiming the scene. The rain started again, the pools all around him suddenly zinging as rings formed across their surface. The car wreck hissed and creaked, the pick-up crackled and popped, and the odd saloon came by, speeding up when they saw Tony, shotgun still at his shoulder, and the body lying on the sidewalk.

He looked up at the open window of the apartment, and across at Don. His old friend was face down, sprawled, a kind of reverse crucifixion. The wind was catching his hair, and it could be mistaken for life, as if his head were shaking. But the body was still. He was dead. Big hole in his middle. Dead. And Tony had no doubt Don wouldn't be surprised one little bit. He had to get out of there now. He'd raise a glass to his old pessimistic pal later. Tony bent down to retrieve the case of money when the small burst of three nine mil slugs hit him, pushing him backwards across the surface of the tarmac, in some kind of crazed moondance, as if he were on rails, his hand just having grazed the handle then plucked away. So near, so far. Almost a million in his fingers.

He hit the ground and felt his lungs explode, a tsunami of white pain crashed through his brain. Don, Lester and now me. Fuck you, Ed, he thought. Fuck you and your games. I should've stayed in the woods.

Ed was watching open-mouthed at the scene below. By leaning out of the window he could see where Lester had rammed the other car, where Backson had been blown away, he could see Tony had made it to the case but was holding a shotgun. And he could see Don, face down, his raincoat wicking up the water from the puddle he had landed in, rain starting to thud on his lifeless back. A pick-up had been engulfed by flames, blown to fuck, and he had no idea why. He could just see a lifeless torso, a set of legs, a rifle, a shotgun, a twisted wreckage of two cars and, glinting like discarded treasure, the spent cartridges from the firefight, fallout from some kind of extreme carnage.

Then he felt the gun forced against his scalp, the hand in his hair, twisting him back, forcing him down, until he was on his knees. He tried to raise the Spitfire but something hard rapped him across his knuckles and he dropped it.

Ed found himself forced by the agony on his scalp to look into Billy's face, and Billy's gun, an inch from his eyes. There was no sign of a wound. He should have no chest – or at least no back left. Billy Moon should be dead. Ed knew that much. He didn't know much about guns but he knew a nine mil slug from two feet was supposed to take you out of the game for good.

Billy grabbed him by the throat, roughly, angrily, homicidally. Ed closed his eyes.

'Just before I blow your fuckin' brains out, tell me why.'

Ed opened one eye. The stench of discharged rounds filled his nostrils, leaking out of the gun that was now denting the flesh of his forehead, but he couldn't feel it, not pain, not even the sensation of touch. He had gone numb. But he could tell by the smell that the gun had been used before. He never thought, had never considered Billy might be the one who was carrying, who was used to this shit. Why? He looked at the girl, at that Candy Clark face, and felt a jolt inside. He wouldn't understand. Or maybe he would. Maybe—

'Why?'

'For Lester.'

Billy pulled the gun back as if he was going to hit Ed with it. He snapped his eyes shut and tensed, waiting for the blow.

'Lester?'

'Yes, fucking Lester. You dumped us back then, you let Lester rot after what happened to him. You dumped the evidence, then you ratted us. You got rich and we got poor and fucked up and we wanted you to know it.' He could feel the molecular pool beckoning, his slot in the empty universe waiting to be filled. No God, no afterlife, just . . . nothing. Another lump of protein and fat and gristle to be digested and redistributed. And he didn't care. 'Now pull the fuckin' trigger.'

The hand twisted harder in his hair and Ed was yanked to his feet. Billy was strong enough. Not street-strong like Don. Poor Don. But there was power in those arms. Billy had looked after himself, part of his brain told him admiringly. When they were level Ed opened his eyes again, looked at the girl, who seemed to have slumped in resignation. Or maybe she was just OD'd on craziness.

'Lester?' asked Billy, his mind whirring. But he knew the answer to his questions already. 'Lester? What you saying here? What you saying? Huh? What you saying?'

'Yes. Lester. Lester who is probably fucking dead across the street. Lester. Me. Tony. Don. Bird. All of us . . .'

'Come on. Grab those keys. In the purse. Honey we got to take the car. You'll be OK. Undo those cuffs, Ed. Come on. Now, we got to go and see a man about an elephant, get fucking moving, shitface.' And he pushed a confused, stumbling Ed ahead of him towards the door.

Shepard tried to sit up and felt his nervous system protest. That was all. No muscle seemed involved, no bruises, cuts, gashes, just a raw burst of electrical energy. Get through it, he thought.

He managed to pull himself onto one elbow and the rest of his body came back to life. Something ground in his leg, there was blood running down his face, glass or grit in one eye, he was deaf in one ear, a large part of an upper arm missing, and his hands started throbbing. But he was alive.

Above him he could see the tangled mess of the cars. The Chevy had ridden over the front of the oncoming Olds, throwing him clear as it crushed the roof line, and popped the windshield. One front wheel of their car was where the driver would have been. But he was pretty sure that driver was dead before he hit them, only some last post-death spasm keeping his foot on the throttle.

And Alice?

It took him an eternity to get to his feet. Wincing as he put weight on his left leg, biting his tongue rather than yelling out. Something gone in there. His head spun sickeningly with the effort. Then he realised the Colt SMG was still at his feet; it took another nausea-inducing crouch to retrieve it.

Then the lights of the lot went out, leaving the whole area bathed only in the thin, white light from the streetlamps and the yellowy radiance from still burning gasoline. He fought off the urge to be sick, and leant on the Olds to guide his way round.

Alice had been caught under the chin by the door as the Chevy bucked up. The metal had buried itself into the flesh under her jaw, lifted her off the ground, and her own weight had helped plunge it deep into the back of her neck. She hung there still, like a grotesque art installation. Lifeless. Had to get her down. Couldn't leave his partner there. Medics be here soon. Too late, but nobody should be found like that. No pictures should be taken to satisfy the gore hounds. Could he hear the sirens yet? Surely someone in the now darkened diner, in the apartment block, some passing drivers, the people in Cecil C's – surely someone had called 911.

The rattle of a gun brought him back. A three shot burst. He looked up at the two characters about ten yards ahead of him on either side of a car parked on the street. Their attention was on the parking lot of the apartments. Shepard tried to focus, but couldn't. His long vision had gone. One eye was filling with blood, the other felt like someone was sandpapering it. But he could see these two all right. He raised the Colt, holding it single-handed in his right hand, and started walking, dragging the left leg behind him slightly, ignoring the grinding in it, the noise he could almost hear, as if the lubrication had failed on a drive shaft and it was about to tear itself apart. Forget Alice for now. Get these two.

'Armed Fed—' His voice cracked, he cleared his throat and inflated his lungs. 'Armed Federal Officer. Drop your weapons.'

Brownie started to turn when Shepard's single shot exploded his right shoulder, throwing him against the car. He grunted, fought the stab of pain. He looked at the flap of skin that had been exposed and checked it as not bad. But he couldn't lift his gun arm. Shock.

Brownie looked at the bloody figure moving towards them, at the blood on his face, the twisted foot, the glass shards glinting in his cheek. This guy don't look like he's got much to lose, he thought.

He turned his head to look over the roofline at Wuzel. It was Wuzel's call. He was on the far side of the vehicle. If he chose to duck, use all that metal as cover then . . . then Brownie would get it first. That was what he would do. And the moment Wuzel dived, the Fed would drop Brownie, so there would be only one to worry about.

But Wuzel had taken three steps into the street, away from the car. It left him more exposed than he would have liked. Stepping back to duck down would take a second too long. The guy may be injured – badly – but he looked like he knew what he was doing. He hit Brownie. Maybe he meant to kill him, but from where he was it looked like good shooting. And he would bet everything in that case lying across the street that the Fed had switched the SMG to full auto now.

'Brownie?' the ATF man suddenly asked. 'Is that you, Brownie?'

'Who the fuck . . .? I know you?'

'Goodrich.'

Brownie nodded. Goodrich. The barfly pawnshop guy. Him, a Ness. Go figure that one. There was a squeal of tires from across the street. Wuzel and Brownie both looked anxiously at the lot, where a Toyota had emerged from the ramp of the apartment parking level and had paused next to the guy they had just dropped.

'Goodrich, look, you got us, but you ought to know the big prize is over there, and it's getting away. Under your nose. Don't you care about that? There's a robbery going down. One million dollars, give or take.'

'I don't care if the President is getting ass-fucked by one of his aides, Brownie. I thought we had lost you when you fucked off out of town. Hoped by raiding the bar we'd get something on you—' he caught a movement from Wuzel. 'Don't think about it pal, you drop that gun. I can get both of you before you raise it. Even with blood in my eyes and one good hand. This is on full blow-you-in-half mode now. Drop it. OK. Brownie, you're the big prize. My guess is Ed Behr is over there, and we'll catch up with him sometime . . .' the sickness hit and the pair blurred, as if they were on a merry-go-round. He coughed to try and bring the spinning to a halt. They steadied. Blurred but steady. He heard and half saw the Toyota come screeching out of the apartment lot and accelerate away.

He waited for time to pass, reminding himself that each second got the cops and his boys closer and closer. He could hear sirens already. Fire boys no doubt. Medics. All he had to do was keep these two covered. Stay awake. That was all he wanted. Then get Alice down. Keep them covered. Stay awake.

Had to talk. To stay sharp. 'Brownie, you are the big p . . .' This time the image tilted to forty-five degrees and blackness started to crowd the edge of his vision, tunnelling it. He tried to shake his head, but it was too late. He staggered once, twice, recovered, tried to focus on Brownie, who was now at the end of a dark, long passageway. He could see life was back in his arm, that he was raising the gun. Shepard squeezed off a burst, felt the weapon judder in his hands as it spat out a stream of shells, but sensed it all went skyward. He had lost consciousness even before Brownie's cluster of three rounds punctured his body.

FORTY-SIX

There was pain exploding throughout Tony's body, sending pointed stabs of agony to his brain. As if trying to block them out, his mind was wandering, tracing the diaphanous thread that led him back to the woods, to Lou and Fred, back to Warren, back to the dope deals, through Boxgrove and back to that night on the bridge.

It had been a wonderful night. Stars, no wind, the highway below, the big trucks rattling through, the block balanced on the edge. All about timing. You had to push the block while you could still see the truck, as if the block was going to hit the cab. It never did, the grey lump rotated in the air in slo-mo, eventually landing with a hollow metal ringing sound right in the empty tipper section. By the time you rushed over to the other side of the bridge you could see the brake lights burning bright as the truck snaked to a halt, the driver wondering what the fuck had happened.

So it was this night as Billy walked up to do the pushing, watching the lights of the truck come towards him, measuring the distance like a pitcher, psyching himself up. Now, Tony remembered thinking. Now. But Billy turned and smiled a cocky smile, a little shake of his head. Not yet, not yet. Then a two-handed push, a look over the edge and a sprint to the other side.

Then the multitude of noises. More than there should have been. The bang of the cinder block hitting metal, a screeching of brakes . . . no, two sets of screeching of brakes wrapped and intertwined with each other, glass shattering, metal crunching, an implosion, a whooshing sound, then a sudden burst of flame.

They ran down the dirt path at the side of the bridge that took them down the bank, onto the shoulder of the highway on the far side from the wreck. Two hundred yards away they could see the sedan embedded in the back of the truck, flames licking around the already dead family inside.

The wind caught the fumes and carried the gruesome smells towards them, pungent carcinogens from melting plastic and boiling, crisping flesh.

'Holy shit,' said Billy.

'Holy fucking shit,' said Ed, fighting back the urge to vomit.

'No, I meant this.'

They turned and looked at Billy. The block must have entered the windshield and hit the driver in the throat, severing the head clean off, the momentum sending both it and the block through the rear window too.

Now Billy was holding up the head of the poor smashed driver by the hair, with his back to the slowing vehicles so they couldn't see it, staring at the mangled, inhuman features and the blood and tissue draining from the severed umbilicals that protruded from the torn throat. As the first sirens wailed he wrapped it in his coat and said: 'Let's split. Now.'

The lifeless eye squeezed out of the severed head, resting on the crushed cheek, that was the last image Tony saw as he slipped out of consciousness.

The Toyota was shot. The engine rattled and squeaked and gave up the fight at around sixty, sixty-five, but Billy pushed it for all it was worth, wanting to leave behind him the carnage outside the block. He had freed Honey before he left, switched off the camera – the guys had had enough excitement for one night – and dragged a compliant Ed with him.

It was just sinking in, now, what had gone down. There had been a little stand-off he had witnessed as they went by what was left of the diner lot. And he had seen Wuzel, he was sure, his old man's sidekick. Vince Wuzel. Now what was he doing there? Sent by his father to chaperone him, because he had suspected something? Sent by his father to whack him? So what did that make the guy who had Wuzel covered? And the twisted form in the middle of the lot? And the pick-up? What was that all about?

In the back seat Tony groaned with pain. Billy had insisted on grabbing the million dollars, Ed had settled for Tony. He was lying full length on the small seat, still cradling his shotgun, a large lake of blood gathering in the hollow of his clothes around his chest area.

It was time to make your mind up, Billy. He still had his gun. He had left the one Ed had been carrying behind. Ed himself was next to him, wild-eyed, panting, trying to stop the movie playing in his head. The movie of the wreckage of two cars, with a dead, shattered Lester just visible beneath one of the wheels that had caved in the bullet-shattered windshield. Of Don, things finally having worked out just like he always thought they would. Badly. If there *was* an afterlife, no doubt he had the whole of eternity to finally say I-told-you-so. Of Fred, split in half and cast aside like a soggy burger bun. And Tony, rattling and whistling as he breathed, like some badly maintained steam pump.

They saw three police cruisers, bells, whistles and sirens full on, race by them, followed by a couple of ambulances and two fire trucks. Kind of slow, boys, he thought.

Billy reached the lights at 35 and stopped on red. The airport was north, the plane waiting for him, the one that was going to take him and his mil away from his wife and father and all that shit. A new life. Not perfect, not with such a little stake, but it'd do. South – well, what was south? Curiosity was south, and maybe some help for Tony, although he suspected it was too late for that. For the first time Ed looked up at him. A horn honked behind. Green. Ed said: 'Well, what is it? France or Italy?'

Brownie knew he had a minute, maybe two. He knew there would be confusion. He had got Wuzel to move the car round the back of the apartment. Maybe someone in Cecils or the diner or in the block had seen them, knew they were part of all this, but he was betting it was going to be chaos when the cops got here. Bodies, officers down, one of them pinned in mid air like a hunting trophy. There was plenty of other traffic on the road, slowing down to gawk. He just had to hide his shoulder, which was throbbing like a mother-fucker, and he and Wuzel could get away in the midst of the mayhem.

He had known which apartment to go to by the open window. In fact, the door was also still ajar, so it was a piece of cake. He pulled out his wallet, but made no attempt to open it. Just as he had figured, the girl was still there, kneeling by the bed as if praying, her eyes red with tears, shaking. What she needed was some authority. Someone to look up to. A shoulder to cry – no, forget the shoulder. That hurt too much. Kind of messy, too.

He held up the wallet quickly. 'FBI, ma'am. Where did they go?'

'They . . .' She looked up at him, took in the bloody stain, and studied his face, the tan, and the wrinkles. 'FBI? Kinda old aren't you?'

He pulled the SAF from under his coat. 'It's an outreach program for third agers. Where did they go?'

As he pointed the weapon at her face he was struck by the other image that had been floating in his head that night. The woman on the ship, *The Alchemist*. They could have been sisters. Twins, almost. What had her name been? Rachel, that was it. The name badge had said Rachel.

Honey realised she didn't care if he was a Fed or a cop or a hoodlum. She just wanted him to leave. She was tired of everything to do with Billy, and his little Honey fantasy life, especially after the full Broadway production that had just gone down in her room. First he's dead, then he's not. She wondered if it was just another one of his deceptions, upping the role-playing to include resurrection and saving. Shit, maybe the poor man was getting a Jesus Christ fixation. Too, too weird. It was time to get back to being plain old Emma Lean from Troy Hills. She played back the last few sentences spoken in the room. They made no sense either. 'Damn, mister, all they said was they was going to see an elephant. I am pretty sure they said elephant. They took my car. A Toyota. Pennsylvania plates.' Trying to be helpful. Now get out she wanted to scream. If only she had the Walther. Fuck the Feds and their five day wait. Then she realised what she was kneeling against.

Elephant? A fucking elephant? thought Brownie. What was this – running away to the circus? He thought maybe she was bullshitting him, but he could tell from her expression she was too beat, too confused to do anything of the sort. OK, maybe Wuzel knew what that meant. Elephant. He'd figure it out later. Problem was, if she told him, then she'd tell the next set of people through the door, and maybe the advantage they had would be gone. Spooky, her looking like that dealer. Still, got one, why not collect the pair? He looked over his shoulder to make sure no neighbours were coming in, flipped the safety on the SAF down to the single shot – the quieter – setting.

The screen suddenly went dead. A message flashed up to tell them that the connection was broken. Anne looked at Sarah and burst into tears. Sarah put her arm around her, felt the sob racking her body. That was the strangest thing she had ever seen on the Internet in her life – and she thought she had seen every bizarre thing.

At the end, from what they could see, Billy was in control, not dead at all, but that didn't seem to matter to Anne, she was crying harder. In fact it looked suspiciously like set-up, as if . . . no. This wouldn't be a piece of Internet performance would it?

Anne turned to face Sarah, perplexed and bewildered, but knowing that what they had witnessed was a *coda* of some kind, to something. 'I'm not going to see him again, am I?'

Sarah tried to smile, tried to give a reassurance she couldn't feel. How was she supposed to know? 'Of course you will, sugar, of course you will,' she said with true sincerity and hope in her voice – because otherwise she was never going to shift that damned apartment.

Left. South. But not on the Parkway, down to pick up route nine. It'd be slow, but someone at the toll stations on the parkway was bound to see the bleeding figure in the back. Also it was there they would set up the blocks. Going to take some time, this. Hour and a half, maybe even two. Billy turned back and looked at Tony. The pool of blood didn't seem to be getting any bigger, and what was there was firming up, forming a crust. Shit, maybe he would make it.

'F-F-France or Italy?' Tony asked weakly, echoing Ed.

'What the fuck you all talking about?' asked Billy with barely suppressed rage.

Ed told him.

'This ain't no movie, Tony. But since you ask, France, I guess. Sort this out once and for all.'

'A-a-amen to that,' said Tony, and slipped out of it again with a long gurgling sigh.

Billy had hidden the dead driver's head in the freezer in the garage, wrapped in plastic bags. The photo shoot had been his idea. Like a bunch of kids with trophies. He lined them up, got them all to grin, got Lester to hold the head like he was a football mascot holding the ball before Superbowl. Snap, snap, snap. Black and white. Develop them at the school darkroom. One for each of them. Help them recall a night to remember. Help them remember they were all in it together, now the cops were following up reports of a group of kids standing on the shoulder immediately after the accident.

'Elephant?' asked Wuzel.

'Yeah, we'll figure it out as we drive. I don't think those lights are the second coming. Come on, they must be heading for the Parkway.'

Wuzel edged out cautiously onto the road, almost blinded by the luminous cruisers screeching to a halt. He looked in the mirror and could see the cops sprinting towards the diner. It'd be ten, fifteen minutes before anything made any sense to them. He just kept driving real slow and easy, like any one of the two dozen cars that had come by in the last ten minutes, wondering whether Cotchford really was the nice, safe town they had been led to believe.

Wuzel said, 'Well, there is only one elephant I can think

of. Two, two – there is the Blue Elephant Thai in Toms River. And Lucy.'

'Lucy? Margate? The Budweiser elephant?'

'Yeah. Well, she's easy to find. It might be some kind of pre-arranged rendezvous. You know – the Oh Shit option? Good place for a regrouping. Got any better ideas? OK. We'll go south on the Parkway.'

Brownie touched him on the arm. 'How's my shoulder look?'

'Like shit. How's it feel?'

'Oh, like shit. But I'll live.' He lifted a big flap of skin. 'Listen, we pull into a gas station, big one, get me some kind of waterproof, something to go over the coat?'

Wuzel nodded. 'What about the girl?'

'The girl?'

'In the apartment? The one you was sure was up there?'

Brownie shrugged with his one good shoulder. He just wondered where the hell that big silver pistol she had pulled on him came from. She held it straight out, two handed, level with his balls. Told him she could keep her mouth shut, been doing it half her life, and she could easily forget someone who came in claiming to be a Fed. And all about an elephant. And if he didn't believe her he would just have to take his chances with how fast she could pull the trigger.

He liked that.

Big, shiny gun, too. Safety off as far as he could see. He looked at the end of the barrel, waiting for evidence of shaking, but it stayed there, sighted right on his crotch. This girl knew how to make a man nervous, alright. Make your mind up time, Brownie. Do you want to keep your nuts on the shelf next to your yet-to-be-won golfing trophies? Or take a chance on the fact that you were sure to be a better, cooler shot?

'Well?' she asked, willing him out of the room, tightening her grip on the trigger, hoping he could see the bunching of tendons in her fingers as she increased the pressure.

Like some kind of supplicant he had walked out backwards, nodding slowly his agreement, and left. He wasn't sorry. It would've been like killing two sisters, what with her and the croupier.

'Don't worry about her,' he finally said.

Wuzel nodded. He could always rely on Brownie.

Ed asked: 'What about the girl?' What about Honey, he wanted to say. My Honey. What about my Honey, how come you were fucking with *my* girl.

They had cleared the snarl at Toms River, and the Toyota was approaching something like its top speed as they threaded through the isolated communities. They were not too far from Ruby's. She could help Tony. But then he remembered the State Trooper husband. Armed at all times. Shit. No, couldn't rely on her. And anyway, everything he had touched with his old friends had turned to shit. Did he want to bring Ruby down as well, force her to make a decision, whether she should break the law or not, get caught in a firefight between hubby and the remnants of the Cotchford boys? 'The girl?' Ed asked again.

Billy ignored the question. Right now he could hardly see. Sheets of rain were pouring down the windshield, and the squealing wipers could barely cope. The film of water was reducing all lights to great streaks of colour, be they brake lights, traffic lights or store signs. His head was beginning to ache. Had he done the right thing, coming south? Shit, would the pilot have taken off in this anyway? This weather system wasn't meant to hit until two or three in the morning, he had checked. The pilot had checked. But the little car was rocking as the gusts from the sea hit it. Still, he reminded himself, flight or no flight, he still had a million bucks behind his seat. He could rent a car, buy one even. It was enough to get away from the claws of BB, keep him going for a couple of years until he figured out what he wanted to do. He wouldn't be rich, but he could be comfortable. And free. He thought of Anne and felt a pang of guilt. He'd call her. Once he got somewhere he felt safe. He'd call her. And Honey. She must be wondering why he didn't ask her to come along. She'd get over it. He'd send her something, maybe.

'The girl?' asked Ed for the third time.

'What about her?' snapped Billy.

'What about her? What about her? She's a dead ringer for Honey, that's what about her.'

Billy put a hand on the pistol on his lap. He realised how ridiculous whatever he said would sound. How could he tell Ed about finding someone who looked almost the same as the girl from Cotchford, about getting her hair cut just as he remembered it, about the little role-playing, a harmless little game to put him in the mood. Tell him that, of all the women, he still thought about Honey. The way she would slip her hand into his pants, so innocent yet somehow practised at the same time.

And when he first found the girl on the Net, he really had thought it was her. He genuinely believed he had rediscovered Honey. And when it turned out not to be . . . turned out to be an Emma, well, he couldn't let it go that easily. They said a little fantasy was good for you, and she seemed happy enough to pretend. Even took on the name full time. Made the site honicam. Where was the harm?

'Maybe that's why I liked her,' he said flatly.

Ed shook his head. 'You are some piece of work. Some piece of shit, I should say. Can't get the real thing, then dress up some whore to look like her.'

Yeah, well, maybe he did like fucking her because he knew that everyone in Cotchford always wanted to get to Honey, including Ed. She was the hottest game in town.

'Listen, we got more to concern us than my sex life.'

'What do you mean?' asked Ed.

So he told him the full story.

One officer had been and checked on her, telling her that someone would be up to take a statement. She had called Matt, asked if she could spend the night with him after it was all over. He got all white knight-ish again and said he would come and pick her up. She liked that. And it was all over, she told him, he could look after her as long as he wanted. Journey's End for Honey. She was tired, real tired. She heard raised voices outside. Now the danger had passed the corridors were full of neighbours, anxious to add their ten cents to what had gone down. It was going to take hours to piece it all together.

Over in the parking lot of Starboards the photographs had been taken by snappers draped in big oilskins. Dozens of cops, water running down their faces and off their noses in rivulets, were busy measuring out distances. No chance of a simple chalk outline in this storm, and the mass of yellow and black tapes were whipping back and forth, tugging at their anchor points like tethered snakes struggling to bust free. The two cars were being prised apart by a recovery crew, and a giant tarp erected across Cecil C's busted curtain wall. Medics were poking at the crispy remains of someone by the pick-up, and the two halves of Fred were being re-mated, like a badly made puzzle.

Some lights had come back on at the diner, and there was an orderly line of customers waiting to get their thoughts down on paper before they could go. A few were being bandaged for flying glass cuts or minor burns from being too close to the gas tank when it went.

The wind was whipping the surface water now, skimming the tops of the puddles, driving it horizontally, drenching the fifteen or so people still out in the open. Someone was pointing up at her window. Most of the cops would give their right arm to be able to take her statement, in the warm and dry.

She had one thing left to do. From the lounge area she fetched a chair, and placed it in front of the closet. She stepped up, level with the camera box, felt behind it for the wires and wrenched. Strange, she thought, there was no cry of anguish, no sobbing, no screaming, nothing as the honicam went out of her life forever.

As they pulled to a halt on the gravel outside Lucy, Ed reached over and felt Tony's neck. Tony opened his eyes. They were cloudy, flat. He managed a smile. 'Hey Billy, you ever seen *Vertigo*?' His voice was soft, a high fluting sound making it harder than ever to hear.

Billy twisted round, puzzled. 'I can't say I have.'

'James Stewart, Kim N-N-Novak. 'Bout a man who . . . falls for a double.'

He's been listening, thought Ed.

'It might interest you.' He even managed a wink.

Billy said without emotion: 'I'll check it out. C'mon let's get you inside.' He stepped out, holding the door to stop it slamming shut, then leant inside to help.

Tony swung the shotgun so it was level with Billy's face and pulled the trigger. The roof of the Toyota exploded into hundreds of small holes, like a pepper pot, the double-O blasting out into the night sky. The noise was like a small nuclear device going off. Tony opened his eyes, expecting to see raw steak where Billy's face had been. Instead he saw the black barrel of a small pistol pressing into his socket.

The report sounded flat and weak after the shotgun but Tony gave one jerk and was dead.

Billy reached in, fetched the shotgun and handed it to Ed. He kept one hand on it. He put a finger in his ear to try and clear the loud ringing and came away with blood on his hand. A piece of buckshot had torn away part of the lobe. Same thing had happened to Wuzel once, he recalled. 'Son-of-a-bitch. You gonna try as well?'

Ed shook his head, numbed by the escalating body count. Billy let go of the barrel. He nodded to the car.

'Fuckin' gratitude for you. Told you we shoulda left him in that puddle.'

Billy pulled the money free and, case in left hand, pistol in right, ran from the Toyota to the door of Lucy and rang the bell, making room for Ed as he too pushed in for what meagre shelter the doorway afforded. The steel lines that held the big beast in place were thrumming in the wind, and some of the tin tiles were flapping loosely, making a sound like Styrofoam on glass.

Billy came close to snarling. 'Well, looks like you got them all killed, one way or another.'

Ed felt like he had been slapped, but had to agree. It had been just what he was thinking. Billy rang again.

Billy heard the inspection hatch open on the other side of the door, knew he was being examined. Then it opened and Bird said: 'Billy?' but stopped when he saw Ed. Without waiting to be asked they pushed in.

'Up,' instructed Billy, waving the .32.

Bird backed up the stairs, glaring down at them. Nothing was said until they reached the living area. Ed fell into one of the couches, fighting the urge to curl up and sleep, to wake and dismiss all this as a nightmare. Don, Lester, Tony, the little litany kept chanting over in his head. Dead, dead, dead.

Billy remained standing. He put the case down, and took off his coat, keeping the gun at his side.

'Drink?' asked Bird.

'A shot of something?' asked Billy. 'Yeah.'

Bird nodded and fetched a bottle of Maker's Mark. He handed them each a tumbler. Ed downed it and squirmed with the gentle burn. He accepted another.

Ed finally said, 'Billy's been telling me.'

Bird nodded.

'Everything. About the payments he made a while back back. Coupla years after we all got out.'

Bird just nodded again, combined with a so-what shrug.

'You thought it would never . . . come to light?'

Bird put a hand on his brow. 'I never . . . I never thought it through that much. Never. I just . . . I always thought I could pay it back.'

'So there was no software sale in California.'

Bird shook his head. 'I was never as smart as you thought. And it was only a hundred thousand dollars. Twenty Gs each. Not enough to buy Lucy. I did go to California. I did, but . . . nothing. When I got this . . . this – it was blood money, Ed. Would you have wanted that? Tainted. He was salving his conscience, paying us off, saying here, sorry for the time you did, take this. Would you have wanted that?'

Ed knocked back the second tumbler of bourbon. 'Yes.' He laid the shotgun alongside his leg as he lay back, sinking into the leather, enjoying the warmth of the drink and the room, trying to hold back the crazy crowd of images jostling for brain time. Images of his dead friends. 'For Lester.' For Honey, the real one. Shit, maybe he could even have made himself a substitute like Billy.

'And that bitch you always went on about. Isn't that what you mean really? Lester was just a convenient excuse.' Realising something was missing, he asked, 'Where is he anyway? And Don? And Tony?'

Billy ignored the question. 'I only sent it to you, because I thought I could trust you. You were always the fuckin' straight arrow.'

'Jimmy never trusted him,' said Ed. 'He told me once. I thought he was crazy. Should have known. Jimmy could always judge a character. Thought Bird was a born hustler at heart.'

'I wasn't even there. So the hundred grand – I deserved it. Out of all of you I got the rawest deal.'

As the net had got closer Billy had gathered them together for one last time. 'Destroy the evidence,' he had said, echoing his old man. 'Always destroy the evidence. They can't touch you then.' And they had thrown the driver's head, and the pictures, into the incinerator. Watched it turn into bone and bone to ashes, while the photographs blackened and curled and blistered, the identities of the boys scorched away forever.

But Don, stupid stupid Don, he'd forgotten about the duplicates he made, the ones the cops found in the garage. There was the image of them grinning with the head, some of them poking fingers into eye sockets, mouth, ears, violating the human remains of the decapitated driver. And there was the other one. The thing about Lester is he would always do anything for a dare, anything he thought would please his peer group. Even this. The last photograph they found was one of Ed holding the driver's head while little Lester got his dick out and pretended to put it in the frozen mouth. Necrophilia and fellatio colliding in one sickening image. That was what had damned them. If the father had been driving, if it had been a man's head they had picked up, then maybe, just maybe it wouldn't have turned out this way. But it was a woman, a thirty-year-old mangled face, still recognisable enough for Lester to think waving his dick around her mouth was funny. A prank. The court didn't see it that way. It was considered so horrific, so degrading, so depraved, that they wouldn't let the papers report it.

They were so shocked nobody thought to ask who took the shot. All assumed it was a self-timed number. And nobody from the group fingered Billy as the head-keeper. He was treated like some poor kid sucked into this depraved circle of friends. And so it began.

'And Lester?' asked Ed.

'Ed, Lester you know was born to be fucked over.'

'Well he is now,' said Ed, 'He's dead.'

Bird hardly registered it, as if he knew all along. 'Want to tell me about it?' Ed gave him the *Reader's Digest* version of events, the way they had gone a week early because Starboards was closing. Bird seemed oddly unmoved, whereas Ed felt like he wanted to be sick, to throw up, to purge his stomach over these expensive carpets and wall hangings.

Billy grabbed a piece of cloth from one of the chairs and dabbed his ear. Blood was slowly dripping down onto his shoulder.

Bird looked like he was about to say something about Billy's choice of material to staunch the bleeding, but thought better of it. 'And them being dead – that's my fault is it? I told you all along to let it lie. We all made mistakes back then – and yes, since you ask, I admit, what I did was wrong. But at least they were alive after what *I* did to them.'

'Fuck you.'

'And what's in the case?' Again, Ed told him. 'So in the end it all comes down to money. Which makes neither of you any better than me.'

The tiredness was a lead coat now, locking his limbs down, pressing on his chest, pulling his eyelids down. 'Bird?'

'Yeah?'

'You got anything to eat? I am fuckin' starvin'. Had to leave my sub behind.'

Bird went upstairs to the kitchen, and when he came down he melodramatically flourished a Colt 2000.

Ed wasn't surprised. There was nothing that could surprise him, short of aliens crash-landing through the roof, and even then they would probably blame him for their spaceship malfunctioning. He had a sudden thought. 'You could've brought the sandwich too.'

'You and your stomach.'

'We been together a long time. We ain't gonna part. I realise that now. Tell me – did you tell the Fishers we were ATF when we went in to get Tony? Hoping they'd shoot the shit out of us?'

Bird nodded. 'I called your pal Dupree. Told him he'd been suckered. He said he'd arrange a little reception.'

'And what were you going to do about us and the heist if we hadn't gone early? Let it ride?'

'Oh, I'd've probably told Big Billy there was going to be a hit. Make sure he . . . took care of you beforehand.'

Billy thought of the Depot and the pool and those burning heads again. Could he have done it to his old friends? A long time ago – last week, say – yes. He said wearily: 'Anyways, you don't need the gun. I ain't going to try and kill you. I just wanted to explain it for Ed here. You got a car, Bird?' He pointed at the case. 'I can pay for it.'

Bird said: 'How much?'

Billy sighed. 'Now let's not get greedy. I don't want to pay Porsche money for a junker.'

'Come, now, surely we could do some caring and sharing here. I always thought a hundred grand was at the low end of the compensation spectrum. Eh, Ed?' Bird gripped the gun tighter and pointed it at Billy. It was a half-hearted attempt to look threatening.

Ed shook his head. 'Count me out, chief. You two want to do that gunfight thing, you go right ahead.' He wanted to close his eyes and sleep, sleep forever maybe, but every time he closed them a hot dog smothered with French mustard drifted by.

Billy said: 'Bird, I reckon that something like half a dozen people died tonight around us. Anyway Ed already shot me dead tonight.'

Bird looked puzzled. Ed said: 'I know, beats the shit out of me as well. He should be dead. Wait till I see Goodrich.' It occurred to him then – maybe Goodrich had loaded up with blanks deliberately. Billy was hit by the wadding. But why blanks?

Bird heard the movement on the stair and turned. Whoever was in the stairwell simply saw a man with a gun pointed his way, period. And reacted appropriately. The two three-round clusters pushed Bird into the bureau, scattering the drinks and glasses.

Ed never knew he had reflexes like it. He rolled off the couch in a smooth, continuous movement, keeping his head up so he could see the stairwell as much as possible, swung up the shotgun, pumped in the new round and fired. The recoil slid him along the rug, and he felt the butt catch his ribs, driving the breath out of him. A massive section of the internal wall around the stairs exploded into a twister of splinters. Billy also loosed off two shots in the general direction and they heard the footsteps descending.

Ed looked at Bird. He had slid to the floor, head slumped forward, a lifeless toy. Christ, he really did have the whole gang dead. Well, almost. Now we are two.

Ed levered himself up, breathing shallowly, trying not to move his tender ribs too much, until he went over and levered the Colt from Bird's hands. 'Cops?' he whispered.

Billy shook his head. They would be all flashing lights and bullhorns, he thought. 'Wuzel.' He said. Which meant his old man meant to kill him. When the bullet whistled past his ear, Ed turned again and blasted the stairs, punching straight out into the night through the skin of the elephant this time. A second burst of rounds came by. The baby grand piano made strange zinging, pinging noises, like something from a John-Cage-with-gunfire performance. A hole ripped through the lid, splintering the lacquer. But still nobody was on the staircase. Then he realised. They were firing through the floor, up through the belly of the beast.

'Upstairs,' said Ed. Over the ringing in his head he could hear the outside world whooshing through the holes in the side of the animal, felt the fine mist of rain on his face.

They took the stairs to the kitchen, bedroom and bathrooms. Ed stopped and found a hunk of bread, which he stuffed in his mouth. There was another flight up. 'What's up there?' asked Billy.

They could hear the thud of bullets in the floor below them, but they didn't have the power to penetrate, not through two thick layers of wood. But Wuzel and friend would probably take the next floor soon and start again.

'Mmmffffah,' said Ed, then swallowed some of the bread. 'The howdah. Open air. What if we went up there and let off a few shots? Get some attention.'

'You think anyone would hear . . . in this weather?' asked Billy.

The carpet next to Billy suddenly started dancing and squirming as the rounds tore through it. They were directly below. Billy staggered as one went through his foot. 'Shit. Shit. Shit.' He fired at the floor in anger, two, three times watching the neat little holes appear. Ed went to the stairwell and risked another random shot down into the room below, the sound deafening as it bounced back from the curved walls of Lucy.

Billy bent double as the pain raced up his leg, but Ed grabbed him and they hobbled for the steps as more sections of the floor erupted into a tangle of splinters and threads. Ed felt the pinpricks of wood shards penetrate his cheek, but ignored them. At the top of the flight he pushed open the hatch to the howdah and felt the wind tug at him. The gale was howling up here, rawer, faster than at ground level. Awkwardly they pulled themselves and their weapons onto the roof. Ed went back down and heaved up the case. 'I guess you want this.'

Billy's face contorted. 'You know, right now, not as much as I once did. I'd trade it for a couple of sub machine guns.' He puffed out his cheeks and panted, trying to regulate the pain, concentrate away from it. Scream his brain said, *scream*. But he pressed it down, isolated the feeling that his flesh was being scorched with a welding torch. He breathed deeply, trying to load up on oxygen, felt the rain squeezing between his teeth.

'You were robbing your old man?'

Billy nodded. 'Time for a new start.'

Ed heard movement below. He swung his head down through the hatch and caught a glimpse of two figures. Blindly he let off another round, and even as it left the barrel he realised it was the last one. But they didn't know that. It might keep their heads down until they could figure something out. He kicked the hatch shut.

It would have been a great view if the storm hadn't wrapped itself around them. The air had mutated from being mere atmosphere to an airborne sea, so heavy with liquid it dashed great waves into their faces, stinging Ed's broken skin, and the roar in their ears made conversation almost impossible.

Billy looked around for any possibilities of escape. He could hear the singing of the great animal's support wires, and they led from skin to ground, but reaching them meant climbing onto the side of the beast, a curve of slippery, treacherous tin. No go.

Billy realised that somewhere a few miles north was life, lights, thousands of people cocooned in the hyper-reality of the casinos, barely noticing the angry turbulence passing over the city. A city his old man wanted to discard as having outlived its usefulness. And, it seemed, he felt much the same about his son.

He heard another burst of fire above the howling in his ears. Billy leant in close to Ed. 'Should I just give it to them?' he pointed at the case.

Ed nodded vigorously. 'My vote is yes.'

They heard a further rattle of fire, this time felt the pressure as the bullets thudded under their feet, but nothing came through. Ed knew the howdah floor was strengthened here to take the tables and chairs that came out in summer. Probably with steel plates. 'You got any more bullets?' he yelled.

Billy held up a magazine.

'The shotgun's empty. I guess we got a full clip here,' Ed waved Bird's Colt. 'I can't find a safety.'

Billy took it and looked it over. He wiped the rain from his eyes and turned his back on the buffeting wind. 'Double action it says. Pull the slide and you get one in the chamber and just fire.'

'Sure?'

'Trust me, I was a member of the Manhattan Gun Club.'

'Shall I give it to them?'

Billy shrugged, wondering if it was money or him they wanted here. Maybe it wasn't Wuzel. Maybe it was a straightforward heist job. 'I don't know any more. Nobody told me the rules of this particular game.'

Ed half smiled, remembering how Tony would bust through whenever he was in a tight spot, releasing him from the alley-o prison. Where was he when he needed him? And he remembered where his rescuer was, and fought back a howl of anguish, managed to keep all the horror he had seen buried within. There would either be time for that later. Or there wouldn't.

The access panel suddenly buckled as the rounds punched through and whistled into the night sky. No steel there. Ed moved gingerly over to the now shattered hatch, kicking the case in front of him. He shouted. 'I'm throwing it down. OK? Don't shoot. Take it and go. OK? You hear me?'

Nothing.

He lifted the few remaining planks and pushed the case in, heard it thud down the steps.

He closed the hatch and they moved to the edge of the howdah, holding onto the rail as the swirling became stronger. The burning was gone, but Billy was getting heavy stabs of big, fat dull pain from his foot now.

Ed said: 'Billy?'

'Yeah?'

'I fucked up. I should have said something in the cab all those weeks ago. After the accident? Said it was me. The story would've come out. Bird's I mean.'

There was another burst of fire from below, and one bullet finally got through the strengthened floor, zinging off crazily into the night sky. They weren't giving up. Maybe because they didn't want anyone around to say who it was. Yeah, he knew now, it was Wuzel.

Billy laughed bitterly. 'I think we all did, one way or another. Fuck up I mean. I did a lot of things in my time.' He loaded the magazine into his pistol. A lot of them for his old man, just like Wuzel. And maybe now Wuzel was after him. Or there was the chance that . . . no, Wuzel double crossing his old man too? And trying to wet the witnesses? He stopped the thoughts before they spiralled out of control. Speculation wouldn't help right now. Nothing would. He motioned to Ed. 'C'm'ere.'

Tentatively they put their arms round each other, and for a moment Ed recalled the end of a game, the final of an alley-o match when the two captains came and shook hands, or maybe did something like this if it had been a hard fought game. All bets off until the next time. If only they had stayed playing that, if they hadn't invented the Bridge game. If Bird hadn't. And now what happened with that block, all those years ago, the cinder block spinning through the air, hitting the metal bed of the tipper truck with the usual clang, and, as they ran to the opposite side of the bridge to see the driver brake as always, lifting again, as if it was a giant eraser – *bouncing* for Christ's sake – tumbling clear of the rear of the truck and growing, filling the windshield of the family following the truck. Now he could see the look on their faces, imagine the last thoughts as it came smashing through the glass, folding it like a transparent envelope and brushing it aside, neatly ripping off the driver's head, dooming everyone else in the vehicle to death in a car smash. And it was just a game. If only they'd stuck to alley-o.

Ed looked at the hatch. There were wisps of smoke rising from it, dancing in the light briefly before being snatched away by the wind. And they were getting thicker, billowing into heavy coils now. He remembered Bird's words about a fire risk. They were burning Lucy. The residents of Margate would not be pleased, he found himself thinking, as if he gave a shit about what the locals thought.

Then, just as he was about to break the embrace to share the bad news with Billy, Ed heard and felt his old friend pull back the slide of the Heckler and Koch, arming the gun with a fresh cartridge in the chamber, and he stiffened. He reached down and did the same with Bird's Colt and felt a round eject. It had had one up the spout already. He watched the cartridge roll across the decking, chased and taunted by the rain, over to where a steady stream of smoke was now bleeding out into the storm.

'We were friends once,' said Billy into his ear.

'Yeah. We just forgot it for a while.' Ed laughed, feeling the streams of water coming into his mouth. If they didn't burn to death they would drown up here. 'Well, more than a while.'

Billy said: 'Whatever happens, Ed . . .' There might have been more but the wind grabbed the words and ran with them.

'I'll understand,' Ed shouted.

'Understand what?'

'Oh, nothing. Nothing.' And he gripped tighter as he heard a sudden muffled explosion from below as something detonated and flames started to join the smoke pouring onto the howdah.

And Ed suddenly could see the scene from above, like an out of body experience, a perfect panning aerial camera shot of Lucy, of the two men waiting on the ground for anyone stupid enough to try and break out of the now smouldering animal, anyone who could put a name to them, and then a crane shot of the howdah, its access hatch a mass of jagged edges, a yellow and orange glow bleeding out into the night, illuminating the rain, turning the spinning drops into liquid fireflies, and a few feet away, just caught at the edges of the glare, two men, no, two boys, the hardened accumulations of the years bleached out by the light so they were young again, clutched together in a rainstorm, both of them frightened to let go, wondering what they would do if they did, yet knowing what they would have to do when they did, feeling that they were going to be on top of that elephant hugging each other forever.

AUTHOR'S NOTE

Although there have been serious proposals to introduce gambling to both Asbury Park and Governors' Island off Manhattan, neither of them looks like succeeding for the moment. The Internet is awash with home pages like Honey's and, I am afraid, the horse. Even the turkey baster story is true. You couldn't make this stuff up.

Thanks are due to Sheelagh Wylie of New Jersey Tourism, although I hasten to add the vision of Atlantic City is all mine. Thanks also to Rick Young, a Senior Special Agent with the Department of Transportation, to Emmett Grogan for ringolevio (although it was called alley-o when I played it in Liverpool) and apologies to AA and Christopher Milne.

Jimmy Jazz is based on the wonderful Ralph John Gatta of Red Bank NJ, who runs Johnny's Jazz Mart, and who has plenty of stories about the old jazz days. However, he does not have a coterie of kids hanging around, and has never sold anything stronger than well-cured ham.

Lucy the Elephant is, of course, safe and well on her plinth in Margate, just south of Atlantic City.

Thanks are due to two fine books – *Making a Killing: the Business of Guns in America* by Tom Diaz (The New Press, New York) and *Lethal Passage* by Erik Larson (Vintage, London), the latter the story of one gun, the Cobray M-11/9, and its role in a high school shooting.

Anne Fousse donated her memories of high school in North Carolina, Sloan Harris gave me Alice's story and

Brandon Holley, Bo's. Susan D'Arcy and Christine Walker bravely read early versions of the book, and David Miller and Bill Massey made it what it is today. I am indebted to all of them.

Rob Ryan

Dead Headers

James H. Jackson

Officially the British Intelligence organisation known as Executive Support doesn't exist. But for its far-from-innocent victims it is all too real. Its aim: to terrorize the terrorists, to eliminate them before they can act. Its nickname: the Dead Headers.

When a sadistic mortar attack turns the streets of Paris into a charnel house, no group claims responsibility and there are no clues to the killers' motives. But the attack is only the first piece of a terrifying jigsaw that leads the Dead Headers from a secretive German pharmaceuticals company to an Iraqi biological weapons base in the Libyan desert, from a gruesome sex-murder in London's Hammersmith to a power struggle at the heart of the Iranian revolutionary regime. And by the time the final piece is in place, the fate of millions will have been decided . . .

'Tense, well researched, fast-paced and hard-nosed'
Frederick Forsyth

'Hair-raising' *Guardian*

0 7472 5771 X

Inheritance

Keith Baker

When retired RUC officer Bob McCallan is killed in a gas explosion in a caravan in Donegal, his son Jack inherits an unexpected fortune. He also inherits a key to the past.

The violence in Northern Ireland has been over for two decades, but there are still secrets that could shatter the foundations of peace. Secrets that Bob McCallan's untimely death threatens to bring to the surface. Secrets that some people would do anything to keep buried.

'A gripping read' Michael Dobbs

'Breathtaking . . . if you buy no other thriller this year, buy this one' *Irish Times*

'Gripping' *Belfast Telegraph*

0 7472 5235 1

The Locust Farm

Jeremy Dronfield

Carole Perceval lives alone on a remote Yorkshire farm, trying to forget a traumatic past. Her life is one of tranquil routine, until one rain-swept night when a dishevelled figure hammers on her door.

Lost and confused, the man has no memory, no idea who he is. His only certainty is that he is being pursued, that he has to flee at all costs. Exhausted, desperate, the farm is his final refuge.

Both of them dream of escape. Of change. Of redemption. And both are about to step into a nightmare.

'A tense page-turner . . . dodging between serial-killer thriller, psychological suspense and full-on action drama' Val McDermid

0 7472 5947 X

HEADLINE
FEATURE

Ceremony of Innocence

Humphrey Hawksley

On a sweltering Asian night, Hong Kong police commando Mike McKillop watches helplessly as his best friend is shot dead at point-blank range during an anti-drugs operation. The killer is a Chinese colonel and the murder marks McKillop for the rest of his life.

Thirteen years later, the colonel has become a general – and Mike McKillop's boss. His role as a special forces officer is little more than political window-dressing for the Communist party's corrupt security machine, until an old CIA friend makes an unexpected appearance. Clem Watkins is on the run, in fear of his life and with an appalling secret which China and America are equally determined to suppress.

'An exciting thriller' *Mail on Sunday*

'Provocative and topical' *Daily Telegraph*

0 7472 5903 8

HEADLINE FEATURE